all the little MOMENTS

G BENSON

Dedication

For my mum:
Because, without you, there is no me.
Forever you've told me I can be anything I ever wanted to be
You gave me wings.
x

Acknowledgements

Where to start?

Lauren. You were the first I told and the first to be stuck as my test reader—you've always been one of my biggest cheerleaders, yet I can always rely on you to yank my feet back down to the ground when I need it—thanks for being there to do the same again.

To Erin, who had to deal with being my first-ever beta reader. Your suggestions and comments had me laughing, smiling, and nodding at your wisdom. I hounded you with questions, and you always replied with honesty. I hope we get to work together again—and again and again!

A massive thanks to the editing team at Ylva, especially Michelle, who edited this into the streamlined, professional piece it is now. I have no words for how much you taught me with your editing; you're all amazing at your jobs, and I can't thank you enough. I'll try anyway: thanks—one hundred percent!

Melissa, if it weren't for you, I wouldn't have learnt to write an essay, let alone a book. You proofread my teenaged ramblings and helped turn them into something acceptable. Ten years on, and you did the same here—thank you.

Lastly, and certainly not least, to Astrid (and Daniela, for pushing her to email me repeatedly): Thank you for not giving up on me. Thank you for the advice, the ideas, the support. This would not be the shiny work it is if not for you. You believed in this story when I didn't, and I think you've ruined me for every other publisher ever. You're gold.

Chapter One

The car turned down a quiet street and Anna blinked rapidly as she realised it was her parents' already. Her neck ached from sitting so stiffly, and she turned awkwardly in the passenger seat. In spite of herself, a smile tugged at her lips: Hayley lay sprawled over in the back, seat belt digging into her neck. The normally poised and put-together lawyer slept with her mouth hung open, and there was a slight sign of drool.

The last fourteen hours had been a kind of hell, and both of them were exhausted.

Swallowing heavily, Anna looked back to the front and clenched her fingers together in her lap. She kept her eyes off her father, scared to look at the expression on his face as he pulled into the driveway. The car had been eerily silent the entire drive from the airport. There were no words for this situation.

Now, with the engine cut off, the silence somehow became even more oppressive.

Heart racing, Anna let out a long, slow breath. The house looked as it always had, white and two story with a simple front garden. It all looked the same, yet everything had changed. How could it be that just yesterday she'd been on a beach on the Gili Islands, Indonesia, relaxing with a mojito in her hand?

Her father cleared his throat and opened his door, sliding out easily. As usual, Anna followed his lead, while Hayley unbuckled herself and got out on Anna's side, squeezing Anna's fingers in comfort. Anna returned the gesture as they stood next to the car, looking up at the house.

If she could just stand out here and not go in, Anna thought, the reality that awaited her could be avoided. Maybe her brother, Jake, would actually be in there, smiling and asking what had taken her so long. He would wink at her and ask if the islands were as romantic as people said. Sally would laugh and punch her husband's arm, rolling her eyes.

Except that wouldn't happen.

She didn't want to go inside. The driver's side door slammed shut, and it made her jump. Warm fingers wrapped around her wrist, and she turned to see Hayley looking at her intently.

"Sandra will want you."

Anna sighed. She didn't know if she was ready to see her mother.

The walk to the house felt like it took forever.

She'd spoken to her mother for less than a minute from the hotel, as Sandra had sobbed the news into the phone. Unable to listen as shock crawled through her belly, Anna had simply handed the phone to Hayley.

The front door pushed open too easily. Framed by the doorway, Sandra looked small and at the sight of her red eyes and pinched face, Anna had to swallow past a lump in her throat. Sandra fell upon Anna, grabbing her like a lifeline, sobs hot against Anna's cheek, her fingertips digging into her skin. Anna wrapped her arms around her mother and ran her hand along her greying hair. Words failed, and the only sound was that of Sandra's grief. Anna felt a powerful urge to look around for Hayley, to find the person who always knew what to say, but her mother clung so hard there would be bruises. All there was to do was to sway gently and bite back the burning in her throat.

"Na!"

Anna flinched at the contrast between the grief-stricken woman in her arms and the delighted shout of her nephew. Throughout the entire panicked trip off the island and the flight to Melbourne, she hadn't let herself think of the kids.

Her mother took a shuddering breath, and Anna felt her tense as she straightened and wiped her eyes quickly.

Jake's fifteen-month-old son Toby was making his way, step by step, down the stairs, ratty blue blanket clasped in one hand while his other hand clung to the rail. He was grinning around his pacifier. As she watched the little boy, the spitting image of his father, stumble his way down, her smile was the closest to a genuine one she'd managed since receiving the news. Still, her heart ached, and her stomach twisted so badly, she thought she'd be sick.

Regardless, she took two long strides towards the bottom of the stairs and threw her arms wide; Toby all but fell into them, his little arms wrapping around her neck and his legs around her middle. He giggled as she cuddled him tightly. Squeezing her eyes shut, Anna hugged him to her. Warm and solid in her arms, he gave another giggle. Out of the corner of her eye, Anna saw her father grimace and disappear down the hall to his study. The door closed with a solid thump.

Toby pulled back from her neck, blanket clasped to his chest with one hand while the other pulled out his pacifier with a pop. Serious big blue eyes looked at her, smile gone. "Na," he said, with a nod. He patted her face, pacifier poking her cheek, then broke into another smile. "Stay!"

Even as her stomach twisted again and nausea rose in her throat, Anna nodded and returned the smile. "Of course I'm staying, Tobes. I've missed you."

She squeezed him to her again and he wiggled in her grasp, already wanting to get down and run around on his chubby legs. The moment his feet touched the ground, he was tugging her towards the living room. Anna looked up at her mother, pretending not to see the fresh tears on her cheeks. "Where's Ella?"

"Upstairs." Sandra's voice was like a guitar string tuned too tight. "She's gone very quiet."

A promise to return satisfied Toby, who ran to a pile of blocks, either to demolish or create. Halfway up the stairs, Anna stopped and turned to Hayley. "You okay here?"

Hayley smiled slightly and nodded. "Sandra and I will have some tea."

Anna nodded absently and continued up the stairs, thoughts already on her niece.

Ella was an incredibly chatty child—an incredibly chatty child who loved her aunty. She'd been a surprise that had come into her brother's life when he and his fiancé were twenty-five—the surprise that had turned Anna's jokester, loud brother into a ball of sap who looked at his tiny daughter like he'd destroy mountains for her. The change in him had been immediate as he held the tiny, squealing bundle. When he'd returned to Iraq after three months' leave, he'd done so with a new love of his life in his heart.

Sudden, overwhelming anger made her screw up her fists. Her brother had survived a war that had claimed thousands, only to be killed years later, along with the wife he'd left active duty for, by one drunk asshole in a car.

Sometimes, the world was a shitty place.

Almost dizzy, she paused outside the room her parents kept for the kids. Taking a deep breath, she knocked and pushed the door open. "Ella?"

There was only silence.

She glanced around the room: a single bed all made up in pink in the corner, portacot along the wall, toys everywhere. A hiccup reached her ears, and her sight zeroed in on the neon orange Converse shoes sticking out from under the bed. Anna almost smiled: she had bought Ella those shoes for her sixth birthday five weeks ago. Jake had laughed and rolled his eyes when he caught sight of them. That was the last time Anna had seen him.

He'd said the shoes were ridiculous, that Ella would grow out of them too fast. Anna had punched his arm to shut him up, and Ella put them on straight away. The night Anna left, Jake sent a photo message of Ella in bed, fast asleep with her shoes still on.

She had no idea how that was only five weeks ago. A lump formed in her throat and she swallowed it down with difficulty. She slid under the bed on her back, wriggling until she lay shoulder to shoulder with Ella.

Her niece was still, staring unblinkingly at the springs over their heads, so Anna didn't attempt to touch her. Ella's auburn hair was a mess around her head, and her eyes were intent on not looking at Anna. Somehow, the sprinkle of freckles over her nose had gotten even sweeter since Anna had last seen her.

"Hey, Ella Bella," Anna said softly.

Ella continued to stare straight up.

Anna wasn't brilliant at this. Becoming an anaesthetist, rather than a doctor or a nurse, had been a choice she'd made because she wasn't great at conversation or small talk. When they lost a patient, she didn't have to give terrible news to parents and loved ones, didn't need to know what to say, how to act. Kids had always been even more of an enigma to her. She could smile at a child in physical pain on her table and make them smile back enough to settle down before she put them to sleep. She could play games with kids, entertain them. She loved to sit with her niece and nephew and read them stories for a few hours, to make them giggle and watch their eyes widen at the things she told them. There had been the weekend she would never forget, when she had stupidly offered to take the kids so Jake and Sally could have two nights alone. But then she'd handed them back and returned to her life. There had been no permanence in that situation—she could handle a few nights because then she got to give them back.

But this? She didn't know how to do *this*, how to comfort a six-year-old who had just lost her parents.

She lifted a hand, grateful that the bed left a little room, and pushed a lock of hair behind Ella's ear. And that was all it took; her little face crumbled and tears spilled as she turned into Anna's arms. The girl's frame was thin, and Anna wrapped her arms around her shaking, sobbing, almost gasping niece as best she could in the restricted space.

"Our class rabbit died last year. He never came back."

Anna's throat tightened, and she squeezed Ella closer.

"Does that mean Mummy and Daddy aren't coming back too?" Ella's voice hiccupped over every word.

Anna didn't know what to say. So, she went with the truth. "No, they're not, honey."

The joint funeral was beautiful and hideous all at once.

Throughout, Ella clung to her grandparents and to Anna in turn, green eyes wide, barely speaking a word.

In the middle of the service, Anna and Hayley had to take Toby outside to play on the grass. The tiny boy didn't understand and didn't want to sit still.

Sally's parents barely spoke a word to anybody, saying hello to the kids before retreating quickly. They had never bonded with their grandchildren, and Anna tried her best to be polite while harbouring a feeling of resentment towards them. The stories Sally had shared didn't foster familial bonds. In spite of herself, Anna had kept looking for them at the wake, thinking that surely they would make an appearance.

That night, Hayley came up behind her in the kitchen, running a hand down her arm and making Anna jump and spin around.

"What was up with Sally's parents?"

Leaning back against the sink, Anna shrugged and crossed her arms. "They're born-again Christians."

Hayley's eyes widened. "Oh."

"Yeah."

She pulled Hayley in for a kiss, relieved she was there as a shield between herself and the crying relatives. Most of her life, Anna had thought herself happier single, but when she'd met Hayley three-and-a-half years ago, the two women who didn't settle down for anyone had settled down for each other. She smiled, remembering how there had been heartbroken women everywhere in Brisbane when she'd taken Hayley off the market.

"Why are you smiling?"

Anna shook her head, pulling Hayley in for another kiss. "No reason."

It wasn't easy to be the partner of someone who was grieving. Hayley ghosted around Anna, offering comfort where she could, which was hard with someone who refused to take it. Anna was aware that it must be maddening, but she didn't want to talk. All she wanted was to squash down the feeling that was threatening to swallow her whole. Whenever she pulled Hayley to her and crushed their lips together, Hayley looked almost relieved. Sex was easier than words, and after five days in her parents' house, they learnt to be quiet.

She was at a loss when people asked how she was doing, when Hayley looked at her in the middle of the night and said, "Babe, you have to be feeling *something* you want to talk about." Silence was the only answer, as Anna would roll onto her side and pull Hayley's arm across her middle. Sleep eluded her even as she pretended to succumb to it.

What could she talk about? Her only sibling had been killed. She didn't have words for losing the man who was half brother, half best friend. It was a bond that had never faded as they'd gotten older.

When he'd been shipped overseas, she had gone as crazy as Sally worrying about him. The two of them had drunk more wine together than was probably appropriate for sisters-in-law.

She wasn't ready to not have her best friend.

How would she talk about the look in her mother's eye? Or about the scotch she could smell on her father's breath, even as he avoided looking at her? Or about how Ella was still quiet, pushing her food around her plate and barely eating? About how poor Toby had started to pick up that something was very wrong, becoming more and more clingy and agitated. He was often calling for Ma and Da, looking confused when it was his grandmother hovering over him, before breaking into the grin he was so good at.

How did she talk about how dreading the lawyer's visit the next day to go over the will? About how she didn't want to watch her mother break down and her father stare stoically as their son and daughter-in-law's last will and testament was read. Something about doing that was so very, very final. And soon—surely it was too soon?

And how did she talk about how it felt like a part of her had died too?

In between sips of tea, the balding lawyer spoke monotonously, seated across the living room on a chair brought from the kitchen. While Anna was trying to concentrate on the complicated legalese the man spewed forth, it felt like listening to something underwater. She leant heavily against Hayley while giving the occasional nod, trusting her hot-shot lawyer girlfriend to pay attention for her. Distracted, Anna focussed on Sandra's hands, running methodically through Toby's soft brown hair as he slept on the sofa between her parents. The tea in Andrew's lap was probably cold, untouched as he sat ramrod straight. He hadn't blinked once that Anna had noticed.

With a twinge of guilt, a part of her longed for this to be over, to go home with her girlfriend and bury herself in work and ignore what had happened. Another part of her just wanted to crawl into bed and never emerge again.

She missed Jake.

The lawyer cleared his throat and Anna blinked, forcing herself to look back at him. "So, really, the will is summed up fairly easily. Anna Foster is to be left the house in Melbourne and both cars—er, the remaining car. All assets, both financial and material, are to be transferred into her name."

Silence descended upon the room, and the words finally registered in Anna's mind. "I'm sorry. What?"

Hayley's hand, which had been rubbing gently up and down her back, stilled.

The lawyer kept going, "Custody of Ella and Toby Foster is to go to one Anna Foster, as unanimously agreed by the biological parents."

Anna's mouth fell open. She blinked again.

The lawyer, the stupid boring man, looked up from his papers and seemed surprised to see the look on her face. "Jake said he spoke of this with you?"

"Uh..." There was a conversation Anna vaguely recalled.

"If I die, you'll take the kids, right?"

She spun on her bar stool, raising an eyebrow at him, "We're here toasting the birth of your first kid, and you're already talking plural?"

"Oh, I'll have more. Have you seen that kid? I make good kids. It's imperative I produce more, little sister."

Anna snorted. "Oh, yeah, you owe it to mankind."

"Glad you agree. Now, that's a yes *then? I won't have my kids going to Sally's parents, they're terrifying. Hell, even Sally doesn't want to go near her parents."*

"Mum and Dad can raise them. Besides, you're not dying."

"Mum and Dad!? I love them, but they're old, and kids don't need old. And Dad's...you know Dad—he's not warm, Anna. It was just me and you growing up. So that leaves you."

Anna threw back a shot and slid one over the bar to Jake. "Right, yeah, I'd be great with the kids."

Anna stared at the lawyer, mouth still open. *Jake Foster, that was not a conversation about me raising your children in your absence.* She suddenly felt irrationally pissed that he wasn't there for her to throttle.

A glance at her parents told her they weren't surprised. Then she looked at Hayley, who was staring at the lawyer with horrified, wide eyes.

Anna's world just kept falling apart.

Chapter Two

Two hours on from meeting with the lawyer and Anna was still shell-shocked. The silence in the car as she drove Hayley to the airport was pressing in on her ears. Both of them stared numbly at the road, Anna's mind churning over everything, ignoring the fact that her girlfriend had retreated completely inside herself. Focussing on the anger bubbling in her stomach was easier.

It probably wasn't healthy to be so mad at her dead brother, but she was—which was almost a relief, because it stopped everything else from overwhelming her.

Being angry stopped the feeling that her chest was restricted and she couldn't breathe, the feeling that everything was spinning while she stood still, the feeling that overtook her when she watched her father close his study door and heard the clink of a bottle on glass or when she caught her mother staring vaguely at a plate, hands covered in drying dish water.

A red light turned green and it took her too long to notice. A loud horn blasted behind her as she tried to forget the memory of Ella staring wordlessly at her untouched food. Anna accelerated, trying to concentrate, but she couldn't stop thinking of the kids. When she and Hayley had left the house, Anna had had to choke down a lump at the sight of Toby sitting in his sister's lap with a book. Ella's arms had encircled the small toddler, and he'd been gripping his blanket to himself as he leant back against her chest, looking up at her and then back at the book with captivated eyes.

That sight hurt. The fact that those two kids didn't have their parents hurt. A six-year-old who would forever remember feeling abandoned and a fifteen-month-old who wouldn't remember anything—what would happen to them now? Would Ella forever be taking on a role too big for her?

Anna's eyes flicked to Hayley, who was steadfastly staring out the window, looking ready to bolt. The worried thought that she would gnawed at Anna, but then anger boiled in her stomach again, overshadowing everything else. How could Jake and Sally put her in this position when they knew damn well how she felt about having kids? The grip she had on the steering wheel turned her knuckles white. Despite what he seemed to think of a random bar conversation, Jake had never spoken about this, had ignored the fact that she didn't want children. Anna's grip on the wheel tightened even more at the implications. This type of commitment was something she had spent her entire life avoiding. Anna had been nervous enough just *thinking* of buying an apartment with her girlfriend. Jake knew that.

Eyes glued to the road, she swallowed heavily, her breathing getting out of control. Jake was dead and she couldn't even yell at him.

Being angry at Jake was easier than being sad about Jake.

Anna hit her indicator harder than she intended and drove into the departures section of the airport. The hideous silence was making her feel like crawling out of her skin.

"We'll figure this out," she said.

Hayley blinked and looked over at her, hand slipping onto Anna's thigh. "We'll figure something out."

"My parents can take them."

Anna found a spot to pull over and killed the engine. They looked at each other, the space wide between them.

"Maybe." Hayley hesitated. "They seemed on board with Jake's will."

"It looks like he may have talked to them about it." Anna suddenly slammed her open palm against the steering wheel. "Damn it, Jake!"

Guilt slammed into her stomach as Anna dropped her head back against the headrest. Tears filled her eyes, and she blinked them away.

Hayley looked at her, grip tightening. "Hey. Like you said, we'll figure it out."

Cheeks burning, Anna didn't open her eyes.

"I'm sorry I have to go when—well—with everything like this. I'm sorry I have to go so soon. I booked your ticket for two days from now—you'll fly back then?"

Anna rolled her head to the side, finally looking at Hayley. "Yeah. I'll talk to my parents. Figure out what all this actually means."

When they slid out of the car, Anna pulled Hayley's bag out of the back, then leant against the passenger door.

Hayley moved forward, kissing her once. "I'll call you when I land?"

Anna nodded.

"Try and survive without the constant sex, hey?" Hayley smiled.

Anna rolled her eyes. "It'll be hard."

Bag in hand, Hayley started to walk off. Metres away, she paused and turned to look back one last time, head tilted slightly. "It's okay to cry, Anna."

Unable to look her in the eye, Anna shrugged, tight lipped, and Hayley turned away again. Anna watched her walk through the doors before sliding back into the car. Heart thudding, she clutched the steering wheel, started the car, and pulled out too fast, trying to remind herself to pay attention as her stomach turned over. Her reality was inescapable. And her brother must have been insane.

Jake had made his decision, but surely she could speak to her parents, tell them it was best they took the kids. They saw them regularly; it made a lot more sense. She was just the fun aunty, and she didn't want this. Kids deserved to be with someone who wanted them.

She slammed her hand into the steering wheel again, saying out loud, "Talk to them, but not to me. Makes real sense." She bit her lip. Now she was talking to herself.

There was a thought that nagged in the back of her mind. She loved her parents, and she and Jake had been incredibly lucky compared to a lot of other children. But Jake had made it a point to her that he didn't want his kids raised by them. What had he said? Their father wasn't warm. Anna gave a snort of laughter. That was the understatement of the year. Andrew could be a distant, foreboding man. What little physical affection he had given when they were small had stopped quickly. He had kept them at arm's length and expected them to be stoic, non-complaining, quiet children. Her father now expected them to be quiet adults.

Anna pulled the car into a spot at a park near her parents' house and rested her head heavily on the steering wheel. A glance at the clock told her she could avoid going back for a little longer, and she shut her eyes tightly as she thought of Jake as a father.

She'd been curious about how a man raised with a closed-off father like theirs would be as a parent, but children had changed her brother, had enlivened him. Parenthood had suited him and Sally both. Bright, loving and warm, Jake had been everything their father was not, loudly encouraging where their father was a harsh disciplinarian. Jake didn't want his kids growing up in that household. That much he'd said.

With a sigh, she finally pulled out of the park an hour later. Sally's parents were off the table without even a question. And as Jake had said, that left Anna. These kids were all that remained of her brother.

And that thought scared the shit out of her.

By the time she pulled into the driveway, the streetlights had switched on, and Anna knew the kids would be in bed. Guilt gnawed at her stomach, but she pushed it down. She had no idea what to do about any of this.

After letting herself in, she padded softly down the hall to the kitchen, where her mother was pouring cups of tea as if she'd been waiting for Anna to appear. Anna leant on the centre bar top and rested on her elbows, accepting the mug with a grateful look.

"He wanted it to be you, Anna."

She looked up and caught her mother's eye, which was red-rimmed and shadowed by dark smudges. "Mum, why? Why would he want it to be me? I live in another city. I've never wanted kids. Plus, I work God-awful hours." Anna wrapped her fingers around her mug, tilting her head to look at Sandra, who sat down opposite her at the kitchen island.

"You don't think I said all of that to him?" Her mother raised an eyebrow playfully.

The half joke didn't even insult Anna. "See, even you agree with me. I'm as nurturing as a teaspoon."

"You and I both know you can be nurturing. And, actually, I agree with Jake and Sally's decision."

"You don't want the kids?" Surprise caused her to raise her voice, and she glanced upstairs, even though it was late and Ella and Toby were fast asleep.

Sandra's look hardened. "Those children mean the world to me. But your brother explained his decision, and it made sense. Your hours are better now that you're out of your internship and residency. You're more settled since you met Hayley—we won't talk about your drinking and partying before then."

Anna avoided her mother's eye and sipped her tea. Maybe she had enjoyed herself a touch too much.

"You're responsible, love those kids, and your job can easily be moved to a hospital in Melbourne. Or you could move the kids to Brisbane, but I don't think that would be fair."

Anna barely managed to push down the urge to throw her tea to the floor and scream hysterically about how unfair all this was. Acting like a child wouldn't solve her problem.

It wouldn't be fair to *the kids*? She was being asked to drop her entire life and move cities to take care of her brother's children—permanently. Her brother and sister-in-law had just died. Since the will had been read, her girlfriend could barely look her in the eye, and now Hayley was on a plane, probably panicking about what had just happened. Her father was comforting himself with a bottle of scotch as he hid in his study, and her mother's eyes were a permanent glazed red. Fair was a concept Anna was struggling with.

Her mother seemed to sense her internal struggle. "It's what he wanted, Anna." The words sunk in, heavy, as Sandra reached forward and rested a hand on her forearm. "Your father and I are, well, grandparents. We're old. J-Jake had a point."

It hurt to hear her mother stutter over his name. It hurt to know she spoke the truth. Everything hurt and Anna just wanted out. She knew it was selfish. But at least she was honest enough with herself to admit that.

Anna was going to be taking her brother's children.

She would be moving to God-awful Melbourne.

Her girlfriend was going to be pissed.

Two incomes, no kids.

Shit.

The next two days passed in a blur of trying to keep the kids settled, calling lawyers, and figuring out the next steps. Andrew stayed hidden away, and Sandra did most of the work with the kids, while Anna tried to hide from the reality of her situation.

Yet she couldn't escape the reality of what had happened.

In the shower, the loss of her brother would slam into her full force, only to be quickly drowned out by irrational anger at both him and Sally. What had they been thinking? Pacing the house like she was caged, Anna would finally go for walks, desperate to escape the grief that followed her. With her heart pounding, she would walk blindly and hope the ache in her chest would cease. Never had she thought she could feel like this; she could still barely believe her brother was gone.

The night before she flew out, Anna found herself tiptoeing into the kids' room before she went to bed. The room was dark, and she could hear Toby's soft baby snores coming from his cot. She padded softly over, and even she was thrown by the cuteness of the toddler, sprawled on his back, pacifier discarded to the side. She pulled the blanket up over him and ran her fingers over the silk of his hair. He really was the sweetest thing, this little boy who moved with a vengeance and had a vocabulary of less than ten words. He was never going to know his father and mother. His future had just been inexorably altered, the man he would have grown into changed. Nature versus nurture was about to take point.

"Aunty Na?"

She turned.

Big eyes stared at her from Ella's pillow.

Walking over, she squatted next to the bed, resting a hand on the blankets. "What's up, Ella Bella?" she asked in a low voice, anxious not to wake Toby.

"Do you *have* to go in the morning?"

Anna smiled softly. "I do. But I'll be back very soon."

"And then we're all going back home?" Ella scrunched up her little face, still trying to wrap her head around all the changes. "You, me and Toby?"

"Yep. Is that okay with you?"

Ella's face remained blank. She didn't respond but rolled over to face the wall, little hand gripping Anna's.

Anna sat for a few minutes, waiting for Ella's breathing to even out and her grip to slacken. Then she made her way out the door and pulled it closed quietly. Jake had always laughed and said Ella was a miniature Anna in personality. Apparently he wasn't far off. She leant against the wall, eyes closed. A long, slow breath left her body.

What was she doing?

"So, you're doing it?"

Heart pounding, Anna nodded.

They both sipped their wine, Hayley almost gulping hers before licking her lips, "And, uh—when do you need to go back?"

Anna tried to calm herself down. It had been a long day, flying back home and trying to organize everything as quickly as she could. None of that had been helped by the fact that she had spent an hour on the couch alone waiting for Hayley to come home, going over and over what she had to tell her. "I spoke to my boss at work today; he's supportive." She let out a long breath. "I'm thinking within a week, depending."

Hayley leant forward, putting her wine glass down on the coffee table and turning to look at Anna. "Depending on what?"

"On us."

Hayley licked her lips, taking her time to answer, as if she was carefully thinking out her response. "Does it have to be so soon?"

"My mum thinks the sooner the kids get settled back into normal—"

"Nothing will be normal for them."

"No. It won't." Sighing, Anna ran a hand over her eyes. "But she thinks the closer we can get them to it, the better."

Anna clung to her wine. This was unfair. They had both built a life avoiding exactly this situation. But where Anna had no choice in it, Hayley did. "This isn't something we ever wanted."

Hayley nodded again.

"You don't have to—we can just—I can go. And you can stay."

With a sigh, Hayley reached for her wine again. "I just—you're right, this isn't anything I ever wanted. I was just promoted. But—we—what if we try? I can't promise anything. But what if we try? I'll still live here, but I'll come on and off and see how we go. I'll come in a few weeks or so and we'll try distance."

Barely daring to breathe, Anna stared at her. "You don't have to do that."

"I want to."

Relief bloomed in Anna's chest and she kissed Haley before pulling back to try to lighten the mood. "I almost had a tantrum at my mother."

Hayley smirked, bringing a hand up behind Anna's neck, pulling her close. "I don't blame you. Can I throw one?"

The next six days were full of boxing up items, seeing friends before she left, sorting out lease payments, and overseeing last-minute handovers at work. Hayley was only home late in the evenings after long days at her firm. Anna kept busy with organising and packing up her life and then by pushing Hayley to the bedroom the second she walked through the door. She managed to not think at all. Compartmentalising had always been her strong point.

She pushed the thought that Jake was dead to the back of her mind, buried it as deep as she could. But there were times, when she was doing something completely mundane, that her chest would tighten and, for no apparent reason, it felt like she couldn't breathe. Before she could lose herself to that feeling completely, Anna would bite her lip to distract herself.

They had decided that Hayley was going to join her for a week, after a month or so, and then try and fly out as regularly as she could on weekends. A newspaper was sprawled on the table, red circles around job offers in Melbourne. Anna really had no idea what she was doing. Uprooting her entire life for two children. Uprooting herself for her dead brother, whom she longed to hit as hard as she could.

The anger hadn't really gone.

Six days in, the night before she flew out, she stood blowing hair out of her eyes, her messy ponytail coming apart as she pulled packing tape over her final box. The whole apartment was in shambles, her own boxes packed up amongst Hayley's things, tape dispensers and stuff scattered everywhere. She sighed heavily. Her love for this apartment bordered on the extreme. She'd made it so pretty—a home with her girlfriend. While they had always been working so much they hadn't spent a lot of time there, it was still home.

A sound from the bedroom made Anna turn. Hayley was half falling over a box on her way into the living room.

"Smooth."

Hayley shrugged, looking around.

Anna bit her lip.

Wide eyed, Hayley stared at all the boxes. She had her freaked-out face on, looking ready to burst with something she needed to say. The expression had been crossing her face regularly the last few nights.

Anna crossed her arms and shifted her weight to her other foot, waiting until Hayley finally made eye contact with her.

"It's okay, Hayley. Say it."

Hayley flinched slightly. "I can't do this."

Anna swallowed. She waited for Hayley to say what she needed to.

"I don't want to delay it. I don't want to come out in four weeks, to leave a week later, and then only see you every few weeks. For us both to be miserable until I finally panic and end it." She gritted her jaw and took a step forward. "We both know that's what I'll do."

Anna didn't move. Internally, everything shifted into boxes, compartmentalised so that shutting down was easier. The talent to do so was one Anna had always been grateful for—now more than ever.

"Anna, I'm sorry. I wanted to try. I didn't want to be the bitch that left you after your brother died and you got dumped with this…this huge responsibility, but I just…I can't do this. It's not me. And the firm…I just got promoted."

"I know."

This was a woman who hardly ever cried, and Anna could hardly look at her glazed eyes.

"I'm—I'm sorry. Kids—I just…I can't. I love you. But I can't."

"I get it, Hayley." The words came out harsher than Anna had intended, and Hayley moved closer. But exhaustion rolled over Anna, and the anger left as quickly as it had come.

Hayley took another step forward. "You can be angry at me."

Anna almost laughed. "Thanks for the permission, Hayley. But I get it."

Bitterness was rising in her gut. She wanted to squash the feeling. She did get it. If she had a choice, she'd bail as well. Over three years together, plans to buy an apartment, plans to build a life, and what did it take to destroy that? A drunk driver on his phone.

"I—"

"Hayley. I kind of need you to go. I can't…I fly out tomorrow night. I need to not see you before then."

Hayley stopped short, looking surprised, "O…Okay."

"I'm sorry."

"I'm sorry. I didn't…I don't want this."

Anna nodded.

Hayley moved forward as if to hug her.

Automatically, Anna took a step back, arms still crossed and eyes glued to a spot over Hayley's shoulder—anywhere but directly at her.

Nodding, Hayley stopped. They looked at each other for a second, and then Hayley turned, grabbed her bag and keys, and walked out.

Anna let out a long breath, falling back on the couch. Pulling her half-drunk wine towards her, she avoided looking around the room. Her brother was dead, her sister-in-law as well. Her girlfriend had left her, and she was moving the next day to a rainy city to take care of her niece and nephew, forever.

She took a sip.

There wasn't enough wine in the house.

Chapter Three

Anna couldn't bring herself to open the door.

Her fingers were numb with cold and her eyelids were heavy as she stood staring at the wood. After flying in late, she had come straight from the airport to her brother's house to drop off her suitcases. All she wanted to do was sleep, and now she couldn't even make herself go inside the house.

Instead, she looked around the front porch. It made her choke up. She'd been here only eight weeks ago, talking with Sally on the steps while they waited for Jake to finish his shower so he could drive Anna to the airport. She and Sally had been laughing hysterically about something, and Anna really wished she could remember what it was. Staring at the step and willing herself to remember, she bit her lip but came up blank. All she could recall was that Jake had come out, shaking his head at the two of them with their wine glasses, and had scooped up Sally, throwing her over his shoulder and carrying her inside despite her shrieks of laughing protests.

Anna shook her head and took a deep breath. If she didn't do this now, she would never do it. The spare key was hot in her hand after being gripped so long, and she finally unlocked the door and pushed it open. Warm air washed over her and smelt like *their* home. Almost dizzy, Anna took a second.

Steeling herself, she dragged one oversized suitcase and then the other up the stairs to the guest room. It was a nice room, one she had slept in many times. The walls were white, decorative touches done with anyone's taste in mind.

There was no way she could sleep in her brother's room.

She unpacked her suitcases, dreading the arrival of boxes that wouldn't fit anywhere. It didn't take long to put her things away, and she ended up standing in the middle of the room, slightly breathless and unsure of what to do next.

Actually, she knew what she should do next; she just wanted to avoid it.

Forcing herself, she wandered down the dark hallway and stood outside the master bedroom door. Repeatedly, her hand rose up to push it open, then dropped back down every time to clench at her side. Was it better for the kids to come back to it packed up and empty, or worse? Should she do something in there, or simply leave it alone for now?

In the end, she turned and left for her parents' house to sleep the night, unable to be in the oppressive quiet any longer.

Groggy and disorientated, an unrecognizable sound drilled into Anna's sleep. Blinding light pierced her eyes when she finally opened them and she slammed them shut again. She flopped over, forcing her eyes open again, and slowly focused on Ella. A book was open in her lap as she turned the pages absently. Without a word, Anna lifted up her bed sheets, and the little girl climbed in. It almost blew Anna away how hard Ella fell against her, fingers digging into her back and cold nose pressed against her neck.

She had no idea what she was supposed to do, but maybe the kids would help her.

They spent the day at her parents', and only at dinner time did they all go back to the house. This time, Anna didn't let herself hesitate, pushing the door open and entering like it was nothing—despite the clenching in her stomach.

Her parents stayed; Sandra cooked dinner. Ella simply pushed the food all over her plate and kept looking around the dining room, pale cheeked and not speaking a word. Toby chattered, instantly comfortable and happy in the place he knew as home. Soon, Anna had mashed potato in her hair from where he'd flung it.

At one point, Toby stopped, head cocked and a half smile on his face, staring off towards the hallway as if he'd heard a noise. "Ma?"

They all paused and stared at him, even Ella, watching as he realised no one was coming and went intently back to his potato. It left a hollow feeling in Anna's stomach.

When they put the kids to bed, Ella didn't say a word the entire time. Anna tried to stay until her niece fell asleep, but she was fairly sure Ella was faking it when she finally walked out quietly.

Her parents let themselves out, Sandra pausing to wrap her arms around Anna. "Hayley will be out soon; that'll help."

It was only then that Anna told her.

Her mother looked ready to burst into tears, but one look at Anna's face seemed to make her rein it in. In the car already, her father beeped the horn. Sandra wrapped her arms around Anna again and told her to call if she needed anything.

Anna stood in the hallway, wanting to rip the door open and scream at her mother to come back and stay while Anna flew back to her life. Instead, fingers trembling slightly, she grabbed a bottle of wine that was unopened in the fridge and sat on the couch. She tried to ignore the fact that the wine was her and Sally's favourite, one they always shared.

The house was horribly still. And her heart was racing.

Distantly, she wondered if she was having an anxiety attack. Her breathing was a little rapid and the trembling in her fingers had intensified. Licking her lips, Anna tried to tamp it down.

The kids were going to stay home the next day, Friday. It had been decided that Ella would go back to school on Monday. Sandra said she'd spoken to the school counsellor, and the sooner they got Ella back into whatever normalcy they could, the better. The same day, Anna would have a meeting with Ella's teacher and the counsellor to discuss how to keep everything as normal as possible. But what *was* normal?

Kids' toys sat in the corner of the room, a haphazard stack of Disney DVDs piled in front of the television. There was so much colour. Knees drawn up to her chest, Anna took in a deep breath and dropped her head down. Home was what she wanted, not this. She longed to be sharing wine on the couch with Hayley, then to fall into bed and throw herself into sex and skin, not go to bed alone in her dead brother's house with his kids sleeping down the hall.

Something poked into her back, and she pulled the remote control out from between the cushions. Deciding against turning the television on, she dropped it on the sofa. She couldn't blame Hayley, not at all, not really. But that didn't mean she didn't feel some resentment. They'd spent three years together, and she thought Hayley could at least have tried a bit harder.

She'd done it. Her life had turned upside down, and she was trying.

Mentally slapping herself, she stood up, put her wine glass in the sink and the bottle in the fridge. Just as she was walking up the stairs, she heard Toby give a cry. Heart pounding, she hovered and hoped he would fall back to sleep. Another cry. Steeling herself, she continued up and into his room.

"Mama." He gave a nonsensical cry again and then, "Da."

The sound almost broke her heart. She wondered how long until he'd forget, until he no longer cried for the parents who had once shown up without fail.

Carpet soft beneath her toes, Anna padded across the room to bend over his cot. He was sitting up, his blanket pulled to his chest, brown hair mussed and little cheeks red and wet. Damp blue eyes looked at her for a minute, not recognising his aunt, only to throw his arms up when he did. She bent down and picked him up, and he nestled into her.

Swallowing, Anna sat on the chair in the corner of the room. She leant back awkwardly and held him to her chest, smoothing the hair off his forehead and rubbing his back. Heavy and unsettled breathing echoed in Anna's ears, and he murmured "Da" several times before he calmed down, fingers clasping rhythmically at her shirt, eyes fluttering closed.

The chair rocked silently, and she rubbed his back, remembering her last phone conversation with her brother.

"Toby's still not sleeping through the night. You're a doctor, right? Is that normal? Ella slept like a log."

"Jake, seriously, how many times? I'm an anaesthetist—kids cry, and I put them to sleep."

"Perfect! That's what we want to happen. What drugs do I need?"

She laughed and rolled her eyes, switching the hand she held the phone in. "Funny. I don't know. Is he waking up screaming or just waking up?"

"Just every few nights, waking up. I only have Ella to compare him to."

"I'd say it's just a phase. Does he settle quickly?"

"Yeah, right back down. Only that quickly for me, though. Sally now has an excuse to kick me out of bed when he cries. Kid loves his dad."

It was hard to keep being angry with Jake when memories like that made her feel like falling apart.

Anna pressed her lips against the finally sleeping boy's head. Not for the first time—and it wouldn't be the last—she really did wonder what the hell she was doing.

Too much TV wasn't good for kids—Anna had read this somewhere. Nevertheless, she spent her Friday morning watching a lot of cartoons. With a job interview that afternoon, surely a little downtime would do them all some good. Her boss at her old hospital had called ahead to recommend her for the job, but Anna still had to go through the formalities.

Plus, it was a good excuse to get out of the house.

Her mother showed up, took one look at the kids—Toby had a Lego bucket on his head that Ella was hitting at with a wooden spoon while staring at the television—and said, "I'll take them to the park."

Anna mouthed "thank you" and grabbed her bag, saying "bye" to the kids and escaping quickly. As she started to leave, she heard Toby make a squawk of protest, but the sound was interrupted by her mother's soothing whispers.

Since Sandra didn't need her car, with the park just down the road, Anna used it. She still didn't feel like her brother's car was hers to use.

Navigating slowly through the streets, she was surprised it only took twenty-five minutes to get to the hospital. Anna parked in visitors parking and wandered to the entrance. The building loomed high, the walls grey and intimidating. The place was huge. Luckily, the receptionist at the information desk was more than happy to give her directions to the office she needed. The familiar smell of hospital relaxed Anna slightly.

As she slid into an elevator, a tall, pale woman slipped in just behind her.

"Are you looking for Luke McDermott's office?"

Anna looked at her, surprised. "Ah, yeah?"

"Sorry, I heard you talking to the receptionist. I was heading there too. I can show you if you like?"

Anna breathed a sigh of relief. "Thanks, that'd be great. The directions weren't overly specific."

The woman slipped her hands into her lab coat. "It's a bit of a maze."

"I'm Anna Foster." She held her hand out.

The woman shook it. "Kym Drew."

"Worked here long?"

"A couple of years now. I'm in Psych."

Anna winced. "Brave. Well, it's nice to meet someone I might run into around the place."

"Applying for a job?" They walked out of the elevator and down a hallway before turning left down another. Already lost, Anna tried to track their route.

"Yeah, actually. Senior anaesthetist. I just moved from Brisbane."

Kym's eyes widened slightly. "Oh, wait. He mentioned the woman from Brisbane—you come highly recommended. Job's pretty much yours, if that helps."

"It does, actually, thanks."

"So what brings you to Melbourne? You leave the Sunshine Coast for all this bright weather?" Kym nodded her head to the window they were walking past. All that could be seen were dark clouds rolling across the sky.

"Uh...some family stuff. Had to move." Anna wasn't ready to explain the whole ordeal to a stranger.

Her face must have given something away, though, because Kym's look sobered. "Sorry, I shouldn't have asked. I talk a bit more than I should. My husband passed away a few months ago, and, since then, I seem to overshare, even more than I used to." She stopped outside a door, fidgeting. "Like now, for example." She gave a wry grin. "I'm probably not suited to Psych at the moment."

She took in Kym's expression, the way her eyes flicked from place to place, how she bounced slightly back on her heels. "No, don't be sorry. I'm sorry about your husband." She hesitated. "My uh—my brother passed away, almost three weeks ago now. Things are kind of...messy? I had to move to Melbourne."

Kym's eyes caught and held hers. She gave a soft smile. "I'm sorry about your brother. Maybe we could get a coffee sometime?"

She had no idea how she would fit in work with the two kids suddenly in her care, let alone coffee, but...

"I'd love that." She indicated the door. "You go first."

"I'll only be a minute." Kym was out again about thirty seconds later. "Thanks."

She smiled. "No worries."

"I told him you were out here, just head on in."

"Thanks, Kym. It was nice meeting you."

"I look forward to that coffee."

Anna smiled and turned, knocking as she walked into the office, thinking: *That woman had the saddest eyes.*

When Anna woke up on Saturday morning, faint light gave away the very early hour. A look outside the window showed a cloudy sky that was just beginning to lighten. Still warm, she buried herself deeper in her covers.

Thankfully, the kids were still sleeping—which gave her the opportunity to panic. The job at the hospital was hers—a promotion, too, as one of the seniors in her department. She wanted to feel proud, excited even. Instead, it felt tainted. She would much rather still be working in Brisbane, with Jake alive, living his life with his wife and kids. Everyone would be where they wanted to be, not where they were obligated to be. Or dead.

She sighed, kicking the blanket off. Sleeping without Hayley was hard.

Work would begin in a week, giving Anna time to sort out childcare for Toby—apparently the staff got a great rate at the day care in the hospital. She needed to make sure Ella was settled back into school and to sort out after-school care for when she finished.

Everything was still too overwhelming. Even after explaining her situation to her new boss and making arrangements so she could be with the kids as much as possible, Anna was worried about work. Emergencies happened, surgeries ran long. And, even excluding all of this, how was she going to handle two kids, full stop?

The sheet tightened in her fist as she tried to ignore the tense feeling in her gut. She missed Hayley, missed the adult company. She missed her brother. And Sally. Really, she missed the life she had barely yet given up.

Rolling out of bed, Anna decided to make noise to wake the kids up and stop herself from thinking.

Cheerios littered the floor, the table, and Toby's hair. Milk was finger-painted all over the high chair tray. Toby sat, hair still bed messy, grinning at Anna as he picked up Cheerios one by one. There was nothing she could do but smile back at him. He'd woken up grumpy, grizzling, and calling for Sally. It had taken a little while, but he'd warmed up.

"Na!" he said through the grin, happily going back to his cereal. Mostly bright and playful, he had especially settled in his own environment. Yet, still, he was constantly calling for his mother and father. The cries at night were the worst.

Ella ate most of her breakfast, for which Anna was grateful, but she tried not to bring attention to it. Not once did she speak, but Anna figured beggars can't be choosers. Her niece was still quiet and introspective most of the time, moody and rarely speaking—except when she was with Toby. In spite of herself, she chatted to Toby, holding his hand and making up stories to tell him.

A Cheerio hit her shoulder, and Anna turned her attention back to Toby.

"Good cereal, Mister?" She took a bite of her toast, smiling softly as he nodded, and tried to ignore the smell she had just noticed coming from him. Nappies were definitely very low on her list of favourite things.

"Can we go to the park again today?"

Surprised to hear Ella speak, Anna whipped her head around. "Of course. It's a great day for the park. Did you have fun with Grandma yesterday?"

Ella shrugged. "It was okay. There were other kids there."

"There'll be more there today, it's Saturday. You can play with them as long as you like."

"Okay."

After finally breaking the silence, going back to it was too depressing. Surging ahead with the newfound conversation, Anna asked, "You looking forward to school on Monday?"

"No."

Blinking at the honesty, she wondered how to tackle this one. Direct seemed the best way. "Why not, honey?"

Ella used the spoon to squash the soggy remnants of her cereal in her bowl before saying, "The other kids will ask me about Mummy and Daddy."

Anna's chewing slowed. She swallowed hard. "Well, if they do and you don't want to talk about it, you just say 'Can we talk about something else?' Okay?"

The cereal bowl still held Ella's attention as she went back to mashing her breakfast.

"You can talk about it, if you want to? With kids or teachers. Or Grandma or me?"

"I don't want to talk about it."

At a loss, Anna nodded. "That's okay."

If there was something Anna understood, it was that. But was that okay for a six-year-old? Should she push her to talk? When was it too long for Ella to be pushing food around her plate? When should Ella be expected to act like a kid again and not like a quiet little adult? Would she ever act like that again?

"How about you go clean up, I'll get Toby ready and we'll head to the park?"

Ella nodded, perking up slightly at the notion. After putting her plate in the sink, she scooted out of the room.

Anna watched her walk out and then turned to Toby, who had brought his bowl up to his mouth and was drinking what milk was left. Most of it spilt all over him. Anna grimaced.

He put it down with a loud 'ah!' noise and grinned at Anna, milk dripping off his chin.

She sat with an eyebrow raised at him, a smile playing on her lips. "Beautiful manners, Tobes."

"Park!"

Anna stripped the giant bib off Toby, glad it had mostly protected him from the milk. Carrying him on her hip, she went up the stairs. "Yup. We'll go to the park. That's a new word for you, by the way. Well done. Grandma teach you that one?"

He just smiled at her and patted her cheek with sticky fingers, legs kicking idly.

Anna entered his room. "All right, we'll face that monster nappy of yours, then go to the park. Deal?"

He giggled at her.

"Easy for you to laugh. You just make the mess. I have to clean it up."

Five minutes later, Anna was making her way down the stairs with a much cleaner Toby dressed in tiny green overalls. She put him down in front of a floor puzzle in the living room, calling in the general direction of the stairs, "I'll just get the pram and we'll go, Ella."

She took a deep breath to calm her nerves. She was handling this. Toby was dressed and clean. They'd eaten. Ella was interested in the park. She was totally handling this.

Walking into the garage off the side of the kitchen, she flicked on the light switch, flooding the space with light. When she saw Jake's SUV, Anna nearly groaned at the idea of driving a soccer mum's car.

The car she had driven in Brisbane, now on the market, was a zippy one that had appreciated her lead foot. As Anna sucked it up and pressed the button to unlock the doors, she froze for a moment. The thought occurred to her: If Jake and Sally had been driving the SUV instead of Sally's smaller work car, could they have survived the crash? Her heart pounded, and Anna squeezed her eyes shut and blocked out the thought. She was getting the pram and they were going to walk to the park.

That was what she was doing that morning.

Small things.

She walked to the back of the car, opening it and pulling out the folded-up pram. Dropping it on the ground at her feet, she eyed it suspiciously. The thing looked more like a mountain-climbing buggy. Since when did prams come with three wheels?

Anna sighed and bent over, pulling at the handlebars and the wheels to try and make it unfold. Sandra had told her it just "popped" open.

Nothing happened.

She shook it, levering it with her feet and tugging again at the handlebars.

Again, nothing.

Anna was a well-sought-after anaesthetist who'd graduated with honours. She could do complex drug calculations in her sleep. Her *mother* could do this. Anna could make the damn pram open.

Squatting, she looked it over and saw a little red lever. She flicked it, which seemed to unlock something as the frame loosened. She pulled at the handlebars again and the whole thing finally popped open, catching Anna in the chin and sending her back on her rear as it did so.

Hand to her jaw, she rubbed, glaring at the pram. Tears of frustration welled up in her eyes.

She really wasn't handling this.

A giggle came from behind her. Anna turned to see Ella standing in the doorway, hand over her mouth as if to catch the noise and send it back in.

Anna couldn't stop the slow smile that came to her lips. "You laughing at me, madam?"

Ella pulled her hand away from her mouth, a stubborn smile still pulling at her lips. It lit up her whole face, her green eyes bright and a hint of dimples on her cheeks. "You're not very good at this stuff, are you, Aunty Na?"

Anna smiled wryly, wiping her hands on her jeans. "Not really, Ella Bella, but I'll get better."

Chapter Four

The groceries were piling up in her cart, yet Anna was only halfway through. Ella was at her second day back at school, and Sandra, taking pity on Anna when she'd said she needed to grocery shop, had taken Toby for the afternoon. Apparently grocery shopping with a child was hard work, and Anna was very okay with her mother helping in that department.

So, alone for the first time in days, Anna was even enjoying grocery shopping.

Oh, how her life had changed.

She couldn't believe how much food she had to buy. Even with Ella's fussy appetite, they powered through bread, milk, and cereal like a small army. And Toby would put anything food-like in his mouth—she'd caught him with a decorative apple clenched between his teeth, looking confused as to why he couldn't chew it.

Anna found herself in the cereal aisle debating types, overwhelmed by the fact that there was enough variety to take up an entire aisle. Coloured boxes lined the shelves, advertising low sugar and no additives and a lot of information about dietary needs for kids. Palms sweaty, she stared at the huge array and missed the days of a simple coffee for breakfast.

Taking a deep breath, she tried to quell the panic that rose inside her. Choosing cereal was a ridiculous reason to freak out. But panic had been her constant companion ever since signing the papers at the lawyers' yesterday. In reality, the panic had been constant since her phone had rung during her vacation over two weeks ago. In a few weeks, or even months, the guardianship would be official. The kids, the house, everything would be in her name. All of this had become even more real after a bubbly social worker had visited the night before and explained she'd be popping in regularly.

Anna stared at the bright, colourful boxes lining the shelves in front of her. It was too much.

Swallowing heavily, she grabbed a packet of Cheerios. There had definitely been enough change lately. She dropped it in the cart, and, on second thought, grabbed another two boxes and dropped them in too. Making any kind of decision felt good. As had so often occurred in recent days, the reality of the situation was catching up with her, as was the headache from the wine she'd drunk last night after the kids had gone to bed. What she really wanted to do was call her brother to talk about it all, partly because he was who Anna always talked to about these things and partly because she was still filled with an inner rage she would love to let loose on him.

Anna headed towards the next aisle, happy to escape the confusing cereal section. Her cart turned the corner, and she heard, and felt, it make loud contact with someone's basket. She pulled up short. "Oh, God, I'm so sorry!"

Completely turning the corner, pushing the cart wider to go around the unfortunate soul, she made eye contact with surprised-looking dark brown eyes.

The woman she'd hit laughed, adjusting her basket to rest against the hip it had just been knocked from. "It's okay, I'm in a bit of a blind spot."

"Still, I'm sorry. I was lost in thought."

The stranger grinned and Anna found herself smiling back.

"Who doesn't get lost in thought wandering the grocery aisles?"

"Yeah, well, the choices between condiments left me pondering the complexities of life."

Anna felt a bit smug as the woman smiled harder in response. She shifted on her feet, shaking her head slightly to get tight black curls out of her eyes. "Mustard versus ketchup, whole egg versus light mayonnaise. Really does parallel with the tough choices we face, don't you think?"

"Don't forget the incredibly difficult one between olive oils." Anna leant against the handle of her cart, enjoying the easy banter.

"See, that's where you lose me. Virgin and light and extra virgin—I didn't know olive oil was a university kid."

Caught in surprise at the words, Anna laughed out loud.

The woman smiled as if pleased with Anna's response. She really was pretty, smile lighting up her face, dark skin and eyes so brown Anna couldn't look away.

"I'm Anna—I usually exchange pleasantries before pushing people over in grocery aisles."

Without hesitating, the woman offered her hand. Strong fingers wrapped around her own, the stranger's grasp firmer than Anna had expected.

"Lane. And you make a regular thing of running people over?"

Lingering briefly a moment, they both let go and lowered their hands. "I'm known for it."

Amusement flashed across Lane's face. "Is that how you got that interesting bruise on your chin? Running a stranger over in the store?"

A flush made its way onto Anna's cheeks. The bruise from the pram incident had only just started to fade. "That...that's a bit of a long story. I had a fight with an embarrassing object."

"I'd really like to hear that story sometime."

Anna winked. "Maybe I'll tell it to you one day."

Lane's phone, clasped in her hand, beeped, and she quickly glanced down at it before looking up again, apologetic. "It's a pity I'm late for a party—I was told weeks ago to bring crackers and cheese, so of course I forgot and had to stop by on my way there."

"No judgment here. I just ran down an innocent bystander in the grocery store."

Lane grinned again and Anna couldn't get over how it lit her whole face up. "Maybe next time you do it, I can hear the story behind that bruise."

"Sounds fair." Straightening up, Anna put her hands on the cart-handle. "Enjoy your party."

"Thanks. Enjoy your Cheerios. Looks like you like them." With a final smile over her shoulder, Lane walked away.

Dark jeans clung to Lane's body far too well and Anna let her eyes trail for a minute, before mentally slapping herself. The rest of her shopping was done with a small smile tugging at her lips.

She made it through the checkout, trying not to react to the cost of shopping for an adult and two small children, instead focussing on the conversation she'd just had. It had been fun, with an edge of flirty. Anna shook her head. She'd probably never see Lane again. And she didn't even want to. She'd just ended a long-term relationship, and her life was chaos.

But Lane had been really pretty.

And pretty could be a nice distraction.

She pushed her cart out and loaded the bags into the stupidly oversized vehicle, sliding into the driver's seat and pulling out her phone. Lane really did have an amazing smile.

Her thoughts still on Lane, she dialled Jake's number, always her first point of contact to talk about women with. A half smile on her face, she froze as the call went straight to voicemail and she remembered that the phone had been shattered in the crash. The sound of his voice flooded the car.

Hey, it's Jake Foster. Leave a message and I'll call you back. Or call Sally, she's more reliable, anyway.

Anna didn't know how long she sat, fingers gripping the steering wheel, knuckles white, staring at her mobile.

She'd forgotten. For five minutes, she'd forgotten.

The thought made her horrified, guilty, sad.

It made her stomach twist with so much emotion that, for a moment, she thought she was going to vomit.

And it made her miss Jake ten times more, as remembering crashed over her and it hit her all over again.

Her brother was dead.

On Thursday night, Anna prepared fish fingers and chips. A lazy meal, but she was over cooking. While chopping up a salad, she tried not to think about the phone conversation she'd just had with her mother.

Sandra had called her up in tears, sobbing because she'd just gone through the baby photos of her and Jake. Anna had listened and made soothing noises as words like "baby boy" and "the poor kids" and "the two of you were inseparable" came over the phone. During the call, Anna had snuck down the hall and hid near the coat rack to be away from the living room, where Toby was destroying the puzzle Ella was patiently doing, so they wouldn't overhear.

She'd gotten off the phone drained and exhausted, instructing her mother to have a hot bath and a glass of scotch, with a promise to spend the next day with her at the park with Toby.

Anna tried to still her thoughts and focus on chopping everything into even chunks. Since accidentally calling Jake's phone, she'd been on edge. The conversation with her mother hadn't helped. How was she supposed to keep the kids, herself, *and* her mother together? When Anna had picked up Ella from school, she hadn't said a single word in the car. Toby was as sweet as ever, a tiny but destructive force of giggles and mess. While he was happy and delightful most of the time, he was clingy and confused at others, crying for Mama or Da. Luckily, he was of an age that distraction and being with people he knew were enough to turn his mind to other things. But when he called for people who couldn't answer and looked so confused when they didn't come, Anna's stomach ached with the fact that she couldn't even explain it to him.

All she had to do was keep herself together and get through dinner. Then bath time, then bed—and then she would sit on the couch and eat a lot of chocolate and surf the Internet, looking at holidays she couldn't go on.

God, the beaches she'd visited before her life had shattered had been incredible.

A shrill ringing sounded, and Anna jumped. Another phone conversation was not something she had the energy for. She wiped her hands on her jeans and pulled it out of her pocket, eyebrows shooting up when she saw who was calling. For a moment, she genuinely considered not answering. With a sigh, she sucked it up and hit the green button.

"Hayley?"

"Hey, Anna."

"Uh...how are you?"

"I'm, I'm good." Silence hovered a second. "I just wanted to see how you were going."

Phone between her shoulder and ear, Anna went back to chopping. "I'm fine. I'm chopping tomato. Not for Ella though, she hates them."

"She's a bit young to have such a big bias."

Anna gave a mirthless laugh. "Yeah, well. I let her hate what she wants right now."

"Fair call."

Tomato on her plate, Anna grabbed a small bowl to put Toby's in. She'd given him a plate the first night with pasta on it. Big mistake.

"So, how are you, really, Anna?"

Anna's throat caught. Why was it that you were fine until someone genuinely asked how you were? "Hayley—I'm fine."

"Anna..."

"Look, I can't do this. I...you walked, Hayley. And that's okay. But you can't call me and be all concerned. We only broke up two weeks ago."

Hayley sighed. "I know, I'm sorry. I just...it's not that I don't care. I know I walked. I'm just worried about you. This is...it's a lot. And I miss you."

Anna closed her eyes and took a deep breath, knife stilled. "I appreciate that, Hayley. But I... I can't do that. The kids need dinner and they have to be in bed on time. Ella has school tomorrow."

They were both silent, the ridiculousness of Anna being in this position, talking about dinner and school and kids, hanging over them.

"Okay. I'm sorry, again. I just wanted to check in." There was a pause. "I'm sure you're doing amazing, Anna."

"Thanks. Take care, Hayley." She hung up, shoving her phone into her back pocket again, hands trembling slightly. Anna didn't have this in her today.

Something hit her leg and she looked down. Finally, she smiled. Grinning up around his pacifier was Toby.

"Hey, Mister. You hungry? And where'd you get that pacifier? According to Nanna, that's just for sleep time."

Hands held up were his answer.

Acquiescing, Anna reached down and picked him up, then carried him to his high chair and set his salad down for him to pick at while she pulled the food out of the oven. She served it onto her and Ella's plates, then chopped some into pieces so it would cool more quickly before placing it in front of Toby. After some advice from her mother, Anna added enough ketchup to drown a small town. She put the plates on the table and called Ella. Anna had to call a second time before Ella meandered her way in and sat down.

Sauce smeared on his face, Toby babbled as he ate with his hands. Ella picked at a few chips, and Anna tried to force herself to eat food she wasn't so keen on either.

"How was school, Ella?"

Ella shrugged.

"Do anything new?"

"No."

Anna bit into her salad and resigned herself to a silent dinner. She wasn't in the mood to force conversation either. Everything had left her feeling ready to crawl out of her skin, exhausted and wired at the same time, her head a mess of thoughts, and all she wanted to do was go anywhere that wasn't here. She tried not to focus on how trapped she felt.

Toby managed to finish everything on his plate, Anna as well, while Ella had a handful of chips and a bite of the fish and then proceeded to massacre the rest with her fork.

Anna sighed. "Ella. You need to eat some more, please."

Ella stabbed harder at her fish. "Not hungry."

"Well, you should be. You didn't want anything to eat after school. Have some of your salad."

"No."

"Ella, for God's sake, eat something!" Anna hadn't meant to snap.

Ella pushed her plate away, so forceful it slid almost to the other end of the table. "Why?"

Ella glared at her, a flush over her cheeks.

"Because you need to eat. Your mum would want—"

"You're not my mum! You don't know what she'd want!"

Anna's eyes widened at the angry tone.

Ella's face was a mirror of her own. They stared at each other for a long minute, both breathing hard, before Ella shoved her chair back and ran out of the room, her feet thumping up the stairs.

Anna swallowed heavily and looked to Toby, whose hand had stilled in the middle of smearing ketchup over his high chair table, his own eyes wide as he blinked at her. Closing her eyes for a moment, Anna tried to gather her strength. Finally, she stood up and dumped all their plates in the sink. After quickly wiping Toby down, she pulled him out of his high chair. The tight feeling in her throat made it hard to act fine. Anna put him in the living room in front of the puzzle, and he went to it, pulling it all apart. Adding some blocks, she hoped it was enough to keep him going.

Then she moved to the bottom of the stairs and steeled herself. She wasn't surprised Ella had finally snapped. But Anna *was* kicking herself for raising her voice. The last two days had been especially terrible, excluding the best adult conversation she'd had in a long time in a supermarket aisle. Still, she shouldn't have let that, combined with her worry that Ella wasn't eating, come out that way.

She took a deep breath and climbed the stairs, pausing outside Ella's room. Eye level with the orange letters that spelt Ella's name out on her door, Anna knocked. Jake had stuck the letters up after Sally had found them in a gift store way before Ella was even born. Sally had loved the name Ella from the get-go, and had been firm in the knowledge that she was having a girl. Jake had put up the letters and sent Anna a photo, with the caption *an Ella for Aunty Anna?*

Anna pushed the door open. Her niece was curled up on her bed, pillow pulled over her face, turned to the wall. Silent sobs were making her whole body shudder.

Once again, Anna was at a loss. "Ella?" Her own voice was hoarse.

"Go away."

Even Anna knew that wasn't what she should do. She walked forward and sat on the edge of the bed. "I'm not going to do that, honey."

A hiccup came from under the pillow.

Her heart breaking for the little girl who was too young to handle this, Anna leant down and lay behind her. She wrapped her arm around Ella, pulling her close. Ella's body still shook with sobs, and Anna ran her hand down her hair and pressed a kiss to the back of her head.

"I…I m-miss Mummy and Daddy." Ella could barely get the words out.

Tears stung Anna's eyes. She blinked them back, screwing her eyes closed and pressing her face into Ella's hair. "I know."

"You don't know." Ella's truthful words were muffled in the pillow, but she was definitely shouting them. "I want things to be how they were."

Anna nodded, even though she knew Ella couldn't see. She wanted to tell her niece that it would get better, but she wasn't so sure about that herself.

"I-I really miss them." Ella's voice cracked.

"I do too, sweetie. I do too."

She swallowed, taking in a shuddering breath. "You do?"

"I really do. So much." Anna's own voice trembled. "Your daddy was my brother, and I miss him so much."

Tearstained and flushed, Ella pulled the pillow away from her face. Glistening green eyes looked up at Anna. "He was?" Her face was screwed up, confused.

"Yeah. Like Toby is your brother. That's what makes me your aunty."

Ella took this new concept in, still hiccupping occasionally. She blinked, and a fresh tear spilled over. They lay for a minute, Anna wrapped around Ella, who was half-turned in her arms.

"Aunty Na?"

"Yeah?"

"I like that you're my aunty."

"I like that I am, too."

She pressed her nose into Ella's neck, shaking her head to tickle, and Ella gave a small, choking noise that was not a laugh but wasn't a cry, either.

Anna sat up suddenly, having an idea. "Ella?"

Ella looked at her.

"Come with me."

In a minute, she had Toby and Ella in the kitchen. After rummaging in a cupboard, Anna pulled out a saucepan and a fry pan. She gave Toby the saucepan and a wooden spoon—which he happily went about smacking together—and put the fry pan on the stovetop.

Ella stood there, looking confused. "What are you doing?"

Anna had gotten out a mixing bowl and measuring cups and was now pulling out flour, eggs, milk, and honey. "We're making pancakes."

A small smile flickered onto Ella's face. "But it's dinner time. And you cooked fish already."

"So?" Anna pulled a footstool up to the bench and picked Ella up, making an exaggerated "oof" noise as she set the girl down. Flour and a measuring cup sat in front of her. "We want two cups of that in the mixing bowl."

Ella's eyes widened. "I can do it?"

"Yup. Who cares about the mess?"

Puffs of flour exploded in the air as Ella dug the cup into the container and scooped some into the bowl. She grinned as a cloud rose up, tears already drying on her cheeks.

They made the pancakes in a floury mess, Toby banging loudly on the saucepan, creating as much noise as possible. Anna cracked eggs, Ella slopped milk over the mix and stirred it with all the vigour of her six years. Flour streaked their faces and the batter turned out a lumpy mess.

Voice hoarse, Ella stood on her footstool, naming shapes for Anna to make pancakes into, Toby adding to the noise just because he could. Anna made diamonds, stars, squares, and triangles and even attempted a dog that came out as a blob. Anything Ella requested, she attempted, earning giggles and mature eye rolls at the messy shapes that ended up on their plates.

They covered the hot pancakes in honey and ate them as soon as they were ready while more cooked on the stove. They were lumpy and, at times, only half-cooked. But Ella tore hers apart and shared them with Toby, who delighted in the sweetness. Her cheeks were a mess of honey and flour, and she was grinning from ear to ear.

And, without noticing she was doing it, she finished every pancake Anna handed her.

They stayed up past ten. Toby fell asleep on the couch under a blanket while Ella sat sleepily in Anna's lap, watching *Megamind* twice over and mimicking the voices.

Anna smoothed Ella's hair off her face, cheek resting against the top of the girl's head.

It wasn't everything, but it wasn't nothing, either.

Chapter Five

Considering the circumstances, the school didn't question Anna when she called Ella in sick. She found herself wanting both kids with her after the night before—a feeling that surprised her. Burying herself in them helped her not to think about what had put her in this situation. The distraction probably wasn't ideal, but it was welcome anyway.

They all slept a little later than usual, Ella in Anna's bed and Toby in his cot. For a little girl, Ella took up a lot of space. Anna had had an elbow, foot or bony knee digging into her back at some point all through the night.

When Toby's babbling woke Anna sometime just after eight, she wandered through to get him.

His face splitting into a grin when he saw her, he was standing up in his cot, hands clinging to the side, his hair spikey and mussed.

"Morning, little man." Anna pulled his pacifier out and dropped it in the cot. Thankfully enough, he barely flinched, still staring up at her. Once he was in her arms, he immediately dropped his head into her neck, melding himself to her for morning cuddles. The way he happily settled into Anna never failed to surprise her. Nor did the feeling of warmth she got when he did it, his little fingers gripping at her shirt.

She stood for a minute, swaying with him and rubbing his back. "Shall we go see Ella?"

He sat up straighter in her arms and pointed out the door, whole body arching into the action. "El!"

Anna quickly changed his nappy, using the opportunity to put some outside clothes on him. When he was back in her arms, she held a finger to her lips and said, "Shh. Let's wake up Ella."

Toby just giggled.

Creeping comically, Anna snuck them into her room. Even as Toby was giggling madly, she deposited him on the lump in the bed. The lump made a groaning noise.

Delighted, Toby tugged at the blankets, pulling them off her. He smacked his open palm none too gently on her cheek.

"Toby!" Ella opened her eyes and glared at him. "I'm sleeping!"

Toby clearly didn't care. "El! El!"

Ella reached her hands up and tickled Toby on his stomach; he squealed and threw himself backwards on the bed. Auburn hair a mess around her head, Ella sat up, instantly awake in the way Anna was learning only a child could be. It amazed her how painstakingly patient Ella could be with Toby at times. She was fairly certain that she and Jake had not been that gentle. Maybe it was the age gap.

Eventually, they went from the bed to the kitchen for cereal. Anna had cleaned up the night before, and flour no longer coated everything.

The morning felt different, somehow. Ella was happy not to be going to school, almost excited at the sneaky day off. As Anna fished through the fridge, she realised they needed more milk and bread—shocking, considering she'd just been to the store the other day.

"Ella Bella?"

"Yeah?" Ella answered around a mouthful of milk and Cheerios.

"What do you say to some one-on-one time with Grandma? I'll go to the store with Toby, bring him back for a sleep, and then the two of us will meet you at the park in the afternoon?"

Ella perked up a little. "Really?" One-on-one time with Grandma was hard to come by with a baby brother.

"Really. She doesn't even know you're playing hooky, so we can surprise her when she gets here."

"Okay."

Anna figured her mother would be delighted, especially considering how upset she'd been on the phone yesterday. And this would mean Anna could have some chill-out time while Toby had a sleep. She really, really needed it.

Ella put their bowls in the sink while Anna was wiping Toby's face with a washcloth. The first morning, Anna hadn't wiped his face, and she'd ended up with yoghurt and who knows what else covering her shoulder and legs. As she pulled him out of the high chair, there was a knock on the door and the sound of it opening.

Sandra's voice called out as she entered the front hall.

"Nanna!" Ella immediately ran to greet her.

Anna dumped a squirming Toby to the ground, and he took off towards the front door on unsteady legs.

"I'm playing hooky!" Ella announced as Anna entered the hall.

"I can see that!"

Ella was wrapped around her grandmother's legs. "We get to hang out just us this morning, Nanna."

Sandra smiled and knelt down, wrapping her arms around Ella. "Well, aren't I lucky?"

Toby hit her then, like a whirlwind, and she wrapped an arm around him too.

She looked over Ella's shoulder and gave Anna a strained smile. "Morning, sweetheart."

"Do you mind, Mum? I thought you could have Ella this morning while I take Toby to the store and bring him back for a sleep, then meet you at the park at, say, two?"

Her mother stood up, wincing as her knees cracked. "That sounds delightful. All day with my beautiful grandchildren. We can go for lunch somewhere, Ella?"

"And get a hot chocolate?"

"I think that's a must. Run upstairs and grab your jacket, and we'll go find something fun to do."

As Ella made a beeline up the stairs, Anna and Sandra made eye contact. "No school?"

Anna crossed her arms and leant against the stair railing, watching Toby pull shoes off the rack one by one. "We had a rough night. I thought she could use a day off."

"Everyone needs a day off sometimes."

Anna nodded.

"You need one, too. I can take the kids anytime, Anna. You're not alone."

Staring adamantly at Toby so she didn't have to look her mother in the eye, Anna nodded again, choking on words she wanted to spew forth. She wanted to tell her mother just how overwhelmed she felt, just how much she did not think she was the one to be doing this. And in amongst it all was this gnawing loneliness. She *was* alone. She missed Hayley. There were nights she woke up with her arm stretched out, wondering why she hit empty space and not her girlfriend's skin. Sometimes she wondered if she actually missed Hayley, or just the idea of Hayley. Either way, most nights she felt as if she was drowning in panic.

Anna finally glanced towards her mother.

"Have you talked to anyone? Vented?" Sandra crossed her arms. "Cried?"

Avoiding her mother's eye, Anna lifted up Toby, who was in the process of methodically putting all the shoes back. His hands moved to her necklace, playing with the chain.

"I'm fine, Mum." She looked at her mother. "Really."

Sandra raised her eyebrows. "I know you. This is what you do, and that's okay for a little while. But then you explode—you're just like your father. Find someone to talk to, sweetie. It's okay if it's not me." She smiled affectionately. "Your father, you, and Ella are three generations of avoiders."

"We do okay."

"You do brilliantly."

Grateful to hear Ella thundering down the stairs, Anna turned her attention from Sandra. The little girl was flushed slightly, her eyes bright. She looked more like herself than she had in weeks.

"Ready to go?" Sandra asked.

Wiggling her foot in the air to indicate her orange Converse shoes, Ella nodded. "I tied my laces myself," she said, little chest puffed out.

Anna smiled at her. "Go you."

"Daddy taught me."

Excitement radiating off him, Toby straightened up in her arms. "Da!"

The pained look on Sandra's face and the way Anna's jaw clenched were missed as Ella pulled on her jacket.

Helping to fix Ella's zip, Sandra forced a smile. "He taught you well, honey. Let's go get some hot chocolate into you."

With a wave goodbye, Ella followed her grandmother out. Toby waved back energetically from Anna's arms, a skill he used vigorously, even if Anna was just leaving the room to walk into the kitchen.

As soon as the door shut behind them, Toby blinked at her owlishly, as if surprised to find them alone together. Anna jiggled him on her hip so he smiled. "Alright, Mister. Shops?"

Looking for a feeling of normalcy, Anna stopped in at a café on the way to the supermarket. A coffee in a café was something Anna lived for. With his Babycino in front of him, Toby made a mess of himself in seconds as Anna sipped her latte. She tried to ignore how people smiled at them as they threw Toby delighted looks, probably assuming they were mother and son. With their brunette hair, dimples, and bright blue eyes, it wasn't surprising people made that connection. It was just so wrong. It felt like cheating to have people assume that she was his mother. Especially considering how torn she had been—still was—about taking the kids on.

It was a strange feeling, to want them around her so much, yet at the same time miss her old life. Anna craved her freedom. She'd lain in bed in the middle of the night, Ella's knee in her back, and almost cried with how much she wanted to be back in her life of four months ago. Feeling hot, flushed, and completely pinned down, she'd gotten up to sit outside on the back step, gulping in cold air to try to calm herself down.

Then that morning, she'd woken up and called Ella in sick so she'd be near.

Anna swallowed her too-hot latte and forced her thoughts back to the minute.

She winked at Toby after the fourth smile from a stranger passing by. "Not surprising, Tobes. You're pretty damn cute."

He waved his spoon at her, grinning back at two women who beamed at him as they walked past the table.

Anna lowered her voice and whispered to him, "And you'd be a pretty good babe magnet, if I could be bothered with anything like that right now."

Toby jammed his spoon in his mouth and giggled.

The words her mother had said innocently enough echoed around her head—so much like her father. And her mother wasn't only talking about her grief—Anna had always handled herself in a way that was very similar to the distant father she'd grown up with.

While Sandra had never understood Anna's lack of desire to have kids, she'd respected it. She knew it had just been a part of what made Anna *Anna*. And here Anna was, with her brother's children, having Babycinos and desperately trying to hold them all together with pancakes and animated movies, all the while slowly drowning in a life she had never wanted.

Anna missed adult company. Work was starting to look appealing, even with all the complications of balancing kids and rosters. Just the idea of meeting some new people and engaging her brain had Anna itching to get started. She missed the challenge, the distraction and focus it required. The woman she'd met in the elevator, Kym, seemed friendly. Maybe she'd try and take her up on the coffee offer—even if Anna didn't feel like talking about her things, it seemed Kym had some stuff she'd openly talk about. It could help, distract her, get her feeling like herself again. Her mother would take the kids, give her a break, and give her some time for adult company.

The sneaky idea that she'd been burying herself in the kids had come over her.

So soon, she'd bury herself in work *and* the kids.

"No no no no nonononono!"

Anna stood stock-still, immobile, afraid any sudden movement would cause this to get worse.

"No no no!"

Her eyes were wide, and she had her hands raised slightly in the air as if someone was pointing a gun at her. The noise was almost ear splitting.

"Nononononononono!" Toby lay on the floor, kicking and screaming, red faced and covered in mucous and tears.

Anna had no idea what had happened. They'd been in the kitchen, unpacking the groceries, Toby his usual sweet and clingy self. He'd grabbed at the packet of doughnuts in her hand. She'd said, "As if. No way am I giving you that much sugar before nap time again," and put them on the top shelf of the pantry. When she'd turned around, ready to pick him up and take him upstairs for a sleep, she'd paused in shock. Toby's little face had been crumbling, his lower lip quivering, and then he'd fallen to the floor in a big floppy mess and was now in the middle of an excellent example of a tantrum.

It almost looked like he was having a seizure. And all Anna could do was stare, her mouth slightly open. Where had the incredibly cute, happy boy gone? He was clingy, yes. Some nights he woke up screaming and when she went in, he cried harder for his parents. But he'd always settled quickly. Nothing like this had ever happened.

Completely lost in this situation, Anna finally closed her mouth and tried to think what to do. You can't talk sense to a sixteen month old, she told herself. She'd never been left in charge of a toddler throwing this kind of tantrum. When Ella had done it when she was younger, Anna had just sidled out of the room, leaving Jake to calm her down, or she'd edged down the store aisle and left Sally soothing her and trying to hide her frustration.

Thank God they weren't in public. How embarrassing.

She stared at him, little fists thrashing, big tears on his screwed-up face, and considered calling her mother. She'd said to call if Anna had any questions, something Anna had taken her up on several times. But she had the feeling her mum would laugh at her for this one.

Apparently, Anna herself had been quite good at throwing tantrums as a toddler. Her mother loved to bring that up.

Slowly, she squatted down. "Uh…Toby?"

He didn't even hear her. Did she do tough love? Or comfort? She kind of just wanted to ignore him. Maybe that was the way to go.

Sally had once made a joke in the store, when Ella was throwing a fantastic one, while people looked sideways at them, that if they were at home, she'd just walk out of the room. Maybe it hadn't been a joke?

So Anna stood and went about unpacking the groceries around him.

He'd stopped saying "no" and was just making squealing noises.

Her ears hurt. She put away everything that went in the refrigerator and freezer and then started on the pantry items.

The screaming slowed down to hiccups.

She started the dishes from that morning and heard the hiccups ebb.

Anna turned around and looked at him.

He was sitting on the floor, face covered in tears and eyes incredibly bright. His little bottom lip was still out, and he was staring up at her with the most pitiful look.

Anna quirked an eyebrow at him. "All better?"

Toby sniffled miserably.

She would have smiled, but the panic that had risen up was still too close to the surface.

Toby pushed himself up off the floor and held his arms up.

She dried her hands on a tea towel and smiled nervously at him. "Are you a happy boy again?" She vaguely remembered hearing Jake say something of the sort to Ella when she'd gotten over one of hers.

And there, through his tears, he grinned at her—a real grin, the way only a toddler covered in tears could.

Relieved laughter bubbled out of her. Anna bent and scooped him up, placing kisses on the softness of his neck. "How about we go for a sleep?"

She walked him up the stairs.

That had been terrifying.

Give her a child under anaesthetic any day.

Feeling lazy, Anna drove to the park at two, even though it was just down the road. She told herself that it was threatening rain, and that was why, but really, she just felt exhausted. Toby had slept for over an hour, and Anna had meant to use the spare time to catch up on emails and maybe make some calls to the electric company and start switching bills over from Jake and Sally's name.

But she'd found she didn't have it in her. Instead, she'd tidied up, restlessly moving around the house, throwing things in the washing machine—kids went through clothes like nothing she'd ever seen before. An inability to sit still had overtaken her. She had even picked up her phone to call Hayley before she remembered that it wasn't her place to do so anymore.

Back in a life that now felt years ago, Anna loved her own company. Yet, now, with all the changes in her life, she couldn't seem to relax anymore.

When she pulled up at the park, her mother was seated on a blanket reading a book while Ella played on the slide, wind whipping their hair around their heads. The park was otherwise empty.

Wrangling Toby out of his car seat, Anna held his back against her front as she pointed in the direction of Sandra and whispered, "Go get Grandma!"

Already wriggling, she put him down and watched him run on unsteady legs, calling, "Danma! Danma!" at the top of his lungs.

Sandra looked up and held her arms out as he collided heavily with her, giggling loudly.

More sedate than the toddler, Anna walked up and sat cross-legged next to them.

"Aunty Na!" She looked up and waved to Ella at the monkey bars. "Watch! I can make it all the way across now!"

"Well done, Ella Bella."

About to ask Sandra how their day had been, Anna heard a squeal and looked up just in time to see Ella plummet to the ground, arms out to brace herself.

Anna and her mother were up in a second, Anna bolting towards Ella while Sandra paused to scoop up Toby. Before Anna's attention focused completely on Ella, she saw her mother's face twisted in worry.

Ella was lying on the ground clutching her wrist to her chest, face pale.

Anna squatted down next to her, heart pounding in her ears. "Ella? Ella, sweetie, are you okay?"

There was no answer.

As gently as she could, Anna scooped her up into a sitting position. Her hands ran over Ella's head, smoothing her hair, feeling no contusions; her fingers came away dry.

Eyes wide, face even paler, Ella sat still, breathing in shallow gasps.

"Ella, can you speak to me?"

Her niece blinked, slightly glazed eyes finally coming up to meet Anna's. She gave a tiny shake of her head.

"What hurts? Your wrist?" Anna felt her mother hovering over them, anxiety coming off her in waves.

She nodded—the wrist was already swollen. Anna ran a gentle hand over it, assessing the swelling, watching Ella's face as she did so. It was definitely broken. She'd seen kids in pain, and many of them, most really, did exactly what Ella was doing now. When they were in pain, serious pain, they retreated to a place inside themselves.

"I need to take her to the ER." She lowered her voice so only Sandra behind her could hear. "I think her wrist is broken. Can you take Toby home? Take the SUV, it has the car seat."

Not waiting for an answer, Anna scooped Ella up and carried her to the car, whispering assurances in her ear. Once Ella was in the seat, Anna buckled her in.

Sandra hovered behind with Toby, watching Ella's face. "It'll be okay, Ella sweetie. Aunty Na's a doctor, she'll look after you."

Ella just stared straight ahead, still cradling her wrist.

Anna closed the door and turned to Sandra. "What time did she last eat? And drink?"

"Uh…she ate at eleven-thirty. She had some water after that but nothing else. Why?"

"In case she needs surgery."

Her mother paled. "Really?"

They exchanged car keys. "Maybe, maybe not—I can only see swelling, the skin's not broken, and I can't feel an obvious deformity. But I can't tell for sure without an X-ray. It's definitely broken though. Everything else seems okay. I don't think she hit her head."

"Call me?"

"I'll let you know as soon as I do." Anna leant forward and kissed her mother on the cheek, then Toby. "Be good, Tobes."

Toby squawked and reached out for her as she walked around the car to the driver's side. She blew him a kiss and tried to ignore the distraught look on his face as she got in without him.

Anna pulled out of the parking lot, heading towards her new place of employment. It was the only hospital location she knew. The entire drive, she chatted to Ella about nothing. Her niece didn't answer, but Anna kept it up, giving them both something else to think about. Anytime there was silence, she heard again how Ella had squealed as she fell; worry clenched her stomach each time.

In record time, Anna pulled into the hospital. As she helped Ella out of the car, she asked, "Can you walk, Ella Bella?"

Ella nodded, eyes still glazed and face still pale.

At the triage desk, it was still early in the day, and the waiting room only held a few people. Still, Anna was grateful that all ERs saw children as quickly as possible. Five minutes later, they were whisked through, a kind nurse taking Ella's vitals and telling jokes, almost bringing a smile to her pale little face.

The nurse fluttered out, leaving in her efficient wake an intern who didn't look old enough to shave. Anna eyed him critically. "What are you here to do?"

He looked at her in surprise, his nerves written all over his face. "Uh…the initial exam?"

"Did you just answer me with a question?"

"Uh…no?"

Ella was sitting on the edge of the bed, still cradling her wrist. With her chair pulled up alongside Ella, Anna sat with her arm around her back, the girl's feet resting on her legs. Protectiveness was rearing its head, and Anna tried to rein it back. Working in this field, she knew they had to learn. But not on her niece. "What year are you?"

His eyes widened further. "Uh…this is my first."

She knew it. "How far into your internship?"

"Three weeks?"

Anna closed her eyes, then opened them, keeping her tone light so as not to alarm Ella. "That's what I thought. How about you just get her some pain relief sorted out, order the X-ray, and call an orthopaedic consult. Her vitals were fine—check the chart."

"But, I—"

Her eyebrows raised. "Run along."

The intern swallowed, nodded, and fled.

When she looked back at Ella, her niece was staring at her. "You were mean to him, Aunty Na."

Anna grinned, glad the little girl had finally spoken, even if it was to say that. "Yeah, I was. I'm getting you a good doctor. And something that's going to make your arm feel better."

A minute later, a nurse appeared with a tablet, smiling at Ella. "Do you feel like you can swallow a tablet, princess?"

Ella nodded. "I'm good at tablets. I take a vitamin every day."

Blinking, Anna stared at Ella. She hadn't known that—she should ask Sandra about it.

The nurse sat next to Ella on the bed, handing her the tablet and a small shot of water. "Okay, do you think you can swallow it with such a tiny amount of water?"

"I'll try."

"Good girl." The nurse tipped the tablet into Ella's mouth, then the water, and Ella swallowed, opening her mouth and sticking her tongue out to show she'd done it.

The nurse clapped. "I think that earned a prize!"

Ella's eyes lit up a little.

Anna breathed a slight sigh of relief. Seeing Ella like that, pale and withdrawn, had almost been worse than seeing her crying the night before.

"A prize?"

"Yup!" The nurse reached into her pocket and pulled out a sheet of horse stickers. "You can have this *whole* sheet for being so brave!"

Still holding her injured wrist to her chest, Ella reached forward with her good hand. "Thank you."

Eyes bright as she looked over the stickers, Ella looked at Anna. "Look, Aunty Na."

"Wow." Mouthing a silent "thank you", Anna smiled at the nurse.

She winked back. "No problem. Just call out if you need anything. The X-ray won't be long. It's time to switch shifts, so the next nurse will be on her way."

For the next few minutes, Anna helped Ella pull off stickers and stick them on her shoes and shirt. Ella, giggling, put one on Anna's cheek. Anna poked her tongue out.

"Ella Foster?"

Recognizing the voice, Anna's eyes widened. Suddenly very aware of the pony sticker stuck to her cheek, she looked up. The woman from the grocery store, Lane, was standing at the end of the ER bed, flicking through Ella's chart. Lane was dressed in light blue scrubs, hair a jumble around her head, where she'd tried to pull it into some kind of order. She looked like a mess. A delightful, gorgeous mess.

Looking straight at Ella, Lane smiled widely. "You're Ella?"

Quieter now, Ella nodded. "Yup."

"And this is your—" Eyes finally on Anna, Lane stopped mid-sentence, grin growing bigger. "Anna!"

For some reason, Anna thought to give an awkward wave. She grimaced internally. "Lane. Hi."

"Uh..." Lane looked back to Ella, then to Anna. "So it was you scaring the intern?"

"Um. Maybe?"

With a knowing nod, Lane shrugged. "I can't say I blame you."

"You work here?"

Lane looked down at her outfit then back at Anna. "Uh…yeah."

"That's a coincidence."

"It really is."

"In more ways than one—I start here on Monday."

"What? Really?"

"Yeah, I'm the new anaesthetist."

"Wow. That really is a coincidence."

Anna nodded. "It is."

Confused, Ella glanced from one woman to the other.

"No wonder you ran off the intern. You know too much."

Biting her lip, Anna cleared her throat. "He—uh, looked incompetent."

"Most interns are."

"I bet you weren't."

An amused expression flitted across Lane's face. "Actually, not a doctor. I'm one of the emergency nurses. We just switched shifts, and I saw the intern fleeing without completing the paperwork I needed. When I confronted him, he told me he had to find someone else and ran."

"I may have been harsher than I intended."

Shrugging, Lane smirked. "Nah, he's a cocky one, he needs it. The nurse handed over that she hadn't completed the initial exam. Is it okay if I do that, and then I'll get the orthopaedic god around these parts to come over? He likes an initial exam done, and since the intern isn't here…"

Still feeling sheepish, Anna nodded. "Of course. I imagine you're ten times more competent than him at it, anyway."

Lane's cheeks flushed slightly as she tore her eyes off Anna and looked to the bemused six-year-old. "Ella? I hear you hurt your wrist?"

Before excited about stickers, Ella suddenly frowned, nodding her head. "It hurts."

Lane pulled up a chair, seating herself so she was facing Anna, their knees almost touching. Her eyes were on Ella. "Let me guess?" She flicked her gaze to Anna, then back to Ella. "Monkey bars or trampoline?"

Wide eyes stared at Lane. "Monkey bars! How did you know?"

"I'm magic." She checked the chart to make sure Ella had had some pain relief before gently examining her wrist, getting the little girl to wriggle her fingers, passively manipulating the joint to see what movement she had. When she was done, she winked at Ella, who was holding her breath. "Well done. You're incredibly brave."

Ella looked relieved that this part was over. "Will I get a colourful thing on my arm?"

"A cast?"

"Yeah. Brodie got a blue one at school."

Lane grinned. "I'd say you will be getting one, honey, and you can have any colour you want. We just have to take some special photos of your wrist, and then we'll see what we can do about that, okay?"

Ella nodded, going back to her stickers.

Lane turned to Anna. "I don't think we'll need the OR. Fingers crossed, it looks like you'll be lucky. I'll have the ortho guy come by. He's nice, you'll like him." She flicked her eyes to Ella to make sure she was still preoccupied. "We'll need the images to confirm, but it looks okay."

Anna let out the breath she'd been subconsciously holding. "Thank God." She smiled. "No OR will make me very happy."

"Oh, I'm amazing in the OR. It's a pity I won't get to work my magic." At Anna's confused look, Lane went on. "I work the casual pool here, but I mainly end up in emergency—sometimes, though, I'm in surgery as a scrub or recovery nurse. So maybe you can see me in action soon?"

Anna's heart sped up at the slight innuendo. "Well, I'm sure we'll work together at some point."

Dark eyes looked up at Anna from under long lashes as Lane gave a slow smile. "I really hope we do. You've come highly recommended from Brisbane."

"The others that worked there were morons. But yeah, I'm a little hard core."

"What's a moron?"

Anna winced. Ella was staring at them. "It's another word for idiot."

"You're not 'sposed to call people that."

"You're right, it was mean."

With a chuckle, Lane said goodbye to Ella before disappearing.

After a quick glance at her arm, the orthopaedic surgeon sent for X-rays, and Lane re-appeared with the intern from before.

"Ah, if it's okay with you, Mrs, um, Foster, I'll take Ella to X-ray."

Lane watched them with a smirk hovering on her lips.

"Of course. And it's Miss, not Mrs—or Doctor, really."

The intern's eyes widened as he clearly realised why Anna had so easily scared him. "O…okay."

Anna saw Lane look at her with interest as she turned to her niece. "Ella Bella? We're going to go take photos of your wrist with a really big camera. I'm going to come and be there the whole time, okay?" Her eyes flicked to the intern, daring him to argue.

Despite his obvious youth, he seemed to sense who had the upper hand, and he just nodded emphatically.

Lane smirked openly. "I'll be around if you need me when you get back. Just press the call bell." She turned to Ella. "I'll see you really soon, Ella."

Ella nodded sleepily. The pain medicine was taking effect.

As Anna brushed Ella's hair off her forehead, she looked up and noticed Lane watching her. "Thanks, Lane. I appreciate it."

"No problem at all. Call if you need me."

Lane started to walk away at Anna's grateful smile. "Oh, Anna?"

"Yeah?"

"That pony sticker on your cheek is, you're right, *incredibly* hard core." She laughed as she made her exit.

Anna blushingly peeled the sticker off her cheek before helping a sleepy Ella into the wheelchair. Still grinning, she walked alongside Ella to radiology and gently helped set her up for the X-ray.

This wasn't how she had planned to learn her way around the hospital, or meet the new staff. Standing behind the protective screen as the radiologist took the images, she sighed. At least she would know where some things were come Monday morning.

The X-ray was over quickly. Ella was soon dozing in her bed, knocked out by the pain relief medication. After Anna called her mother with a quick update, she had nothing left to do, and stared blindly at her phone, lost in thought.

Lane worked where she worked. So much for never seeing her again. Anna couldn't stop her thoughts from going back to the woman. Lane's smile made her heart rate speed up in the best way, a relief from the racing pulse she'd been experiencing since Jake had passed away. She missed easy adult conversations—the type that didn't revolve around sympathy.

Ella, peaceful as she slept with her hair smoothed off her face reminded Anna that she really didn't have time for work, let alone women.

But a flirtation was harmless.

"Anna?"

Her head whipped up and a delighted grin crossed her lips as she saw who was standing in front of her. "Kym! Hi."

"What on earth are you doing here?" Kym looked to the sleeping girl and back to Anna. "What happened?"

"Broken wrist. Monkey bar incident."

They shared a wry look. "She going to be okay?"

"She's in good hands. Some ortho God man and a nurse named Lane?"

"She's definitely in good hands then." Kym cocked her head as she looked at Ella. "You must've been worried."

"Scared me to death, actually. I've never seen her like that."

"Kids are resilient—you should know that."

"All my knowledge and experience, and I was still terrified."

"It's always different when they're you're own."

Anna hesitated. This hadn't happened yet. It felt rude to the kids, to quickly deny them as her own, but she couldn't let people assume she was their mother. "Uh. Actually, she's my brother's daughter."

Kym nodded, then her almond eyes widened as she put two and two together from their last conversation. Her face grew sympathetic. "Poor thing." Her eyes were trained on Ella. "Her mum must be struggling."

Anna swallowed. She wasn't normally a sharer, but something about Kym, even from their first meeting, made her feel comfortable. Maybe it was because Anna could just tell she was drowning in her own grief. "Sally—Sally passed away as well; they were in a car accident."

Kym's face became even more sympathetic. But to Anna's relief, it wasn't pity, the way many people reacted when they found out. She could handle empathy.

"That sucks," Kym simply said.

Anna nodded. They shared a look—two women hit down by life.

Kym's pager went off and she checked it quickly. "I gotta run. It's Friday, so the very high people are already starting to roll in." She paused. "Coffee on Sunday? We can discuss the impending moment of your first week as a newbie. Though, you already know two of the best people, so it's looking up."

"You and Lane or you and Ortho Guy whose name I have already forgotten?"

"Definitely Lane and I…you'll like her."

Actually, Anna was grateful Kym didn't know just how much Lane interested her.

"So, coffee?"

"That'd be great. Uh—" She didn't know if Kym had realised she was actually the kids' guardian. "I'll just have to check some stuff out."

"No worries. Here, write your number down and I'll send you a text." She tapped some buttons on her phone and handed it over for Anna to input her number. Anna did so and handed it back. "I'll hopefully see you Sunday, Anna."

Anna smiled. A coffee date; her mother would be so proud.

The ER was hectic, patients rolling in, doctors and nurses moving quickly. Anna's roving gaze landed on Lane. She was standing at the desk, looking at something on a computer screen. Anna raked her eyes down Lane's form, then made herself look back up to her face.

Perving while her niece was in the ER was not a classy move.

Lane grabbed a chart and gestured to the orthopaedic doctor who was standing next to her. They both looked at the screen, the doctor nodding before he started walking towards their bed. Lane looked up and caught Anna's eyes, giving her a thumbs up as both she and the doctor stopped at the end of the bed.

"Good news," the doctor said softly, glancing at the sleeping Ella. "It's a clean, hairline fracture. No manipulation needed, only a back slab cast for a week to accommodate the swelling. Then you can bring her in to the cast clinic and we'll X-ray again to ensure nothing's shifted, and change her to a fiberglass one."

Anna relaxed into her chair as the tension in her muscles finally let go. "Thank God. I really didn't want to put her through a manipulation, even with sedation. Just the pain relief knocked her out."

Lane chuckled, looking down at Ella. "It really did. That cast will only need to be on for four weeks, and then, hopefully, all going well, we can take it off and she'll be good to go."

The doctor nodded. "I'll leave you to sort it out, Lane. I have an emergency coming in." He turned to Anna. "I hear I may work with you in the future. It's been a pleasure meeting you; maybe I'll see you soon." And with an almost friendly smile, he was gone.

They gently woke Ella, explaining to her what would happen next. Her main concern was that she'd have a "boring" cast for a week, but she perked up when she heard that everyone could draw all over it.

Lane was called away, unfortunately too busy to do the casting herself, as much as she looked like she wanted to. With Anna's approval, Lane paged the intern to do it and walked away with a shadow of regret in her eyes.

In no time, they were ready to leave, Anna with some simple pain meds in her pocket that Ella should only really need while the wrist was swollen. They signed some paperwork and made an appointment for the next week, then started to walk out. Ella walked stiffly, adjusting to the collar and cuff sling.

"Anna!"

They paused at the ER exit doors and turned around to see Lane running up behind them.

Anna and Ella both smiled.

Lane raised her eyebrows at them. "Whoa. Same dimples."

Laughter lit up her face in a way that made Anna want to bat her eyelashes like a fifteen year old.

Ella giggled. "That's 'cause we're related."

The giggle was high pitched and Anna tried not to show her amusement. The girl was still a little high.

Lane raised her palm up to her forehead. "Oh! Of course it is." She winked at Ella. "Silly me."

Lane knelt down in front of the girl, pulling a pen out of her pocket. "I was wondering if I could be the first to sign your cast?"

Ella nodded eagerly. "Okay." She held it up, uninjured hand supporting the heavy cast.

Lane drew a large, simple flower.

Anna chuckled.

Not looking up, Lane simply said, "Hey, I'm an artist with patients, not so much with a pen."

"I like it, Nurse Lane."

"I knew you'd appreciate me, Ella." Lane was adding some detail Anna couldn't see. With a flourish, she finished. "There!" She stood up.

Anna laughed out loud at the sight of Lane's phone number.

"If you have any broken bone concerns, Ella," Lane said with utter seriousness, "you can call me."

Ella bounced a little. "Okay!"

"But if not, I'll see you in a week." Lane looked at Anna, smiling as she folded her arms. "And if not, feel free to call me if you want a tour of the hospital on your first day, Anna." She held Anna's eyes for a second, then looked back to Ella. "Now, be careful on those monkey bars!" She threw them both a casual grin, turned, and walked off.

Ella slipped her free hand into Anna's as they both looked after her. "I like her."

Anna looked down at her.

"Me too, Ella Bella."

Chapter Six

Being in such a silent house could be unnerving, especially when guilt was gnawing at you.

Anna snuck down the hallway and tiptoed up to Toby's cot. All she could see was the back of his little brunette head and a fist flung up next to it, fingers curled around his thumb. He was fast asleep and snoring softly. Carefully, Anna picked his pacifier up and moved it to the far corner of the cot. Lately, he was waking up less and less without it, slowly not asking for it during the day. It was a quiet war, a battle of wills, and Toby—a stubborn toddler who she had learnt could throw a fit one second and bat his big beautiful baby blues at you the next—was losing. The truth was that Anna would have been content to let him have all the little comforts he wanted. But her mother had told her that Jake and Sally had almost completely weaned him off it, so Anna was trying to get back to that.

Quietly, she padded out and walked to Ella's room, pushing the door open slightly; Anna had learnt quickly that a shut door and no hall light apparently invited monsters. She rested one hand on the doorframe and one on the door handle, leaning in to see the light falling across the bed. She smiled softly as she looked at Ella, who was sprawled on her back, arm in its cast over her head. It was Saturday night, and, after having to keep the cast dry in the bath with a plastic garbage bag, Ella was already fed up with her broken wrist and it had only been twenty-four hours. But she was out cold now, vulnerable, completely trusting that, in her sleep, she would be kept safe.

Assured that the kids were asleep and everything was calm, Anna made her way down to the kitchen. She pulled out a half-empty bottle of white, grabbed a wine glass, patted her pocket to make sure what she really wanted was there, and headed out the back door. The screen door shut quietly behind her but she made sure the back door stayed open so she could hear sneaky six-year-old footsteps or baby cries. Finally, with a sigh, Anna sat down on the back step, set the bottle down next to her foot and leant against the banister, the wood digging into her shoulder.

One sip, the wine rich on her tongue, and Anna guiltily put the glass down and fumbled for her packet of cigarettes. Lighting one, she slowly blew the smoke out and tilted her head to watch it drift slowly upwards. She blinked sleepily and took another drag, staring at the stars overhead.

Anna could look at stars all night.

Another sip of wine, and her jangling nerves began to settle. Her mother would kill her if she could see her now. When Anna was sixteen, her mother had caught her with a packet of cigarettes and then had stood behind her yelling father with her arms crossed, an incredibly disappointed look on her face.

It hadn't stopped Anna at the time, but she had smoked less, seen it as less of a rebellion, not as fun. She'd learnt to hide it better, too. By her second year of college, she had pretty much stopped. Smoking became a secret vice she succumbed to when she felt guilty.

Hayley had found her once in the place they had shared together. Anna had poked her head out of their tiny bathroom window in an attempt to hide the smell. Yet, still, Hayley walked in, eyebrows raised and arms crossed. Apparently, she had been able to smell the smoke all the way from the living room. Hayley had simply looked at her and asked, "What did you do?"

This time, Anna had broken her brother's daughter. There was even a cast to prove it.

She was logical. She knew these things happened. Sick and injured people surrounded her at work. She knew children broke bones, caught terrible diseases, fell down. And nine out of ten times, they got right back up again, none the worse for wear.

But she'd seen the parents as she floated through pre-ops, had seen the guilt, the terror. They tore themselves apart with blame and angst. "These things happen" was a token line she heard said a lot.

So yes, Anna *knew* she wasn't to blame. But, still, it was barely past the fortnight mark of being the kids' guardian, and she'd already broken one of them. Anna bit at her thumbnail, then took another drag.

This, right here, was one of the big reasons she'd never wanted kids. Anna snorted. Now here she was, instant family, just add Anna—and one of the members was broken, literally. And she had used part of the time Ella had been broken to flirt with an incredibly attractive emergency nurse. Who had flirted with her first. And had given Anna her number—kind of. But whoever had started it, surely it was breaking some kind of guardianship rule?

Therapeutic smoke filled her lungs. She needed to ask her mother if she'd ever been this overrun with guilt any time she or Jake had hurt themselves. Jake had broken his arm twice as a kid, both times falling out of a tree, and Anna had once fractured her tibia, something she remembered blaming Jake for at the time. She had a vague recollection of riding her bike down a dirt track and him poking a stick at her wheel.

Anna stared up at the sky again with a wry grin. God, she'd been mad. She'd missed the beach that summer because of him. Granted, he'd spent the entire time at home with her, feet up on the coffee table next to hers, decorating her cast and watching movies. He had even let her play with his precious Nintendo.

A lump swelled in her throat, and her eyes burned. Her head, for one second defeated by her feelings, dropped to rest on her palm, cigarette smouldering near her hair.

Fuck, she missed her brother. She missed talking to him, hearing his laugh. While accidentally calling him had ripped a new hole in her, she kind of wanted to do it again just to hear his voice, like a balm—the sound could wash over her and take her away for just a minute. All she wanted was to have a conversation with Jake. She wanted to ask him about raising kids, and if he was mad Ella had broken her arm while under Anna's care. She would have loved to ask if he thought that she was doing okay with Toby—and did he think they could be happier or that she could be doing anything better.

She sucked in a deep breath and sat up straighter. Her eyes felt swollen, but her cheeks were dry. She let out a slow breath, a shuddering noise. Sometimes it felt as if she let herself fall into that feeling, she'd never crawl out. And she just couldn't let that happen. Not with the kids, not with that terrifying loss of control.

Pulling at her phone, she looked down at the text she'd received that morning from Kym.

> *Anna! Coffee? Tomorrow? I'm free all day, like morning or afternoon or whatever. I don't want to sound like the desperate widow, but I am. So hang out with me? Coffee?*

Anna knew it was getting late, but she figured it'd be okay to text Kym back anyway. She glanced at her watch, and her eyes widened in amusement. It was just going nine. It wasn't late by any means in her old life. How these kids had changed her.

She sent a quick reply.

Coffee, say, two? Though I have no idea where to go in this city. I know lots of nice places in Brisbane. ;)

And a quick text to her mother:

Hey Mum, can you come over and watch the kids from two tomorrow for a couple of hours? I thought I'd get coffee with one of the women from work.

She sipped her wine as she stubbed out her cigarette, hiding the butt in the packet. Her phone gave a single bleep.

Well, I know you know where the hospital is. Two streets over, Campbell Drive? There's a coffee place called Campbell's. Meet you there at two? Their coffee is not as bland as their name.

Anna smiled and texted Kym back.

Campbell's it is. I'm looking forward to it, bland coffee or not.

And she genuinely was.

Anna was looking up at the sky again, finding shapes in the stars, when her phone gave another bleep. Looking down at it, she snorted.

Her mum.

Oh thank God, you're not turning into a hermit. I'd love to have Fella and root for the afternoon.

Smirking at the hilarity of autocorrect, she waited. Sure enough, it bleeped again six minutes later. Anna sipped her wine in amusement.

Ella and Toby! I hate touchscreens. How do you communicate like this all the time? Call me from now on.

"So my husband caught a tragic disease because he thought he was the new Crocodile Hunter and was in the north hunting them or something, which I found despicable. He got a cut on his leg, and played the hero, and didn't get it seen to. It got infected, then spread, and, eventually, he went septic. Turns out he had some underlying kidney thing. They gave out, and *bam*, he died."

Anna tried to stop her mouth from dropping open. "That's terrible."

Kym shrugged, "Tragic rating of nine, I'd say. We'd just started trying for kids."

"Jesus."

"Yeah. Your turn." Kym looked at her expectantly.

Anna drew in a deep breath. She could do it like this, this half-joking, off-the-cuff way that they were sharing. She put her half-finished coffee on the table. "Okay. My brother and his wife died in a car accident, leaving behind two tiny children. My girlfriend of the time, Hayley, and I flew over for the funeral, and when they read the will, we found out he had named me guardian of the kids."

Kym's eyes widened, but she just kept looking at Anna, waiting for more.

"I never wanted kids, ever. It was why Hayley and I worked; we wanted the same things. But I agreed to take them on, and so Hayley left me. Now I live in my dead brother's house and am attempting to raise his kids in a city that I hate." Anna picked her glass back up. "No offense."

Kym leant back in her chair. "Whoa." A playful smile crossed her lips. "Wait, you're gay?"

"That's what you focussed on in all that?"

"Yeah, well, the rest was too much like a soap opera. I'm glad it's not just my life that reads like one."

"Nope, you're not special at all."

"Obviously."

Surprisingly Anna was enjoying this. She barely knew Kym, and Anna was the kind of person who normally took a long time to warm up to someone enough to share intimate details. But here? Sitting in a coffee shop, rain pouring down outside, with a woman who could somehow get the grief she felt? Kym was funny, dry in a way that Anna enjoyed. There was no pity party, no woe-is-us. There was just truth and a joke and the odd eye contact that spoke volumes. It made her comfortable, able to share.

Maybe Melbourne wouldn't be so bad.

"Your husband was in Iraq?"

Kym nodded. "Yeah, for years as a medic."

"And he ignored the highly inflamed, infected leg wound?"

"Don't get me started."

"Well, he did amazing work over there, I'm sure. My brother was there too, serving." Anna still had trouble saying Jake's name. It was something she found herself tripping over. "He spoke highly of the medics."

"How long did he serve?"

"Six years. He moved into administration when Sally fell pregnant with Toby. He didn't want to take the risk anymore."

"Were you and Sally close?"

Anna ran her finger around the rim of her glass, eyes downcast. "We were."

"That must've been hard, losing your brother and a friend."

"It really was."

Kym tilted her head, waiting.

"Sally and I got along the second we met. We used to stay up for hours drinking wine and just chatting. J—he loved that we were close. Since we were so close, he wanted me to like his wife."

"You and your brother were best friends?" Kym's look softened. "That must have been nice."

"My father was a structural engineer; we moved a few times as kids. We stopped trying to make new friends every time and just...glued together."

"That's actually really sweet. I don't have any siblings."

"How did you meet your husband?"

"He needed an evaluation post upon returning from Iraq."

"You got involved with a client?"

"What? No. No, no." Kym shook her head adamantly. "I need to remember to elaborate. It was before I worked in the hospital; I had an office with another psychiatrist. We met in the lobby of the building and ended up walking the stairs together. He was there to see my partner for a standard debriefing thing. Nothing dodgy."

Anna feigned relief. "Thank God. That would be a terrible beginning."

"Oh, completely." With a soft look, she studied her coffee. "We were talking kids before it happened. He'd left the army and was working in a GP clinic, and everything seemed...like it was time."

"That sucks." Anna rested her hand on Kym's forearm. "Maybe we could get that printed on a T-shirt."

That made Kym crack a small smile.

"You know," Anna squeezed her arm gently. "I have two kids, if you want 'em?"

The laughter was a relief. "You can keep them."

Pulling back, Anna relaxed against the back of her chair. “How is it? Getting through work in the hospital he passed away in?”

“That’s the million dollar question.” Kym studied her almost-empty cappuccino. “It’s shit. He’s everywhere—in that hospital, at home. I’ve thought about leaving, but I don’t know. My life was always here. I like it here. I just don’t like that he’s not here with me. But,” she looked up, a small grin on her face, “there’s this great new anaesthetist starting.”

“I hear she’s awesome.”

“Is it a similar thing for you—living in that house?”

“I guess it is. I avoid their room like the plague, though I really need to do something with it.” Anna fidgeted with her spoon. “Ella avoids it, too, but I’ve had to distract Toby a few times from sitting outside it, banging on the door.”

“How young is he?”

“He’s just gone sixteen months.”

“Too young to get it.”

“Exactly. Mostly I’m scared he’ll forget—or that he’s already started to. But then there’s Ella, who can’t seem to remember anything else. I don’t know what’s better for either of them.”

There was a beat of silence. “How are you doing there?”

Anna moved from the spoon to a sugar packet. “Some days I just feel like screaming—Like: Is this my life now? Really? Two kids and working? My time and energy dictated by their wants and needs? That’s not what I wanted.”

Kym pressed her lips together, nodding.

Guilt made Anna drop her eyes down to the table. “And that just sounded so selfish, didn’t it?”

“Not at all. I was just thinking how incredibly selfless you’re being.” Kym seemed to sense the need to change the subject. “How’s Ella’s arm?”

“Okay. She’s cranky and over the cast. I think the fibreglass one will make it easier; it’s lighter and waterproof.” Anna thanked the waitress as she put down another coffee for each of them. “And it’ll be colourful.”

“The important things, then.” Kym smiled, pulling her new cup towards her.

“Toby had his first tantrum the other day.”

Kym winced. “How was that?”

“Terrifying. Thank God we were at home. I’d rather a patient with malignant hyperthermia.”

“So, you really weren’t a kid person before?”

While she considered how to answer that one, Anna took a sip of her coffee. "I loved being an aunty. But kids just, they were something I knew a long time ago I didn't want. It was never a decision I wavered in."

"And then you were forced to."

"Exactly. I...I don't resent the kids, at all. For a while, I wanted my parents to take them, because kids don't deserve to be with someone who doesn't want them one hundred percent."

"What changed your mind?"

"My brother." Anna sighed. "I remember him saying once that he never wanted the kids to grow up with our parents. He'd talked to Mum, even, to explain that he wanted it to be me. He just never really had the conversation with me—not in a way I realised we were having it, anyway."

"Seriously?"

"I think he knew I would've said no."

"Well, can't really argue with him now."

"Right?" Anna's voice raised, and she winced as she looked around. "I may still be angry at him."

"Angry's the easiest thing to be."

They exchanged a knowing look.

Kym brought her mug up, elbows balanced on the arms of her chair as she leant back in her seat. "So. Lane's nice, hm?"

"Most unsubtle segue ever."

"I feel this coffee date has removed the need for me to be subtle."

Huffing, Anna looked up at the ceiling. "Lane's nice, yes."

"I hear you ran her over with a shopping cart?"

A flush spread over Anna's cheeks. "Ah—maybe." A thought occurred to her. "Wait, she told you about that? She talked about me before the ER?"

Kym just grinned like the Cheshire Cat.

Anna walked through the front door, and, before she could blink, a blur hit her legs. She looked down to see Toby wrapped around them.

"Na!"

Anna melted as he stared up at her with an adoring look in his eyes. She felt better than she had in weeks. It was amazing what joined grief between adults could do, how it could bring two people together.

Toby tugged harder on her pants and she bent down and lifted him up, swinging him onto her hip. "Hey, little man." She pressed her face against his soft baby cheek, and he pressed back against her. "What you been doing? You have fun?"

"Poo!"

Anna stopped dead in her walk to the kitchen and raised her eyebrows at him. "I'm sorry, what?"

"Poo, Na!" He was grinning, a smear of what looked like icing sugar on his face.

Sandra poked her head around the door. "We went to the *pool*, Aunty Anna."

"Oh! Did you have fun at the pool, Tobes?"

"Poo! Poo!"

Biting back her mirth, she walked them into the kitchen to try and put him at the table where he had been destroying a piece of paper with a yellow crayon. The second she lowered him down, Toby immediately tried to crawl back up her again, making whining noises. She made eye contact with her mother but picked him up; he settled back on her hip, content.

Anna leant over and kissed Ella on the top of her head. She was colouring in, a serious look of concentration on her face. "Nice job, Ella Bella."

"Thanks."

Kids took praise so readily.

Her mother was icing cupcakes. "Busy afternoon, Mum?"

"We went to the pool for an hour and then made cupcakes—I thought you could take them to Toby's day care."

Take cupcakes? Good God. She needed a handbook. "Thanks. They look great."

"The kids helped me ice them."

Eyeing the uneven blobs of pink frosting, Anna pursed her lips. "They look… amazing." The wink Sandra sent her made her look away to hide her amusement.

Finally, Toby was settled at the table with some crayons and paper. On a whim, she walked over and wrapped her arms around her mother from behind. Sandra put down the icing spatula and turned, wrapping her arms around Anna. As her mother's fingers dug tightly into her back, Anna realised she needed to do this more often. Releasing her, Sandra eyed her. "What was that for?"

"Nothing. I just love you." Anna's eyes widened as her mother's welled up. Desperate to stop any tears, Anna pulled her back in for another hug.

"Why are you hugging Grandma?"

Over Sandra's shoulder, Anna smiled at Ella, who was kneeling on her chair, looking at them both curiously. "Because sometimes people just need a hug."

Ella nodded and went back to colouring. "They do."

Sandra gave a sniff, a quick wipe of her eyes and went back to her cupcakes.

With a smile still on her face, Anna walked around the kitchen bench and stood behind Ella's chair, wrapping her arms around the girl's middle. She lifted Ella up and squeezed her before plopping her back down again. Face buried in the back of the Ella's neck, Anna blew raspberries until her niece finally giggled and tried to wriggle away.

"Aunty Na! That tickles!"

"What? I was giving you a cuddle."

"That wasn't a cuddle!"

"Oh, really?"

And Anna did the whole thing again, while Toby yelled, "Poo!" repeatedly.

When Sandra left, she grasped Anna's forearm briefly and forced her to make eye contact. "You're handling this, Anna. And not only that, but you're doing brilliantly."

Anna swallowed past a lump as her mother whisked out the door.

Hours later, after the kids were in bed, she wandered downstairs and opened the fridge. Her mother had prepared two lunch boxes, ready to go for the morning. Anna sent a silent thanks to her. At seven-thirty tomorrow morning, Anna would drop Ella off at her mother's and Sandra would take her to school. Anna would get Toby to day care at the hospital and be ready to go for an eight a.m. start. They were yet to sort out night shifts and on calls, but they figured they'd just take them as they came.

Guilt already plagued Anna about putting Toby in day care—he'd always been at home with Sally. Anna was worried he'd hate it, or she would be doing some kind of permanent damage, or Sally would've been disappointed.

Really, she worried constantly.

With more force than necessary, Anna closed the fridge and wandered over to the kettle, switching it on and pulling out tea bags. She placed one in a large mug, then stood and stared vaguely at it while waiting for the hot water.

Ella was doing a little better, but Anna had caught her walking back from the bathroom that evening. She had edged along the wall past her parents' room as if scared of it. When Anna had gone to read to her, she'd been quiet, almost pensive. Despite the times Anna could get a laugh from her, she was still mostly quiet and reserved.

Anna supposed she should expect this behaviour to come and go for a long time. Maybe she should talk to Ella's counsellor again. She'd chatted to both the counsellor and the teacher earlier in the week, a basic "let's get everything back to normal for Ella" talk. But maybe the counsellor could offer more advice on what was normal and what wasn't. Maybe there wasn't any normal in this situation. The teacher had mentioned that Ella wasn't playing with the other kids at school anymore, but, for now, everyone seemed to agree on not pushing her.

The kettle boiled, and Anna poured the hot water into her mug before adding a splash of milk, then sat herself down on the floor in the living room. Warmth from the tea washed over her face as she took a sip and leant against the couch, legs stretched out in front of her. She turned the TV on and flicked channels.

It was so early, and the house was so still.

In her earlier life, she would be at dinner or after-work drinks or simply sprawled on the couch with Hayley, exhausted yet relaxed. Here, though, everything was so permanent. Even though the kids were asleep, she had to sit here, stay near them. Out of nowhere, panic crawled up her throat. Even with the television playing, it was as if she could hear her own heartbeat speeding up.

The reality of this life pressed in on her.

And she felt very alone.

Swallowing heavily, Anna tried to focus on her breathing and think about something else.

Starting work tomorrow felt like she was really starting this new life, cementing herself in it. The tea was suddenly bitter on her tongue, and she tried to ignore the lingering traces of panic.

She hadn't heard from Hayley since the phone call that had left her irrationally angry. While she missed Hayley, the feeling was distant, like something Anna couldn't quite let touch her, something removed from the life she was living now. Hayley felt like years ago.

The life they had shared felt like years ago—a life focussed on their careers and, in reality, rarely seeing each other as they floated through work and social circles. But that didn't stop this panic, this ache in Anna's stomach. It didn't stop the feeling that she was alone and very, very stuck.

Reaching forward, Anna grabbed her phone and stared at it for a moment, debating.

She needed a distraction. Desperately.

Swallowing, she went for it.

Hey, Lane. It's Anna. Still up for that tour? I'm in HR until nine tomorrow.

Six minutes later, her phone went off.

Definitely still up for the tour. Turn down the HR one, the guy that takes you smells like BO. I'll meet you at nine at HR with a coffee from the good coffee cart, and I promise to smell nice.

Anna tried not to flirt.

I'll judge the outcome of that promise in the morning. There's a bad coffee cart?

She sipped her tea and waited.

Isn't there always? Don't worry, the tour will show the places to avoid. Like the level three on-call room. You'll get pregnant just sitting in there.

The laugh that burst from her grated against the oppressive silence in the house. Anna felt lighter.

Can't wait. Nurses are able to just leave their shift whenever they want?

She leant back against the couch.

Haha, you're in luck. I'm working in one of the day clinics tomorrow, and we start at ten. See you at nine, Anna. :) Glad you ran into me with the shopping cart. Never thought I'd say that.

Thumb resting on the screen, Anna sat for a moment, contemplating.

I've never been happier to cause a bruise.

Innuendo wasn't necessarily flirting. Anna sipped her tea and waited for a response.

Tomorrow I demand the story of that chin bruise as payment for the tour. :)

In spite of herself, Anna smiled. A frown quickly replaced it. She didn't know if she wanted to share her history with Lane. The reason behind the bruise, while a pretty damn funny story, now came with a big backlog of "I'm a recent full-time guardian of two charming but rather traumatised children." Sharing with Kym had been cathartic. And Anna had filled her boss in so that he knew where she stood.

But sharing that with Lane? Something made her want to hold it back. She was worried about scaring her off. Which Anna shouldn't be, because she was recently single and had no time for this, anyway.

Groaning, she dropped her head back. She had a crush on a crazy hot, incredibly flirty nurse. How perfect. What a great side note to the drama that was her life right now. But she couldn't help herself:

That story is worth more than just a tour.

She gnawed at her thumbnail for a moment. Lane's response was quick.

I'll think of something...

A grin took over Anna's face.

See you at nine.

She barely took in any of the TV she stared at, anticipation spreading through her limbs as the house settled around her.

Chapter Seven

The day had barely started, and Anna was already exhausted. How did single parents do it? How did single, working parents do it? How did parents with three nannies do it?

They'd been up at six a.m., the hour not a problem, but getting two children ready in time was going to take some practice. Especially as one of those children's idea of feeding himself was pouring his cereal on the floor and putting the remnants up his nose.

Yawning, Anna walked into the hospital, Toby on her hip and his SpongeBob backpack on her back. She had just over five minutes to drop him off and find HR. When she reached the day care, she was shocked to realise she was reluctant to hand him over to the attendant. The woman didn't look a day over twenty.

But the redhead gave Toby a friendly smile, and it worked on Toby. He grinned back.

"Hello! You must be Toby Foster?" She looked at Anna. "And you're Doctor Foster? We spoke on the phone—I'm Tanya, the coordinator here."

Already, Anna was feeling slightly better. "Hey, Anna is fine, and this," she jiggled Toby on her hip, causing him to beam again, "is my nephew, Toby."

Tanya looked from Anna to Toby. "My gosh, you two look alike. Hi, Toby! You want to come do some puzzles?"

Anna hugged him harder to her. "He loves blocks. And trains."

"We have lots of those here!"

Anna slid Toby down her body until he was standing on the floor. His little arms were wrapped around her legs and he tried to crawl back up her again.

"Tobes, they have lots of trains."

Big blue eyes widened. "Twain, Na?"

Tanya knelt down so she was eye level with Toby, her face open and friendly. This woman was made for child work. "We have lots of trains. I think there's some Thomas ones."

Toby's eyes lit up, but his arms didn't move from Anna's legs.

When Anna had called the day care and spoken to Tanya, she'd filled her in on the situation as much as she could. They'd ended up chatting about the first day and how Toby might struggle with being left, especially in the circumstances; about how, often, the easiest thing was to get him occupied, give him a quick goodbye, and leave.

The one thing Tanya hadn't mentioned was that Anna might struggle to leave *him*.

All she'd wanted was some semblance of her own life back. She hadn't been away from Toby for longer than a few hours in a fortnight. Some away time from the kids had seemed like a great idea, but now she felt anxious for him. Anna rested her hand on his head. "Shall we look at Thomas, Tobes?"

Toby grabbed her hand, and Tanya, ever perky, jumped up and led the way. Tanya sat herself down cross-legged on the floor and started pulling out trains from a bucket. Anna sat down across from her, and Toby sat himself in her lap, reaching over and grabbing at a train, holding it up in delight to show them.

Tanya chattered to Toby as he rammed trains together in the violent manner of play he had sometimes, and Anna slowly lifted him off her lap so he sat on the ground. With a look at Tanya, she left his backpack on the floor and slowly slid back, stood up and took a few steps backwards.

Toby had his head buried in the giant bucket as he fished for more toys.

A reassuring nod from Tanya prompted Anna to turn away, saying a nonchalant, "Bye, Tobes."

"No! Na!"

Wrenching her eyes back, Toby was standing, a train in each hand, wide-eyed, and with a look of utter betrayal on his little face.

Forcing herself to look cheery, Anna waved. "I'll be back soon, Toby!"

In an instant, the trains fell from his hands, and Toby ran at her, wrapping his arms around her legs again, clinging, tears already spilling down his cheeks. "No! Na! No! No!" He looked up at her, trying to scale up her body. "Stay!"

Anna's heart broke for him. She gazed helplessly at Tanya, and the woman walked over, obviously realising Anna couldn't do it. She reached down and tried to pull Toby away.

His fingers clung to Anna's pants, and she had to fight the urge to reach down, pick him up, and walk them out of there. She took a deep breath, smiling at the boy who was crying hysterically in a stranger's arms. "I'll see you soon, Tobes. You play with Tanya and Thomas, okay?"

Toby hiccupped and reached for her.

Anna flicked her eyes up at Tanya, who was giving her a reassuring look as she mouthed, "Go, it's okay."

With a smile at Toby that made her feel a little ill, Anna stepped back, "Na! Na!" echoing in her ears as she walked out.

Another deep breath didn't do much to make her feel better as she walked down the hallway. Adjusting her bag, she checked her watch. Only five minutes late. She figured the HR people would let it slide. She swallowed hard as she got into the elevator.

Toby would be fine. Anna knew that. But it still didn't feel good. It was as if his fingers still clung to her jeans. But he would be fine. Anna would phone later, and he would be fine. Before her lunch break, she could even stop by.

Suddenly, her hand slapped to her forehead: she'd forgotten to tell Tanya about the cupcakes in Toby's bag. She could call after the meeting. And it would also be an excuse to check on Toby.

She made her way to HR and got sucked into thirty-five minutes' worth of paperwork and a fifteen-minute DVD on hand hygiene. Her eyebrows had raised at the movie the entire time. Seriously? She'd been in the surgery room for years.

They wrapped up ten minutes early, and Anna was approached by a squat balding man in a terrible suit. Introducing himself as Barry, he handed her a security pass and offered to give the tour. Trying not to breathe in the strong smell of BO or give away her amusement, Anna politely shook her head and said she'd be okay. Unconcerned, he wandered off, leaving her to back out of the room to escape the stench. Relieved, she shoved her copies of various bits of paperwork into her bag and pocketed her ID, then leant against the wall outside the HR offices to read a text from Lane.

> *Seriously, don't breathe in through your nose when he stands near you. I, on the other hand, smell like Mark Jacobs...the perfume, hopefully not the man himself. Getting coffee now, see you soon for the tour. :)*

Anna quickly sent a reply.

> *Please tell me it's Mark Jacobs, Lola. Actually, don't tell me. I'll take a guess when you get here. All done and dying for a coffee. :)*

She hit *send* and then "3" on her speed dial before raising the phone to her ear.

"Hi, Tanya? It's, ah, Anna Foster. I just wanted to see—"

"Toby's doing great, now."

The amusement in the woman's voice was clear. Anna tried not to let the sheepishness she felt creep into her tone. "I figured he would be. I just wanted to hear it."

"I don't blame you. What you saw is a daily show for some of the kids. And Toby's got lots of adjusting to do—but they all settle within a few minutes and have a great day. He's currently gluing macaroni to a piece of paper. Well, and to his hair. It's washable glue, don't worry."

Anna chuckled, feeling far more relaxed. "Thank you, Tanya."

"No worries. Call at any time, or stop in if you need. But I promise, he's all good now."

"I believe you. Thanks, I'll see you tonight—oh, and there's cupcakes in Toby's bag for everyone."

"Well isn't that sweet! Thanks—we'll see you tonight."

Anna hung up, feeling a lot more at ease, and caught sight of Lane walking towards her, two giant coffee cups in hand. A huge grin broke over Lane's lips as their eyes met.

Trying to ignore the way her heart sped up, Anna couldn't help but smile back. "Hey there." She tried to not look Lane up and down, those legs going on forever in black jeans and a shirt cut just low enough to show cleavage. Fighting the urge to stare openly, Anna instead focused on the coffee Lane held out to her.

"You survived HR. Well done."

Anna tilted her cup. "Thanks. And yeah, I did." Her voice went mock serious. "They made me watch a DVD on hand hygiene, Lane."

"Oh, you get to watch that one annually."

"Seriously?"

Lane nodded over a sip of her coffee. "Yup. I just saw it last month. I love the bit about how if you sing "Happy Birthday" in your head, that's how long you should wash your hands for."

"Or how long to rub in the alcohol hand rub, don't forget." Anna grinned.

"That's about when I vague out and start answering emails on my phone."

"Nice work ethic." Anna's voice was playful.

"Oh, I'm impressive."

She fought the urge to wink over her coffee cup. "I believe that."

Lane's eyes widened slightly before she cast her gaze to the ground, grinning. "Shall we start the tour?"

"Lead the way."

They started down the hallway, then waited at the elevator Anna had come out of earlier. "I thought we'd start back down at the entrance and go from there?"

"Start at the beginning?" said Anna.

"Best way to do it."

Anna was grinning as they stepped into the elevator. Every conversation with Lane seemed to leave her feeling lighter.

Two people quickly got on after them, and they moved back into the corner to make room, smiling politely at the two intruders. Their shoulders brushed, and Anna turned her head as Lane shifted to look at her. They were close enough that a sweet, soft scent invaded her senses.

Anna tilted her head as their eyes locked. "Lola," she whispered.

Lane's smile widened, her voice low. "Live up to expectations?"

Eyes still on Lane's, Anna gave a small nod. "Definitely."

An annoying ding sounded, and the doors opened. Reluctantly, Anna tore her eyes away and followed Lane out of the elevator. Feeling that she was acting too boldly, she slid her hands into her pockets. She just couldn't help it, the woman smelt good. And seriously, that smile...

Lane led her around the entrance, showing her the staff entry to the ER, then introduced her to a few of the staff and orientated her to the location of the copious amounts of paperwork she would need. Eventually, the tour brought her through to the theatres, and Anna bounced on her feet as they stood in an empty operating room. She looked around, the space familiar, comforting.

Anna caught sight of Lane grinning at her. "What?"

"You look like a kid at Christmas. Your eyes are practically shining."

"I've not been at work for three weeks." Anna paused, and her mouth dropped open. "Oh, shit, more like a month."

Lane's eyes widened. "A month? God, I'd be climbing the wall without working that long. Unless I was on some incredible holiday. What's stopped you?"

Pretending to take in the gleaming surfaces surrounding her, Anna kept her voice light. "Oh, just, the move took a while." The fluoroscope now held her attention. "But I can't wait to get back into it. What are the anaesthetic nurses like?"

"We have a great team of nurses here." Lane led the way through to the corridor. "Though I might be biased. I can take you through to the surgical nurses' room if you like? I know most of them. I work everywhere."

Letting Lane lead her down a hallway and into another elevator, Anna nodded enthusiastically. "That'd be great. If there's anything I've learnt, it's be friends with your nurses."

"Yeah, the new generation of doctors and surgeons are finally getting that. Unfortunately, the dinosaurs are a bit slow on the uptake. When do you finish today?"

"Five."

"Five? Scoring an early finish. Nice."

"I'm just lucky." She studiously avoided looking sideways at Lane, fairly certain the woman was looking at her like she was a puzzle to solve.

It wasn't long until the smell of cafeteria food warned her they were at that part of the tour. With a flourish of her hands, Lane gestured to the ugly metal tables and boring walls that constituted an eating place in a hospital. That part of the tour included a warning to not buy lunch on Tuesdays because it was always "something surprise."

"And seriously, the surprise it's given many people's gastro tract was not fun."

Anna wrinkled her nose, following Lane up a flight of stairs. "Ew. Too much information."

Walking through the door Lane held open for her, there was a moment she thought she caught Lane's eyes looking her up and down. The idea of it brought a smile to Anna's lips.

"Yeah, I tend to overshare gruesome details. Sorry."

Rapidly, they took in the laboratories and various locker rooms. Most importantly, Lane pointed out the coffee cart on level two that served burnt, old coffee but the best muffins and then the coffee cart on level four that served the only decent coffee in the hospital but had the worst snacks.

"It's all about combining the positives," Lane explained.

Their next stop was the surgical ward. Lane showed her the various staff rooms, then confidently led her into the surgical nurses' room where Anna played meet and greet with the nurses and doctors present. Before she knew it, they were at the end of the tour, leaning against a railing at the top of the emergency stairs. From there they could take in the city view outside, their shoulders almost touching, not quite making contact.

"So, do I get to hear the story of that bruise?"

Even though she felt Lane's eyes on her face, Anna continued staring forward. Her cheeks warmed. "I told you that story was worth more than a tour."

"Oh, come on, that was a *great* tour."

Anna finally caught Lane's eye. "That was an amazing tour. And, as promised, there was good coffee and you smelt delightful."

Lane's grin widened.

"But, still, it's worth more than that."

"Drinks, then." Lane kind of blurted it out, her own eyes widening to match Anna's.

"Ah—" She knew she should say no. This morning, she had barely had time to brush her teeth and make it to the bathroom, and that was only the beginning of her problems. Yes, she was single, but Lane had no idea what she'd be getting into.

Yet, it *was* just drinks. Casual. Was there anything wrong with welcoming a distraction into her life? It didn't have to be anything serious. Anna crossed her arms and gave a small nod. "Drinks would be great."

A look of relief flashed over Lane's face. "Will that earn me the story?"

Anna was going to have to tell her sometime. She smiled, her tone playful. "If drinks with you is as amazing as I would imagine it to be, then yes. You'll get the story."

Lane's phone went off in her pocket. She checked it with a roll of her eyes. "I gotta run. But, great. Friday night?" When she looked back up, she was grinning.

Anna would have to speak with her parents. And wow, did that thought sound strange in her head at thirty-two. "Friday night sounds good."

"I'll talk to you during the week about it. Maybe we could get some of the work guys out, give you a proper introduction?" Lane started backing away.

Anna grinned after her. "Sounds perfect."

It did sound perfect. A group was casual. Not as much expectation as a one-on-one catch up.

Also known as a date.

When Hayley had left her and she'd taken on this role with the kids, the notion had entered Anna's head that women would be something she wouldn't think about for a while. But Lane? She just couldn't *not* think about her. The last hour had been relaxed, chatty. And even when she tried to say no or tried to rein in the flirting, she couldn't do it. Lane was so fun. In fact, she was the most simple, enjoyable thing in Anna's life right then; light-hearted, easy.

It didn't have to be anything serious.

Her phone vibrated in her pocket.

Lane.

PS: I'm impressed you picked the perfume.

Fun texts, fun conversations—nothing serious.

It's my favourite...It suits you.

She would have to tell Lane about the kids, about her brother. But it was so tempting not to. To keep this one uncomplicated, fun thing that she could embrace. But the two kids made not telling Lane the truth impossible. And Ella and Toby, they deserved her full attention. She shouldn't even be thinking of dating at this point. Everything was still so difficult. And she'd only been single for three weeks, though it felt like that phone call in Indonesia had happened a year ago.

She sighed and pushed off from the bannister. Time to meet with her boss to go over the schedules. Vibrations in her pocket pulled her attention back to her phone.

I'll have to wear it Friday night, then.

Anna's smile could be seen from space, she was sure.

Chapter Eight

You know, in all the excitement of the tour, I didn't ask: how is Ella and her broken arm? Did you know I actually thought she was your daughter? Kym corrected me this afternoon. haha :)

Anna considered the text message over a glass of wine. Guiltily, she put out her half-smoked cigarette, even though there was no one to see it. So, Lane had thought Ella was her daughter. And now she knew she wasn't. It almost would have been better for her to keep assuming that. At least then she'd know Anna came with some complications. Lane didn't even know about the toddler with the charming smile and killer ability to throw a tantrum.

Her bum had started to go numb on the wooden step after sitting there for two hours flicking her lighter before succumbing to the temptation of a cigarette. Toby and Ella were in bed, Toby still with remnants of "washable" glue in his hair that had *not* come out. Ella had initially refused to talk, but Anna had coaxed her out of it a bit by asking what colour cast she was going to get. Even then, the responses had been minimal.

And now, Anna sat with a text that held a perfect lead-in to explain the catch to dating her, and she couldn't bring herself to do it.

After a long internal debate, she sent a reply.

Haha, that's a mistake often made, more so even with my nephew. Ella is in fine form, just deciding cast colour and rambling on and on about the nurse she's excited to see Friday. I gloated that I spent this morning with you and made the six year old jealous.

Anna put her phone down and took a long sip of wine. Yes, she was kind of a coward. But this wasn't a bombshell she wanted to drop through text—or so she told herself.

Amazingly, her first day at work had gone well. She'd done a few assessments for surgeries that were scheduled for the next day, met with families to go over consents for said surgeries, and ended up with even more paperwork in the afternoon. She had managed to see Kym for lunch, and had made the mistake of mentioning that there might be drinks on Friday evening. After seeing Kym's eyes light up, Anna got the feeling that it was going to turn into more than just four or five of them coming. So much for a casual, getting-to-know-people evening. The niggling feeling in the back of her mind told her that she really wanted it to be just her and Lane out for drinks.

Or, you know, naked and in bed.

But you couldn't say no to a grieving widow.

Anna's phone buzzed and she looked down.

Your nephew must be incredibly cute then. You gloated to a six-year-old? Seriously?

Anna laughed out loud.

His smile is lethal, it's true. And yeah, I did. Judging me?

The reply came quickly.

To be honest? I just like that I'm something worth being jealous over, even if she's only six.

Anna grabbed her cigarettes and wine glass, dropping the latter off in the kitchen and tapping out a reply as she walked up to her room.

Wait until she hears I'm spending Friday night with you. :)

As silently as possible, Anna walked through to her room and got her pyjamas, then headed to the shower, on the way pausing outside her brother's room. She really needed to sort it out. The wood was smooth against her fingers as she rested her palm on the surface of the door. The light feeling from talking with Lane turned heavier as she stood in the silent hallway.

This room had an ensuite and was adult size. She could sleep in there, clear everything out, box up their things. It made sense to do so; Anna was living there now. Hell, the house was in the process of being put in her name. It was *her* house, technically.

But it wasn't.

It was her brother's house, and Sally's. Ella had almost been born on the stairs. They'd repainted every room—Sally's taste was splashed everywhere. The living room held a feature wall of an amazing deep blue and the hideously ugly rug in the hallway had been Sally's great-grandmother's. Her brother's Air Force papers were framed and hung on the stairway wall, along with the kids' baby photos.

The house was a shrine to the deceased, and Anna didn't know if that was healthy or not. For now, though, she was happy to keep sleeping in the tiny spare room.

"Mummy!"

Anna's gut clenched at the cry, and her head whipped around, hair flying around her face.

Ella.

She walked to her niece's room and pushed the door open, heart pounding. A whimper came from the bed, and Anna padded forward and squatted next to it, hand hovering over the lump that was Ella. The little girl was curled into a ball, eyes clamped shut. She was still asleep.

Anna stroked her fingers through the soft strands of Ella's hair, but something stopped her from waking her niece. Instead she stroked Ella's head and just watched her, at a complete loss as to what to do. The whimpers slowed, but even after they'd stopped, she sat for a long while, hand stilled on Ella's shoulder over the blanket. The sound of even, settled breathing filled the air. Ella might not be as young as Toby, but here, lost in sleep, she was tiny.

After pressing her lips to Ella's forehead, Anna tiptoed to the door. A glance back assured her Ella really was fast asleep before pulling the door over slightly. Once she checked that Toby was still settled, Anna, throat burning, made her way to the shower.

The water was scorching hot, and yet, she turned the cold down even more as the water beat at her back. She pressed her palms against the tile, fingers pressing against the cool ceramic. Resolute, she bit back a sob, refusing to give in to the feeling that clawed at her chest.

Seeing the kids grieve like they were ate at her, and there were times when the sorrow simply washed over her. She would be okay, they would all be okay, and then something as simple, yet really complex, as Ella calling out for her mother while asleep left Anna drowning in a feeling she spent all day holding at bay. The sight of her brother's door, or his car parked in the garage, or the wine glasses with the blue decoration that she had shared with Sally pulled at threads until she suddenly found herself unravelling.

Her throat tightened, and she pressed her hand over her eyes, turned to stand directly under the spray of water, and took a long, deep breath. Nights like tonight—when she was about to climb into the bed in her brother's spare room after checking on his kids, and it was starting to feel normal—almost felt worse than when things had constantly been strange and uncomfortable. In spite of herself, Anna was enjoying moments in the car with Toby, the time spent unwinding from her day by chatting with him. And then Ella would be sitting at her parents' window, hand pressed to the glass, waiting for them, and Anna always warmed at the sight.

She was constantly exhausted by the competition between normalcy and the silent moments that left her wanting to bolt. Missing her brother, and missing Sally, left Anna beyond fatigued. The swirl of mixed emotions was too much, and she wanted to just stay in the boiling water of the shower forever.

Fingers shaking slightly, she finally turned off the tap and stepped out, running the towel over her pink skin. As quickly as she could, she pulled on her clothes and turned off the light. One last peek at the kids, and she went to her room and slipped between the cool sheets.

She needed a diversion, Anna decided, as she picked up her phone from where she'd put it on charge.

> *Well, I'd say bring Ella, but I'd much rather have you to myself. Though I think there's going to be quite a few people there now. Maybe I could take you to dinner next week, if Friday goes well? ;)*

Anna tapped out a quick reply and relaxed into her bed, ignoring the dry feeling in her eyes and the way her stomach churned.

> *If all goes well, consider me in.*

Distraction achieved.

Anna soon discovered that she loved her job at the new hospital—the people she worked with, the patients, the feeling of being busy. When she completed her first surgery, she felt elated. It had felt so good to be in a role that she innately understood. In the operating theatre, monitoring the patient's airway, intubating and administering drugs, cannulating and murmuring quietly to the anaesthetic nurse—all of this—had come naturally.

Anna washed her hands and then went to the elevator, delighted to see Lane leaning against the back wall when the doors opened. She looked adorable in her scrub cap, and a grin spread over her face when she saw Anna.

"You look happy."

After hitting the button she needed, Anna leant her shoulder against the back wall, arms crossed. "I just rocked surgery."

"I'm sorry I missed it. I was scrub nurse for Patel. I'd love to see you in action."

"You will, I'm sure."

Lane leant slightly forward, her face inches from Anna's. "At home or the hospital? Either is fine with me."

With a ding, the doors opened. Anna was left with her mouth slightly open, an amused expression on her face but unable to respond as Lane threw her a smug look and walked out. Just as the doors closed, Lane shot one last glance over her shoulder, a delighted laugh escaping her lips at the look on Anna's face.

Friday morning came, and Anna walked into work anticipating drinks that evening with a mixture of guilt and excitement. Ella held Anna's hand and Toby bounced along on her hip. Her mind was half on Lane and half on the need to hurry to get Ella to her casting appointment and then to school. She gave a furtive look around and breathed a sigh of relief when she didn't see Lane. She had meant to slip the fact that she was her niece and nephew's guardian into conversations throughout the week, but it just hadn't happened.

Or maybe she hadn't wanted it to happen.

Ella snapped Anna out of her thoughts. "I think I want an orange cast."

Anna gently squeezed her hand. "Orange is cool."

"But what if I want purple?"

Anna led them down the hallway leading to the day care. "What about green?"

Ella made a face. "Yuck. No. Peas are green."

Anna nodded. "That's a good point."

They'd been having this conversation for three days now.

"Do you think I could get purple *and* orange?"

"As awesome as that would be, the type of cast you're getting won't let that happen."

"A fiverclass one?"

"Fibreglass. I think orange sounds cool."

"You keep saying that."

"That's because that's what I think."

"Ogen! Na, ogen."

Anna turned her head and blew a raspberry against Toby's cheek as they entered the day care. "See, Ella? Even Toby thinks orange."

"He's a baby."

As soon as Toby was on the floor he ran to the tub of trains and cars and started pulling them out. One in each hand, he showed them to Ella, pressing them against her stomach to get her to notice. "Twain, El. Twain."

"Is that Thomas, Toby?"

Shaking his head adamantly, Toby dropped the trains he was holding and ran to the bucket to pick up a Thomas one, which he brought over to Ella, holding it up.

"Cool, Toby! It's bigger than your one at home."

Once Toby was signed in, Anna put his backpack away. Thankfully, he had sat down at one of the train tracks and was pushing Thomas along it. Ella sat next to him, helping. Another little boy sat next to them, whom Toby also showed the train to.

Discreetly, Anna tapped Ella on the back, and put her finger to her lips.

Ella stood up and they tried to casually walk away, quickly kissing Toby's head and saying goodbye. He looked up and his little face dropped.

This had gotten easier than the first time, but not by much.

He was clasping two trains in his hands and his face was threatening to crumple completely.

"Tobes, we'll see you soon. I'm coming in for lunch with a cupcake today!" She hated the false cheer in her voice.

He shook his head adamantly. "Na, no."

Tanya swept in and scooped Toby up, whispering something in his ear that almost made him giggle before he went back and reached for Anna, who kept smiling and waved "bye". It was not getting easier for her to turn around and walk away. At least this time he didn't scream. She did hear his crying pick up in pitch, though.

Worry gnawed at Anna's stomach. This was exactly why she was partially dreading drinks that evening, as much as her mother had readily agreed to take the kids. They needed her, and throwing dating into the mix of work, kids and grief seemed impossible.

Hand in hand, they walked to the orthopaedic clinic, Anna trying not to dwell on the emotions that had stormed through her all week. Spending each evening alone in that house, torn between conflicting urges to protect her brother's two kids and to flee, was taking its toll on her.

"Why does Toby get so sad when you leave? You're not Mum."

Anna had to appreciate the fact that when Ella did speak, she got right to the point. Considering her response, Anna finally said, eyes forward, "I think Toby misses your mum and dad and so gets a little worried when the only people he knows leave."

"Does he think you won't come back?"

Anna swallowed at the nugget of truth. "Maybe." She glanced down at Ella, but like her aunt, the little girl was staring ahead as they walked.

In the end, she said, "The last thing Mummy told Toby was she'd see him in the morning." Anna nodded. Ella continued, "I think Toby now doesn't know what's true."

Ella blew Anna away sometimes.

"I think you're right, Ella Bella." Anna squeezed her hand.

They walked quietly for a minute before Ella said softly, "The last thing Daddy said to me was I had to be a good big sister, because Grandad is scared of monsters."

Anna choked a chuckle over the lump in her throat. "He said that, yeah?"

"Yeah. Will Nurse Lane be there today?"

It was a sudden change, but Anna went with it. "Yup. She's going down there just to help change your cast. She said she couldn't wait to see you."

"I can't wait to see her. She was nice."

"She was, wasn't she?"

"Can she come over to play one time?"

Clearing her throat, Anna tried to hide the fact that choked on nothing. How she wished Lane could come over to play. And she didn't mean dolls. "Nurse Lane is really busy, Ella. But you'll get to see her when you get this new cast off."

"Really?"

"Yup. She told me that she'll take it off herself."

"Cool."

They walked into the clinic and approached the receptionist, who ushered them straight through to a cast room and told them that the nurse wouldn't be long. Anna tried not to smirk—Lane had said she'd pulled some strings to get placed in the clinic that morning.

At just that moment, Lane walked in with three takeaway coffee cups in a carrier. "Well hi, Miss Ella."

Ella grinned at Lane, and Anna was unable to stop herself smiling either.

"Hi, Nurse Lane."

"There's those two matching grins again." She handed one of the cups to Anna, and then held one out to Ella. "If it's okay with your Aunty Anna, I got you a hot chocolate since the adults get coffee."

Ella's eyes widened and she batted her eyelashes. "Please, Aunty Na?"

Anna pretended to consider it for a second. "I don't know, it's barely quarter past eight in the morning."

"You get coffee!"

"Kid has a point, Aunty Na."

Anna rolled her eyes at Lane. "You, shush. Of course you can have it, Ella."

"Thank you!" She grabbed the cup, taking a long sip. "There's marshmallows!" She looked like all her Christmases had come at once.

Anna chuckled, happy to see Ella behave more like a kid. "Thanks, Lane."

"No worries. Now, Ella, let's save that hot chocolate and get this cast done, then you can have it as a reward."

Momentarily bummed, Ella handed the cup over.

"Thanks! Now have you decided on a colour?"

"It was a pretty hard choice-but I want orange."

"Interesting colour choice."

"I like how Toby says 'orange.'"

"How is that?"

Ella mimicked Toby's baby voice perfectly. "Ogen."

"Well—that is ridiculously adorable. Orange it is, then."

Lane easily removed the old cast first before starting with the new one, chatting the whole time with Ella about all the current Pixar movies that Anna had only recently become acquainted with.

Soon Lane was putting on the final touches, going over cast care, explaining that it set really quickly—more for Ella's benefit than for Anna's, who obviously knew what to do already.

As she was finishing up, Ella stared intently at her, head tilted in a mirror image of Anna's. "You're really pretty, Nurse Lane. You have really pretty skin."

Lane looked up from Ella's arm and smiled in a way that made Anna's heart speed up again. "You're really pretty too, Ella. You look a lot like your aunty."

"Everybody says that."

"They do?"

Ella nodded. "Yup. Toby looks even more like her, 'cause they both have the same brown hair and colour eyes. It's weird."

Lane laughed. "Why is it weird?"

"Cause he's a boy."

Without taking her eyes off Anna, Lane said, "He must be a very pretty boy, then."

Anna felt her cheeks flush slightly.

"Well! We're all done. No more bags on your arm in the bath." Lane had turned back to Ella, who sighed in a very adult way and rolled her eyes.

"Thank God."

Lane hid a smile at the dramatic behaviour. "Now, you look after that arm and I'll see you in a month."

"So I'll see you, and not someone scary?"

"I promise."

"Good."

Anna steered Ella out with a hand on her back, the hot chocolate practically glued to Ella's mouth.

"I'll see you tonight, if I don't run into you today," she said.

Lane stood with her arms crossed, watching them walk out. "Can't wait, Anna. See you soon, Ella!"

Ella turned and waved with her newly orange arm, yelling, "Bye! Thanks!" from around the cup.

Glad that the school would be dealing with the sugar high that had steadily started to hit Ella in the car, Anna dropped her off.

The day passed quickly after that, mostly in consults and sneaking down to spend her forty-minute lunch break with Toby. Ella's insight into how Toby must feel echoed in Anna's mind. She could only hope just being around all the time helped him.

Before she knew it, she was dropping the kids off to her parents and waving goodbye. Toby settled with his grandmother fairly well, the only person besides Anna whom he clung to now. Ella was already asking to run a bath, wanting to try out her new waterproof cast. Anna's father, as usual, hid away in his study.

She drove home, had a quick shower, and then stood in front of her wardrobe, debating what to wear. Six outfits later, she went with tight jeans, ankle boots, and a cream jersey. A scarf wrapped around her neck, plus a tailor-cut jacket and some perfume added the final touches just in time for the taxi to honk outside.

As she got in, she quickly checked her phone.

> *No fair, you get to go home and shower. I have to shower at work because I was in a surgery that ran long.*

Lane. Anna grinned and replied.

> *You'll still look great.*

Sometimes, a simple sentence was best. Her phone buzzed. At the sight of Kym's text, Anna shook her head.

> *Got here early with lots of the work people. We found some shots. Help me.*

When her taxi pulled up to the bar, Anna paid the fare and slid out. She stood outside and took in a deep breath, trying to quell her thoughts about what to tell Lane about the kids, then walked inside.

The heat and noise hit her, and she felt herself relax a little. How she had missed this. She and Hayley used to go to bars a couple of nights a week, just for a quiet drink—or sometimes a not-so-quiet one. They'd been social, with a wide circle of friends. They'd both had their own circles, too, back then. Anna found herself almost excited to have a few drinks and unwind with people she'd have at least one thing to talk about with, even if it was their jobs. Nights in the house had been sending her a little insane; this might help her feel a touch normal again.

After stopping at the bar, Anna took a sip of her wine while she turned to look for Kym. Finally, she caught sight of her in a far corner booth where several chairs were pulled up to fit more people.

Kym caught her eye and waved enthusiastically from where she sat wedged between colleagues.

Smirking at the obviously tipsy state of her friend, Anna made her way over. Kym made a loud noise at her arrival, still waving. Anna smiled and raised her glass in acknowledgement.

"You made it!" Kym grinned at her.

"Wouldn't have missed it." She took another sip of her wine, because, judging from the look of everyone, she needed to catch up. Anna greeted the staff members she knew and shook hands with those she hadn't yet met. About fifteen people were spread over three tables. Taking a seat, she took another sip of her wine, then turned around to peer behind her when she saw Kym's eyes light up as she waved again.

Anna practically had to restrain her jaw from dropping. Lane had walked in wearing a clingy white dress that draped over every curve like it had been made just for her. It was cut low—low enough that Anna was concerned she wouldn't be able to look anywhere else. The white set off Lane's dark skin in a way that had Anna mesmerised. In that moment, she couldn't remember a single reason why seeing Lane was a bad idea.

"Oi, do you need a napkin to get that drool?"

Anna turned around to find Kym and a nurse friend of hers grinning. Thankfully, the others were all wrapped up in conversation. "I have no idea what you mean."

Kym sipped at her whisky. "Sure. Tess here has a friend that works in plastics, we can get your jaw re-attached later."

Tess gave a snort into her beer and winked at Anna. "We love a good nurse and doctor romance. Gives us something to gossip about in the nurses' room."

Anna figured finishing her drink was probably the best fix for this situation.

Lane slid into the seat next to her and put a glass of white wine down on the table. "You looked like you were almost out."

Anna put her now empty glass down and reached forward to pick up the new one. "Thanks."

Shit-eating grins appeared on Kym's and Tess' faces.

"What?"

Tess grinned wider. "Nothin'."

"O-kay." Lane narrowed her eyes. "You can stop staring now."

Their only response was to chuckle.

Lane turned to Anna. "Sorry about them."

"Don't be. They caught me staring at you as you came in." Anna leant slightly forward. "I was wrong—you look better than great. Nice perfume, by the way."

Lane winked. "I thought you'd like it."

"But how? I was so subtle."

"About as subtle as your niece. Did she learn to tell women they're pretty from you?"

"No, she just learnt to tell the truth from me."

Lane sipped her wine, looking Anna up and down before meeting her eyes. "You look good."

"Thanks." Anna tried and failed not to flush.

They got pulled into conversation with the others, Lane chatting with an emergency resident while Anna talked to Kym and Tess, who could probably have a comedy show. Anna spent her time nodding and adding in the odd comment, amused by the two of them, and throwing Lane flirty looks, which she returned in kind.

An hour or so in, Anna stood to get another drink, and Kym clambered over people's laps to join her. As they stood at the bar waiting to order, Kym swayed, watching her.

"What?"

Kym shrugged. "Nothing."

Laughing, Anna ordered their drinks. "Okay."

"It's just..." Kym leant forward as if to whisper, still talking at the same volume regardless, "...you. And Lane. It makes me happy."

"Nothing's happened."

"Oh, please. It may not have *yet*."

Anna paid, handing Kym her whisky and picking up the two wine glasses. "It may not at all, Kym."

Kym had stopped dead and put her glass down in her mission to do up the zip and button combination of her handbag, something she was failing at miserably. "What do you mean?"

"She doesn't know about the kids, Kym." Anna leant against the bar.

Visibly relaxing, Kym waved her hand. "So? Lots of people with kids date. You're allowed to date. Kids aren't a chastity belt." She paused. "Most of the time."

"The kids need attention. I barely have enough time with work, and—"

Kym grabbed her by the shoulders. "Anna. Shut up. Get laid. Have fun."

"Um—"

"No." Kym shook her head, squeezing Anna's arms to keep her balance more than anything. "One of us needs to. I'm horny as hell, but I miss my husband. I'm all emotionally traumatised and stuff. You're allowed to have a life. Your brother wouldn't have wanted you to suffer because of this. He'd want the kids happy, but he'd want you happy, too."

"What about your happiness?"

Flippantly giving a wave of her hand, Kym went back to her handbag. "One day. It's been six months, and he's still all I think about." She raised her hands up triumphantly when she got one button done, then realised it was through the wrong hole. "Damn it."

Smiling affectionately, Anna watched her struggle. On a whim, she gave Kym a quick hug.

Eyeing Anna suspiciously, Kym gave up on her buttons. "What was that for?"

"Nothing. I just like that I met you. We can talk. It's nice." Maybe the wine had gone to her head.

The emphatic nod Kym gave looked like it might send her off balance. "Me too. You're a good find, even if you're also emotionally scarred. Maybe because of it."

With a laugh, Anna picked up the wine glasses and led the way to their table where Lane was loudly debating the necessity of extra nurses with their boss. She slid one of the glasses in front of her and blinked at it, then grinned.

"Thanks."

"Anytime." Just as she slid into her seat, Lane stood up.

"Toilet break." She turned and walked away, looking back over her shoulder to catch Anna watching her again.

"Seriously, follow her." Kym had one eye half-closed as she gave the order.

"What?"

"Go, follow her. You've been eye-fucking all night! Go do something about it."

"What? We have not!" Anna protested indignantly.

The loud snort Tess gave shut Anna up. "Oh, please, some of those looks even made *me* squirm."

Sliding an arm over Anna's shoulder, Kym slurred, "I don't know what's holding you back, but woman, go follow her."

"The kids."

"Do something for you."

Anna stared at her for a minute. Maybe she was right.

Tess sighed loudly. "Go, or I'll ensure you're stuck with every intern wanting to learn anaesthetics for the next month. I know people."

"Mean. I'm new."

"Don't care."

With a resigned shake of her head, Anna stood up to walk quickly after Lane. Her hand rested against the handle of the bathroom door for a second as she took in a deep breath, then exhaled.

She pushed it open.

Lane was just walking out of a cubicle and grinned as she moved across to wash her hands.

Anna smiled back, unsure of what her next step should be.

Drying her hands on a paper towel before throwing it in the bin, Lane positioned herself against the sink and crossed her arms. "Hey."

"Hey." Anna's heart was pounding in her ears, and she had no idea why. She swallowed. "I, uh, I think it's only fair, to tell you something; though it's really tempting not to."

Lane's grin softened.

"You don't know everything about me," Anna began.

Lane chuckled, stepping forward. "No one knows everything about a person—that's why you do things like go out to dinner, chat...?"

Anna returned the smile but stayed against the door as Lane took a few more small steps forward, arms still crossed.

"That's true. But some things, you should know beforehand. Like, if I was leaving the country in a month, I'd have to give you a heads-up."

Lane's confusion was evident. "Uh, okay. Are you?"

"What? No. Not leaving the country." Anna tapped her fingers against the cold door, more nervous about this than she wanted to be.

Only a tiny distance separated them now, and Anna tried to ignore the urge to grab her so she could finish what she started. "Just—there's some things, in my life. It's, uh, complicated."

"Everyone's complicated, Anna."

Taking a breath, Anna closed her eyes from a moment in frustration. She was terrified Lane would see it all as too much, and run. And she was terrified that this terrified her. She hardly knew Lane, really. Yet not telling didn't seem right. Her eyes opened.

And what if she did blow it? What if Lane ran? Anna wouldn't blame her. Hayley had run. Anna might have, had their positions been reversed. Hell, she had wanted to and it was *her* niece and nephew. Sometimes, she still wanted to.

Her eyes locked on Lane's. Without thinking anymore, Anna slid forward to close the last small gap between them. The scent of Lane's perfume surrounded her, and her cheeks were flushed from the wine. Lane's eyes darted to Anna's mouth and back up again. She bit subtly at her bottom lip, the gesture drawing Anna's attention directly to her mouth. If Lane was going to run, Anna wanted something to remember her by. The gap closed completely as Anna pressed her lips to Lane's.

The kiss was supposed to be simple. Chaste. But then, Lane's hands came up to gently cup her cheeks, and Anna pressed her body flush against Lane's, hands on her waist. She pressed her lips harder against Lane's, giving in to the sensation. Their lips parted, and she felt Lane's tongue flick against her own and almost groaned.

For a month, Anna had closed herself off. She had tried that entire time to be what she needed to be for the kids. Whenever she had felt overwhelmed, she'd taken a breath and clamped it down. Whenever she'd felt anything at all lately, she had clamped it down.

As Lane's tongue slid against her own, Anna felt that thing inside that held it all down shift. Her fingers gripped at Lane's dress, pulling them tighter together. Lane responded, hands slipping up to wrap in Anna's hair. Their mouths moved slowly, tongues languid.

It was intense and a little sloppy, and it tasted like wine, and it was perfect.

They parted, both slightly breathless, and Anna leant her forehead against Lane's, hands still grasping her close.

"Wow." The sound of Lane's low, husky voice made heat settle deep in Anna's stomach.

"Yeah." Her own voice sounded much the same.

"Was that what you wanted to tell me? Because you can tell me that anytime you want to."

Anna couldn't help but chuckle at the charming grin Lane threw at her. "No, that wasn't it. That just happened."

"Again, really, that can happen any time."

Suddenly feeling cold, Anna stepped back. "I'd like that to happen any time."

Lane was looking intently at her again, head tilted. "What is it?"

She took another step and, breaking eye contact with Lane, Anna created more space. With her back against the door and Lane in front of her, watching her expectantly, she felt caged in. Couldn't she just go back to kissing Lane? To keeping this as her fun, flirty escape?

"I come with a catch."

"You *are* a catch."

Anna actually laughed this time. "And you're too smooth." She crossed her arms again, wishing the wine was making this easier. Lane's lips were red, swollen from the kiss, and Anna just wanted to lean forward and get lost in her again. "You know Ella? And I've mentioned my nephew, Toby?"

Lane nodded, still playful.

Rip it off like a Band-Aid, Anna. "My brother, Jake, died over a month ago, with my sister-in-law, in a car accident. They named me the kids' guardian. I... uh, they're kind of, mine."

The smile faded from Lane's lips. She blinked in surprise, her mouth dropped partly open.

Anna hovered for a minute and then, after a beat of silence, decided she couldn't take seeing Lane turn away. She turned on the spot and fled the bathroom.

Anna had said his name. And it had hurt, had caught at her gut and made her feel almost ill. And now, after an incredibly amazing kiss, she'd gone and scared Lane off. Anna walked out quickly, swinging by the table to grab her jacket.

Kym looked up at her in surprise. "How'd it go? Thought you'd be in there for ages. I've been fielding the door." She tried to give a wink that ended up as a drunken blink.

"Um…fine. I gotta run. I'll see you later."

Grateful that everyone was now a little too drunk to really pay attention, Anna escaped out the door. The cool air hit her burning cheeks as she pulled on her jacket. With no real thought as to where she was going, she turned left and powered down the street. Breathing heavily, irritated at herself, she walked blindly.

She'd kissed Lane, blurted out something huge, then turned and ran. And now she was alone in the street, a little drunk, and God, she wanted to talk to her brother about it all. Or to Sally. All she wanted was to call them and have them pass the phone back and forth between them, alternating between teasing her and offering advice. Jake would be calling her a coward right now. Sally would slap him on the head, steal the phone, and laugh down the line as she said, *"Not coward, exactly, Anna, more…cautious."* And Jake would be yelling in the background, *"Coward!"*

She missed his laugh.

Anna used to call them when she got home from work, and Sally would answer, and both would drink a glass of wine while they caught up. Jake would eventually steal the phone, and the two of them would chat for ages, each other's confidante, a constant since they were children.

And right now? She missed that more than anything. Her throat was burning, and she bit back tears. She wanted to talk to her brother. She wanted to have a simple life, one in which when she met Lane, they could fall into bed together and never turn back. Though, if the damn accident hadn't happened, she'd be with Hayley. So what did she really want? Anna didn't know anymore.

"Anna!"

She spun at the sound of her name.

Lane pulled up in front of her, out of breath and concerned, eyes searching Anna's face. "Why did you leave?"

Anna wrapped her arms around herself. "Uh, I don't know." She really didn't. In hindsight, it was a little dramatic. "Your face, you looked—"

"Surprised? Shocked?" Lane stepped forward, hands coming up to rest on Anna's shoulders as if to hold her in place. "I was. That—that is just, horrible. For you. And for those kids. To lose your brother, and their dad. Their mum." Lane shook her head. "God—how have you been coping? All your lives have been turned completely upside down."

Anna swallowed over a lump in her throat and gave a tiny shrug.

"Why did you leave?"

Anna didn't trust herself to speak.

Lane was watching her with wide, concerned eyes, and the feelings in Anna's throat were going to choke her. More forcefully than intended, she kissed Lane. With her eyes still closed, she pulled back, afraid to open them and give herself away.

"Anna, open your eyes."

After a moment she did, and a tear slipped onto her cheek. Lane reached up to brush it away, her thumb gentle on Anna's skin.

"I'm sorry."

"Why? Because you ran away, or for the tears? You're not allowed to apologise for tears."

"Um, for both." Lane's hands were resting against Anna's neck, while her own hands clenched Lane's jacket. "I, uh, I thought it might be too much. The kids, all this baggage. My brother." Her voice hitched slightly over the last word, and she took in a deep breath and let it out slowly.

Lane's voice was soft. "You're an idiot."

The laugh trapped inside Anna's body came out almost like a sob. "Can you blame me?" She looked down. "Did I mention my girlfriend left because of the kids?"

Lane ducked her head to catch Anna's eye. Her voice was soft. "Well, she's an idiot. Can't say I'm sad though. That means you're definitely single."

"I don't kiss girls in bathrooms unless I'm single."

"Good to know."

Anna drew in a shuddering breath, and Lane pulled her forward. Resigning herself to the sensation, Anna buried her face in the warmth of Lane's neck. Strong arms wrapped around her, and Anna unravelled. The sob that forced its way out of her chest was painful, as if she was parting from something. The tears came hard and fast, finally, soaking Lane's jacket under her cheek.

"I'm sorry." Anna rasped the words against soft skin, hands clinging to Lane.

Lane's hands came up into her hair, pulling Anna tighter against her. "I'm not."

Chapter Nine

Anna Foster didn't like to lose control.

Growing up with a father who favoured discipline and a firm word and a mother who was loving but always bowed to her husband, Anna and her brother had been the strong ones. She liked to be the one who fixed things and people, the one who held it together while everything crumbled. It was what she knew how to do. She had held Ella and Toby as their little worlds flipped. She had held her mother while she sobbed and asked questions Anna just didn't have the answers to. She had nodded to her dad stoically, chin up and lips pursed, instead of breaking into pieces and collapsing in a heap. Needing someone was not something Anna did.

But Lane's arms around her felt incredible, and letting go enough to cry was like bursting out of the water and getting air for the first time in far too long. She didn't know how long they had stood on the sidewalk, only that eventually, Lane had murmured something, and they had started walking down the street. Arm firmly around Lane, Anna had leant her head on the taller woman's shoulder, and the tears had just kept falling. She'd definitely opened a floodgate.

After a short taxi ride, Anna was directed into a building that looked incredibly out of place in the modern area. They made their way inside and up the elevator to Lane's floor, where she fluidly opened the second door on the right and ushered Anna inside.

Curiously, Anna stared around the room while Lane took their jackets and dropped them over the couch.

Turning on the spot, Lane gave her a bemused look. "Tears on your cheek, yet you're smirking?"

"Nice place."

"Nice place, but...?"

Her smirk strengthened, though her cheeks were still wet. "It's incredibly... vintage."

"Uh—I like old stuff?"

"You're so...sleek, and put together. I imagined you in a shiny, modern apartment."

Lane sat on the back of the couch, crossing her arms. "Well, I grew up with parents who treasured anything that had been owned by at least two other people before them. My father loved carpentry, and my mother liked anything my dad fixed up."

Glancing around again, Anna tried to ignore the slight shake in her fingers. "In retrospect, this suits you far more than modern."

Lane raised an eyebrow playfully. "Mhm."

The emotions that lingered just below the surface made being playful impossible, and fresh tears spilled down Anna's cheeks.

The second Lane stood, staring at her with concerned eyes, Anna shook her head, stepping back and crossing her arms across her chest.

"Anna." Lane's voice was almost a whisper.

"I...I'm sorry." Her own voice was hoarse.

"Please, stop saying that."

This time, when Lane stepped toward her, Anna didn't match it with one step back but let her close the gap. Anna buried her head into Lane's neck again, hands pinned between them as she fisted the cloth of Lane's shirt. "I can't s-stop, now that I've started. I don't even feel like crying, now. It just won't stop."

Lips against Anna's ear, Lane asked, "Is this the first time you've cried?"

A nod was all Anna could manage to answer.

Lane's grip tightened. "Then you're definitely banned from the *sorry* word." After a few minutes of quiet rocking, Lane finally broke the silence. "Now. Do you want to keep hugging it out or would you like to sit and stare at a movie? Or sit and talk and I can ignore the tears? Or...whatever you want to do?"

Forehead still pressing against Lane's shoulder, Anna drew in a shuddering breath. "Sit and talk and ignore the tears."

"Okay. Wine? I know we've had a few, but wine fits most situations."

"Wine, yes."

"Right, you, sit." A gentle push nudged Anna towards the couch and she went without resisting.

Strangely exhausted, Anna flopped on the couch, unwinding her scarf and throwing it on top of her jacket. Wiping her cheeks, she took in another quiet, shuddering breath. She didn't know what was wrong with her.

Lane manoeuvred easily, pulling out a bottle of red and two glasses. She held the red up. "Do you drink red at all? I don't have any white."

"I do." Anna's nod was accompanied by a soft, watery smile.

After pouring them both a glass, Lane sat down next to her, mimicking Anna's pose. They both took a sip of wine. Lane leant her elbow on the back of the couch and rested her head in her hand, looking imploringly at Anna. "How have you not cried?"

Anna took another sip and tried to ignore the stinging way her eyes still watered. "I don't know. I had to…my mum, she needed me. And then the kids. And then Hayley. And then I, it was like I'd stopped it so much that I couldn't, even if I felt like I wanted to."

Shifting forward ever so slightly so that their knees touched, Lane put her wine down on the coffee table. She rested one hand hesitantly on Anna's knee. "Were you close? With your brother?"

Anna closed her eyes as if bracing herself. She nodded as she opened them slowly. "We were. Very."

Lane's furrowed brow caused tears to spill over Anna's eyes once more. She was grateful it happened without sobs, without the catching of breath. Lane didn't move forward to comfort her, obviously honouring Anna's instructions to ignore the tears.

"Were you always close? Because me and my sisters fought constantly as kids. It wasn't until we were out of high school that we started to get along."

"You have sisters?"

"Yeah, two. My older sister and I get along great, but my younger sister and I argue like you wouldn't believe. We're too different—she's a good person, though."

"I can't imagine her being related to you and not being."

"I could be a horrible person."

Anna laughed, the noise loosening the restricted feeling in her chest. "We may not know each other very well, but I know you're not a horrible person, Lane."

"So you grew up close? I don't know if there are a lot of brothers and sisters that can say they did that and stayed that way."

"Jake and I…" She just wanted to be able to say his name without it making her stomach ache. "We were just, close. We moved a couple of times, and it just made us closer. We got along well, there was barely a year between us. We were kind of inseparable."

"Who was older?"

"He was. Though people used to assume we were twins."

Lane's hand traced patterns on Anna's knee, but her eyes were solely focused on Anna's face as they talked. Wine glass balanced on her thigh, Anna relaxed sideways into the couch.

"Did he like being a big brother?"

The question was like a punch in the gut. Despite that, Anna softened as she pondered her answer. "He did, I think. Even though we were close in age, he was protective. He punched a guy when I was sixteen for calling me a dyke."

"Some guy did that?"

"Yeah. Jake heard him, grabbed his shoulder, spun him around, and clocked him in the chin."

Lane smirked. "I shouldn't condone violence, but that's awesome."

"Yeah, it was. Later, I told him I was one. He just said to tell him something he didn't know."

"He sounds awesome."

"He really was."

"Were you close to his wife?"

Anna glanced down. "Yeah. Sally and I got on like a house on fire. I met her when I was twenty-one, and we bonded over a mutual love of white wine and torturing Jake." She smiled softly. "They were so in love, those two. There was no…hesitancy? No *ifs*, or *maybes*. They were just so solid."

"That's really nice."

"It was. Jake got drunk one night after their third date and called to tell me he was going to marry her."

"Third date? That's the sex date."

"I'm fairly certain their first was the sex date."

"Go Jake." Lane sounded genuinely impressed. "Sounds like the Fosters have a way with the ladies."

Anna laughed again, the sound less like a choking noise, almost bordering on genuine. "I don't know about that. But he was certain about Sally. Even while he was deployed, they were fine."

"He was in the army?"

"Air Force. Over in Iraq. When Sally fell pregnant with Toby, he moved into administration. There was a near miss with an air strike, he was lucky. He told me once that he didn't…" Anna paused and looked down at her wine, "he didn't want to leave his kids without their dad."

Fingers tightening on Anna's knee again, Lane stayed silent.

Without looking up, Anna continued. "I wonder so many things, Lane. If he had stayed in Iraq, would they both be okay? If they had taken his stupid SUV instead of Sally's tiny work car, would they have survived?"

"It's normal to do that. But being in the job you are, you know there's no point wondering."

Finally dragging her eyes from her wine, Anna blinked back tears. "I know. But I can't help it. He was so brave in Iraq. Jake survived a war, and then a drunk asshole wiped two of the most amazing people off the earth, and left two kids orphans."

The ticking of a clock from the mantle was overly loud as Lane seemed to not know what to say. Finally, she said, "Life's shit. And unfair, sometimes."

"It is."

"Those two kids, though? They're lucky, they have you. It's a shit situation, but they have you."

Anna swallowed heavily, eyes dropping again. "Yeah."

"What is it?"

Sitting straighter, Anna closed in on herself slightly as she cradled her wine glass. "This is a crap first date."

Lane looked affronted. "This is *not* a date. My kind of date will knock your socks off and have you throwing yourself at me."

In spite of herself, Anna smiled. "I believe that. Well, this is a crap first proper conversation."

"Shut up, Anna. There's nothing crap about this. I've wanted to get to know you since you tried to kill me with a shopping trolley."

"Well, I'm learning you're an exaggerator. Almost killed you? Please."

"Close enough. Now, don't avoid it. What was that a minute ago? Those kids are so lucky you're in their lives."

Running her fingertip around the rim of her glass was easier than responding to that. But Lane seemed determined to make her talk.

"I didn't want to do it." Saying it out loud made the guilt swell up fiercely in her stomach. "I never wanted kids. Let alone someone else's." Her cheeks burned and Anna stared at her fingers.

"So?"

Anna's head whipped up. "What do you mean, so? I didn't want to do it. I liked my life the way it was. Even now, there are days—most days—where I just want to open the door and run as far away as I can. Those kids deserve someone who wants them; they deserve parents."

"Anna, so what if you didn't want to do it? You still did it. You dropped your entire life, sacrificed your girlfriend and moved cities to look after your brother's kids. So what if you didn't want kids? Or if you wanted to say no, at first? Look at what you're doing, now. I just have to watch Ella for a minute to see she dotes on you."

Cheeks still burning, Anna stared at Lane. "Sometimes I want to run. Sometimes I'm lying there, in bed, after putting on mountains of washing of tiny children clothing, after running around after dinner and bath time. I think about how Ella barely speaks and is obviously so broken for someone so little, and how Toby is starting to forget. I think of how Ella sits on the couch and stares at the wall, not the TV. And I think about how I want my life back. It's so selfish, but I just want my life back. I lie there and I feel like I'm going to explode."

"That would be the lack of sex."

Anna choked on a gulp of wine. "Excuse me?"

"The need to explode? There are things you can do about that."

The snort that Anna gave was not attractive. "Way to ruin a serious moment."

"Look, of course you feel like that. You're grieving, you're in a new city, you've been dumped, and you've gained two kids. You're allowed to have some feelings about that. You can be angry and resentful and hate it if you need to." Lane tucked her fingers under Anna's chin, tugging her head up so Anna was forced to look her in the eye. "You can feel all that. It's allowed. But it's what you're doing that matters. And those kids? You love them, and you're there for them. Even though it wasn't what you wanted. How you feel, I'm ninety percent certain every parent on earth has felt, so I think you're allowed to feel it, too."

Moving closer, Anna's eyes fluttered closed at the last minute as she pressed her lips to Lane's. She pulled back slightly, breath mingled between them. "You're some kind of amazing, Lane Bishop, you know that?"

Lane rolled her eyes. "Like you've implied, you barely know me."

"I'd like to."

"You would?"

"I would."

She placed Anna's wine glass on the coffee table, sliding one hand behind Anna's neck, the other sliding over her knee. As she pulled Anna gently forward into a kiss, Anna's lips parted and Lane's tongue traced her lower lip, tasting of wine and salt. She sucked gently on the sensitive flesh before letting it go.

With a groan, Anna followed Lane as she slowly sunk back into the couch. Arms braced on either side of Lane, Anna half fell between her legs. What started gentle quickly turned intense. Anna's wrought emotions were still raw. Their lips were forceful, tongues and teeth colliding.

Anna shifted so her thigh rested between Lane's legs, gasping as Lane's pressed up between hers. She dropped her weight slightly, one hand bracing herself, the other buried in Lane's hair. Her fingers tangled in curls, tugging gently, and a groan escaped Lane.

Heat settled low in Anna's stomach. Lane's skin felt better than Anna could even have imagined. The feel of her lips took her breath away. The way Lane's hips moved under her, her thigh pressing up and against Anna's body, drove her crazy. She wanted to drown in this feeling, to drown in Lane. Her life had been a giant mess for so long, but here, with Lane against her, moving under her, Anna felt okay. More than okay, she felt like she could breathe, like she could escape. She'd been afraid that telling Lane would make her run. Instead, she'd found someone who listened, who was interested. She'd found someone who caused the most amazing shudder to course through her body. Anna could barely suppress a moan.

Desire clouded her thoughts as Lane's hands ran down her back, fingers trailing on the skin where Anna's shirt had ridden up. Nails bit into her skin, and Anna groaned, hips rolling, her hand dropping from Lane's hair and running down from ribs to hip, fingers grasping at the bunched up material of Lane's dress. The soft skin of Lane's thigh was hot against Anna's skin, as insistent fingers pulled the edges of her dress up further.

As Anna's lips trailed over Lane's jaw and down her neck, her tongue met against skin. Lane's head fell back against the arm of the couch, her thigh pressing into Anna in a way that was driving her mad.

"Anna." Her voice was low, husky, like it had been in the bathroom earlier. Lane's nails slid from the skin of Anna's back to bite into her jeans, her other hand raising goose bumps on the back of Anna's neck as it stroked the sensitive skin. Rhythm built in their hips, and Anna's lips touched Lane's collarbone. "Anna?"

"Mm?" The combination of wine and Lane was making her head foggy.

"Bed?"

Finally, Anna paused. "Is that a good idea?" She didn't remove her hand, and her lips pressed against the unbelievably soft skin again.

"Right now?" Lane's fingertips dug into her shoulder as Anna's lips pressed back against her neck. "Yes. Yes, it's definitely a good idea."

After a soft kiss, Anna nodded. "Okay." She stood up, holding a hand out to Lane.

With her cheeks flushed, Lane really was stunning.

She took Anna's hand, and Anna tugged her up, turning to lead before pausing. Sheepishly, Anna smiled at Lane's raised eyebrow. "I was going to be all smooth and lead you to the bedroom, but I don't know where it is."

Lane wrapped her arms around Anna, stepping them backwards, kissing her neck. "Well, this is the living room." They stumbled back, Lane leading their joined steps. "This is the hallway."

Anna gave a loud giggle between kisses as they half tripped, nearly falling through a doorway.

"And this," Lane pushed Anna's hair off her face, eyes impossibly soft, "is the bedroom."

Anna didn't take her eyes off Lane. "It's nice."

"I like it."

Anna kissed Lane again, pushing backwards until the back of Lane's knees hit the bed.

As she sank down and sat on the edge, she pulled Anna down with her. Anna's legs slid to either side of Lane's hips and Lane's hands dropped instantly to rest on Anna's waist. Her tongue traced Anna's lips before it slid into her mouth and Lane's fingertips gripped her waist.

"Before," Anna said between kisses, "you said 'right now', it seemed like a good idea." Her foggy brain was telling her something.

"Yeah?"

"Maybe that's the wine and the making out talking?"

Lane chuckled softly. "Maybe."

"Something tells me we should stop, or we won't stop."

"Something tells me I wouldn't hate that idea."

Anna pushed a curl of hair behind Lane's ear, skin soft under her fingertips. "I think hating it would be far from my feelings on the matter."

Smiling, Lane leant forward, kissing Anna's neck. "But we should stop, anyway?" Her lips trailed down, slow and teasing.

Anna's eyes fluttered closed and her head tilted up to allow Lane more access. "You've made me feel…amazing. But I-I'm worried. I'm all, um, fragile. I may end up in tears. And that wouldn't exactly be hot."

Lane straightened up. "You're always hot." She raised her hands up, cupping Anna's cheeks. "But I understand."

"I don't want to sleep with you because I'm sad and burying feelings." Anna's eyes widened. "Not that that would be the only reason. It's just, that's kind of my MO, and—"

"Anna. I get it. It's okay. You still look on the verge of tears—I understand." Lane pulled her down and kissed her, softly. "Really."

"Thank you."

"What for?"

"You've been awesome, tonight."

"You don't need to thank me."

"Still." Anna's voice was soft. "Thank you."

"Okay, you're welcome. Now," Lane dropped her hands to the tops of Anna's thighs, then flopped backwards on the bed, looking up at her, "What are we going to do? I'm not sending you home when you're fragile. We're being good, even after making it to the bed. Which, in my eyes, deserves a medal. I may be understanding, but I'm still human." Anna laughed again, linking her hands with Lane's. "You can stay here. We'll both behave."

Anna hesitated.

"You don't have to stay, of course. I just—I'm guessing the kids aren't at your place?"

Anna shook her head. "They're with my parents, tonight. I'm picking them up at nine."

Lane made a face. "That's early for a day off. Okay, so your place is empty? I just thought you might prefer to stay here. But it's totally okay if you don't want to."

Caught between one delicious option and her own fear, Anna hovered . If she was honest with herself, she didn't want to go home, but she wasn't so sure she should stay, either. "Maybe we could watch a movie?"

"Sounds great."

Anna pulled Lane to her feet, and Lane grinned at her when they were eye to eye. "If we're going to watch movies, we need comfy clothes."

"What?"

"Comfy clothes." Lane turned and went to her dresser, rummaging around the drawers. A pair of track pants and a hoodie emerged. Lane threw them to Anna, who caught them. "You put those on in the living room, and I'll change out of this inappropriate dress."

Anna pouted and clutched the clothes to her chest. "I like the inappropriate dress."

"Too bad. I want movie-watching clothes."

Sighing, Anna turned and went back to the living room. As she changed, slipping the too-long pants on and rolling them up once, she peered around the living room. The furniture really was spectacular, the coffee table clearly hand carved. Lane's dad obviously knew what he was doing.

Anna sat on the couch, admittedly much comfier. Lane appeared and twirled in her grey track pants and simple red shirt.

"Still hot?"

Chuckling, Anna nodded. "Still hot."

Triumphant, Lane walked over to the TV. "Now, what to watch?"

"All I've watched the last few weeks are kids' movies. Have you got anything incredibly dramatic, or scary—something completely inappropriate for children?"

Lane peered at the DVD rack next to her television. She scanned the titles. "Okay, we have a couple of choices." She bent over and Anna perved more than she paid attention. "*Shawshank Redemption*, the *Scream* movies, *There's Something About Mary*, oh! I have *True Blood*?" Lane turned around, DVDs in hand, and caught Anna out with a pervy look still on her face.

Lane raised her eyebrows. "I thought we were behaving?"

"I can look. I've spent the last week at the hospital doing it, it's a habit. It's not my fault—stop being hot."

"You weren't subtle at work, either."

Anna shrugged unapologetically.

"Any of those DVDs sound okay?"

Anna really hadn't been paying attention. "Um…maybe?"

Lane rolled her eyes. "Have you watched *True Blood*?"

Anna shook her head.

"Well, it's definitely in the category of not appropriate for kids. You're not—wait..." She went red, looking amused at herself. "Never mind."

Anna eyed Lane as she went about loading the DVD and then walked over to the couch. "Not what?"

Lane looked ready to laugh. "Nothing."

Under Anna's questioning look, Lane caved. "I was about to ask if blood makes you squeamish. Then I remembered you're an anaesthetist who's constantly in surgeries."

Anna cracked up.

"Yeah, yeah. That's why I stopped asking. Watch the DVD, you."

Still snickering, Anna lay down, tugging at Lane's hand, pulling her behind her. Lane's arm slipped around Anna's middle, and she propped her head up so she could see past. As the opening scene aired, she leant forward, pressing her lips to Anna's shoulder.

Wriggling around, Anna stared up at Lane until she glanced down curiously. "What?"

Turning completely, Anna asked, "We can still make out, right?"

Warm breath washed over Anna's lips as Lane dipped her head.

"Definitely."

Chapter Ten

Anna woke up and almost fell off the couch. Groaning, she rolled over so that Lane's front was pressed to hers and their legs tangled together. Lane had gotten them a pillow at some point before they'd fallen asleep, and Anna couldn't remember the last time she'd felt this comfortable, especially after sleeping on a couch. She tilted her head and pressed her lips softly to Lane's neck.

Lane's arms tightened around Anna's waist and she sighed softly. Much calmer than she would have expected after the uncharacteristic outburst, Anna pressed closer.

"Morning." Lane's voice was thick with sleep.

Anna smiled against her neck. "Morning."

"We slept on the couch." Half-asleep, Lane was adorable. She sounded confused. Anna could feel her head shifting slightly as she looked around like she didn't know where she was.

"We did. It was surprisingly comfy."

"You're comfy."

Anna chuckled, kissing Lane's neck again.

Lane's head dropped back to the pillow, relaxing as she sighed. "And you feel good."

"Shit!" Anna sat straight up and stared down at Lane. "Shit! What's the time?"

Disgruntled at the loss of warmth, her hair a mess around her head, Lane lifted her arm from where it had fallen to Anna's thigh. Her wrist hovered over her face and she squinted at it. "Um..."

Smirking and rolling her eyes, Anna grabbed Lane's wrist and turned it gently to look at her watch. Lane dropped her head happily back to the pillow and flopped her other arm theatrically over her eyes to block out the light.

"Good, it's only six thirty," Anna said with a sigh of relief.

"Six thirty!" Lane lifted her arm slightly to glare at Anna. "That's way too early. It's a day off."

"You really aren't a morning person, are you?"

Lane hid her eyes back again behind her arm. "What gave me away?"

With a snort, Anna tried to stand up, but Lane grabbed her wrist and yanked her back down. Anna wriggled backwards so Lane was pressed tighter against her back.

"Gee, I don't know. I have no idea how you cope with shift work."

She felt Lane shrug behind her, her face buried in Anna's hair. "The promise of money and coffee, so much coffee."

"Coffee sounds amazing right now."

"Oh, thank God. You like coffee. I dated someone who didn't, years and years ago."

"What kind of person doesn't like coffee?"

"Abnormal ones. How do they function?"

"Probably quite well, without an addiction that leads to a blinding headache by eleven if you don't get your fix."

Lane attempted a sleepy chuckle, the hand around Anna's middle sliding under her shirt to splay over her stomach. "Yours doesn't kick in until eleven? Lucky."

"Yours?"

"Ten minutes after I wake up."

"Oh, dear God. I have about six minutes to get caffeine into you." Anna made as if to get up again and chuckled when Lane's arm held her firmly in place. "Coffee, Lane."

"Yeah, but you're comfy." It was almost a whine.

"Did you not hear me? *Caffeine.*"

The arm loosened. "Fine."

Anna tugged her shirt back into place as Lane rolled onto her stomach and buried her face in the pillow.

Anna raised her eyebrows. "I'd love to be all chivalrous, but much like last night, where I tried to take you to the bedroom, I don't know where anything is."

Lane nodded into her bedding.

"You're staring at me, aren't you?"

"Mhm."

Her voice light, despite the attempt to be grumpy, Lane rolled back onto her side. "You're lucky you're cute."

"I've been told that before." With a wink, Anna walked to the kitchen.

"And you have a cute ass." Lane sat up on the edge of the couch.

"I've caught you staring at it enough at work."

"Good to hear I was about as subtle as you."

"What was that?"

"Coffee's in the cabinet under the toaster!"

They moved around each other in the kitchen, not quite fluidly, but strangely comfortable for the short time they had known each other. Lane giggled sleepily as Anna pressed her against the kitchen bench, kissing her slowly as the kettle boiled.

Coffee in hand, Anna sat on the same bench taking small sips, while Lane stood between her legs. Anna's free hand clung to Lane's shirt, maintaining a grip while they drank, contented silence surrounding them. Anna could drown in this feeling.

Lane rested her coffee on the bench next to Anna, leaning forward to press her face against Anna's neck. Warm lips kissed her skin and Anna sighed.

"Do you really have to be there by nine?"

Lane's breath against her neck sent a shudder down Anna's spine. "Yeah. I promised the kids. We're going to the zoo today."

"I could come?"

Anna froze slightly, saved from answering as Lane continued, "Crap, never mind—I promised a friend I'd help him move today."

Trying to hide her reaction, Anna took a sip of coffee. "I may need to be at my place by about eight thirty? To get to my mum's by nine."

Lane pressed her lips against Anna's neck, tracing an agonisingly slow line to her collarbone. The caffeine was obviously hitting her system. "That means having to leave here pretty soon, yeah?"

"Unfortunately, yes."

With Lane's hands kneading her thighs as her lips moved slowly to the other side of Anna's neck, Anna didn't want to go anywhere. "What if I dropped you at your mum's at nine, instead?"

"Uh—" Her head fell back slightly as Lane's tongue pressed to her skin. "I need my car, with the car seat, to get them."

"Damn." Lane's voice was a whisper against Anna's ear. "Shall we shower and stuff here, then I can drop you at your place?"

The image of a naked Lane in the shower made Anna grin widely.

"Shower separately, pervert. We're on a time restriction. And we're being good. Or something."

Anna shrugged unashamed. "You're the one who put the idea in my head."

"Well, it's a pretty nice image."

They showered—separately. Lane made them both a second coffee in travel mugs while waiting for Anna to finish, both their heads slightly sore from the wine the previous evening. They were putting on their jackets at the door, Anna pulling her arm through her sleeve and taking the proffered cup, when she paused to watch Lane.

Lane raised an eyebrow. "What?"

"You're awesome."

"I am?"

Her fingers tucked a loose curl behind Lane's ear. "You are. Thank you."

"No more *thank yous*. Or *sorrys*. Those be the rules."

Lane pulled the door open, Anna running a hand down Lane's arm to link with her fingers and tug her with her as she walked out. "Rules?"

"Oh, I'm bossy."

"That could be fun."

Lane smirked, pressing the button for the elevator, and they made their way to the garage and into Lane's car.

They drove in silence, sipping their coffees, Anna working to quell her rushing thoughts until the car pulled up smoothly in front of the house.

Lane looked across at her. "I had a really nice time last night."

"With all the tears and—"

"Hey. We banned that."

"Look, you *are* bossy."

"Yep."

Suddenly a little shy, Anna flicked her nail against the lid of her takeaway cup. "I had a really nice night, too. Thanks for, you know, listening."

"It was my pleasure." Lane smiled. "And you're hot even with the tears."

Anna chuckled. "Shut up."

When Lane leant in to kiss her, Anna met her halfway. Their lips touched, Lane pressing into the kiss. Anna rested her palm over Lane's heart, soothed by the steady beat.

As they parted, Lane leant her forehead against Anna's. "I know everything's really complicated for you right now. But I'd really like to see you, however I can."

"I'd like that too." Anna threw Lane one last smile and slid out of the car.

She turned at the front door to wave at Lane before she went inside. The door closed behind her, and she leant back, looking around the empty house. It was eerily quiet. A slow, deep breath left her body.

She had meant what she'd said, that she would like to see Lane too. Anna really had no idea where the tears had come from, the talking about Jake and Sally—the entire thing, really. It was as if once she'd started, she couldn't stop.

Yet, while she felt scrubbed raw after it all, her shoulders felt less tense than they had in weeks. The lump in her throat that had been her constant companion had eased.

And Lane really had been perfect.

Fingers pressed to her lips, Anna smiled; she could still feel traces of Lane.

The woman captivated her. That was really the only word for it.

She knew it was too soon. She and Hayley had ended less than a month ago. Yet, with everything that had happened in those first few weeks, it felt like forever. Anna had shut down any feelings she'd had about the matter, along with those about her brother. Everything had been too much at once, especially with Ella and Toby in her life.

And even though it felt too soon, Lane felt incredibly right.

Yet, still, she'd stiffened when Lane had pushed for more. While she was over her fear of Lane's reaction to the kids, her other concerns weren't gone—about it being too soon for the kids, about it being too selfish of her to pursue this. Ella and Toby needed her.

She rubbed a hand over her tired eyes. Why did it all have to be so complicated?

How was it so complicated, when the last few hours had been so easy?

Anna pushed off the door and went upstairs to change.

In a previous life, or alternate universe, she and Lane would have stayed in bed all day having mind-blowing sex—and Anna had no concerns that it wouldn't be mind blowing, if last night had been anything to go by. They would have had a lazy breakfast in bed and stayed there all day. Or, if they weren't quite there yet, they would have met up and spent the day getting lunch, flirting loudly and openly, and making out in the cinema.

But in Anna's new reality, she had to go pick up her niece and nephew and take them to the zoo, and then bring them home and play parent.

She in no way resented the kids, but buried deep down was still a little resentment at the situation. And at her brother. She wasn't sure if that was very healthy.

Talking to Lane last night, actually voicing some of those feelings she'd had bottled up and locked away, had made her feel better this morning—better than she had in a long time. Lane made her feel like it was okay to feel like that. She had expected shock or disgust but, instead, had seen sympathy and understanding.

She padded down the stairs and grabbed the car keys. She loved the kids, and life here was starting to feel a little more...settled—if that was the word. Starting something as new and distracting as Lane was unfair to them. Kym had said last night that Anna's brother wouldn't want that, that he'd want her to be happy. But was this all moving too fast?

Just thinking about it gave her a headache. How would she manage this thing with Lane, the two kids, and working full time? And on top of it all, she still hadn't moved past the grief that, at times, threatened to swallow her whole.

Maybe it didn't have to be a relationship. It could be relaxed. Casual.

With a sigh, she parked in her parents' driveway, softening when she saw Ella pressed to the front window, waving madly. Anna waved back and grabbed her bag, checking her phone before she slipped out of the car. A text from Lane caught her eye.

> *Even after that simple kiss in the car, I need a cold shower. We really do deserve a medal for last night. What are you doing to me, Anna Foster? :)*

Anna wasn't sure she could stop even if she wanted to.

"So go on a date with her, for Christ's sake! I've been watching you two deliver coffees to each other and flirt over stale cafeteria food for a week now."

Anna blinked over her coffee at Kym. She'd been driving herself so mad with worries about being fair to the kids, she hadn't realized she was being *that* obvious.

"Uh...okay?"

Kym leant her shoulder against the wall, facing Anna with her arms crossed. "Look, I'm sorry, but you want to see her out of work? Do it. So you have those two kids—that doesn't mean your life stops."

"But what if they—"

"They won't feel like you're neglecting them, Anna."

Clearly, she'd verbalised this to Kym more than she had realised. "But—"

"No. They won't. Keep it all separate for now, if that's what you need to do. Really, that makes sense. All three of you have had huge life changes. It's okay to do that. But, seriously, go on a damn date so I can live vicariously through you. Since the bar last weekend, you've been itching to see her outside of work."

Anna sipped her coffee, eyes wide. "You know me far too well."

"It's creepy, considering this friendship is younger than the carton of milk in my fridge."

"Ew."

"I'm not home much."

"Still sleeping at the hospital?"

Kym shrugged. "Most of the time."

"When do I need to start to worry about that?"

"When I try and move a cat into my office lounge. Then, *then* you may have me committed."

"Check. First sign of feline in the hospital, I worry." She tilted her head slightly, taking Kym in. "Though I may before then, too."

Kym smiled softly, reaching over to accept the coffee the attendant handed out to her. They stayed against the wall, Anna content to completely avoid starting her workday. The mountain of paperwork she had waiting couldn't be delayed for much longer, however.

"Deal. Now, date. You. Soon."

"Okay. Fine. I just don't know when."

"Well, you have Saturday off. I recall Lane saying she has an early finish that day, and when I was a creep last night, I checked the nurses' roster. She's on an afternoon shift Sunday. What about a good old Saturday night date?"

"You've been planning this."

"Well, you weren't going to get off your ass and do it. And Lane's being so overly respectful of you and your life that she doesn't want to push it, so that left me."

Anna laughed out loud, trying to hide the sappy look that the mention of Lane surely produced on her face. "What about the kids? My mum's been dropping everything to take care of them for me. I don't know if I can ask this of her."

"And I'm sure she'd do it again; but if you don't want to ask, how about I babysit?"

Anna's mouth almost dropped open. "You'd do that?"

"Why not? I'm not some fifteen-year-old who's going to have my boyfriend come over and put cigarette holes in your couch. I'm a doctor, kind of, and I vaguely remember what kids like to do in their spare time."

"Kym, that would be amazing."

"Well, I'm fairly amazing, so that's a given."

"Okay. I'll ask Lane."

"Excellent. I'm like a skinny Cupid, only mildly taller and with more swag."

Anna nearly spit her coffee out. "Did you just say you have swag?"

"Can't pull that off?"

"No. But try, more often, please. One question—are you free tonight to come over and meet the kids first?"

Kym grimaced. "No, sorry. I've taken the on call."

Anna gnawed her lip, then shrugged. "No problem. I'll talk with Ella, and, if it doesn't seem to go smoothly, we'll do it another night."

"Are you worried?"

"A little." At Kym's expectant look, Anna sighed. "I spoke to Ella's counsellor at school the other day. Ella's doing, you know, okay. But she is still withdrawn and quiet. The woman said that she probably feels isolated."

"That's not surprising." Kym's words were gentle.

"That's what I said—I mean, her friends can't understand how she's feeling. I don't think *Ella* can know how she's feeling. I just—she was so, vibrant, before. A ball of energy. Chatty. Inquisitive."

"Her whole life changed."

Anna flicked her nail against the plastic lid of the coffee cup, warm in her hand. It felt good to talk about this with someone who understood a little. Her mother was wonderful, but Anna found herself supporting *her* in her grief—not that she minded; it was a good distraction. And her father still stayed locked in his study.

"It really has. Sometimes the old Ella kind of shines through for brief moments—especially with Toby. But it's so rare and short-lived." Anna didn't mention the way protectiveness now washed over her in waves when she watched the two kids. She gave a half shrug as they started walking towards the elevator. "I'm sure she'll be fine with you at the house. It's just…I want to be careful with her."

"If there's any problems, I'll call. And if Ella is uncomfortable, we'll try another time."

"Good plan." Anna shot her a grateful look, then grinned. "I just thought she could use a warm-up to get used to you."

"Uh, excuse me. I'm skinny Cupid and also a tenacious child whisperer. It will go amazingly—just you watch. Maybe I'll show up in a ballerina outfit."

They went their separate ways, Anna chuckling at the image Kym had given her. Before she could pull out her phone to text Lane, her pager went off, and she was pulled into the intensity of an emergency surgery.

It had been a smooth operation, which meant she had sat most of the time writing vital observations and reading an article to try to catch up on her professional development hours. But, by the time she found time to get in contact with Lane, it was the end of the day and time to pick up Toby from day care. She hadn't even eaten lunch.

Toby hit her legs at a run before she'd walked more than three steps into the day care. Once he was in her arms, he wrapped his chubby arms around her neck and patted her in his funny little way.

"Hey, little man." She looked up at Tanya, waved, and signed Toby out on the register. New dinosaur backpack in hand, they headed out.

"Sorry I didn't make it in for a visit this afternoon, Tobes. Work was hectic."

Anna usually went into the day care at least twice a day if she could. The sight of Toby barrelling towards her, ecstatic at her visit, always left her feeling warm inside.

She pulled out her phone and tapped out a text quickly, holding it high as Toby tried to grab it from her. It was scary how well he could flick through things on her iPhone.

Hey, Lane. Are you free this Saturday night? I was wondering if you wanted to knock my socks off with that date...

She hit *send* and slipped her phone back into her pocket. "Did you play trains today, Tobes?"

"Thomas."

"Thomas, huh? Doesn't Percy get jealous that you don't play with him very much?"

Toby just blinked at her.

"Yeah, never mind."

"Anna!"

She had been so focused on the text and then Toby that she hadn't even realized she'd entered the lobby. When she stopped in her tracks and turned around, there was Lane, quickly walking up behind her.

"Hey."

Lane waved her phone hand in the air, her eyes on Toby, who was staring back at her, wide eyed. "I just got your text. Hey there, cutie!" She looked from Toby to Anna. "Wow, I see what Ella meant when she said he looks even more like you than she does."

As Anna jostled Toby gently on her hip, he raised his hand to his mouth to suck on his fingers, something he'd started to do when he didn't have his blanket.

"Yeah, people always assume he's mine." She smiled sadly as she reached up and tugged at his hand to pop the fingers out of his mouth. She was rewarded with a long train of saliva that fell on her shoulder. Sexy.

Toby kept staring at Lane, little face serious even though she grinned at him.

"He's gorgeous, Anna."

"I think so." She looked at Toby. "And you certainly know it." She poked him in the tummy, trying to get the serious look off his face. He yelped, giggling and burying his face into Anna's neck, wrapping his arms around her.

Lane looked like she wanted to scoop him up and cuddle him. "He always this shy?"

"Not even remotely."

"I didn't think so." Lane caught Anna's eye. "I'm in for Saturday, by the way. As if there was any question."

Anna ran a hand up and down Toby's back. "Great."

"Can I pick you up? Say, six?"

"Six thirty okay? Then this one will be asleep."

"Six thirty is perfect. Be prepared to have your socks knocked off."

"Awesome."

"What do you say, Toby?" Toby peeked up at Lane from Anna's shoulder. "Can I steal your aunty for a little while?"

"My Na." He buried his face back into her neck.

Lane grinned, and Anna rolled her eyes, poking him in the ribs again so he gave a squeal of laughter. "You can share, little man."

"My shift is nowhere near finished, so I have to run. But I'll see you for lunch tomorrow?"

"Definitely."

Lane hovered for a minute, looking like the last thing she wanted to do was leave. Finally, she took a step backwards, smiling ruefully. "I'll see you, then. Bye, Toby!"

At the last moment before she left, Toby sat up, waving. "Bye-bye!"

Anna tickled him again, and he wriggled.

With a final wave, Lane walked away, Anna's eyes on her until she disappeared from view. There was an idiotic look on her face, she knew it; she just didn't care.

She looked to Toby, who was looking after Lane as if he regretted not being nicer, now that the lady with the pretty smile had gone. He looked to Anna, almost confused.

"You'll see her again, Tobes, I'm sure."

He nodded seriously and stuck his fingers back in his mouth.

Chapter Eleven

"Why are you in a dress?"

Anna turned from the mirror and saw Ella peering around the doorframe at her.

Tattered blanket in hand, Toby stood in front of her. He grinned at Anna before running forward and colliding with her knees. Unable to say no to the blue eyes staring up at her, Anna swung him onto her hip. Instantly, he dropped his head on her shoulder, hand coming up to splay his tiny fingers over her collarbone, blanket held tight between them.

She ran her fingers over his hair, soft after a wash. He was incredibly sweet and endearing at this time of night, sleepy and cuddly. She'd had no idea a child possessed the ability to melt her this much.

Looking down at herself, Anna asked, "Is it a bad dress?"

Strawberry-blonde hair flicked around her face as Ella shook her head adamantly. "No! You look really pretty." She sat on the edge of Anna's bed, cradling her marker-covered orange cast in her arm. Her face scrunched up as she continued to peer at Anna. "But you never wear dresses."

Smiling wryly, Anna turned back to the mirror and, without thinking, said, "I used to, Ella Bella."

"Why don't you now?" Ella's voice was curious.

Anna paused, gazing at the half-asleep Toby on her hip. Her red cocktail dress had never seen a child near it before. It had always been Anna's go-to dress, the neckline low enough to catch someone's eye without being too out-there, the skirt swishing around her knees as she moved in a way that she loved. However, it was the back that sold it, cut down between her shoulder blades. Her light brown hair was out and loose, blow-dried straight. Anna made sure to keep the smile on her face, running her fingers through Toby's hair again and turning away from the mirror to look at Ella, who was watching her innocently.

"I've just been so busy with my new job."

Ella nodded, eyes serious. "You have an important job. Grandma told me you help save lives. Like Nurse Lane saved my arm."

"Exactly."

"Can I do that when I grow up?"

"Is that what you want to do?"

She took a second to think, then shook her head. "I want to own an ice cream truck."

Anna bent down and rubbed her nose against Ella's. Ella shook her head back and forth to reciprocate the motion.

"You can do that, if you want. You could be like Ben and Jerry, and make whole new flavours of ice cream."

Bouncing on the bed, Ella's eyes lit up. "I could make macaroni and cheese ice cream!"

Anna wrinkled her nose. "Mac and cheese ice cream?"

"Yeah."

"As a flavour?"

"My favourite dinner is mac and cheese with ice cream as dessert. That way I get all of it."

"Just 'cause it mixes in your tummy doesn't mean it should mix in your mouth."

"Oh."

Anna reached out her spare hand, still holding Toby with the other arm. He was blinking steadily to ward off sleep. Wrapping her fingers around Ella's small hand, Anna lifted her to her feet.

"If you want to make it a flavour, you can, Ella Bella. Actually, we had mac and cheese for dinner. So you get some i-c-e c-r-e-a-m after Toby is in bed."

Ella's eyes lit up as they walked out to the hallway and down the stairs. "I do?"

"It's Saturday night. I don't see why not."

"No school tomorrow."

Anna shook her head as they walked into the living room. "Nope. You can stay up with Kym and watch a DVD. Have you picked one?"

Flopping onto her beanbag, Ella crossed her legs in front of her. "Yup. *Beauty and the Beast.*"

Taking a seat on the couch, Anna shifted Toby so he sat on her lap with his legs wrapped around her, head nestled into her neck. She rubbed his back up and down. "Good choice. I think Kym will like it."

"Will I like Kym?"

Purposefully fiddling with her cast, Ella avoided Anna's eye. "I think you'll love Kym. She's kind of funny."

"I like funny."

"You'll like Kym, then."

It was times like this, when Ella got nervous about meeting someone new, that Anna was reminded of the changes the loss of her parents had caused. She had lost some of her confidence, the once overly friendly girl now reserved and pensive. The anxiety was new. Anna gnawed her lip.

"Okay." Ella kept her eyes down.

"You all right?"

She stared at the floor. "Yeah." There was a quiver in her voice.

"Come up here, chicken."

Ella shook her head, and Anna put her arm out along the couch, inviting her into the Toby cuddle. Slowly, Ella stood and wormed in, pressing tight to Anna's side and tracing patterns over Toby's dinosaur pyjamas. He was almost asleep and didn't notice.

"What's wrong?"

She shrugged.

"You can talk about anything."

"When..." She drew in a shuddering breath. "When Mummy got ready before, I'd help her do her make-up. I helped her that night."

Anna swallowed. "Do you miss that?"

"I miss lots of things."

"I know, Ella Bella." Anna dropped a kiss on her head. "Want to help me with my make-up?"

Ella thought for a minute. "Next time?"

"Of course. Tonight you get ice cream?"

Finally, a smile tugged at Ella's lips. "Yeah. And a DVD."

"Just one, right?"

Ella's smile grew a little. "Just one."

"I know *Beauty and the Beast* came in a dual cover with *The Little Mermaid*, but that's still two movies."

"But—"

Anna raised her eyebrows.

Collapsing back against Anna, Ella sighed. "Fine. Can I watch it tomorrow?"

"When Tobes is having a sleep, how about we make some popcorn and watch it together?"

"Okay."

"And Ella, remember what I said—if you don't want to be here with Kym tonight, you just have to tell me and instead, I'll hang out here with you, okay?"

"I know."

She squirmed a little when Anna poked her. "I mean it. Or you just say you want banana for breakfast, and that will be our code."

"Okay. I remember." Ella looked up at her with wide eyes. "So when is Nurse Lane getting here?"

Anna stood up. "Soon. Kym will be here any minute. I'm going to put Toby down—wait for me, if the doorbell goes."

"I know, Aunty Na."

"So you should." Anna poked her tongue out.

"Night, Toby!"

Toby waved his hand at his sister, barely raising his head.

They'd gone to the park before dinner, and he'd not stopped running for over an hour, chasing the ducks and generally causing chaos. The plan to tire him out had apparently worked.

In the kitchen, she handed him a premade bottle. A sweet "Ta" left his mouth seconds before he shoved the bottle into it.

"You're welcome," Anna replied.

As they made their way up the stairs, Toby's eyes were already closing. Anna stood with him next to his cot, patting his back as she rocked him, though she didn't need to bother on his behalf. Toby was practically asleep. It was more for her to enjoy him when he was this still, his long eyelashes casting shadows on his cheeks. He was so very like Jake, but he had a perfectly straight little nose, the way Sally's had been.

The doorbell went, and she pressed a kiss to his head, putting him down gently. His blue blanket was tucked under his arm and Anna pulled his thicker covers over him. "Night, Tobes."

She walked down the stairs to see Ella hovering at the front door.

"Here she is!" Ella practically yelled through the door, presumably in answer to whatever the person on the other side had asked.

"Ella, inside voice. Toby is asleep."

"You said I couldn't open it."

"True, I did." Anna pulled open the door to find Kym, dressed comfortably in jeans and a hoody—with a bright pink ballerina skirt floating around her legs. Anna stared at her, wide eyed, a smirk working its way over her lips. "Hey, Kym."

Kym refused to acknowledge her smirk. "Hey." She looked Anna up and down, eyes widening. "Nice dress, you're *so* going to get lai—"

Anna pushed the door open wider to remind Kym that Ella was standing there.

"Lai—uh, lame. Your foot will go lame, if you wear high heels with that dress."

Anna pressed her lips together tried not to smirk. The look on Kym's face showed utter panic. "Kym, this is Ella. Ella, this is Kym."

"What's lame?"

Kym cleared her throat somewhat lamely herself. "Uh, it means you can't walk properly. If you hurt your foot."

Ella looked up at Anna worriedly. "Don't get lame."

Anna laughed, resting her hand on Ella's shoulder. "I won't, Ella Bella." She looked back at Kym. "Come on in, you're in for a night of *Beauty and the Beast* and ice cream."

Kym's eyes lit up. "*Beauty and the Beast*?"

Ella eyed her. "Yeah?"

"That's my favourite Disney movie!"

Anna felt relieved as Ella's eyes widened. "It is?"

"Yeah! I always wanted to have the library Belle gets."

"Me too!"

Ella grabbed Kym's hand and dragged her into the living room. Anna heard Ella state approvingly, "I like your skirt. I have one in purple."

"I'm just going to finish getting ready!" Anna called through the door as she walked past it to the stairs.

They both waved a hand at her in acknowledgement, Ella grabbing the DVD box and probably already telling Kym that they could watch two movies tonight.

Anna made her way upstairs and put the finishing touches on her make-up. One bathroom, an adult, and two kids were not fun. She sighed and threw a yellow duck that had somehow made it onto the hand basin into the tub—where it belonged. At least the bathroom in her former life had always been clean.

She hesitated as she walked past her brother and Sally's room. There was a big, clean en suite bathroom in there that she wouldn't have to share. But it was full of all of their things and too many memories, including the make-up that Sally had been using with Ella the night they'd died.

With a deep breath, she walked past it, ignoring the decision she would have to make one day. Back in her room, she slipped on a pair of black heels before taking one last look in the mirror. She'd cleaned up all right. Anna adjusted the dress, slightly looser than she remembered from the last time she'd worn it. Stress and grief had apparently led to a little weight loss.

The doorbell rang again. Anna's heart beat a bit faster, and she sighed at herself. She grabbed her bag off the bed and went down the stairs. Poking her head into the living room, she saw Ella and Kym sitting in front of the TV on bean bags next to each other, bowls of ice cream already in their laps. Ella had clearly dug out her skirt and the lace puffed up around both of them.

Shaking her head, Anna pulled open the door.

Her breath caught in her chest and she almost fell over. Lane pulled off that dress like nothing she'd ever seen before.

A grin crossed Lane's face while her eyes flicked down Anna's body and back up. "Hey."

"Hey, yourself. You, ah, you look amazing." And she did, wrapped in a black dress that clung everywhere it should, hair half swept up one side, tight curls loose at the back and other side, make-up perfect, minimalistic.

"You, too. You look great."

Anna ducked her head. "Thanks."

"Nurse Lane!" The yell came from the living room.

At the shout, Lane looked almost scared. Anna shrugged apologetically. "She's been excited since she found out you were coming yesterday."

Lane chuckled. "Good to know, because I've been excited since Thursday."

"Want to take Ella out then?"

She shook her head. "I don't even want to joke and say yes." She was still smiling, but there was a look in her eye that made Anna grip the door a bit tighter. "Tonight, I just want you."

They stared at each other for a minute before Anna managed to answer. "Good—I don't want to have to compete with a six-year-old."

"Nurse Lane!" The yell was much louder now, showing zero regard for a sleeping sibling.

"You better come in before she wakes up Toby."

Lane stepped through the door, pausing for a minute, her shoulder brushing by Anna's front. Her eyes darted to Anna's mouth and back up again before she turned and walked down the hallway, following the yells into the living room.

Anna blew out a slow breath and shut the door, then followed. She crossed her arms and leant against the doorframe as she saw Ella staring at Lane, who was squatting next to the beanbag.

"How's the arm, Ella?"

The cast-covered appendage waved in the air. "Doesn't even hurt anymore."

"That's great. Can you wiggle all your fingers?"

She did, earning her an approving look from Lane.

"Good. Now, most important—do you still have space for people to draw on?"

Ella's eyes widened and she shook her head. "No! It got covered really quick."

The cast really was covered in every spot possible with crude six-year-old writing and drawings, all in different colours. Ella had come back after her first day at school with it that way, so happy that everyone had wanted to draw on it.

"That's cool. I like the horse one of your friends drew."

"That was Aunty Na."

A smile playing on her lips, Lane looked up at Anna, who gave them a look that dared them to tease it.

"Art's not my strong point."

"Clearly."

"I like it, Aunty Na."

"Thanks, Ella Bella."

"Can't you two stay and watch DVDs with me and Kym?"

"Aw, I would, but we have a booking. Maybe next time?"

"Okay." Ella's eyes went back to the TV.

Lane ruffled Ella's hair and stood, gazing down at Kym, who looked ridiculous with her ice cream bowl laid out on a tiny child's bean bag with her tutu puffed out around her. "You good there, Kym?"

Eyes trained on the screen, Kym waved her spoon. "Great. You crazy kids go out." She finally pulled her eyes away from the TV. "Have fun, and don't rush home. I'm all good here." With a comical wink, she looked back at the television.

"Where did you buy that, Kym?"

"I'll have you know I got this from the Queen Vic Markets."

"Well, you look beautiful."

Without looking away from the TV, Ella chimed in. "Everyone looks beautiful in a fairy skirt, Nurse Lane."

Eyes still on the movie, Kym gave a nod. "Truth delivered by a six-year-old."

Grinning, Lane waved at them and stepped over to Anna.

"Thanks again, Kym, bye Ella!" Anna said.

Both of them just waved their spoons.

"You have my cell number—if Toby wakes up, he should settle fine with just a back rub. If you get desperate, you can use a pacifier."

Kym waved her spoon again, this time more vehemently. "We'll be fine. Go. Enjoy!"

A little nervous to leave, even though her niece looked so comfortable, Anna kept a wary eye on them. "Ella?"

Her niece didn't look up.

"Ella Bella?"

Ella still didn't look away from the TV. "I don't want banana, Aunty Na. Sh."

Smothering a grin, Anna tiptoed out the room with Lane in tow. Behind them, Kym's voice was audible as she said, "They interrupted us, Ella—rude. Want to rewind?"

Anna and Lane were still chuckling when they walked out the door. Anna pulled it shut and then gasped as she was pushed back against it.

Lane was pressed against her, face inches from her own.

"Hey."

"Hey."

Lane gently pressed her lips against Anna's. Soft fingers stroked Anna's cheek. Their mouths parted, and fingers grasped at the material of each other's dresses as Lane's tongue slid against her own.

Lane pulled back slowly, forehead resting on Anna's, a smile on her lips. "I've wanted to do that constantly all last week."

"A week is a stupidly long time to go without that."

"Why did we again?"

"We were stuck at work and...I actually don't know why."

"Let's not again."

Anna nodded. "Deal."

Lane kissed her once more, lingering a second. "Okay. I have a booking for Italian, and if we keep doing this, I'll happily miss it."

"Let's miss it."

"And stay on your doorstep all night?"

Anna looked around. "True. Dinner it is."

At the car, Lane opened the passenger door for Anna with a faux bow, then walked around and entered the driver's side. She started the car before leaning back against the seat, looking at Anna seriously.

Uncomfortable under the gaze, Anna shifted. "What?"

"You just look gorgeous. I really could spend all night kissing you."

Anna's breath caught. She leant back in her seat, head turned and eyes still glued to Lane's. "Right back at you."

"Okay. I'm driving now, or we won't go anywhere."

Enjoying the feeling of being dressed up and out of the house—and being looked at like she was all Lane could see—Anna relaxed back into her seat.

The drive was quick and filled with easy chatter. Anna couldn't help but revel in Lane's company, watching her and snickering as Lane told her about a patient that came into the emergency room with a questionable object in an interesting area.

They eventually pulled up to a restaurant, and Lane handed her keys to the valet attendant before she took Anna's hand and led them inside. Anna hummed appreciatively at the intimate atmosphere. Soft candles lit up the room, and classical jazz played over hidden speakers. There was a soft buzz of conversation; almost all of the tables were occupied. The restaurant was in the heart of Melbourne city, and Anna had never been there before.

They were seated the instant that Lane gave her name for the reservation. Wine was brought over before Anna could even blink.

"Fast service." Anna eyed Lane over her wine glass as she took a sip.

"My father knows the owner; they're old friends from the States."

"You're from the States? How did I not know this? Where's your accent?"

"Oh, God, I moved when I was ten and worked really, really hard to lose it. The accent's not loved here."

"I think it would be cute. So, why such a big move?"

"My mother's family is Australian, and she moved to the US after meeting my father when they were both backpacking. Her father passed away, and they decided to move here to be closer to her family, especially my grandmother."

"Wow. How was that for you?"

"I was excited, Australia was very exotic." Anna made a face and Lane shrugged. "No, really, it is, especially in the US. It was a huge adjustment, though."

"I bet. And your parents, or your dad, never wanted to go back?"

Lane ran her fingertip over the pattern on the tablecloth. "He thought about it. But it just, I don't know, became home. And now, I would never want to leave, anyway. But it was my mum who wanted to go back the most."

"That's surprising. Do you mind me asking why?"

Lane shook her head. "Her family never liked that she married a black man, especially because she moved to the other side of the world for him. Her mother could still be difficult at first, but she got over it, and now it's mostly fine."

Anna's eyes were huge. "That must have been really hard for your dad."

"He was actually okay about it. My mum got really angry. But that drama's over, and now everyone is a mostly happy family. Except at Christmas, but that's normal."

"That's for sure."

Lane gave a smile and dropped her eyes back to the menu briefly. "So, what looks good to you?"

"Everything—what do you recommend?"

Lane glanced down at the menu. "You should try the linguine. It's amazing."

"Linguine it is." Decision made, Anna put the menu down. She was excited to eat anything that wasn't aimed to please small children.

"So why were you in Brisbane?"

"It's not as interesting as your story."

Lane looked up.

"I'd lived there when I was twelve and loved it, and when we moved to Melbourne, I always kind of wanted to go back. When Jake was posted overseas, I really didn't feel like I had a lot to stay for, so I moved."

"It must have been hard having him over there."

"It really was. Though, at first, it gave Sally and me an excuse to drink a lot of wine."

"Did the two of you ever really need an excuse?"

Anna gave a soft smile. "That's what Jake said."

The waiter came over and they ordered. They chatted idly about Lane's family as they waited, Anna asking more questions about Lane's sisters. The stories made Anna glad that there were only two children in her care, not three. Watching Lane talk so animatedly, Anna found a question bursting out of her mouth before she could stop it.

"Lane—why on Earth are you still single?"

Lane looked up sharply from her glass of water, amused. "What?"

Grimacing, Anna tried to reword her question. "Uh, I mean, how—never mind, I can't fix that. You're, you know—funny, understanding, gorgeous. How are you single?"

She added a charming grin to try and make the question less strange.

Lane gave an awkward shrug, smiling slightly at the compliments. "I don't know—I guess I had a bad break up."

Nodding, Anna pulled a piece of bread apart on her plate. "Crazy ex?"

Eyes dropping down to watch Anna's hand, Lane smiled tightly. "That's one way to say it. It was a bad start and a bad ending. I guess I was just…avoiding dating for a while after that."

Anna wasn't sure how to ask for more details when it seemed obvious Lane didn't want to talk about it. "What—"

The waiter appeared and placed their food in front of them, steam rising from the plates. At the interruption, Lane seemed to relax, and Anna decided to let it go. For now.

She stared at the linguini in front of her, inhaling the aroma of cream sauce. "This looks amazing." The first bite brought a moan to her lips as the rich flavour spread over her tongue. She looked up to see Lane watching her, eyes wide and fork paused partway to her mouth. "What?"

A blush spread over her cheeks. "Nothing—you, just, um—you're very vocally appreciative of that linguini."

It was Anna's turn to blush. "Well, it's good." Desperate to change the subject from her embarrassing noises she said, "I'm glad we skipped appetizers. I really want to have dessert here."

"Yeah, they serve some of the best food in Melbourne."

"So your mum's family wasn't okay with the black thing, but they're fully accepting of the lesbian thing?"

"Yeah, go figure. I think they thought it was a phase and just figured I'd settle down with a man." She winked. "Oops."

Anna gave a delighted laugh. "Oops, indeed."

"Your family had no issues with it?"

"I was lucky. My dad struggled, I think. We just didn't talk about it, really."

"And now?"

"Now, fine. He never talked about emotional things, anyway."

"See, my dad was always the one who opened discussion. The dinner table was a bombardment of questions and conversation."

"He sounds fun."

"Oh, he is. My mum is constantly exasperated with him."

"How did he cope with three girls?"

"He loved it—my mum struggled more I think."

Anna winced. "I'm not surprised—it must have been fun when you were teenagers."

"It was loud."

With a contented sigh, Anna put the last piece of pasta in her mouth. "That was so good."

Lane nodded. "Just wait until you taste their chocolate torte. Your continuous use of the word 'good' will look pathetic—divine doesn't even begin to describe it."

"You're leading me to the dark side."

"You bet." Lane's eyes sparkled.

The waiter came over and took their plates as well as their dessert orders.

Anna glanced down at her watch. "I wonder how Kym's holding up."

"She looked pretty comfortable when we left."

"I'll have to invite her over more. She did seem really content."

Lane smirked. "You can send a text to check up on them, Anna. I don't mind."

"What? I—" Anna gave up and started fishing around in her bag for her phone. "That obvious, am I?"

"Completely."

As her fingers swiped over the phone, Anna laughed aloud.

"What's so funny?"

Without answering, Anna held the phone up to show the selfie of Kym and Ella, both poking their tongues out. "This was sent five minutes ago. Clearly, Kym knew I'd want an update."

Amusement playing over her features, Lane winked. "Clearly. Is it just me, or does Kym have more ice-cream on her face than Ella?"

"Definitely not just you."

"Speaking of dessert…" Lane's face had lit up.

The waiter placed one plate of dark temptation in front of them. Anna's mouth watered. "This is evil."

"Yes, but evil tastes good."

Catching Anna's eye, Lane spooned some of the chocolate torte into her mouth, eyes closing in ecstasy as she swallowed. "God, that's amazing. Yeah, Kym looked more relaxed than I've seen her in ages."

Anna tore her eyes from Lane's lips, taking some cake herself, trying not to think about the expression on Lane's face. "Ella has that effect. As does *Beauty and the Beast*."

Lane laughed.

In the end, it was Lane who won the argument of who paid.

"I organized this one. You can get the next one."

"Next one?" Anna asked, fluttering her eyelashes.

"Yeah, next one."

"I like that."

They exited, and when the valet brought Lane's car, they both slipped in.

Something heavy settled into Anna's lower stomach. She didn't want the date to end, and, in her situation, it wasn't like she could take Lane home. Or go to Lane's, even if Kym was with the kids. She couldn't leave the poor woman there all night, and it was already well after ten. The old worries about how she was supposed to manage this, dating and the kids, started to flare up. She pressed her hands on her tights, forcing aside those worries.

"Hey, what's wrong?" Lane's soft voice interrupted her thinking.

"Nothing—I just don't want to go home yet."

Lane grinned. "Good, because we aren't."

"Oh, really?"

"Trust me. I want to show you a reason to love Melbourne."

Anna was starting to think she had quite a few reasons she'd never expected for just that.

"Do I get to know where we're going?"

"Nope, but we're almost there. In fact, close your eyes."

Anna eyed her in the dark of the car. "Seriously, Lane?"

"Yes, seriously. Close your eyes."

Sighing playfully, Anna shut them. She was nearly lulled to sleep by the soft music and the equally soft movements of the car. Minutes later, she felt the car slowing down until it eventually stopped, then heard the clicking of Lane's seatbelt.

"Okay, open them."

Anna opened her eyes, blinking while she adjusted to the sight. Her mouth dropped open slightly. In front of them was an incredible view of the city skyline. The buildings were lit up, yet they were just far enough away to also be able to see the stars lighting up the sky.

"Lane, that's gorgeous. Where are we?"

"Ruckers Hill in Northcote. It's where we used to come to watch the fireworks."

"It's incredible."

"See...Melbourne's not all bad."

Anna turned to look at her. "I'm starting to get on board with that."

Lane leant forward, reaching out to tuck her fingers into the strap of Anna's dress. "Good." She tugged gently and met Anna in the middle for a kiss.

Anna let out a soft groan as Lane's hand came up to her hair, fingertips gripping, and she unclicked her seatbelt so she could lean forward better. She sucked slightly at Lane's bottom lip and dug her fingers into the soft skin of her hip as a moan washed over her lips. Manoeuvring herself in a way she hadn't done since she was a teenager, Anna slid her leg over to straddle Lane. Both started giggling as Lane had to help her adjust her dress up her thighs so she could fit. Smiling, Lane pulled Anna's face back against her lips.

As Lane's tongue brushed against hers, Anna ground her hips down in response. The hand on Anna's thigh slid up and under, and Lane dug her fingers into her ass. Their kiss broke, and Anna's head fell back as she felt soft lips against her jaw, trailing down her neck to settle against a spot behind her ear that sent shivers down her spine.

"That feels so good, Lane."

Lane smiled against her neck, and Anna shivered when Lane's tongue ran over sensitive skin. A moan fell from her lips before she pulled Lane back up to her. Their mouths crashed together, the gentleness of their movements gone. Anna rocked her hips again, seeking contact and not finding enough. Lane was driving her to a frenzy. A gasp fell from Anna's lips when she felt a touch against her breast. Lane's other hand pulled Anna in closer, fingers digging into her neck.

Playing at pulling away again before pressing her lips to Anna's neck, Lane sucked gently, teeth nipping at the flesh. Anna finally felt Lane's hand cup her breast through her dress at the same time as Lane sucked again at her pulse point.

"Don't stop." Anna moaned. "Don't you dare stop."

Lane chuckled.

Headlights washed through the car, moving away as another vehicle parked a few spaces away from them.

They paused, breathing hard. Lane's hand was still on Anna's breast.

"Shit."

Anna dropped her head down, pressing their foreheads together. "We're never going to catch a break."

One hand falling back to rest on Anna's thigh, the other still buried in her hair, Lane grinned. "Probably a good thing. First time in a car? What are we, sixteen?"

"Like that's not why you brought me up here."

"Onto me, huh?"

"Romantic view of the city in an apparently abandoned car park?"

"Can you blame me?"

"Did you hear me complain?" Anna kissed her again. She sighed. "I don't want to move."

"Unless you want to keep doing what we were doing while a couple does the same thing metres away, you may have to. Because if you stay pressed to me like this, I can't be held accountable for my actions."

Anna chuckled and slid off Lane as gracefully as she could, settling herself back into the passenger seat. She had to wriggle her hips to pull her dress back down. They both sat, heads pressed back against the seats. Anna tried to focus on the view in front of her, but her body was still thrumming from Lane's touch. It took a moment before her breathing slowed down.

"I think I just heard sex noises from that car."

Anna wrinkled her nose. "Ew, okay. Time to go."

Buckling herself back in, Lane pulled out of the car park. "I'm currently very resentful of that car."

Anna turned her head, smiling softly at Lane and reaching a hand over to rest against her thigh. "Me too."

Way too soon, Lane pulled up at the front of Anna's house. For a moment, they were silent, until Lane said, "I want to walk you to the door..."

"But you're worried Kym will ambush the both of us?"

"Exactly."

"It's safer not to. We'll end up against the door again, she'll interrupt, we'll get cranky—it's probably for the best."

Lane laughed. "I had a really great time, Anna."

"I did as well."

"Um, I'll see you Monday?"

"You'll be getting texts from me tomorrow, I'm sure."

"Good."

Anna kissed her, once, and forced herself to end it, not trusting herself to do more. She raised a hand, pressing it softly against Lane's sternum. "You're incredibly patient."

Lane looked at her as if she was an idiot. "Why wouldn't I be? I'm enjoying this—all of this."

Anna eyed her.

"Okay, yes, I'd love to go inside right now." Lane grinned. "You caught me. But still, I'll take what I can get."

"Me too."

This time, Lane closed the gap between them, kissing Anna once more. "Go, before I kidnap you to my house."

"Is that a threat?"

"No, it's genuinely what I'll do in a minute. You're addictive."

Anna kissed Lane once more, then unclicked her belt and opened the door. "Thanks for a great night, Lane."

"Thank you, Anna."

Grinning to herself, Anna slid out and walked up her front steps. Lane's car didn't drive away until Anna closed the door behind her.

Pale blue TV light washed in from the living room, and Anna paused in the doorway, trying not to laugh out loud.

Ella and Kym were top to tail on the couch, a blanket pulled over them, both fast asleep with a pillow each. Pink and purple tutus peeked out from under the cover. Ice cream was smeared on Ella's cheek.

Anna pulled out her phone and quickly took a photo, then sent it to Lane with a message.

Pretty sure I'm going to leave them like this.

After she walked over and switched the TV off, she looked back to the couch to make sure she hadn't woken either of them up. They were both still fast asleep. The modular couch was wide and spacious, and they looked comfortable. Anna didn't see any reason to move either of them.

Her phone vibrated.

That's stupidly cute. You definitely can't wake them. Aunty Kym-aw!

Anna smiled and replied, walking up stairs as she did so.

Done, they're left. There's still ice cream on Ella's cheek.

She peeked her head in on Toby. He still woke up every second or third night, simply needing a cuddle to get him back down, occasionally a nappy change. Tonight, though, he was out to it, on his stomach with his legs tucked up under him, bum in the air, blanket clasped close. And there was no pacifier. Anna was winning that battle.

She quickly brushed her teeth and washed her face, slipping on her pyjamas and sliding into bed. She really still had no idea what to do about any of it. Yes, Ella liked Lane, and Toby would, too. Yes, she liked Lane. But it wasn't as simple as that. Dating Lane was different, and having a girlfriend, a partner, in her life? That would affect the kids, and maybe not in a good way.

It was complicated, and hard.

But tonight? Tonight Anna was relishing in a first real date, in the memory of Lane's lips against her own, against her neck. The feel of Lane's hands on her.

She looked at her phone, realising Lane might have replied to her text.

She's a kid, the ice cream can stay there.
Inappropriate to say that I'd love to lick ice cream off your cheek?

Anna had no idea how she did it, but Lane always brought a smile to her face.

Chapter Twelve

Anna's hip leant against the nurses' station and she twirled a pen around her fingers absently. A quick glance at the clock told her it was close to twelve. Disappointment swept over her—she was tired and looking forward to getting home with the kids and relaxing. The twirling of the pen slowed. That was a surprising feeling.

There had been days, when Anna had first arrived in Melbourne, when she'd woken up and, for a split second, thought she was back in her old life. And then she'd be struck with an ache of grief so deep and startling it made her nauseous. A grief not just about two deceased people she loved dearly, but also for the life she no longer had. Beneath the grief and shock, behind the learning curve of looking after two small children, she ached to be back in her old life. She had missed Hayley, especially. When she'd lain in bed in the spare room, shell-shocked and exhausted, she'd missed her girlfriend and she'd missed her life. While Anna knew they hadn't been perfect, at times barely seeing each other as they'd focused on their careers or disappeared to bars with friends, she still *missed* Hayley. They'd been great together, supportive and adventurous and incredibly understanding of each other's utter focus on their careers. Anna had missed having a partner.

But, slowly, she wasn't waking up with the feeling that she was drowning in grief anymore.

Instead, she was waking up with thoughts of the kids and, now, often of Lane.

Anna stopped twirling the pen and stared at it. As Ella and Toby stole into her life, they were taking up the space her old life had left. They had floated in and settled into that void in a different way, sure, but Anna was starting to wonder if they fit in even better than her past life had. She still struggled. She still felt that flicker of resentment, pushed way to the back. Sometimes she still *pined* for Jake to be alive purely so she could punch him in the arm and yell, "Seriously, what the *fuck* were you thinking, big brother?"

But the last week, she had barely thought of her old life at all. She woke up with the kids; mornings were the most hectic time. She ran around getting Ella to her mother's and Toby ready for day care, all in time for rounds. She spent her days at the hospital working, laughing with Kym, and flirting with Lane.

Anna was aware that Lane was a big part of the reason she was coping so well. Since their date, they'd spent all the time together they could at work. They had even discovered a stairwell not many people ventured into that was an excellent make-out spot. They managed to grab five minutes here and there to see each other, disappearing to the particular stairwell or chatting in a corridor. But it was never very long before Anna was dragged away by a resident's page or to paperwork, or Lane had to go back to emergency, her break over.

Anna's reservations about dating and the kids were still there, plaguing her mind, usually right before sleep. But Lane, it seemed, was happy to take her time. It was as if she realised that if she moved too quickly, asked for too much, Anna would bolt.

By the time her pen had dropped onto the chart she was supposed to be working on, Anna had completely given up on looking productive.

Sometimes, when she thought about it all too much, she found her mind spinning. Dating would mean more dates—how did she balance that with the kids? How on earth would she find time for a new girlfriend when sometimes she barely had time for a shower? How would they be able to enjoy the fun, the spark, when Anna was tied up with two charming yet demanding children? Would Lane get bored and walk? Hell, she and Hayley had been committed for three years and *she* had run.

And was she damaging the kids by wanting to spend time with Lane? Ella and Toby deserved to feel someone was there no matter what. She really didn't want to mess up the only two things her brother had left for her.

"If you stare much harder at that pen, I'm thinking it'll explode."

Anna looked up to see Kym holding out a coffee to her, a look of amusement on her face.

"Well, that's what I'm trying to do."

Smiling, Kym leant against the nurses' station. "How's that working out for you?"

Anna winked. "Not so well."

"Want to share the complex thoughts that had you sticking your tongue out of your mouth a little?"

"I did *not* do that."

"Oh, you did."

"Can I help you, Kym?"

Suddenly looking a little off, Kym shrugged, eyes flicking to the ground then back to Anna. "I brought you coffee?"

Anna eyed Kym over the coffee cup as she took a sip. "That you did, and it's amazing." They held eye contact for a second. "What's up?"

Opening her mouth, Kym quickly closed it again. Her fingers pulled at a loose thread on her sleeve, eyes flickering.

Without pushing her to answer, Anna simply watched her.

"I...I haven't slept in our bed for, well, since he died."

Head cocked slightly, Anna ran her thumbnail along the edge of her takeaway cup as she watched Kym, waiting as her friend took a deep breath, trying to smile.

"Not once. It's been six months. I sleep here, mostly, or on the couch when I have to go home; once it was on the kitchen floor. I know it's not normal that I *should* sleep there. But I'm so scared of waking up and reaching for him and him not being there. I...I think about moving, but that would be like giving up on him completely." Her eyes swam with unshed tears, none falling as her lips stayed curved up. A subtle waver caught her voice as she fought to sound casual. "That's not normal, is it? I should be...doing something. *Anything*?"

There was nothing Anna could think to say to that. "You're doing what you need to do. There's no guidebook for this." She waved her hand between the two of them to indicate the "this" she meant. "I don't think you *should* be doing anything, specifically."

"I went to a support group." Kym blurted out the words. "I left because I felt like I was ten giant steps behind the rest of them."

"It's been six months. That's nothing, not really."

"Sometimes I can't stand it, Anna, that I'm alive and he's gone." Kym's stricken features twisted as she fought to stay blasé. "All the air goes out of the room and I just, I can't stand it."

A lump caught in Anna's throat, and she grasped Kym's forearm. "I know, Kym."

Kym nodded with tears in her eyes, rotating her arm to return the grasp, fingers tight.

Anna's voice was as tight as her smile. "I haven't been into their room. Not once." She tilted her head, chin jutting up slightly. "It's probably covered in dust and serving as a creepy shrine to them, but I can't bring myself to go in there." She squeezed Kym's arm. "Neither can Ella. I sleep in the tiny spare room and share a bathroom with the kids in a house that's apparently mine but I won't let feel like it, because going in there and packing it up? Facing that? It's the step that makes all this reality."

Kym let out a slow breath that Anna was sure she had been holding for months. "Thank you."

"There's no guidebook, despite how useful that would be."

They let go of each other's arms as one, both placing smiles on their lips, taking a shaky sip of coffee.

Some of the forced edge slipped from Kym's smile. "If your pen leaks in your pocket later, I'm going to be amazed at the power of your mind."

Anna did the only thing she could think to do, now that Kym had changed the subject: she went with it. "We had this caseworker, Lorna, stop in to check up, the other night."

Kym's eyes widened. "What, like someone who's keeping an eye on you?"

"They warned us that will happen the first six months, a couple of random visits. She's called a few times, too."

"I thought everything was sorted, the paperwork and everything"

"Oh, it is. I've not had the confirmation, but they said it could take months and it's only been six weeks or so since I signed it all. Sometimes there needs to be a hearing thing, or if there's no issue, they just sign off on it." Anna flicked her thumbnail on her coffee lid yet again. "It was their wishes, so it should all be fine."

Kym pushed off from the nurses' station, face still a little watery, and led a slow wander towards the elevators. "How did it go, with the caseworker?"

Anna shrugged, keeping her face deadpan. "She came at six thirty at night, Toby was stark naked running around the house after his bath and Ella was chasing him with one of her old dresses to try and get him to put it on. I was in the kitchen being lazy and heating a frozen pizza."

Kym stopped dead at the elevator and pursed her lips, face going red with what Anna was pretty sure was concealed amusement. "Oh. Well, um…" She looked sideways at Anna and finally laughed loudly. Anna couldn't help but join in. "I'm sorry, but of course. Of course she shows up *then.*"

Anna was glad to hear the tension had left Kym's voice. "Right? She's lovely, though. It was her second visit. She came in the beginning, too. She even managed a smile and said she once made her brother wear her gymnastic leotard and perform in the backyard."

"So, basically, she gave Ella more ideas?" The buttons in the elevator lit up slowly as they made their way to the top floor. "So while it wasn't the best circumstances she could have come over in, it was fine?"

"Yeah. I was worried she'd be out to find fault or something, but she really is just there to check in."

"Good." Kym hesitated a moment. "Hey, can I ask something?"

Anna looked sideways at her as they walked into the cardio wing. "Sure?"

"What about Sally's parents? You told me why not yours, but what about them?"

Anna bit her lower lip. "They, um, didn't have a great relationship with Sally. Or rather, Sally didn't see them much at all."

"Oh."

Anna shrugged. "We got stupid drunk one night and she ranted about them being bigoted, closed-minded, judgemental assholes she didn't want in her life any more than she had to, and that she didn't want around her kids."

"Oh."

"Yeah."

Sadly, Sally had told her a lot more, too. But as far as Anna was concerned, that summed it up enough.

"Well, they sound delightful."

Anna grabbed the file she needed from the nurses station. "Oh, they are. They told Sally she was condemning Ella to hell because she was conceived before they were married."

"Right. Got it. They suck."

"Exactly. Now, I have to get to a surgery."

Kym sighed. "I should get back to Psych. My resident is useless."

File held to her chest, Anna watched Kym walk around the corner and disappear. Bracing herself for consultations with worried parents, she checked she had everything she needed in the file and headed for her first patient's room.

Surgery completed earlier than she had hoped, Anna was walking past a stairwell door when she felt fingers wrap around her bicep and tug. Suddenly she was through the door and pressed against it and Lane was in front of her, delicious body pressed against her, smiling.

"Hi."

An involuntary grin spread over Anna's lips. "Hi. This isn't our usual stairwell."

"I thought I'd branch out. Wouldn't want to get stuck in a rut."

Anna grazed Lane's lips as she said, "Good idea."

"I thought so."

Their lips pressed together with more urgency than Anna had anticipated. Lane's thigh moved between Anna's, causing Anna to groan into Lane's mouth. Her fingers slipped under Lane's scrub shirt to cling to her skin.

It had started to become like this, in these brief moments. They fell on each other, hungry. Their constant flirting, the verbal sparring, the looks and touches—they all built so that in the rare times they were alone, one of them escalated soft, playful kisses into something much more frantic.

Lane's teeth bit at Anna's tongue, and Anna's nails dug down. Pinned, she was being driven crazy as Lane's thigh built a rhythm. Soft lips pulled away from Anna's, and her groan of protest turned to delight as those lips pressed against her neck.

The sound of a mobile ringing echoed, bouncing off the cement walls.

"You have," Lane bit at the sensitive skin of Anna's neck as she spoke, "to be," her tongue traced a trail to Anna's collarbone, "kidding me." Lips kissing Anna there once, Lane then met Anna's irritable look. She snickered.

"What?"

"You look so disgruntled."

"I hate your phone."

Lane didn't move, obviously enjoying the close contact. "Well, yesterday afternoon I hated your pager."

"Yeah? Yesterday morning, your mobile rang."

"Should we even mention the evening before?" Lane fished her phone out blindly.

Anna flushed. "Tess should have knocked."

"Yes, she should have. In a public stairwell."

"We need to stop making out like high schoolers all over the hospital."

Mouth dropping open, Lane stared at her. "But I don't want to stop."

"Yeah, well, the entire hospital knows what we're doing—Tess is a giant gossip. The cafeteria lady winked at me yesterday and said she liked that doctors don't snub nurses anymore."

"Seriously?"

"Yes, now, go. Return that call—save patients or move wards or whatever you nurses do."

"Yes, Doctor." Lane gave a mock salute with two fingers. "See you later?"

"Of course."

Lane kissed her, pulling back with a groan when her phone started ringing again.

She glared at it. "Okay, I get it!" Lane looked back to Anna, slightly sulky. "Bye."

Anna pouted as she pulled away. "Bye."

Hovering a minute, looking like she wanted to fall forward once more, Lane's eyes flickered to Anna's lips. With a groan, she turned and walked down the stairs, calling over her shoulder. "You'll be the death of me, Foster."

Lane answered the call. "Dad, you have terrible timing." There was a pause. "Yes, I am supposed to be at work."

Anna sighed happily and dropped her head back against the door.

Hurriedly washing her hands after surgery, Anna breathed in the smell of coffee. Next to her, Lane waited patiently as she held the take-away cups. They only had five minutes, and Anna didn't want to waste them. Drying her hands with a paper towel, she'd just thrown it away and turned to face Lane when her phone rang.

With a heavy sigh, Anna shot Lane an apologetic look and pulled the offending item out of her pocket.

"Yes?"

"Anna! Dinner, tonight. Lasagne. Are we still doing that?"

Anna chuckled. "Of course we are, Mum. I've been looking forward to that food all week."

"I bet the kids are, too."

"What's that supposed to mean?"

"Nothing! Nothing. One question—why don't you ask Lane?"

Panic flipped in Anna's gut. What was she supposed to say with Lane in hearing range? She glanced at Lane, who was ostensibly reading the small print on her coffee cup.

"Uh…maybe, Mum?" Did you ask the girl you've had one real date with over for dinner with your mother? Was she even comfortable with that concept? The answer to that was, "hell, no." Anna was trying to keep the two of them separate from the kids, to keep boundaries there. Having Lane over for dinner on a Friday night for her mother's homemade lasagne was not a notion Anna was particularly excited about.

But, damn her mother, because Anna heard Ella yell in the background, "Nurse Lane is coming? Awesome! I didn't even get to see her last time, Aunty Na hogged her."

Pursing her lips, she prayed Lane couldn't hear the conversation. Anna chanced another glance at her. Still staring at the coffee cup, Lane's eyes weren't even moving—faker.

Now Ella thought Lane was coming. Really, damn her mother and her excellent lasagne.

Sandra's voice came over the phone again, "Oh, honey, you should see her, she's so excited." She dropped her voice. "And she had a bad day at school."

Anna closed her eyes and counted to five. "Will Dad be there?"

Her mother's voice changed. "Ah…no. He's staying in."

Still avoiding her and Toby, then. He seemed to cope with Ella, but she and Toby apparently reminded him too much of Jake.

Lovely. At least that was one less mess to introduce Lane to. "Sure, I'll ask her. Tell Ella not to get her hopes up. She might be busy."

"She sounds like the kind of girl who'll drop everything for you, but whatever, sweetie. I'll see you at Ja—your place." It was a slight hiccup, one she tried to glaze over but didn't completely manage to. Her mother rushed to keep talking. "I'll bring Ella over and meet you and Toby around six thirty. Tell Lane six thirty sharp. Ella and I will start the food prep here."

"Yes, Ma."

"Love you."

"Love you, too, Mum."

The phone dropped heavily into her pocket.

Giving up the pretence of reading the three sentences on her cup, Lane looked up. "That sounded, um, fun?"

"Parents."

"Tell me about it."

"Ah, Mum is cooking at my place tonight, with the kids—lasagne. She asked if you wanted to join."

"Oh. Uh…are you okay with that?"

Could this woman be any more thoughtful? "Um, sure, Ella heard, she's incredibly excited. She'll talk your ear off about how her cast is coming off in a few weeks."

"A week, actually."

"That flew by."

"Yeah. I'd love to join tonight." Lane's smile lit up the darkened scrub room.

Guilt joined the panic that was swirling around Anna's gut, but she forced her voice to remain neutral, unsure if she was managing to keep the panic off her face. "Six thirty?"

"Sounds great." Lane grabbed a fistful of Anna's scrub shirt and tugged her close. As the softness of Lane enveloped her, Anna calmed down slightly. "You can get that look off your face, Anna. It's just lasagne."

Lane was onto her. "Sorry. It's lasagne that involves my mother and hanging at my house and—"

"I don't have to come," Lane said. "If it's going to make your complicated little head explode, I'll just go get drunk with Kym at a bar and talk her ear off about this *totally* hot anaesthetist I'm seeing."

Anna laughed, relaxing completely into Lane and dropping a kiss to her lips. "No. It's fine—complicated, like you said. Come. Ella would be incredibly disappointed if you didn't."

Kissing her once, Lane asked, "Just Ella?"

"Maybe my mum, too."

Lane actually pouted. "Mean."

"Fine." Anna gave in. "I'd miss you, too."

"I knew it."

Their kiss was interrupted as Lane pulled back, eyes wide with realisation. "Shit. I'm meeting your mother."

Smug that Lane finally got it, Anna leant back against the sink. "My point exactly."

Reaching for one of the coffees, Anna took a triumphant sip as she watched Lane stare straight ahead.

"At least there'll be lasagne."

Lane's voice had never been so high.

Anna got a full half hour at home alone with Toby before the house was invaded. She was trying to swallow down her conflicted feelings.

It wasn't like she and Lane would start a romp on the table.

She eyed the spacious dining room table when that occurred to her and had a lot of trouble quelling thoughts of a half-naked Lane spread over it.

Anna read books with Toby, enjoying quiet one-on-one time that wasn't possible at the day care. He leant against her as he sat in her lap, revelling in it. He pointed delightedly at every page, his lips rounded, saying, "Oo!" at everything. "Oo! Na! Oo!"

They were interrupted at six thirty by the tornado that was her mother, the mouth-watering smell of pre-cooked sauce, and an incredibly overexcited Ella.

The lasagne was quickly thrown together and into the oven. It would only need twenty minutes to cook.

Deftly pouring two glasses of wine, Sandra handed one over. "Here, you need this."

One gulp and Anna instantly felt a little better. Under her mother's orders, she started to make a salad, grateful someone else was directing dinner. She had quickly discovered why parents complained about having to cook something every single night: without the option of going out to eat every second night, it was hard to find meals that a fussy toddler and six-year-old would eat; it was incredibly tedious. Anna heaved a sigh as she sliced tomato, amazed that, over such a short period, so much had changed. Every now and again, she just wanted slow-cooked lamb from her old favourite restaurant.

Ella was floating around like a very cute but bad smell, and Anna enjoyed seeing her move out of the quiet headspace she spent so much time in.

"When's Nurse Lane getting here?"

For the fifth time, Anna looked at the clock. "In about fifteen minutes. Three minutes less than when you asked me the last time."

Ella clung to the bench with the fingertips of one hand, taking the carrot Anna held out with the other and jamming it in her mouth.

The hope that it would quiet her for at least a moment was soon dashed. "Is she staying for all of dinner?" Ella asked while chewing,

Anna actually laughed. "Yes, Ella Bella. She's not going to get up and leave halfway through."

"How long now?"

Anna's eye actually twitched.

Sensing Anna's patience waning, Sandra held out an armful of plates. "Set the table, please, Miss Ella."

Ella nodded, grabbing the plates and walking into the dining room, still talking a mile a minute without noticing that no one was listening.

Anna let out a deep breath and took another long gulp of wine as the oven sounded.

Pulling the lasagne out, Sandra didn't try to hide her amusement. "You were so much like her."

The knife in Anna's hand sped up as she chopped cucumbers and tried to smother a groan.

"You were. You could be incredibly introspective and closed like she can be; then there were days your father and I considered muzzling you for five minutes of silence."

"Gee, thanks, Mum."

"Well, it's true."

Anna drizzled over dressing to touch up the salad. Not taking her eyes off her work, she tried to sound casual. "I miss Dad, Mum."

She sensed her mother tense behind her. Silence rang around them, the only sound coming from Toby as he smashed blocks against each other.

"I do, too, honey."

"He won't look at me." She leant on the bench to check on Toby, who was under the table and oblivious to the conversation. "Or Toby."

"He doesn't know how to do this." Her mother's voice was tight. "He, just... he..."

This was a subject Anna knew she should not have pushed. Finally turning around, Anna pulled her mother into her arms when she saw the tears threatening to spill. For a minute, they rocked back and forth. Beneath her hands, her mother felt skinnier, frailer.

"Sorry."

Sandra shook her head against Anna's shoulder, then stepped back, sniffing and wiping at her eyes. "No, I'm sorry. He's hard, at the moment. Hard to be around."

One of the many reasons Jake had put her in this position. Choosing not to say this, Anna rubbed Sandra's arm.

"Come here whenever you need, Mum. Or take the kids. They love sleepovers with you, and they used to do it at least once every two weeks."

"Back to their routine. It might be good for them."

Anna winked. "That, and you love having them there."

"Of course."

Ella burst back into the room. "Nurse Lane's here! Nurse Lane's here! I saw her car! Nurse Lane's here!"

"Inside voice, Ella."

Ella stage-whispered, "Nurse Lane is here!"

At the sound of his sister's voice, Toby had run around the kitchen bench and now stood looking at them all with wide blue eyes.

"Okay, when the doorbell rings, you may answer it. *But*," Anna yelled after her as Ella bolted from the room, "ask who it is!"

Toby wavered and fell onto his nappied bottom. The whirlwind that was Ella was too much for him to try and focus on as he followed her too quickly with his head, feet tangling when he tried to turn, and then lost his balance. Surprised blue eyes blinked at Anna, and then he burst into a giggle.

Shaking her head, Anna picked him up. "You're a dork, Tobes."

She handed him a piece of tomato he'd undoubtedly smear everywhere, kissing his cheek before plopping him back on the ground. Tiny feet carried him out of the room, one hand squashing the whole piece of tomato into his mouth.

The doorbell rang.

Ella yelled, "Who is it!" while wrenching the door open at the same time.

"Ella, it's not effective if you open the door before they even hear the question, let alone answer!" Anna called out.

"Nurse Lane!" Ella squealed.

"I wouldn't bother, Anna."

As usual, her mother was right, and Anna turned back to putting the finishing touches on the salad. The sound of Toby's feet pattering on the tile as he ran back in made her turn. He reached up to her, eyes anxious.

Sandra chuckled behind her. "Oh, Tobes. Did you follow your sister and see a stranger in the hallway?"

He looked from Anna to the direction of the front door, then pointed. "El!"

"She's not a stranger; you met her the other day. Let's investigate, shall we?"

As they moved towards the front door, they heard the quiet sound of Lane's voice, followed by Ella's louder and more excitable one. Toby pointed the entire way, showing her where to go.

"Are they out here, Toby?"

Face serious, he nodded, still pointing.

They rounded the corner to see Ella literally hanging off Lane, pointing to all the new writing and drawing on her cast. Kids had started to draw over what was already there.

Nodding at what Ella was saying, Lane looked up, grinning under her lashes at Anna.

As Lane's smile hit them at full force, Toby stilled in Anna's arms. Right there and then, Anna realised that this woman was going to have them all under her spell if she wasn't careful.

Lane mouthed a "hi" and Anna waved her fingers.

"It's Lane, Tobes."

Barely looking up from her cast, Ella said, "*Nurse* Lane, Aunty Na."

Winking, Lane nodded. "Yeah, Aunty Na. *Nurse* Lane."

"Oh, my mistake." Anna looked at Toby's face as he stared openly at Lane, mouth slightly parted—he looked comical. "Hey, Ella Bella, fairly certain you didn't finish setting the table."

"But I *did*."

"Glasses? And cutlery? Toby's cup and your Transformer glass?"

"Um..."

"Scoot, missy. Lane's here for all of dinner."

Sighing loudly, Ella turned to Lane. "Excuse me, Nurse Lane, I'll be back."

With an amused purse of her lips, Lane watched her go before looking back to Anna. "You know, she has a lot of you in her."

"Don't you start."

Lane looked at Toby, who was still staring at her, wide eyed. "Hey again, Toby. I like your shoes."

Instantly, Toby kicked his feet against Anna's thigh and the new Velcro do-ups lit up along the soles. Finally grinning at Lane, he pointed down to his shoes. "Na!" Toby stared at them for a second, leg held out and still pointing, then looked back to Lane.

"Aunty Na got them for you? Spoilt boy."

At Toby's adamant wriggle, Anna put him down. He clung to her hand with one of his own tiny ones and jumped, a motion he couldn't quite manage without holding onto something. When his shoes lit up again, he squealed, pointing to them.

"How cool, Toby!"

Letting go of Anna's hand, Toby turned and ran, giggling as he disappeared into the kitchen.

"Where on earth is he going?"

"He has the attention span of a gnat. Who knows where?"

"At least he liked me this time."

"He's a smart man: he figures a lady out first."

"Wonder where he gets that from."

"Whatever. Hi, by the way."

Closing some of the distance between them, Lane held the bottle of wine. "Hey, here." She hovered a minute, smiling softly at Anna.

They both took a small step towards each other, and Anna almost closed her eyes at the sensation of Lane's breath on her lips. Despite wanting to kiss her, Anna forced herself to pull back.

"Later," she whispered.

Lane's eyes lit up like Toby's shoes.

There was no way Lane could stay, or *that* could happen. But that didn't mean Anna wasn't going to abuse some boundaries, now that Lane was here.

"Ready to meet my mother?"

Lane's eyes widened. "Sure."

"Your voice always that high pitched?"

"Shut up."

Laughing, Anna led the way to the kitchen, where her mother was cutting up the lasagne in the pan.

"Mum, this is Lane. Lane, this is my mum, Sandra."

Wiping her hands on a tea towel, Sandra walked around the bench.

"Nice to meet you, Mrs Foster."

Sandra stopped in front of Lane, grinning, and wrapped her in a hug.

Sometimes her mother made Anna wince. However, she smiled at Lane as she caught her eye over Sandra's shoulder. Lane's hand awkwardly patted Sandra's back for a moment before she pulled away.

"Call me Sandra. Lovely to meet you, Lane. I've heard a lot about you."

Avidly avoiding Lane's smirking look, Anna added another time to the list of the moments her mother drove her crazy. She hadn't spoken of Lane that much, but Ella must have been blurting out details. Or maybe Anna had said a thing or two without meaning to. But definitely not a lot.

"I hope it's all good."

"You helped fix my granddaughter's arm, of course it's all good. And you got my daughter out of the house."

"Okay!" Anna interrupted, clapping her hands together. "How about we eat? Lane brought over an amazing red, Mum. Would you like a glass? I might stick with white."

After successfully getting everybody moving and mock-glaring at her mother, Anna led the way to the dining room. Predictably, Ella insisted on sitting next to "Nurse Lane." Anna wrestled Toby into his high chair next to her, so she could help him eat when needed. Instantly, he sunk down into the seat, trying to hold his foot out for Lane to admire his shoe. He kept kicking it against the leg of the chair and yelling a nonsensical word, making sure everyone acknowledged it lighting up.

Anna regretted buying those shoes.

Ella dominated most of the conversation, and thankfully, Toby discovered a love for lasagne and dug in with his spoon and hands, mostly distracted from his shoes.

In between Ella's chattering, Sandra questioned Lane without even trying to hide what she was doing.

"So, Lane, where did you grow up?"

Lane looked from Toby, who was again pointing at his shoe. "Yeah, Tobes, they're really cool." She took a sip of wine, measuring her answer. "I grew up here, though I moved from the US when I was ten."

"Anna mentioned that. What did your parents do?"

"Mum." The look Anna threw her mother could silence even Ella, but Sandra was unfazed.

Lane chuckled at the exchange. "My father's an accountant, my mum stayed at home with us kids, but then worked in my dad's company, helping in the office."

Toby, who had managed to get lasagne sauce in his hair, threw his spoon on the floor, grinning as he waited for Anna to pick it up. Handing it back to him with a look that clearly said this wasn't a game, she considered wiping him down. In the end, she thought better of it, figuring she would just be doing it all over again at the end of the meal.

After dessert, Sandra stood up and started clearing dishes. Anna and Lane attempted to help, but Sandra waved them away and instead enlisted Ella, who joined in with only minor grumbling.

Anna grinned across the table at Lane, sipping her second glass of wine.

"Welcome to my crazy world." It wasn't all a joke. Did Lane really know what she was getting herself into?

"They're adorable."

"Na!" Toby hit his spoon against his plastic bowl, which he'd turned over on his high chair table.

Anna poked him gently in the stomach. "Time to clean you up, little man."

"No." Toby's little face scrunched up and his eyebrows pushed together.

Lane gave a snort of laughter at his petulant expression, which Anna ignored. She poked his side again. "No?" she asked playfully.

Giggling now, he still managed a, "No!"

"I'll be right back, Lane. Grab another glass of wine if you want." Anna left Lane playing with Toby's shoe, which he had just remembered; the sight made her smile.

In the kitchen, her mother was elbow deep in suds and Ella stood on a footstool quietly, doing her best to dry the dishes.

"Working hard, Ella Bella?"

"Grandma's telling me about how when you were little, you were just like me."

Anna squeezed between them to run water over a cloth. "Is that so? It seems to be the theme of the evening."

With a nudge, Sandra said, "Well, your influence is making it more prevalent."

Resisting the urge to roll her eyes again, Anna dropped a kiss on Ella's head and started to walk back out. Her mother's voice followed her. "Lane's lovely, by the way."

"Thanks, Mum."

"Nurse Lane is cool, not *lovely*, Grandma."

"Right, sorry."

When she re-entered the dining room, Toby was relaxed and quiet on Lane's lap, playing with the fine chain around her neck. He had settled right into her arms, little legs draped over hers.

"He got fidgety, I hope that's okay."

"Of course." Anna didn't want to word how much the sight made her want to melt.

The glass next to Lane was still empty. "Didn't want another glass?"

She shook her head. "I'm driving."

Anna squatted down next to Lane's chair, surprise-cleaning Toby's face, which was the only way to manage it. If he saw the cloth coming, he bolted as fast as his little legs could take him. She quickly cleaned his hands, and, by that point, he was a squirming mess, sliding off Lane's lap and running to the living room to his toys.

Shoes lighting up as he left, Lane watched him go. "He really does look like you. It's uncanny."

Anna smiled softly, still squatting, hands resting on Lane's thigh. "He looks like Jake. People really did confuse us for twins."

A sigh left Anna's lips as Lane ran fingers through her hair, the look in her eyes soft as she asked, "Would it be weird to say I wish I could have met him?"

Anna leant her chin on top of Lane's thigh, too, looking up at her. "No. I think he would have really liked you."

The door to the kitchen swung open.

Anna stood bolt upright, taking a step back from Lane, but Ella noticed nothing out of the ordinary as she walked in.

"It's not a school night—can Nurse Lane stay and watch a DVD with us?"

Ella, who was giving her with a perfect puppy dog face, added, "Please, Aunty Na?"

Turning to look at Lane, Anna was greeted with a mirror of the look that was on Ella's face. "Please, Anna?"

Anna threw her hands up. "There's no way I can compete with the power of those two looks combined. If Lane would like to stay for a movie, she's more than welcome."

"Yay! I'll go pick, you put Toby to bed." Ella bolted off.

"Yes, ma'am." When Anna turned back to Lane, she was grinning. Anna shook her head, exasperated. "Did you like how she asked you in the end?"

"And told you to get Toby to bed."

"She's lucky she's cute."

"Like her aunt."

"You really are good at smooth talking."

"You make it easy."

"See!"

Holding her hands up to call peace, Lane leant back in her chair. "Are DVDs a Friday night tradition?"

"Yeah, we watch Disney and get hopped up on ice cream once Toby's asleep." Anna bit her lip. "Really, Lane. You don't have to stay."

"Are you kidding? Ice cream and Disney. You better hope Ella and I leave you space on the couch." She stood up, grabbing Toby's bowl. "You heard Ella, get your nephew into bed." She winked and walked out.

Sighing, Anna was realising there could be a small tradition of being ganged up on starting. In the living room, she scooped up Toby and hung him, giggling, upside down for Ella to kiss goodnight. She did the same for her mother and Lane in the kitchen, grabbed him a bottle and headed up the stairs. As she changed him, Anna murmured quietly and dimmed the lights.

In his cot, bottle to his mouth, Toby's eyes were getting the drunk look Anna had discovered was incredibly endearing. Anna rested her hand on his chest and watched him slowly drift off. When she went to pull away, his chubby hand gripped her wrist and held it in place, fingers clinging to her. A lump formed in her throat, and she stayed until he was fast asleep, unmoving until his hand relaxed and slipped down to the mattress. The only sound in the room was his steady breathing.

Downstairs, Lane and Ella sat on the couch, Ella firmly in the middle with Lane on one side. Both had ridiculously giant bowls of ice cream on their laps.

Lane shrugged at her and took a bite. "What? Your mum served them."

As if summoned, Sandra entered in her coat, another bowl of ice cream in hand. "Alright lovelies, I'm off."

"You're not staying for Disney, Mum?" Taking the proffered bowl, Anna looked suspiciously at Sandra, who busied herself doing up her buttons. Normally her mother stayed to enjoy the quiet time with Ella and Anna.

There was a smirk playing at the edges of Sandra's face, and her eyes flicked from Anna to Lane and back again. "Uh…I have some, paperwork to do at home. You girls have fun though."

Anna gave her a quick kiss. "Mhm. Paperwork?"

Managing not to look at Anna by using a cuddle from Ella, Sandra nodded. "Oh, yeah. Paperwork. Mountains of it."

"Sure, Mum." There was no paperwork Sandra could have, as far as Anna knew. "Thanks so much for dinner."

Not even attempting to extract Ella's arms from around her neck, Sandra instead blew a raspberry on the girl's neck to incite giggling. "No problem, leftovers in the fridge."

Lane put her ice cream down and stood up, holding out her hand. "It was so lovely meeting you, Sandra. Thank you for dinner."

This time, when Sandra pushed Lane's hand away to hug her, Lane looked more relaxed.

"It was *delightful* meeting you, Lane." Her mother stepped back and waved to the room. "Enjoy your DVD. I'll see you over the weekend, my girls." And then she disappeared.

Subtlety had never been her mother's strong point. Anna took a spoonful of ice cream, looking at the two on the couch. "So, what did we go for?"

Ice cream sprayed from Ella's mouth as she all but shouted, "Nemo!"

"Ah, good choice."

"Nurse Lane chose. Come sit next to me, Aunty Na." Anna sat, settling back into the couch and taking a big bite of ice cream. "I get to sit next to *both* of you!" Ella was utterly delighted.

Turning her head to catch Lane's eye, Anna bit her lip; Lane was smirking. "You're lucky, hey. You going to press play?"

Oblivious to what she sat between, Ella grabbed the remote and hit play.

They almost made it to when Nemo was caught in the fishing net before Ella succumbed to sleep, curled into Lane's side under a blanket. They let the movie play out, both more invested than they would admit. In the end, Anna lifted Ella up and carried her upstairs to bed, where she left her with her favourite panda tucked in under her arm. Anna closed the door partway and checked her watch. It was only nine thirty and she already felt like yawning.

When she walked into the living room, two glasses of wine sat on the coffee table. Lane leant back into the couch, a leg pulled up under her.

"That's a sight for sore eyes."

With a chuckle, Lane handed one of the glasses to Anna, who accepted it gratefully. The one with considerably less in it stayed in Lane's hand.

Sitting on the couch, knee pressed to Lane's, Anna held her glass aloft. "Cheers."

They clinked their glasses together and both took a sip, then Lane rested her wine glass on her knee. "You're awesome, with them, you know?"

Anna looked at her, slightly puzzled.

"They love you, a lot. You're awesome with them. I just thought you should know that."

"Thank you," Anna said softly, willing herself to take the compliment without squirming or dismissing it.

The glass clinked as Lane set it on the table. "Want to know a secret?"

Anna put her own glass down, intrigued. "Always."

"I own *Finding Nemo*. And a whole lot of other kids' movies." Delighted at the random revelation, Anna laughed as Lane kept speaking. "When you asked me that night to watch a DVD that wasn't a kids' movie, I had trouble finding some. Most of the ones I offered were Kym's."

"That's hilarious. I never watched them until now. I mean, I used to watch the odd one with Ella when I visited. Now I can recite some of them."

"I can sing almost every Disney song."

With one hand on Lane's knee, Anna tried to look serious. "Dear God, don't do that here, or Ella will end up with a flaming crush on you, and everyone will blame the gay auntie's influence."

Lane looked insulted. "Uh, no, she would crush on me because I'm awesome. It has nothing to do with you."

"This conversation is getting weird."

Soft fingers played with Anna's hand. Lane chuckled. "Yeah, it is." She looked up at Anna under her lashes. "It's getting kind of late, I suppose, especially for someone who has to get up to kids in the morning. And I have to start work at seven."

"Yeah, it is getting a bit late."

Lane grinned, moving towards Anna. "I should head off."

With a nod, Anna gripped Lane's shirt and pulled her in. "You really should."

They collided, half giggling, half groaning into the kiss. Lane pressed forward, and Anna fell back against the couch. Lane's hand brushed against her cheek, something gentle in the touch that made Anna's stomach ache. The feel of Lane's tongue, her lips, had Anna dizzy.

She trusted her. The realisation dawned as Lane's hand slid softly from her cheek, fingers stroking at her neck. Anna had trusted Lane instinctively, and trust was not something she usually did lightly. She paused as a thought occurred to her: Lane wasn't just a distraction. She wasn't just a rebound. Something was there.

Anna kissed Lane hard, the upswelling of emotion in her chest making her seek more. Fingers trailed over her collarbone, the touch raising goose bumps. Anna's leg wrapped around Lane's, holding them closer together.

When Lane's hand slid up and under her shirt, stroking the skin at her hip, Anna let out a groan. Pressed against her neck, Lane's lips teased the skin, while keeping her hand against her breast. She felt Lane push at her shirt, felt a hand pull the cup of her bra aside in one smooth motion, and Anna bit her lip too hard when Lane's hot breath washed over her nipple, tongue pressed against the sensitive skin. She wrapped a hand in Lane's hair, holding her head in place. Teeth grazed her, and Anna was *sure* that Lane was someone she could lose herself in.

She felt Lane stop moving.

Anna couldn't believe it.

The sound of a half-asleep toddler drifted down the stairs. Indistinct, not at the demanding point he had usually reached by the time Anna woke or got to him other nights, but starting.

A dry laugh escaped Lane's lips and her forehead dropped against Anna's shoulder. "This one's your fault."

"Yup. This one's on me."

When Lane lifted her head, Anna had to restrain herself from kissing her again at the sight of flushed skin and swollen lips.

Groaning, Lane dropped her head back down. "Don't do that."

Confused, Anna asked, "Do what?"

"Bite your lip like that, all fucking sexy. You do it at work sometimes when you look at me, and it's hard enough to ignore it there, let alone like this."

"Well, don't look at me all drop dead gorgeous and frustrated."

Lane lifted her head back up, smiling. "We're kind of stuffed, you know. I just can't think straight around you."

"Obviously."

Lane sat up, helping Anna tug her shirt down. The disgruntled noises upstairs were getting a touch more persistent. Anna sat up and kissed Lane, trying to keep it chaste.

"He can take a little while to settle."

"I should go, like we said before." Anna resisted the urge to pout as Lane continued, "If I stay, well. With the kids around, you're a little hesitant and seem a little unsure of everything?" She hurried on, linking her hand with Anna's, fingers entwining, "I may be wrong. But like I said, that's okay. I know your life is complicated. I'm okay with that."

"Even if we keep getting interrupted by babies?" How did Lane always know what to say? She always had an intuitive idea of where Anna's head was at. Sometimes Anna barely knew that herself.

"We get interrupted by pagers, and mobiles, and stupid, clumsy friends. What's a baby, in all that?"

As if to challenge that statement, Toby made a squawking noise, and they both grinned.

Lane stood and pulled Anna up next to her. Anna didn't let go of her hand as she led the way to the door. They hovered in the open doorway, pressing kisses to each other's lips. Just as Lane deepened one, Toby got a bit louder.

Anna winced. "Sorry."

"Never be." Lane took a step back. "Thanks for a fun Friday."

A warm feeling spread throughout her chest as Anna watched Lane walk to her car.

She closed the door and walked up the stairs to Toby's room. He sat in his cot, dishevelled hair sticking up on his head, giving her a disgruntled look.

"Little man, look at you." She leant down and scooped him up, softening when he reached for her and buried his head into her neck. She sat in the old rocking chair, rubbing his back as he hiccupped quietly. "You know, you only do this once or twice a week now. So, nice timing, Tobes." Anna kept her voice low, soothing him as he snuffled against her neck.

She waited for the resentment that, before, was always present underneath everything, but there was nothing there. All she felt was soft, the toddler in her arms and a warmth in her chest. "When you're older and understand these implications," Anna rubbed his back in circles, feeling him start to drift off, "I'm going to get you back so badly. Sixteen-year-old you won't know what hit you."

She sat with him a long time after he fell asleep, his presence a comfort, the warm weight of him secure.

This felt normal.

And that made Anna miss her brother even more.

Chapter Thirteen

Hell was the only word that came to mind for this day—from protocol changes that made their lives a nightmare to a patient dying on the table to feeling weirdly nauseated all day. Worse, Anna was running late and was stuck in her office.

She'd only gotten to see Lane for twenty minutes at lunch before being snowed under with paperwork. She'd gotten Toby as the doors were literally closing at day care, and now he sat in her office while she slugged through it all. She texted her mother to ask her to feed Ella, if she wouldn't mind, and to say she'd be there as soon as she could. Her mother's reply was the highlight of her day, a statement to the day's overall awfulness, really.

Of course I'll feel fella, take your wine.

Anna couldn't even be amused by the obvious autocorrect error as Toby tried to crawl up her legs. The phone on her desk rang incessantly, and the paperwork pile in front of her swayed precariously.

Her cell phone beeped again.

Feed Ella! Take your time! What is wrong with this damn thing?

This time, Anna managed a small puff of air that would have to substitute as laughter. Toby made a whining noise, her phone started ringing again, and a ward clerk brought in another file and put it on her desk with an apologetic grimace. A deep breath did nothing to help. Toby was stamping his little feet and holding his arms up, looking three seconds from a tantrum.

"Okay, Tobes, you can sit on my lap, but you have to be still, okay?"

Grinning triumphantly as she swung him onto her lap, Toby immediately threw himself forward and grabbed at the paper she'd been signing, scrunching it up in his hands.

"Tobes, no. C'mon!"

Anna pulled his hand back and plopped him back on the ground, where he proceeded to blink at her in surprise and then start crying.

It was an incredibly long hour and a half. Worse, when Anna finally got to her mother's, Ella was sulking, and Sandra handed her over with a smirk and a "Good luck."

When they got home, she cheated and fed Toby Cheerios for dinner, which he refused to eat, instead crunching them in his hands while Ella sulked at the end of the table and threatened mutiny.

"I want ice cream."

Anna tried to force a spoonful into Toby, who clamped his mouth shut and glared at her in a way only a toddler could. "Ella, you had ice cream at Grandma's. It's eight o'clock and past both your bed times."

"Yeah, well, you picked me up late."

She gave up and dumped the spoon next to the bowl, which Toby proceeded to push away with both hands. He arched his back, trying to force his way out of the high chair. Little fingers pulled at the straps, and he managed to look like he was locked in a torture device.

"Go hungry then, Toby, that's fine." She looked to Ella. "I know I was late. I was held up at work, Ella. That doesn't mean you get extra ice cream."

"Whatever." Ella stood up, tears in her eyes and her face red, and turned to walk out.

"Ella Bella, what's up?" she called after the girl's retreating back.

"Nothing!" She didn't even turn around.

Anna sat blinking after her. She looked back to Toby, who was staring at her with wide eyes, hands trying to prise open the safety belt over his lap.

"Something's definitely up."

No sooner had she said it than vomit landed all over the tray of the high chair and Anna's lap. The pungent smell burned her nostrils, and Anna had to choke back her own gag reflex. She hated vomit. Eyes closed, she counted down from ten.

Toby's crying started at eight.

Anna let herself get to zero before she pulled patience from a place she didn't know she had, trying to swallow back tears of frustration.

"Okay, Tobes. Let's clean you up." She looked down at herself. "And me."

Upstairs, Anna threw on a pair of clean track pants and got Toby into the tub.

He sat in the warm water, miserable, staring at her with huge, watery eyes as she cleaned him up and wiped his flushed cheeks. There was only one more throwing-up incident, which thankfully went over the edge of the tub and not into the water. With a sigh, Anna used an old towel to clean it and threw it in the corner of the bathroom, figuring she could wash it tomorrow.

Not wanting to keep Toby in the bath for too long, she pulled him out and wrapped him in the warmest, fluffiest towel she could find.

Now that she thought about it, he had been a little warm when she'd picked him up from day care, but she'd been too distracted at the time to pay it much mind. Guilt stabbed at her stomach. She bundled him into a clean nappy and a grow suit, then sat in the chair in his room and patted his back as he made unhappy little grunting noises. His bright red cheeks were warm against her skin, and diamond tears glistened on his eyelashes. Anna brushed his hair off his forehead, feeling how warm his skin was. She gnawed her lip as she rocked him gently: he was hot, but not incredibly so. Tummy flu was her guess. She took his temperature, which was hovering around 37.9, and managed to get him to drink a bottle of water. She'd check it again later and, if it was higher, hunt for the baby paracetamol that was somewhere in the bathroom.

Only through using the pacifier he hadn't asked for in a week did he eventually go down, albeit fitfully. She didn't think it would be very long before he woke again.

The empathy and exhaustion mixed in a strange fashion as Anna looked down at him. She just wanted to go to bed, pull the covers over her head. If naked Lane was next to her, that would be even better.

None of that was going to happen right now. Her life, their relationship, this night—everything kind of felt impossible.

A headache clawed behind her eyes. Anna didn't want to feel irritated at either of the kids, Toby sick and not able to help it, Ella unhappy about something and acting out the only way she could.

Anna didn't *want* to feel that at them, but she did. She'd had a long day herself. She wanted to be looked after, to be handed a glass of wine and dragged to bed, not to have to do it the other way around. Come to think of it, whenever she had been sick, Hayley had usually disappeared.

Anna walked through to her room, grabbed her phone, and read a text from Lane. For the first time in half a day, a small smile played on her lips.

Missed you today, hope your day got better since I saw you. x

Anna sighed and tapped a quick reply.

> *Definitely not better. Have been yelled at by the Ella Monster and thrown up on by a toddler. Twice. All is not well in the Foster house. Literally.*

She hit *send* and went to find Ella, who had firmly shut her door when Anna had carried Toby upstairs. She knocked. "Ella Bella?"

There was no reply, so Anna pushed the door open, and felt her stomach clench when she saw that the room was empty.

Where had Ella gone?

Her eyes flicked wildly around, taking in the fluttering curtains, the mess—there was no sign of her. Anna dug her nails into her palms as anxiety pulsed through her body, adrenaline acting quick enough to set her heart racing and dry her mouth. She heard the toilet flush and almost felt lightheaded at the relief that rushed through her.

Anna paused at the bathroom door, hearing the sound of horrible retching. She screwed her eyes shut for a second and genuinely wondered if she was cut out for all of this.

Taking another deep breath, she pushed the door open. Ella hunched over the toilet, tiny palms gripping the rim as she heaved. The position looked ridiculous on one so small.

"Oh, Ella," she murmured, then walked forward and pulled Ella's auburn curls up behind her neck, feeling the clamminess of her skin as her fingers brushed it. She tucked the hair into the back of the little girl's nightgown, then ran a cool washcloth over Ella's neck as she threw up again.

"Aunty Na," Ella whimpered.

"I know, chicken."

Ella turned her head slightly, tears on her flushed cheeks, lower lip quivering. "I threw up." Her croaky voice was utterly miserable.

Giving Ella a sad smile, Anna rubbed her back soothingly. "I know, Ella Bella."

Nothing came up as Ella gagged again.

"Aunty Na?" Ella whispered, not looking up from the toilet bowl.

"Yeah?"

"I want Mummy and Daddy."

The crack in her voice broke Anna's heart. She pulled the little girl into her arms and Ella wrapped herself into her, flushed face pressed into her neck as Anna rubbed up and down her back. Her shoulders shuddered while she sobbed.

"I f-feel yucky and Mummy w-would always make it better."

Anna slowly fell back against the wall, pulling Ella with her so the little girl lay against her chest. Like she would with Toby, Anna wrapped Ella against her and discovered she was not too big for it at all.

They sat there until Ella's sobs slowed. Anna rested her chin on top of Ella's head and rocked her back and forth gently, humming one of the only songs she remembered her mother singing to her as a child.

Heat radiated from Ella and her hand gripped Anna's shirt over her heart. When she finally spoke again, it was a whisper. "That's what Daddy used to sing to me when I was sick."

Anna paused mid-rock, the hum dying in her throat.

"Don't stop." Ella pressed her damp face into Anna's shirt.

Anna started the tune again softly, not ceasing her rocking. Her eyes welled up, and her own cheek was damp where it pressed against Ella's hair.

Two sick little children, both who wanted their parents. Parents know how to make everything better.

Decisive, she nevertheless stood awkwardly, hefting Ella with her. She wasn't sure if this was a good idea or not. Ella still shuddered with the odd sob, her face hot against Anna's skin as she wrapped her arms around Anna's neck and whimpered. Anna walked out to the hallway, then hovered outside the door for a second before struggling to reach a hand out from under the weight of Ella. The door swung open slowly.

Jake and Sally's room was cast in shadow. The blinds were open, the street light outside throwing a tiny amount of light into the room. To the right, the door to the walk-in wardrobe was partly open, left in a hurry to get dressed for a dinner they never made. The bed was tidy, pristine—a habit Jake had never broken from his Air Force days. There was a lonely shoe on the floor, a heel. The roof was angled down over the bed, and, at the sight of it, a memory slammed into Anna.

Her phone rang incessantly in her pocket as she desperately tried to get some sleep in an on-call room. After three days straight at the hospital, sleep deprivation was starting to get to her. She pretended not to hear it.

Unable to ignore the third call, she pulled out her phone out and glared at her brother's name flashing on the screen.

"Jake, seriously? Do you know what time it is?"

"It's only four in the afternoon."

"Do you know what time it is in hospital world?"

"Suck it up."

Anna finally clued in to the panic in her brother's voice. She sat up slightly, alert, her elbow taking her weight.

"Is everything okay?"

"Uh…no. I fail at parenting, and Sally is going to murder me."

Anna blurrily scrunched her eyebrows together. "What now?"

"So, I was dancing and singing with Ella—"

Anna snickered at the image.

"Ha ha, I'm a softy. Shut up. Focus. I had her on our bed, and the stupid roof slopes down over it, something Sally loved when we bought the place; I may have encouraged Ella to bounce and she may have hit her head. Hard."

Anna fell back down against the bed. Seriously, if it wasn't bad enough to warrant an immediate 000 call, her brother was most likely overreacting.

"Is she bleeding?"

"No."

"Did she black out?"

"No."

"Screaming? Crying?"

"At first. Now she's watching Elmo."

"She unsteady? Any more so than a normal two-year-old?"

"No."

"Vomiting? Staring weirdly at things?"

"No."

"She's fine. Keep an eye on her. Any of that happens, take her to the ER."

She heard Jake let out a long breath. "You sure?"

Anna threw an arm over her eyes. "Well, I can't see her, but she sounds okay."

"Okay. Now. The important part: can I hide this from Sally?"

"How bad is the bump?"

"Size of an egg."

Anna grimaced. "Poor Ella. Probably not."

"Shit."

"Shush. Your daughter will hear you. You don't want to corrupt her as well as give her permanent brain damage."

"Brain damage!"

"Jake. Calm. I'm teasing. She's fine. Besides, she totally rolled off the changing table when she was a baby, and Sally called me in the same state. You two can be on even ground now."

"She did?"

"She did. And a million other parents have done what you two have done. You're doing fine."

"Sometimes I have no idea what I'm doing."

Anna laughed wryly, "I think that's how all parents feel."

"You ever going to join the ranks?"

"Christ, no, Jake. When we were kids, you were the one who dragged my cabbage patch doll to feed at the table while Mum dragged me from the mud."

"I played in the mud, too. And it's not my fault Andy liked potato."

"You are a very strange person, Brother."

"Back at you. Now go to sleep."

"Thank God."

"Hey, and thanks, Doctor Foster."

"You know, one day you'll have to stop saying that like it's a joke. I'm an actual doctor."

"Never in my eyes, kid."

"Said the child breaker."

"I hate you."

"Go away, I'm very busy and important."

They both hung up laughing.

In the dim light, Anna could see dust floating in the air. Besides a slight musty smell, it appeared like it always had. Her throat ached as she looked around.

Ella turned her head and stared with wide eyes. "It smells like Mummy."

A lingering whiff of perfume Anna hadn't noticed at first registered. "Wanna sleep in their bed?"

Ella blinked, looking around. She nodded. "I'd sleep in the middle, when I was sick. Daddy called me his hot water bottle."

Anna took in a deep breath and stepped through the doorway.

Nothing happened.

She didn't really expect anything to; maybe she'd just hoped something would. Entering this room had been built up into something, into a symbol of their avoidance.

As gently as she could manage with the uncomfortable weight of a child, Anna put Ella on the bed, Ella clinging to her shirt. Climbing on next to Ella, they slipped under the sheets. Ella sighed as she wriggled backwards. Wrapping her arms around her, Anna pulled her close.

They lay quietly. Not a lot of dust had gathered in these two months after all. She had really built this up in her mind.

Ella's little voice cut through the semidarkness. "I miss the way Mummy knew when I was having a nightmare and would come into my room and scoop me up."

Anna rested her chin on top of Ella's head, the little girl completely folded into her front. Ella's voice was almost contemplative, a tone Anna thought must be rare in someone her age.

"I miss the way your mummy laughed with me after we'd put you rascals to bed."

"I miss how Daddy's cheek felt in the morning when he'd cuddle me, all scratchy."

Anna smiled softly at that. "I miss how your daddy always knew what I was thinking."

"'Cause you two were like twins?"

"Exactly."

"I miss how Daddy made eggs. His eggs were yum."

"I miss how your mummy would choose me awesome presents but let your daddy take the credit."

"I miss how Mummy was always at home."

"I miss your dad's stupid jokes."

"Daddy had good jokes."

"Hey Ella, what do you get hanging from trees?"

"What?"

"Sore arms."

Ella let out a little squawk of laughter. "Was that my dad's joke?"

"It was his favourite."

"See? Funny."

Anna could feel the smug little grin that came off her niece.

"Let's agree to disagree, Ella Bella." Anna pulled her in closer. "I miss how your mummy and I used to go shopping."

"I miss Mummy's cuddles."

"I miss your daddy's hugs."

"Me, too."

They played that for who knew how long, before Toby's cry cut in. Anna sat up and looked down at Ella, whose face was flushed as she blinked sleepy eyes at Anna.

"Are you okay here while I get Toby?"

Ella nodded, burrowing down.

Anna slipped out and went to Toby's room.

The little boy stood up, clinging to the cot rail. The heat coming off him was palpable before she even touched him. Anna pulled him into a cuddle, his tiny limbs wrapping around her, then stripped him of the onesie, leaving him in a nappy and vest. After checking his temperature, she found the baby paracetamol. A few gulps of water, and he quietened.

Cradling him to her front, she cupped his head to her chest and quietly padded down the hallway to Jake and Sally's room, leaving the door open to let in the soft hallway light.

Engulfed in the middle of the king-sized bed, Ella blinked owlishly.

"Ella Bella, what are you wearing?"

Ella looked down at the jumper that was swimming on her. "This is Daddy's military jumper."

Anna slipped into bed next to Ella and sat cross-legged with Toby still wrapped around her. She rubbed his back and kept her voice light. "Where was it?"

"Under Mummy's pillow. She wore it whenever Daddy went away." Ella wrapped her arms around herself. "It's like a hug from both of them."

Ella said it simply, but Anna felt the words tug at her.

She lay down on her side, Toby wiggling to cuddle into her front. Reaching her hand out, she wrapped her arms around both the kids.

The three of them drifted off. Ella didn't wake calling out and Toby slept through.

Anna didn't take her hands off either of them all night.

"You're kind of addictive."

Lips pressed against the back of Anna's neck and an arm wrapped around her middle. She'd been staring vaguely at a spare computer in the surgery lounge, and then suddenly, the bliss of Lane enveloped her.

"You should join a support group." Anna smirked to herself, pretending to keep her eyes on the screen as Lane's chin rested on her shoulder, her front pressed tight to Anna's back. Surely it wasn't normal to feel like turning and pushing someone against the wall and yet feel so settled and at peace all at the same time?

Lane's eyes sparkled. "Anna Addicts Anonymous. I can get Jenny to join."

A laugh puffed out of Anna even as she rolled her eyes.

Lane turned to nuzzle her neck, smiling against the skin. "Laugh all you want, that intern has an insane crush on you."

Turning, eye to eye with Lane, lips barely apart from hers, Anna said, "Too bad I'm only interested in emergency nurses."

Lane's mouth dropped open. "I knew you were seeing Tess!"

With a delighted giggle, she pressed her lips to Lane's.

"How are the kids feeling?"

Anna shrugged. Even though the room was empty, she stepped back to put some space between them before they got too comfortable. "Better. It was a short-lived bug."

"Ella happy to have a day off school yesterday?"

Anna nodded, leading them out of the room and down a hallway to the elevator. "She was. She and Toby were mostly better by the morning but I figured I shouldn't share their bug around. Apparently it's sweeping through the day care, so we'll blame them."

"Good idea. Enjoy your lazy morning yesterday?"

Anna let out an exasperated breath. After the night she'd had, she had started late to ease the kids up slowly before dropping them with her mother.

"Actually, yes. It was delightful. Someone lovely had left a coffee on my desk when I got in."

Lane widened her eyes, pressing the up button on the lift. "Who could that have been?"

When the doors opened, Lane led the way in. The second the doors started to close, Anna pushed her against the back wall. "You?"

Wrapping her arms around Anna, Lane grinned. "It's no fun if you guess."

Anna melted into Lane—it had been days since she had gotten to. First, the day from hell, and then yesterday had seen Lane swamped in Emergency all day. Their session on the couch had been almost a week ago.

Anna could fade into their kisses forever. The feel of Lane's tongue against her lip brought out a groan. She pressed harder against Lane, whose hand entwined in Anna's hair, fingers pressing into her scalp.

The lift slowed to a stop, and Anna stepped backwards, turning on the spot as the doors opened—as innocent as if they'd been in the position the whole time.

Kym kept a straight face, eying them with raised eyebrows before she turned and pressed the button she wanted.

Anna bit her lip as she felt Lane's shoulders shaking with badly-hidden mirth.

"And I'm supposed to believe you two weren't just going at it like horny high schoolers?"

"Anyone else would have believed it." There was a pout in Lane's voice.

"Anna's face is bright red and your shirt, Lane—" She turned, flicking her eyes down and then back to Lane's face, "is unbuttoned almost completely."

Anna hid a smug grin as Lane's indignant voice sounded out. "Holy shit, Anna, how fast do you move your hands?"

Lane had no idea.

"I bet Lane would love to know how fast."

She and Lane gaped at Kym, who feigned confusion. "What? That was funny."

Leaving Lane to do up her buttons and laugh at Kym, Anna slipped out of the elevator.

There were nights like two nights ago, where everything felt impossible, and days like today, where she felt a peace settle over her as her life seemed to calm. She didn't know what it was about the other night with the kids, but, as she lay wrapped with them in a room she had avoided at all costs, she had wondered where they would be now if she wasn't doing this. And when they had woken up in the morning, things had felt different. There was still a constant ache in her stomach, but now it was being pushed out by something much stronger.

She might sometimes wonder what she was doing, but never why she was doing it.

And then there was Lane. Lane made everything a little bit better. And that alone was a little bit scary.

The rest of her day was spent in consults, and, at three o'clock, almost on the dot, an eruption of pagers occurred around her. Anna looked down at hers, scrolling through the abnormally long message it presented. As the surrounding surgeons, doctors, and anaesthetists read through their messages, she watched their expressions—mirrors of the one that must be on her own face. Their boss, looking longingly at the late lunch he wouldn't get to finish now, called out, "Okay, listen up. This is an emergency coming through. A truck has T-boned a school bus, causing a huge pileup on the freeway. We have multiple traumas on the way—we're in for the night, guys."

Anna spun on her heel and started for the stairs, pulling out her phone as she moved quickly down them. As soon as she was through the door, she placed the call. "Mum. Hi, it's me."

"Hey, sweetie."

"I'm really sorry, but there's been a huge accident and I can't leave work this time."

"Oh, no. Don't tell me about it, I don't want to know."

She nodded grimly, feet pounding rhythmically on the stairs. The door on the next level swung open as Anna passed it and she saw Lane, who waved as she started down the stairs next to Anna.

"I think I'll be here late—as one of the senior anaesthetists, I really can't leave. There's going to be multiple surgeries. Can Ella and Toby stay with you?"

"Of course. I can wash Ella's uniform for tomorrow—I've got her from school already. How do I get Toby?"

Anna relaxed slightly when she felt Lane's hand on the small of her back as they made their way to ground level.

"Remember, I told you? You're on the list of people who can get him from day care, just take your license in."

"Okay, honey. I'll get him in an hour."

"Thanks, Mum. Sorry about this."

"Don't be silly. It's what grandmas are for."

"Tell Ella I'm sorry. Tell her we'll go to the movies on the weekend."

"She'll be fine. I'll keep Toby with me tomorrow. I'll let the day care know when I pick him up. Good luck, honey."

"Thanks Mum, bye."

As she put her phone away, Anna flashed a smile at Lane. "Hi."

"Hey. Just got told I'm needed for a double in emergency. Ready for a long night?"

The door that led into the emergency room finally appearing in front of them, Anna nodded and pulled it open. The place was a mess, set up for mass trauma, sirens wailing outside, the first patients already on their way in. Just before they walked through the doors, Lane's fingers linked briefly with hers for a moment before letting go. Adrenaline already moving through her body, Anna bounced on the balls of her feet.

"You bet."

Chapter Fourteen

The night was chaotic, the noise level high. It was all hands on deck, and Anna loved it. Not that there were children and adults in a critical condition after a truck crashed into a school bus—but she was definitely loving the action, the incredibly fast pace, the thinking on her feet. Adrenaline hit her system as she was engulfed by it all. It was her job, after all. A job she was damn good at, that she had lived for—once.

In no time at all, Anna was directed to a bed to take over guarding a patient's airway. The boy was no more than ten, shirt cut open, an emergency doctor inserting an intercostal catheter. Eyes on the monitor, Anna saw that the boy's heart rate was dangerously fast and his oxygen saturations were far too low. The catheter caused only a slight improvement. Anna elbowed out the intern standing at the head of the bed and checked the placement of the endotracheal tube. She tutted and glared the man down as her hands moved quickly, deflating the balloon and removing the tube.

"You've been blowing air into his stomach."

The intern was pale. "I-I thought it was in the correct place."

"Check, don't assume. Watch." Anna inserted a new endotracheal tube, the correct size this time, and bagged the patient. The intern and Anna turned to watch his sats slowly creep up.

"Anna, we need a patient intubated here and we have no hands!"

Anna and the intern's heads whipped to the bed next to theirs, where Lane knelt, performing compressions while a surgeon from trauma worked to control a lower abdomen bleed.

"You got that one?" she asked the intern.

He gave a nod and slipped away, off to apply what he had hopefully just learnt to Lane's patient.

Looking to the doctor at her patient's chest, Anna asked, "This boy for surgery?"

The man gave a swift nod. "He's first on the list, shattered femur and," he pulled the blanket back for a moment, showing a penetrating injury. "We're taking him up now he's stable. You're Doctor Foster, anaesthetics?"

"That's me, and I'm with you guys."

They started to move the bed out, and Anna climbed on to continue bagging. Her eyes flicked up to check the stats on her monitor before darting to the bed next to theirs.

The intern was looking relieved as he bagged the patient, his eyes glued to his own monitor, and Lane had paused her compressions while the surgeon monitored the screens. At his nod, Lane slid off the bed, hands immediately adjusting the intravenous pump.

Brown eyes flicked over and caught Anna's as the bed wheeled away. Lane gave a wink, eyes quickly going back to her patient, and it was probably inappropriate to think the thoughts Anna was thinking.

The next few hours went quickly; at eleven, Anna wasn't even feeling tired. When she finally found a free moment, she ducked into the surgeons' lounge. As she turned from the sink, desperately chugging a glass of water, Lane walked into the room wearing a scrub cap. Anna could have collapsed in a grateful heap when she noticed the two coffees in Lane's hands.

"Oh my God, you are amazing. Thank you." Anna took a long gulp, relishing the taste.

"I see how this is. You're only happy because I gave you coffee."

With a contented sigh, Lane settled next to Anna, leaning against the bench. They watched in amusement as a surgeon ran in, rummaged in a bag, and triumphantly pulled out an apple. Not even noticing them, he shoved it into his mouth before rushing back out.

Taking another sip, Anna shook her head. "Not totally true. I was very happy when you walked in. Especially when I saw you in your cute little scrub cap. I was just ecstatic when I saw the coffee."

"I'll accept that. Though you weren't as happy as that guy about his apple."

"He probably hasn't eaten since three."

Lane leant sideways to press a kiss to Anna's lips. As she tried to end the kiss, Anna grabbed at the material of Lane's scrub top and pulled her closer, deepening the kiss.

They separated after a minute, Lane smiling happily. "If coffee gets me that, what does this get me?" She held up a paper bag.

Anna literally bounced on the spot. "Food!"

Ignoring Lane's amused look, Anna snatched the bag and looked inside. "Microwaved pizza rolls." She looked up at Lane again. "Where did you find these?"

"I stole them from Tess's locker when I was told to find twenty minutes to have a break before the union broke down the doors."

After shoving one in her mouth, Anna handed the bag back over. "I hadn't even realised how hungry I was." She took another bite, chewing quickly and swallowing. "Or how caffeine-deprived." Anna smiled. "Thank you."

"My pleasure. How were your surgeries?"

"Awesome. One of my patients started to have a temp spike, and I thought I had a reaction going on, but it turned out to be nothing exciting. What's up with the sexy scrub cap? I thought you were in emergency?"

"They roped me in to be instrument nurse the last two hours."

"Why didn't you go into medicine, or surgery?"

Lane rolled her eyes. "I love nursing, I do lots of hard core stuff *and* I get to speak more with patients."

"Just a question."

Lane poked her tongue out.

"It's going to be a long night."

Lane nodded. "It really is." She eyed Anna. "Something you don't look too sad about."

Anna had the sense to look a little sheepish. "I know. I can't help it. I've really missed this. I haven't done a late night in months. This kind of pressure, having them wheeled in and out, all a little dicey."

Lane grinned at her. "You really are a little hard core—why didn't *you* do something more hands on?"

"Touché. I don't know. I enjoy that my patients don't talk back much."

"If they do, you haven't done your job correctly."

"You're so funny." Anna grinned. Lane's hand slipped behind her neck, thumb brushing her cheek as Anna pushed back against her. When they parted, Anna pressed a final chaste kiss against Lane's lips for good measure before resting her forehead against Lane's. Eventually, she settled back against the bench, sipping her coffee and watching Lane.

They didn't take their eyes off each other until the sound of people rushing into the lounge to find food finally tore them apart.

"I need to get back downstairs now that surgery is done. It's chaos." Lane winked at her. "Don't fall asleep on your patients."

"You either."

They walked out together, parting ways at the stairs.

"And Lane?" Anna pressed her back against the door to push it open.

Lane looked at her. "Yeah?"

"I owe you one for that coffee."

Lane seemed incapable of wiping the grin from her face.

It was three in the morning when Anna finally left her last surgery. They were done, every staff member wiped, all surgeries that needed to be completed, finished. She had secretly hoped that she would end up in a surgery with Lane at some point, but even though Lane was technically casual pool, she seemed to spend most of her time in emergency.

Now they all gathered in the emergency room's meeting office; nurses, surgeons and doctors standing shoulder to shoulder as the emergency coordinator gave them a speech. "That was great work. I want you all to go home unless you were actually rostered on tonight. Those doing doubles, leave. Your pay will be sorted out, don't worry." He grinned, and everyone gave a tired laugh. "Those rostered on to start this morning, sleep. I'll see you at noon. The night staff that came on at eleven tonight can stay late. You all need it."

Anna stood between Tess and Lane, her hands buried in her pockets. She gave a sigh of relief, happy she wouldn't have to start until twelve the next day after such a long shift.

Tess looked sideways at them both. "Well, I'm going home immediately. No nookie in the hospital, you two."

"Aren't you rostered on tonight?"

At Anna's words, her face fell. "Oh. Yeah." And with a wave she was gone.

"I suppose you should get home to the ki—" Lane stopped suddenly, a wicked grin creeping over her lips. "Ella and Toby are at your mum's."

The realisation dawned slowly on Anna, too. "Yeah, they are. My house is empty."

"I have tomorrow off. Need some company?" Lane stepped backwards, eyes wide with fake innocence even as she led the way to the exit.

Not hesitating, Anna followed. "I think I do."

"That does *not* mean I have more relationship experience than you."

Laughing at the indignant tone in Lane's voice, Anna held the door open for her to walk through. "Please, Lane, you were *married*. Totally does."

Lane shook her head, hanging her jacket up and following Anna down the hall into the kitchen. "I wasn't *married.* We had a civil partnership and a cat." Lane paused. "Okay, fine, in the lesbian world that's married. But I was young and naive. How long were you in your last relationship for?"

"Over three years." Anna peered into her fridge. "Beer okay?"

"As long as it's cold, great. I'd take anything right now."

Anna wriggled her eyebrows as she fished out two beers.

"Okay, I could have worded that better." Lane shrugged. "See. Three years! That's commitment. We were only living together for two."

The sound of the beer opening made Anna happier than she was willing to admit. "Yeah, but you had a cat. That's like, having children." She paused. "Actually, since acquiring two children, I can safely say that no, having a cat is not the same. Still, though, it all adds up to count as more experience than mine."

Lane shook her head. "Nope—my ex ran off with the woman who was painting our front porch and gave me emotional scars." Lane winked. "Doesn't count."

She hadn't known Lane's ex had had an affair. "Really?"

Nonchalantly, Lane blew a raspberry. "It was a long time ago. That part's not important. Your relationship wins. Three years."

"Civil union."

Lane looked thoughtful for a moment. "Okay. Maybe. Maybe it adds up to more experience. But three years is major."

Sipping her beer, Anna slid Lane's to her and took a seat. If her ex had cheated on her, she probably wouldn't be so relaxed. But Lane already seemed to be focussed back on what they were talking about.

"I suppose. It was my first real relationship, though, besides the odd longer thing in college."

"Seriously?" Lane put the bottle on the table and blatantly looked Anna up and down. "*How?*"

Anna rolled her eyes. "I was so focussed on work and my career. I was happy, doing that. I didn't want commitment."

The suspicion in Lane's eyes made Anna uncomfortable. "What?"

"You were a bit of a player, weren't you?"

"What?" At that moment, Anna hated how her voice tended to go high when she lied. "What? No."

"Oh, you so were."

"Whatever. I just didn't do commitment while I was focussed on work."

"Mhm."

"*Anyway.* Then I did a three-year commitment. So there."

"Do you mind me asking what changed? With your ex, I mean? Or is that not something the current date can ask?"

"I think it's fine." Grateful for alcohol, Anna sipped her beer again. "I don't know, really. We were incredibly similar, driven. We both understood our careers came first and that was okay. I'm not sure many women would be okay with that. Now that I think about it, I wonder if that was the main thing holding us together. We didn't spend that much time together, considering we lived together."

Lane nodded. "That makes sense."

"At the beginning, I was such a commitment rookie. Now? I'm plopped into a life with kids, something I never planned. I'm definitely a rookie now. At least before I could kinda make it up as I went along." Anna looked intently at Lane. "You? You seem to have this settled, comfortable thing down pat."

Lane laughed out loud. "Anna, everyone is just making it up as they go along."

"Really?"

"Really." Lane sipped her beer. "I'm certainly happy to be here. New to everything and two kids included."

Unable to resist, Anna kissed her before pulling back slightly to look her in the eye. "You've been amazing." Lane shook her head but Anna interrupted. "You really have, Lane. Amazing."

Before sitting back down, Anna kissed her once more.

Lane was grinning. "Even despite the whole I-owned-a-cat-with-my-ex thing?"

"Even with that."

"What if I told you it was two?"

"I'll laugh at you, but yes."

"What if I told you I met her at work when she came in with a broken femur?"

"A patient, Lane? How risqué."

"A *former* patient."

Anna drained the last of her beer. "Still, point stands."

"Going to report me?"

"Ha. I think if I did, I'd have to report the multiple times I know you've been making out in stairwells."

Lane poked her tongue at her. "Shot yourself in the foot."

"Damn."

Anna picked up her empty bottle, intending to get another. About to ask another question about the ex, she heard Lane's chair push back. When she turned around, Lane had stepped into her space, gently pushing her so the small of her back pressed into the bench. Lane cocked her head at her.

"I got pretty burned coming out of that relationship."

Anna trailed her fingers down Lane's soft cheek. "I don't know how anyone could do that to you."

"It was a long time ago now. I'm just saying that, because I don't get this urge to run and protect myself with you. I wasn't innocent in it all, but—"

Acting on impulse, Anna surged forward, digging her fingers into Lane's neck as she kissed her. Pulling back, she looked searchingly into Lane's eyes. "Do you want another beer?"

Lane shook her head, fingers toying with Anna's shirt. "I don't really want any more beer."

"What do you want, then?"

Anna's eyes closed of their own accord as Lane's gently kissed her jaw, tracing a pattern to behind her ear. Fingers rested lightly against Anna's hips, and her hands fell to grip the bench behind her.

When Lane spoke, it was in a whisper, her breath light against Anna's skin. Anna held back a shudder. "I want you. Just." Lane's tongue snaked against her neck, then her lips pressed against the same spot once. "You."

Anna threaded her hands in Lane's hair, the dark tight curls clamped in her fist. She pulled Lane up so that their lips crushed together. An involuntary groan fell from Anna as Lane pressed her full weight against her, pinning her to the bench.

There were no children in the house. Lane had the day off, and Anna didn't need to be in until twelve. Life was glorious.

At Anna's smile, Lane stopped. "What?"

"We aren't going to be interrupted by work." She kissed Lane once. "Or Kym." And again. "Or crying babies."

Lane grinned too. "Oh, okay. Good reason to smile."

Using her body, Anna moved them towards the kitchen door, lips barely leaving each other.

"Well, you always make me smile."

Anna gently guided Lane to the stairs, eyes flicking to look up before she decided it was too hard and just pushed Lane against the banister. Lane's hands fell on it to balance herself as Anna's lips moved to her neck.

A sigh reached Anna's ears as she ran her tongue along soft skin. When her teeth grazed the hot flesh under her lips, the sigh turned to a moan.

"Upstairs." Anna planted another kiss on her. "Upstairs is a bed."

"Right." Lane's hands pulled Anna tighter. "Right. Bed."

"If we don't go," Anna tried to untangle herself from Lane, "I'm going to shove you onto the stairs, and as hot as that'd be, there's a bed."

With a pout, Lane looked at the stairs. "They don't even have carpet."

Anna laughed, grabbing Lane's hand. Within moments, they were in her bedroom.

For a second, they simply stood next to each other, hands linked. Then they met in a tangle, hands in hair, lips parting against each other, stumbling back against the bed.

Lane sat down on the edge, pulling Anna with her. At the tug on her hips, Anna straddled Lane, not breaking the kiss. Goosebumps erupted over Anna's skin as Lane's fingers ran along her spine under her shirt. Lane kissed her neck, and Anna sighed.

"Finally."

"What?" The whispered question against her neck made Anna shiver. She hadn't meant to say that aloud.

"Nothing."

Lane kissed her again, and Anna couldn't speak anymore as the sensations Lane's fingers caused made all thoughts fade. All there was in that moment was Lane.

Their kiss finally broke as Lane pulled away.

Anna's protest turned into a soft sigh as Lane's lips moved over her cheek and jaw. Teeth grazed her neck. Thumbs brushed the underside of her bra before trailing back down over her stomach, tracing just over the waistband of her pants and back up her spine.

Anna giggled, and Lane looked up, bemused. "Um. Anna? Not really the reaction I was looking for."

With a sheepish look, her hands shifted to cup Lane's cheeks. "No, I'm sorry. I just…this position is very deja-vu, in your bedroom. It just crossed my mind how different it is this time."

A slow look of pleasure crossed Lane's face. "No tears this time."

Happily, Anna shook her head, pushing Lane back so she lay down on the bed. Lane gave no resistance whatsoever, hands sliding out the back of Anna's shirt to rest on top of her thighs. Anna rested a hand on either side of Lane's face, smiling down at her, hair falling around them.

"Nope. And no stopping."

"No medals required."

Anna chuckled, leaning down further to press her lips to Lane's. "I think we deserve medals. It's been a long time that I've wanted you like this, with no interruptions. I don't care that it's four in the morning."

Lane's hands came up to either side of Anna's face. Her eyes were soft. "Totally worth the wait."

The gesture made Anna melt. "Totally." She leant forward as if to kiss Lane, but then pulled back, smiling at the disgruntled look on Lane's face. Instead, Anna toyed at the hemline of her own shirt, head tilted as she waited for Lane's reaction.

Understanding crossed Lane's face, her eyes dropping to Anna's hands then back to meet her eyes. That smile that would forever make Anna's stomach flip lit up Lane's face. This was what Anna had been waiting for.

She tugged the shirt up slowly, pulling it over her head and dropping it on the floor. Briefly, shyness overtook her, an emotion she sometimes thought would never completely leave a woman, no matter how confident. However, when she saw Lane's eyes trail over her and then her mouth drop open, all feelings of inadequacy fled, and all Anna felt was the burn of Lane's eyes.

Lane pushed herself up on her elbows, her gaze intent on Anna's. "You are so fucking beautiful."

Overwhelmed with emotion, Anna leant down, capturing Lane's lips in a kiss.

For a moment, it was Lane who took control. Her fingers stroked Anna's stomach and back, and shivers ran over Anna's body at the touch. She nipped at Anna's lips, teeth dragging over the skin before pulling back. Then her hands dropped down to her own shirt, her gaze boring into Anna, a cheeky smirk on her lips.

Anna pulled those hands away. "I want to."

Lane's smile became sassier. "Assertive? I like it."

"I just know what I want." Anna gripped the shirt, giving a playful shrug before she slowly pulled it off. Heat rushed through her at every inch of skin and curve that was exposed. She tugged the garment over Lane's head, and dark hair tumbled to her shoulders. Anna threw the shirt behind her and pushed forward, pressing Lane down on the bed. Lips crashed together. Legs slid between each other, both of them moaning at the contact. Smooth skin ran under Anna's hand as she grazed it over Lane's thigh, across her hip and up her side.

Her bra was somehow on the floor.

"Anna."

Trembles ran through her at the soft voice against her ear.

"I just want to feel you."

Smothering a groan, Anna slipped her hand under Lane and removed her bra, their torsos pressing together as Lane wrapped her arms around Anna's back, pulling her in. Hot skin pressed flush.

With her palms gliding over Lane's sides, Anna pressed her lips against the thumping pulse at Lane's neck. Her thumb brushed over a nipple, and Lane's head fell back with a groan. Her hands were tangled in Anna's hair, urging her head down to replace the thumb with her mouth.

Anna gripped Lane's hip as her tongue coaxed moans from soft lips. Caught between wanting to drag this out as much as she could and wanting to hear how Lane sounded, *right now*, when she came, Anna kissed a path down Lane's ribs, tongue tracing against her skin.

"You," Anna said between damp kisses, slowly moving down Lane's writhing body, "do things to me I can't even explain." She looked up, her lips pressed just under Lane's navel.

Lane's black eyes sent a jolt through her—a jolt that settled straight in her centre. With trembling fingers, she undid the button and zip of Lane's jeans. How was it possible for Lane to feel so good? Compliant hips lifted as Anna tugged the trousers down and off Lane, pulling her underwear with it.

Lane exhaled deeply. "Believe me when I say, I understand."

Anna smiled as she stood, tugging off her own pants before she crawled back up the bed, dropping wet kisses to Lane's skin. Lane's legs came around Anna, pulling her down. And finally, warm skin enveloped Anna as she lay flat against Lane, naked skin to naked skin.

The site of Lane's mouth dropping partially open as Anna rocked her hips caused her to bite her lip. That groan drove Anna wild. Dipping her head, she kissed Lane again, rolling her hips in a slow rhythm. Lane's legs tightened their hold, pushing Anna harder against her.

"That," Lane moved her hips forward to meet Anna's, "feels amazing."

Distracted by the sensation of nails dragging against the skin of her back, Anna kissed her neck, teeth grazing gently before biting down softly.

"I've wanted to feel you like this for too long."

Their kisses grew more insistent as Anna built a rhythm, soft groans echoing in the room. Heat shot through her when Lane's nails dug into her ass, guiding Anna's movements to greater satisfaction. The friction between them wasn't enough, but it wasn't a sensation Anna wanted to end just yet. Electricity danced over her skin. Lane dragged her other hand between their bodies, thumb brushing over Anna's nipple before cupping her breast.

Anna rocked herself into Lane's body, feeling with every move the heat of her, all of her underneath. "You're so fucking wet."

Nails dug into her back as she thrust against Lane again, and fingers twisted her nipple, making Anna gasp.

"You've worked me up a little."

"Just a little?"

Lane rasped a laugh. "A fuckload, actually."

Despite her distracted state, Anna smirked, elbow bracing her body on one side, her other hand on Lane's breast rolling a nipple between her fingertips. At the feeling of Lane spread under her, the heat of them pressed together—an instinctual rhythm took over.

"I'll come like this, just so you know." Lane's hand pulled almost painfully at Anna's hair, her voice low, words coming out between fast breaths. "You feel so good."

Forcing herself to slow down, Anna brushed her lips against Lane's cheek. "Not that there's anything wrong with that, but..." She shifted one leg, straddling Lane's thigh, hissing slightly as she pressed against the taut muscle, "I really want to be in you when you come."

Lane groaned, one arm still wrapped around Anna, fingertips digging into the small of her back. She pulled Anna down against her thigh, then turned her head, lips seeking Anna's, her free hand reaching up to Anna's hand on her breast to guide their joined hands down. As Anna's fingers slid against her, Lane's head fell back against the pillow.

Blissfully, Lane's eyes closed and her lips parted as Anna ran one finger along her, teasing her.

"Fuck." Lane's voice echoed loudly in the room, her eyes snapping open as Anna pushed the one finger slowly into slick heat. A groan at the sensation fell from Anna's lips as she pressed her lips to Lane's shoulder. The hand on her back slid to her ass, pressing her harder against Lane's thigh. The rhythm Anna set with her hand was matched by the gyration of her hips. She was so wet, she slid against Lane's thigh easily. Too much. All of Lane was too much—the taste, the sound, the smell.

Lane's heel pressed into the mattress, fingertips digging into Anna's ass, still guiding her movements, while her other hand gripped Anna's wrist almost painfully as she moved in her. The desperate feel of Lane's fingers against her wrist almost made Anna lose control.

"Anna."

If she could, Anna would listen to her name fall from Lane's lips like that every day. Husky, dead sexy. She wanted to spend forever seeing just how many ways she could make her name sound like that.

"More?"

Anna's lips collided against Lane's in a messy kiss, slow pace never altering except to add a second finger. Her fingers curled, deep in wet heat.

Grunting into the kiss, Lane's hand finally let go of Anna's wrist to come up and grip the back of Anna's neck, holding her close.

Anna concentrated on the sounds Lane made, slowly pulling her fingers almost completely out before pushing them back inside. The sound of how wet Lane was, coupled with the feeling of Lane gripping her fingers, drove Anna to the edge. She sped the tempo up—slowly, her eyes never leaving Lane's face. Anna's hips kept pace with her hand, her forehead pressed to Lane's, lips pressed against her cheeks as they panted, the odd swear word coming from Lane's lips as Anna moved inside her.

Lane's hips met Anna's fingers thrust for thrust, Anna now having to match Lane's pace. Her own hip movements started to lose their rhythm as a familiar tingling started in her lower stomach and she desperately sought whatever friction she could get.

Anna curled her fingers, meeting Lane's request for, "Fuck, harder, please" instantly. The rhythm of Lane's groaning matched perfectly the thrusting of Anna's fingers. This was heaven—hot, sensual heaven.

Lane's head fell back against the pillow. Anna's pressed against her shoulder, biting down as she felt herself start to come undone, orgasm washing over her, hips thrusting forward uncontrollably one last time against Lane's thigh.

Through the haze of her own orgasm, Anna pressed her palm down and felt Lane's whole body tighten around her fingers. She thrust forward a final time, and Lane came with a groan, nails dragging up Anna's back. Anna hissed as pain clashed deliciously with pleasure. Lane's thighs shook before her legs fell limply against the bed.

Anna let her arm go out from under her, collapsing half on top of Lane and half on the bed, face pressed against sweaty skin. Her hand stayed between Lane's thighs, not willing to lose the connection just yet. With a slight turn of her head, she pressed her lips to Lane's neck.

Humming, Lane rested a hand on Anna's forearm. Their bodies lay still, trembling slightly, erratic breathing calming slowly.

"I think you broke me."

Anna chuckled. "Right back at you." She finally gave in, slowly removing her hand and resting it on Lane's stomach. Her head came up to rest on her other arm, face inches from Lane's.

Lane's brown eyes were dark, soft in the light coming in off the street. "You kind of broke yourself." Lane smirked and it provoked another laugh from Anna.

"True." Again, Anna's lips moved against Lane's lazily, the kiss ending naturally. "That whole thing felt incredible."

"You're incredible." Lane had a dreamy look on her face.

Anna's smile widened. "You're a sap." She fell back on Lane's arm. "Are you comfortable?"

"Incredibly so."

"Excellent." Anna burrowed into Lane's side further, relaxing completely. "Then we don't have to move."

Lane wrapped her arms around Anna, pulling her closer. "Sleep?"

Anna nodded against Lane's shoulder. "God, yes. It must be nearly five."

Lane groaned. "Call in sick tomorrow—I mean, today."

Anna gave a snort that was probably not very attractive, but she was too relaxed to care. "Hi. It's Foster, can't come in. Instead of sleeping like we were meant to be, since I was given a late start, I was busy having mind-blowing sex with one of your casual pool nurses."

"I see nothing wrong with that."

"You wouldn't."

"Are you really sleepy?"

Anna tilted her head up, smiling slyly at the twinkling in Lane's eyes. "Not as much as I should be."

Lane moved quickly, rolling over so she hovered above Anna. "Good. Because," Lane kissed her, once, before pulling back, "I *really* want to taste you."

Anna actually gulped.

Sleep be damned.

The smell of coffee awoke Anna to an empty bed. She stretched her arm out to make sure, and forced her eyes open when it confirmed that there was definitely no Lane. Glancing at the alarm clock, she groaned. It was only nine. Three hours of sleep meant that Anna was in for a very long day.

With languid slowness, she slipped out of bed and pulled on a pair of pyjama shorts and a tank top. Before heading downstairs, she stopped by the bathroom.

As she turned to dry her hands on a towel, something in the mirror caught her eye. Turning so her back was to the mirror, she looked over her shoulder and raised her eyebrows, a smirk playing on her lips. There were four very red lines peeking out from the racer back of her tank. Pulling her shirt up, Anna peered over her shoulder again to see that she had some very impressive scratch marks starting from the small of her back. Trying not to feel a little cocky at that, Anna pulled her shirt back down and headed downstairs.

Music reached her ears halfway down, and Anna smiled as she walked into the kitchen. Lane sashayed around the room, radio up loud and two mugs of coffee on the bench. The mouth-watering smell of eggs and bacon hit her. Lane was wearing a pair of Anna's shorts, deliciously tight on her, and her shirt from yesterday. Spatula in hand, Lane turned, grinning when she saw Anna standing in the doorframe. Lane danced up to her, hips moving in a way that Anna found incredibly sexy and stupidly adorable at the same time.

In one smooth motion, Lane wrapped her arms around Anna's waist and kissed her. "Good morning."

Reciprocating the embrace, Anna grinned. "Morning."

"I hope you don't mind." Lane nodded her head behind her to the stove. "I kind of helped myself."

"Oh, I hate it when hot women get up and make me breakfast and coffee after a night of fantastic sex." Anna shook her head. "Just terrible."

With a swat on Anna's bottom with the spatula, Lane danced away, turning down the radio slightly as she did so. "I do spoil you."

Not wasting any more time, Anna went for the coffee. "You really do. By the way, I think you should wear those shorts every day."

Lane looked over her shoulder wriggled her hips. Turning, Lane put the spatula down, walked up to Anna and pressed her back against the bench. With deliberate mischief in her eyes, Anna held the coffee up against Lane's lips, tipping it back slightly to give her a sip. Lane swallowed and licked her lips.

"I make good coffee."

"You really do. Another check on the girlfriend list."

Lane's eyebrows shot up, and Anna's own eyes widened as she realised what she'd said. They stared at each other a second.

"Uh...girlfriend?"

Anna's eyes were still wide. "Um..."

"Stop looking like you're about to throw up. It's fine, slip of words, or whatever."

As Lane started to turn back to the food, Anna quickly grabbed her hand and yanked her back. "No, Lane. I don't want to throw up." She smiled a little. "Uh, that kind of just came out."

Lane just watched her and waited.

"Everything is...complicated. My situation is complex. You know that already. I don't know how to do this, with the kids."

Slowly, Lane nodded. Her dark eyes were soft as she watched Anna.

"They've had so much change already, that me dating someone, having someone else who needs lots of my time, I don't know if I want to do that to them." Anna paused, eyes looking searchingly into Lane's. "But I don't want this to stop. You—well, I have so much fun with you. You make me feel, I don't know..." Anna gave a little shrug. "You make everything make sense." She grabbed a handful of Lane's shirt, pulling her harder against her. "But we definitely are not just messing around. If you want, I'd like to say girlfriend." Anna looked up at Lane from under her lashes, almost shy.

A slow smile worked its way to Lane's lips. "You like to give speeches a little, don't you?"

"That's what you have to say to that?"

"Well, my answer's so obvious." Lane kissed her, once. "Of course I want to be."

Anna reached up to cup Lane's cheeks, pulling her in for another kiss. Her heart was pounding—the words had been so unplanned, this commitment not something she had thought she wanted. Forethought was normally a priority for Anna, yet, this time, it had felt right to just say what was on her mind.

In one swift motion, Lane's hands ran down Anna's sides to her thighs and she tugged, lifting Anna up onto the bench. Anna wrapped her legs around Lane, crossing her ankles to lock them together.

"Food?" Anna asked between kisses.

"Fuck the food." Lane practically growled, pushing her hand up under Anna's tank top, automatically going to her breast.

Anna arched her back, pulling at Lane's shirt, lifting it up. Just as she was about to yank it over her head, groaning at the feel of Lane's fingers on her nipple, a knock sounded from the front door.

They both paused almost comically, staring at each other.

"Expecting someone?"

Anna shook her head. "It's probably Mum, needing something for Toby or something."

Heaving an overdramatic sigh, Lane tugged her shirt down and turned to the stove, switching it off. "Alright, you get the door, I'm going upstairs to the bathroom, then we eat?"

Still sitting on the bench, Anna grinned. "Or we can resume on the kitchen bench, then eat?"

Lane chuckled, looking over her shoulder on her way out the door, eying Anna flirtatiously. "Deal."

Tugging her shirt back in to place, Anna watched Lane leave the room. That woman really would be the death of her.

As she made her way to the front door, Anna realised that she actually missed Ella and Toby, and it had been less than twenty-four hours since she'd seen them. If they were home, Ella would be loudly running for the door and Toby would be trying to scale Anna's legs as she tried to get there before Ella.

Cool air hit her as she pulled the door open. Before she could control her reaction, her mouth dropped open when she saw who was standing there.

"Uh…"

Sally's mother gave a short nod. She was a mousy woman of approximately Anna's height. Her greying auburn hair was cut in a stylish bob. In her hands was a plastic bag, overly full. She looked Anna up and down, one eyebrow arched, and quirked her lips in what was probably a smile.

"Anna. Hi."

Anna swallowed. "Hi, Mrs Larsen."

"Call me Cathy, Anna."

"Right. Cathy. This is unexpected. Did you want to come in?"

Cathy stayed put, looking behind Anna questioningly. "I thought I'd come to see my grandchildren. Ella would be at school, I know. But I thought I could say hi to Toby."

Anna was surprised. Where was the phone call beforehand? The warning? Sally's parents saw the kids on important occasions, with the odd smattering of visits over the year, and that was all, as far as Anna was aware.

However, in spite of this knowledge, Anna felt herself softening slightly towards the uncomfortable-looking woman standing in front of her whose daughter had died. She probably wanted to make a connection to all that was left of Sally.

"I'm really sorry, Cathy, Toby's with my mum. He'd normally be in day care right now, anyway. Are you sure you don't want to come in?"

Cathy ignored the question. "He's not here? And what do you mean, in day care?"

"Well, it's Friday, I'm normally at work, so he goes to the day care there."

"You don't stay home with him?"

"Um, no. I'm an anaesthetist. I work full time."

Cathy nodded to herself. "Oh. I thought Sally stayed at home with them."

"She did." Anna wasn't sure what was going on.

"Yet you aren't working today?"

"I start at twelve." Why was she explaining herself to this woman?

"So why on earth would Toby not be here?"

Anna was starting to get a little bit irritated. She stood straighter, levelling her shoulders, careful to watch her tone. "There was an emergency at the hospital, and I had to stay late last night."

Suddenly, Anna desperately hoped that Lane wouldn't come down the stairs in those stupidly tiny, sexy shorts.

Cathy's expression didn't alter, but her eyebrows raised slightly at Anna's words. "I see."

Her mouth opened to make excuses, to say it was a rare occurrence, the first time; she closed it though. She didn't have to explain herself to this woman. Instead she said, "You're welcome to see the kids, Cathy. Maybe a call beforehand would be best, however?" Trying not to sound confrontational, Anna kept her voice light.

Cathy nodded, holding out the bag for Anna to take. "I brought over some toys for them. Would you mind giving them to the kids?" Her face was so blank, Anna didn't know what to think. She took the bag.

"Of course. I'm happy to. They'll be very excited."

Cathy nodded once, opening her mouth to say something. The sound of footsteps distracted her, and she looked behind Anna to see who was coming down the stairs.

Anna closed her eyes briefly and took in a deep breath. *Of course.*

When Anna opened her eyes again, the look on Cathy's eyes had hardened and a small polite smile had appeared on her lips.

Anna looked over her shoulder, suddenly incredibly grateful her back was away from Cathy, scratches hidden. She was careful to not turn to her side.

Lane was walking down the stairs, those shorts looking tinier than ever on her amazing legs, shirt in slight disarray.

Anna was just thankful it covered the bite mark she knew was on her shoulder, though Lane was sporting very distinct bed hair. Anna was fairly certain she herself looked like she had just rolled out of bed after a night of sex and little sleep. This was not going well.

Lane caught her eye, giving her a curious look before her gaze reached Cathy. Lane smiled widely, friendly as always. At the bottom of the stairs, she hovered, obviously unsure if she should walk forward. She settled for leaning against the banister, self-consciously tugging at the shorts, smile still wide.

"Uh, hi," she said to Cathy.

Anna finally turned her head back to look at Cathy, trying not to roll her eyes at the woman's hardened look.

Light blue eyes looked from Anna to Lane and back again. "Hello." Her voice was cool.

Anna wanted her gone. This was uncomfortable, and, from what Anna knew of the woman, she could tell she was currently having her entire lifestyle judged.

"Cathy, this is Lane. Lane," she looked over her shoulder again, widening her eyes slightly at Lane before neutralising her expression, "this is Sally's mum, Cathy."

Lane's smile, to her credit, didn't falter. "Pleasure to meet you, Cathy."

Anna looked back to Cathy, who nodded again. "I'm sure." She turned to Anna, eyes hardening properly. "I wasn't born yesterday."

That look almost made Anna step backwards—she wanted to be as far away from that as she could.

"I always wondered about you."

Anna dug her fingers harder into the door knob. She had, before this, been incredibly lucky and had never had true bigotry directed at her. Which was a good thing—she was not enjoying it.

"I think it might be best for you to leave, Cathy."

She could almost feel Lane's hesitation behind her, as if unsure if she should move up to stand beside Anna or stay put. Anna was relieved when she stayed put.

Cathy's lips had paled slightly. "I agree. Please, give those gifts to my grandchildren."

Anna nodded. "Of course." Her heart was racing in her ears.

At the bottom of the steps, Cathy stopped, turning to face Anna again. With the light hitting her face, Anna could see the red sheen in her hair that had been inherited by Sally and Ella, could almost see Sally in her features. The sight knotted her stomach.

"Anna, you should really think about what's best for those two children."

Anna's nails bit into the door handle harder. "That's all I do, Cathy."

The answer was quick. "I've not seen much that says that."

Cathy took her in for a minute, eyes squinting in the bright light, before turning on her heel and walking down the front walk.

Anna let out a long breath, lips pursing as she blew the air out. She closed her eyes for a second, trying to calm her racing heart, then closed the door behind her and looked at Lane, who was staring at her.

"How dare she?" Lane's voice burst out and Anna almost jumped. "Aren't you livid, Anna? How dare she come to *your* house and have a go at you like that."

In other circumstances, Anna would have smiled.

"And she was so smarmy! Smiling all cold while glaring at us both like we were a pair of hussies."

Anna finally spoke. "Well, that was all just spectacular timing, wasn't it?"

Lane paused and cracked a smile. "It was."

"I mean, of course the zealously religious grandmother of the kids I've taken on shows up when I've left the kids with my mother to stay at work into the wee hours of the morning and then have loud lesbian sex in the house her daughter lived in."

Even as she laughed, Lane asked, "How are you calm?"

"I'm not. At all." She really wasn't. "But that was nothing compared to stories Sally told me." Anna stepped forward, hand gripping Lane's and pulling her forward against her. "I'm not okay with being judged like that, but that's just who she is. She would've found out I'm gay eventually."

"Yeah, but—" Anna cut her off with a kiss. When she broke it, Lane was smiling. "Is it weird that I'm totally okay with being shut up like that?"

"No."

"Good."

Pushing Lane backwards, Anna looked at her coyly. "We have a couple of hours before I have to drag my tired ass to work. Bench?" She gave Lane a charming grin.

"Then food. That was the deal."

"I can get on board with that."

Lane grabbed her by the hips as they walked through the kitchen doorway, spinning Anna so her back hit the bench when they stumbled to it.

Lane leant back, appraising Anna with her eyes. "Okay, shorts off."

Complying wasn't a difficult concept.

Chapter Fifteen

"Someone's happy."

Anna tried to wipe the smile off her face that had been a permanent resident since arriving to the hospital. It was three p.m. and she'd only been at work a few hours, but she was practically dead on her feet as the last few days caught up to her. It didn't stop the grin, however. Anna handed cash to the coffee attendant and turned to look at Kym, who stood behind her, amused, hands in her lab coat pocket.

"Anna, go back to smiling, now you look like you've sucked on a lemon but you secretly enjoyed it."

Quickly, Anna relaxed her face. "Can we add a skinny latte to that order?" she asked the attendant, handing over more cash.

It wasn't until they were standing to the side, waiting for their orders, that Kym went back to staring at her. Anna simply stared back.

"You had sex."

At Kym's words, Anna whipped her head around, thankful to find that no one was in earshot.

When she looked back to Kym, the woman looked gleeful. "Well, that answered that."

Opening her mouth, to argue, Anna shut it with a shrug.

"About time you two got there. Worth the wait?"

"Definitely."

"You're not going to give me details, are you?"

Anna shook her head, cheeks hurting from trying to smother her happiness.

"Not one? Help a widow out."

"Are you seriously playing the widow card?"

"Without shame, too."

Anna narrowed her eyes. "What do you want to know?"

"Was it as good as you'd think it would be, considering doing something simple like holding a door open for her led to you oozing sex?"

"We aren't that bad!"

"Oh, it was that bad."

Finally caving, Anna grinned. "Yes, it was that amazing."

"The widow card won't get me any more information than that, will it?"

"Nope."

"You look disgustingly happy."

"I shouldn't, I only slept three hours."

"Ha! Detail. I win."

Anna laughed as she accepted their coffees, handing one over to Kym.

They turned and started heading towards their offices. Kym bumped her hip playfully against Anna's. "I'm glad you showed up. I've never seen Lane so happy."

"Really?"

"Really."

Now rather smug, Anna sipped her coffee. "Did you go home last night at all?" Together, they leant against the back of the elevator wall.

"Got caught up. I was Psych liaison with the families. I got a little sleep in an on-call room."

As gently as she could, Anna said, "Maybe you should move, Kym."

"Not yet."

Looking at the elevator buttons, Anna nodded. "Okay."

It was suddenly silent, and Anna could tell Kym needed a topic change and was coming up blank. So, she said the thing that first popped into her head. "Wanna come for a sleepover?"

"What?"

"Come for a sleepover. Again."

"Well, the last one wasn't intentional."

"Yeah, but you and Ella asleep on the couch was cute as hell."

"That kid is cute as hell. You putting it on Facebook was not cute in any way." Kym led the way out of the elevators as the doors opened.

"It got seventy-one likes. Don't change the subject—come."

"Of course I'll come. When?"

"What about tomorrow night? Saturday night is a big night in kid world."

"How so?"

"Well, Ella doesn't really have a bed time. Exciting stuff."

Kym laughed. "Count me in. Will Lane come? Oh! Girl night!"

Anna had been thinking of attempting to move a little slow, not see Lane too much, focus on the kids. But then Kym's eyes lit up like they just did, and she didn't think she could say no. "What about Tobes?"

"He's under six, he doesn't count. And he sleeps early."

"Fair call. I'll ask Lane."

"As if she'd say no."

Anna rolled her eyes, following Kym down the hallway.

"So I get to see Nurse Lane *and* Kym tonight?"

A laugh huffed out of Anna as she chopped a carrot. "Yup."

"*And* I get to see Nurse Lane on Monday to take off my cast?"

Anna laughed again, adding the carrot to the plate with the crackers, cheese and dip she was compiling. "You definitely do."

"Awesome!" Ella spun on her heel and dashed out, careening upstairs and yelling about getting into her pyjamas.

Shaking her head, Anna looked down at her feet, where Toby was currently pulling at her laces. "Hungry, little man?"

Toby looked up at her, neck craning and blue eyes huge, grinning as he tried to shove her shoelace into his mouth.

Anna bent down and pulled it out, lifting him up and onto her hip. His little hand grasped at her tank top. "Want some pasta?"

He widened his eyes at her. "Pata?"

She widened her eyes back at him. "Pasta! Hey, that's a new word. Too clever for your own good, you are." She walked him around the bench and plopped him into his high chair, putting a carrot stick down to keep him occupied while she reheated pasta from a previous evening.

Betrayed, Toby looked down at it, brow furrowed. "Pata?"

"It's coming, Tobes."

He eyed Anna for a minute as if to make sure she was telling the truth, watching her walk to the fridge and pull out the bowl. Finally, he smiled, picking up the carrot stick and only hitting himself in the cheek once before getting it into his mouth.

As she waited for the microwave to ding, Anna tried—and failed—not to overthink her situation. Lane was coming over, but she'd left the sleepover part out when telling her, just mentioning girls' night with the three of them and Ella—and Toby. Anna would have loved nothing more than for Lane to stay over, but the idea also filled her with dread. She didn't think they should be doing sleepovers yet. They were new, and Anna had her heart set on not confusing the kids. Kym staying and sleeping on the couch was one thing. But Lane staying, in her bed? A completely different thing.

The microwave's beeping pulled her out of her reverie. Anna pulled out the just-warm pasta—a dish even she couldn't mess up—gave it a quick stir and put it in front of Toby. She sat in the chair next to him and watched him attempt to feed himself. Eventually she took over, since his efforts generally led to food on the floor, in his hair and on his lap. Anna had found peas in Toby's ears more times than was probably normal.

The first spoon was just making it in when she heard Ella thundering down the stairs again, pyjama clad and practically bouncing. She climbed up on a chair opposite Anna.

"I got my pjs on and I brought some stuff to make Nurse Lane and Kym a card and do you think we can have ice cream after pizza tonight—wait, what DVD can we watch? Can we watch two?"

Anna blinked at Toby, who was looking at her with an equally bemused expression. Both of them turned to look at Ella. Toby's mouth still hung open as he leant forward for the spoon blindly, staring at Ella like he'd never met her before. Anna put the spoon in his mouth and tried to figure out how to respond to Ella's overly excited speech.

"Uh—wow. Slow down, Ella Bella. We can try for two DVDs, though we may sit in here for the start of the first one, okay?"

Ella looked absolutely devastated and almost dropped her pencil. "What? Why?"

Anna felt a little terrible. "We might have a glass of wine and talk about work."

Ella screwed her nose up. "Ew. Work."

"Exactly. Work." Anna laughed, spooning more food into Toby's mouth. "But, I promise we won't be too long, and then we'll all come snuggle on the couch with you, okay? You can eat your pizza in there in front of the TV, and we'll have ours here, then we'll all hang out."

Happy with this, Ella nodded, wriggling in her chair. "I can really eat dinner in front of the TV?"

Anna winked at her. "This once."

The kid was going to burst with the excitement of it all.

Ella went about colouring in, while Toby happily finished up his dinner. When he got to the stage of clamping his mouth shut and shaking his head adamantly, Anna wiped his face and put him on the ground to go and reign unholy terror, just as the doorbell rang.

"They're here!" Ella almost fell in the attempt to get out of her chair, then bolted off to the front door.

"Ella!"

"Check who it is first, I know!"

Sighing as she followed, Anna heard excited words and the door swung open to show Kym and Lane, Kym clutching a bottle of wine and Lane holding pizza.

"Hi!" Ella squealed.

Both Lane and Kym grinned down at the over-excited girl, Kym stepping forward to have arms wrapped around her waist.

"Ella! Ready to share the couch again?"

Ella looked up at Kym, absolutely delighted she was there. "Silly, I have a bed."

Kym's mouth dropped open in fake shock, looking up to Anna. "Did I just get rejected by a six-year-old?"

Lane poked her in the back gently with the two pizza boxes she was holding. "Afraid so, Kym."

Ella shook her head. "No! I'll share the couch with you. Can we make pancakes in the morning again?"

"We sure can."

Ella then threw herself on Lane, her attention at once completely refocused. "Nurse Lane!"

Kym made her way to Anna, kissed her cheek, and handed over bottles. "I come bearing wine."

"Thank you."

"Nurse Lane, you're taking my cast off before school on Monday."

"Am I? I'll have to check with my personal assistant that I can make it and I'm not all booked out."

Ella's face fell. "You might not be there?"

"Kidding, Ella, it's written in my diary! Of course I'll be there."

Ella followed Kym into the kitchen, pulling Lane after her. Lane was dragged past Anna, grinning all the while, and Anna just wanted to kiss her; she looked so delicious. They settled for staring at each other and mumbling a completely enamoured "hey" back and forth, Lane's arm brushing Anna's front as she went by.

Eventually, they managed to settle Ella down with some slices of pizza and a DVD while the three women ate their own dinners with glasses of wine and Anna's cheese plate in the kitchen.

Toby sat happily on Anna's lap, starting to look sleepy, leaning back heavily against her as he chewed on a cracker.

"So, I went back to group therapy yesterday." Kym looked nervous at the admission.

Lane unsuccessfully tried to hide her surprise. "Yeah? How did that go?"

Kym shrugged, eyeing her food. Anna wondered when she should be worried about the amount of time Kym spent staring at food and not eating it.

"Fine. I even stayed the whole time."

"That's great, Kym."

Finally taking a bite of pizza, Kym gave another half shrug. "So, you two are finally sleeping together."

Lane literally spat out her wine and Anna choked on her pizza, looking pointedly down at Toby.

"Oh, please, Anna, he's almost asleep and he's a baby. He doesn't know what I mean."

"Bo-bo." Toby murmured around his cracker.

"See."

Anna squeezed Toby against her, and caught Lane giving her a soft look as she did so. "He's asking for his bottle; he's a little genius. See, he completely knows what's going on."

Lane fake-glared Kym as Anna got up to get Toby's bottle ready. "No talk about s-e-x in front of the baby."

"You two just want to hold out on details. I already know you were going at it pretty much all night." Kym took a triumphant sip of her wine.

Whipping her head around, Lane stared at Anna. "You told her that?" She appeared torn between smugness and feeling appalled at the over-share.

Wide-eyed, Anna looked at her as she put the bottle into a jug of hot water to warm it up. "What! No, I just said *I* only got three hours sleep. Kym's dirty little brain took it elsewhere."

With narrow eyes, Lane watched Kym drink her wine happily. "You are evil."

"You're just so easy to rile up."

Chuckling, Anna started to walk out of the kitchen. "I'll be right back, guys, just going to put Tobes down. Say g'night, Toby."

Toby lifted his head up from Anna's shoulder and waved his hand. "Bye-bye."

The two at the table all but swooned.

"You certainly help with the ladies, little man."

Toby rested his head back on her shoulder and yawned.

Anna got him down with no fuss, and left him tucked up with his blue blanket under one arm and bottle in his mouth, eyes already closed. In the kitchen, the bottle of wine was looking dangerously close to empty.

"Are you two getting drunk to make it through Disney?"

"We're already both self-confessed kids' movie lovers."

"True. I didn't know how much I liked them until recently."

"Maybe that's another fault with your ability to look after the kids." Lane winked at her as she reached for a cracker.

"Yeah, maybe." At Kym's confused expression, Anna filled her in, "We may have had a visit from Sally's mum at an inconvenient time."

"The bigot we don't like? Please tell me you were clothed?"

Wincing, Anna shrugged. "Mostly. It was more the timing—she stopped in to see the kids just before nine. Instead she got me, Lane in shorts that may as well be underwear, the kids 'dumped' at my mother's and me a full-time worker. She was *not* impressed."

"Yikes. What did she do?"

Lane was only too happy to jump in. "Gave stony 'death to you all' eyes," she said. "Implied Anna wasn't good for the kids."

"Are you *fucking* kidding me?" Kym did not seem to find it as amusing as Anna was able to find it now.

Obviously happy that Kym was as outraged as she was, Lane looked triumphant. "Sadly, no. Anna was awesome though. She was all 'you should really think about what's best for the kids, Anna' and Anna was all smooth and 'that's all I ever do.'"

Anna flushed as Lane threw her a look.

"It was sexy as hell, actually." Lane wiggled her eyebrows.

"Break up the eye sex."

They tore their gazes away, and Anna shot Kym a sheepish look. "Sorry."

"At least you stood up for yourself."

"I know how to. Besides, she's just an angry lady filled with angry words. It doesn't matter."

"You're not mad?" Kym looked surprised.

"That's what I asked!"

"I was—I am, even. But it was also kind of funny and ironic and it doesn't matter. I need to let it go. She'll still be a part of the kids' lives, at least a little. I'm not going to keep them away from each other completely. So, I'll just think she's an idiot but play nice."

Kym nodded. "Very mature."

"I can be, sometimes."

They slowly finished their wine, Anna soaking up the company. The three had an easy banter, a way of talking things over without getting serious. And Anna was relieved that Kym ate two pieces of pizza and would be staying somewhere that wasn't the hospital.

They eventually moved after the third cry of, "Come *on,* guys!" from the living room. Kym flopped onto the modular couch next to Ella, who immediately crawled onto her lap, head resting back on her shoulder. Kym wrapped her arms around the girl, and Anna couldn't help but smile at the two—she was quickly learning that a cuddle from Ella or Toby made anything feel a little better.

Lane sat next to Kym, and Ella threw her arm out to rest on Lane's leg without taking her eyes off the screen. Anna dragged a giant blanket over all of them and sat next to Lane. Who would have thought sitting at home with kids and DVDs on a Saturday night would be something she'd enjoy so much?

They were all pressed in close, and when *Aladdin* finished, Anna lost three to one in *Monsters Inc.* versus *The Fox and the Hound. Monsters Inc.* won because it made everyone less sad. They settled in again, debating favourite characters and gasping theatrically at the mean monster.

Halfway through, silence settled over them as Ella began to slowly succumb to heavy lids. Kym pulled Ella down so that the small girl was lying in front of her, sharing Kym's pillow and blinking tiredly. The scene was cuter than Anna would expect from Kym, and she nudged Lane, then looked to Ella and Kym.

Following Anna's eyes, Lane chuckled quietly and looked back to Anna. "That's actually ridiculous."

Anna nodded, leaning more heavily into Lane now that Ella was starting to drift off. Lane's hand rested on her thigh, thumb rubbing small circles, a touch that started off sweet and comforting but soon started to make Anna's mind wander to what else they could be doing. She glanced over and saw that Ella was out and Kym was probably soon to follow. Would it really be so bad if they snuck upstairs quickly? She looked to Lane, who was looking at her like she'd read her mind.

They stared blankly at the TV for another ten minutes, Lane's hand slowly working its way up her inner thigh, the teasing making Anna have to focus incredibly hard on not breathing too erratically.

Anna finally tore her eyes from the TV, looked to see that Kym was fast asleep and snoring softly, Ella curled against her chest. She grabbed the hand that had been torturing her, standing and pulling Lane after her.

They both ran up the stairs, careful to keep their footsteps quiet. Without hesitating, Anna tugged Lane into her room and shut the door quietly. She grinned as Lane backed her against it gently, both careful not to make any thumping noises.

The whole being-quiet-but-burning-with-need thing was just making Anna hotter.

She bit her lip as Lane pressed her against the door and actually gave a soft moan. "Seriously, you have no idea how fucking hot you look when you do that."

"And you have no idea how much you just touching my leg works me up."

Lips inches from Anna's, Lane said, "I can *show* you how much simply touching you like that affects me."

Anna tilted her head, lips whispering against Lane's, their eyes intent on each other. "We have to be quick."

"I don't think that'll be an issue."

Lane kissed her, teeth dragging against her bottom lip, tongue demanding in Anna's mouth. Just as eager, Anna responded, thighs between legs as they rocked against each other, both careful to not make a sound.

In no time, Lane's hand was up her shirt, pushed under her bra, and her thumb swiped against Anna's nipple; she arched her back at the sensation and dragged her nails across the small of Lane's back, swallowing Lane's groan. Easily, Anna undid the button on Lane's jeans, slowly pulling down the zip.

"Shh."

Lane dropped her head onto Anna's shoulder as Anna pushed her hand down past Lane's underwear.

"Fuck, Lane."

Looking back at Anna, Lane's lips parted. "It's what you do to me."

Lips distracting Anna, Lane's hand left her shirt and pushing past Anna's waistband. A hiss escaped her lips as Lane's fingers moved against her.

Lane groaned into the kiss again. "You're so wet."

Fingers clawing, Anna wrapped a hand behind Lane's neck to press their foreheads together. Lane's spare hand wrapped around her waist, holding them steady.

Their movements were rushed, almost rough. As Lane pushed two fingers into her, Anna dropped her head back. Lane's lips were pressed to her neck, more nipping than biting. Anna pressed her fingers more firmly against Lane, feeling her teeth bite down harder. The movement of Anna's hips was uncontrollable as Lane moved her fingers.

She brought her head down, face pressing into Lane's shoulder, breath hot and fast against her skin. "Faster, Lane."

Lane complied, and Anna didn't know if she could be quiet anymore. She sped her own fingers up, their rhythm lost as they both started to come undone.

Anna came first, leg lifted up, wrapped around Lane, hips rolling forward. It was only minutes later that Lane's orgasm washed over her, Anna's name a whispered groan.

Breathing erratically, a giggle escaping her, Anna dropped her leg to the ground and let her head fall back against the door, cheeks red.

Lane grinned slowly, eyes slightly glazed. "What?"

Anna brought her head up to look into Lane's eyes, which now appeared almost black. "I've never come that fast."

Lane kissed her. "That was intense."

"I can't feel my legs."

"I think I have fingernail marks in the back of my neck."

Anna grimaced. "Sorry."

"Sorry? It was hot."

They stood for a few more minutes before Anna finally sighed. "I think now is where I sneak you out."

"I don't think you have to sneak me out when they know I'm here."

"True."

"I know I'm not going to stay the night, Anna."

Anna looked at her almost guiltily. "That obvious, huh?"

Lane brushed slightly dampened hair off Anna's cheek, then left her hand hovering against it. "I get it."

Anna's hand came up to rest on Lane's wrist, fingers wrapping around it gently. "You are far too understanding."

"I don't think so."

"Well, you are."

Anna kissed her again, trying to convey the emotion that always welled in her chest when Lane seemed to just *get* what was going on. Lane smiled into the kiss, and they parted, both grinning stupidly.

"Okay, let's go downstairs or I'm going to push you onto the bed and I'll never leave."

"That really doesn't make me want to go downstairs."

Lane shrugged. "Good." With a wink, she excused herself to the bathroom.

Anna slipped quietly into her brother's old room to use the en suite, not letting herself pause before walking in. She tried to not smirk at her flushed cheeks while quickly rearranging her hair to its pre-romp neatness.

She met Lane at the landing. Entwining their hands, they quietly went down the stairs. They both peeked into the living room and chuckled to see Kym and Ella still sound asleep, *Monsters Inc.* playing quietly on the screen. At the front door, Anna brought a hand up to cup Lane's cheek, pressing her lips to Lane's in a chaste goodbye.

"Talk tomorrow?"

"Definitely," Anna agreed, reluctantly pulling open the door.

"I'm looking forward to seeing the munchkin on Monday."

"So is she, trust me, Nurse Lane."

Finally, Lane stepped through the doorway. "Bye. Sleep well."

"I will now."

A chuckle was all Lane left behind as she disappeared down the walk.

Trying to contain a contented sigh, Anna closed the door and walked into the living room to shut off the TV. She made sure Kym and Ella were completely covered with the blanket before making her way out of the room.

"You're not kidding anyone."

Anna froze and turned back to the couch. Kym had her head propped up on her hand, elbow digging into the couch, voice low so as not to wake up Ella. She was grinning widely.

"Oh, shut up, Kym."

Kym's snickering followed her up the stairs.

Chapter Sixteen

"One day a child is going to come careening through that door."

Anna chuckled at Lane's words and burrowed further into her side. "Probably."

"I think I'll be more traumatised than the kids."

Sleepily lifting her head, Anna looked down at Lane. "I'm teasing. The door is locked. We would hear Ella yelling at me through it, and Toby's baby monitor is on."

Lane's face visibly relaxed and Anna lay back down. An easy silence settled in around them.

"Have you heard from Crazy Cathy?"

"No, she's left us well alone."

Already half-asleep, Lane hummed her approval.

Despite the bad taste Cathy had left in Anna's mouth, everything had slowly begun to settle over the last week. Kym came over for dinner, and the kids revelled in her attention. Lane and Anna acted like any friends would in front of the kids and used the night-time and days in the hospital to lavish affection on each other. Ella, now cast-free, seemed to enjoy having Lane and Kym around.

Anna and Lane slowly learnt how to map each other's bodies, until sometimes, during sex, Anna wasn't sure where Lane ended and she began. They'd move, coming together urgently, a dance that began when Anna first walked through the doors in the morning to see Lane holding out a coffee and smiling. More than once they met in inappropriate places around the hospital.

Never had she been with someone where conversation came just as easily as the physical side. And what an incredible physical side that was.

"You know," Anna pressed her lips to Lane's clavicle, "someone told me something last week."

"Mm?" Lane turned her head, face against Anna's hair.

"They said they'd never seen you happier than the last couple of months."

"Bloody Kym."

"I'm just—I'm glad. That I make you happy."

"Good." Lane murmured. "Because you really, really do."

Lane rolled suddenly so Anna was under her, head perched on her hand, elbow digging into the pillow. Their legs slipped together easily, smile fading at the intense look that had taken over Lane's face.

"You keep saying thanks to me, for being understanding, and for everything."

Anna was mesmerised by the way Lane's lips moved, the way her eyes darkened, the way the light played across her skin—skin Anna could easily touch all day.

"But you have no idea how grateful I am that you ran me over with a shopping cart."

"So glad I bruised you."

"So was I. I went to that party and told Kym I'd been run over by the hottest brunette I'd ever seen."

At Anna's disagreeing look, Lane stamped a kiss to her cheek. "You are."

"You're just saying that because I put out."

"True."

"I mean it though, and Kym was just being polite in her wording—you really have made me stupidly happy. It isn't just that I wasn't really happy before, I was actually just coming out of a patch of being pretty miserable."

Anna's face darkened with concern. "Miserable?"

"I had been feeling a little stagnant. I loved my job, but things here were rough. When Kym's husband died, well, I knew him fairly well, and she was a mess, and it seemed like all the women I met were crazy. My ex and I had been over for a while, but the sting of her cheating lingered."

As she listened to Lane talk, Anna pushed Lane's hair behind her ear and let the tendrils play between her fingers. She knew much of this, but it had mostly come out in banter.

"I wasn't sure if I would trust someone again." Lane licked her lips nervously, and when Anna went to speak, Lane rushed on, "I wasn't blameless in that break up though, Anna."

"What do you mean?" Anna watched her intently. "Did you cheat on her too?"

The thought made Anna's heart speed up. Everybody made mistakes, but the idea of Lane cheating seemed so foreign to who Anna thought she was.

"No. Not that. But just as bad."

Lane dropped back so she lay on her side, leaning on her elbow. Anna mirrored her, leg hooked over Lane's hip to keep them connected. Despite how close their faces were, Lane avoided eye contact.

"What happened, Lane?"

A flush had risen on Lane's cheeks. "When I met Alex, she was in a relationship. The first time something happened between us, I didn't know that. But I did after. And it kept happening. I—there's no excuse. I guess I thought I believed her when she said they were having problems and were going to end. But it took a long time. I was the other woman for a long time, waiting for that relationship to end."

Anna blinked. She would never have thought Lane would put herself in that position. They were silent for a minute as Anna digested the information.

Obviously nervous, fingers picking at the sheet over Anna's hip, Lane gave a half shrug. "It was a bad move, and I didn't feel good about it. I really did think they were ending, but at the same time, I knew they weren't over and I let it continue. I found out a year into our relationship through someone that knew them that Alex's girlfriend had been blindsided when she ended it." Lane paused. "Clearly Alex was lying to both of us."

"You didn't know it was that serious, Lane," Anna said. The grim smile on Lane's lips tugged at her heart.

"I knew something. I wasn't innocent in it. I was infatuated with her, I don't know why. I thought that she and I had something, and whenever I had doubts she was so good at talking me around to waiting."

"Everyone makes mistakes."

Lane finally met her eye. "Before that happened, I didn't think I was the kind of person who would do something like that. I was really critical of other people who did. When she finally ended it, I thought that was it. That was the reason I had kept going—because Alex and I were serious. We lived together, did the civil partnership thing. But then..." Lane sighed. "Then Alex slowly became really distant. Wasn't home as often. Didn't answer her phone..."

"The woman who was painting your porch?"

"It had been going on for six months."

Anna's mouth dropped open. "Six months!"

Lane flopped onto her back. "I felt so stupid, Anna. Of course she cheated on me. She'd done it before, why would I be different?"

At the tightness in Lane's voice, Anna shifted forward so she was pressed along her side. "What do you mean?"

"I thought we had something serious, which was why I let it start so terribly. Then, though...then it ended the same way it started. There was no justification to what I did."

"Hey."

Lane kept her eyes trained on the ceiling.

"Lane, look at me." Finally, those dark eyes caught her own, and Anna gave a soft smile. "Okay, what you did wasn't the greatest. But Alex was in the wrong. She was the responsible one in both of those relationships. She obviously has no respect for relationships or women."

With a slight huff, Lane looked back to the ceiling.

"Hey! It's true. And she's an idiot to give you up." This time, Lane completely rolled her eyes. Anna's fingers gripped her cheek and tugged gently so Lane had to look at her. "She is an idiot."

"Anyway, I just wanted you to understand. After that, I was pretty burned. I'd rushed into a relationship in the worst way possible. And it ended terribly. It was a really bad year after that, and then Kym's husband and—I was down."

The look on Lane's face was so sincere, and Anna surged forward, kissing her firmly. "Are you still down?"

Pushing Anna onto her back, Lane half sprawled on top of her. "No. I'm not. And that's thanks to you."

Black eyes stared down at her, and Anna ran her fingers against Lane's cheek. Strangely, Lane's past didn't make Anna question her morals; rather, it made her even more sure of them. The look on Lane's face as she'd confessed and told the story, the way she accepted her part of the blame. How she had obviously taken something away from that lesson.

Lane leant into the touch slightly as she continued, "So, stop saying thank you to me. Because I will do the same and say it to you over and over again but, trust me, it's annoying."

Lane's nose nuzzled against Anna's cheek, lips pressing against her mouth.

Lane pulled back, eyes soft. "What we have—this is pretty amazing."

"It is."

They held eye contact, skin to skin.

Breathless with the feeling that bubbled up in her chest, Anna didn't know what to say. The emotion Lane induced was almost overpowering at times like this. Everything just said made Anna want to wrap Lane in her arms and protect her. It all felt so fast, but in other ways so slow. Anna wrapped her arms around Lane, flipping them over smoothly, and settled between Lane's legs. With an intensity that left them both gasping, Anna kissed her.

"What was that for?" Lane asked, hands entwining in her hair as Anna moved her lips against Lane's neck.

She couldn't answer, emotion swelling in her throat. Instead, she kissed her again as hard as she could, fingers biting into the skin of Lane's hip. Lane returned the kiss in kind, both hands holding Anna's face to her.

Everything Anna felt, she poured into that kiss.

Lane arched against her.

It was two hours later that Lane finally rolled her way out of the bed.

On her stomach, Anna lay with her chin resting on her forearm, lying with her head down the wrong end of the bed. Her legs were bent at the knees, ankles crossed, feet in the air.

As she pulled on her clothes, Lane looked down at her.

"I think you should pull that sheet off."

"It's barely covering me."

Lane bent over pressing a kiss to Anna's bare shoulder as she did up her jeans. "Any cover is too much. You have the perfect ass. Why cover it?"

"I'd argue yours is better."

"You'll lose."

Reaching forward, Anna wrapped her fingers around Lane's wrist. When Anna tugged at Lane for a kiss, she shook her head as Anna tried to pull her back down onto the bed.

Anna pouted as Lane pulled back, sliding her bra on and smiling down at Anna's puppy eyes. "If you insist on these hideous rules that include me sneaking out at stupid hours, you have to deal with me leaving your bed."

"Fine."

"Easy for you to be grumpy, you don't have to work in…" Now fully dressed, Lane checked her watch, stifling a groan, "ugh, six hours."

"I do get jumped on in approximately four. Five if I'm lucky."

"Yeah, and then you have a hard day of hanging out with two cuties and going to the park."

Anna rolled onto her back, arm under her head and eyes on Lane. A smirk played on her lips as Lane's eyes automatically slid to her chest. Anna closed her eyes.

"You make it sound like they aren't hard work. Plus, I have grocery shopping." She opened her eyes again. "You can do that instead if you want?"

Blinking, Lane tore her eyes away and grabbed her bag off the floor, slinging it over her shoulder. "I think you make up the stories of them being a handful."

"Don't make me leave them with you all day."

Eyes wide, Lane raised her hands. "Touché."

"Go before I drag you back into bed."

Leaning over Anna so her face hovered above Anna's, Lane's hair fell around them. "You can drag me back to bed. But I won't get out of it twice."

"Damn."

With a laugh, Lane kissed her again. As she pulled back, Anna was grinning. "What?"

"Spiderman kiss."

"You are a dork."

Rolling onto her stomach, Anna watched her walk away. "Lane."

Lane paused in the door and turned to look at her. "Yeah?"

"Thanks for telling me."

"Thanks for listening."

With one last look, Lane walked out.

Coffee with Kym started as it usually did—whoever was there first ordered. So this time, when Anna walked up, Kym was seated at one of their tables with two takeaway cups in front of her.

Anna slid into her seat. "Oh, we're sitting at the hospital coffee cart today? Fancy."

"I thought we'd step it up a notch."

"Great, because I actually have time."

"No appointment?"

Anna shot Kym a confused look. Kym stared innocently over her coffee cup.

"What do you mean?"

"Oh, I thought you might have had a page to meet in a cleaner's closet." Kym laughed in delight as Anna flushed.

"I—you—oh, shut up Kym."

"What, no denial?"

"We don't go to the cleaners' closets."

"A bit late, Anna."

Anna sipped her coffee almost desperately. "*Anyway.* How was yesterday? You said Sunday night one of your patients was reacting to his meds?"

"Nice change of subject. I'll allow it."

"Only because you want to talk about your work."

"Well, it was fine. I fixed it."

Anna laughed. "I wouldn't expect anything less. Ella was asking when you're coming for dinner this week."

"Because we share a special bond."

"Of course. Oh—guess who we had a visit from last night?"

"Sally's charming mother?"

Anna made a face. "Ew. No. Some new caseworker, George Coleman."

"Toby clothed this time?"

"Yes, thankfully. And Ella wasn't trying to force him to cross-dress."

"Why was it someone new?"

Shrugging, Anna answered. "I don't know. He wasn't the friendliest guy. He said something about Lorna being unavailable."

"So, it's all routine?" Kym eyed her over her coffee.

"Yeah, all routine. And it went fine. He didn't stay long. Just kind of popped in, drank some tea, asked how everything was, looked at the house and left."

"Well, you're probably the least of their concerns. The will dictated you as guardian, you're in a stable job, the kids are settling in as well as they can be."

"Yeah, well, Ella was well behaved and in one of her quiet moods, and Toby was shy but charming."

"I'd expect nothing else from him."

Anna rolled her eyes. "You can't adopt him, Kym."

"No, but I can claim him any time I'm over. And Ella."

Anna couldn't really argue with that—the kids loved Kym. "That you can. By the way, Ella requested you read her a story. Between you and Lane, these kids are getting spoilt."

"Between *you* and Lane, *you're* getting spoilt."

Anna's pager went off, saving her a retort. She glanced down at it and stood, drinking the last of her coffee. "Anyway, smartass, like I said, Ella asked if you could come to dinner again. See you tonight?"

"Definitely. Lane calling again?"

"No, I'm off to practice actual medicine." Anna turned and started to walk off before looking over her shoulder. "Then I'm seeing Lane." She could practically feel Kym's smirk as she walked away.

Maybe they needed to stop meeting all over the hospital.

A buzzing in her pocket pulled her attention to her phone as she stood waiting for the elevator. Anna turned for the empty stairwell to give herself more time to chat.

"Hey, Mum."

"Anna, hello darling."

"How are you?"

"I'm good, just wondering... I'm going to do a big cook up of meatloaf Thursday, I thought maybe I could bring some around Friday night for you to freeze and have for the kids?"

Excitement shot through Anna: she loved her mother's meatloaf, and so did the kids. "That's something I would be very okay with you doing, Mum, thanks."

"Lovely. Maybe I could stay for dinner?"

"If you didn't I'd be concerned."

"And maybe, I could stay for a few hours?"

"Of course."

"And maybe, you could use this as an opportunity to go out on a date with Lane." Anna actually stopped mid-step, a smirk on her face. "Subtle, Mum."

"Nothing's subtle about playing Cupid, Anna. He uses arrows, I have to use my brain."

Anna bit her lip, thinking as she started climbing the stairs. "That would actually be amazing."

She could hear Sandra's sly grin over the phone. "Excellent. You can get out of the bloody house."

"Mum! I leave the house."

"Grocery shopping doesn't count, Anna."

"I—"

"Nor does work."

She had nothing.

"Precisely. We both miss Jake. We both want what is best for the kids. But we both need to try and have a life, too. Now, you take Lane on a nice date. There can be flowers—oh! Definitely buy her flowers! And go for a walk."

"It's freezing out."

"A drive then. A romantic one. I hear there's this spot people go to—"

"Yes, Mum."

"Good. And I can be with my lovely grandchildren."

She turned up the last flight. "They'll love that. They love any time with you." There was a pause, and then a sudden silence on the phone. "Mum?"

"That—that's just so nice to hear."

Panic rising in her, a soft sigh left Anna's her lips. "Oh, Mum. Are you okay?"

"Yes, yes. I'm fine, just being silly. Your father's disappeared into his office again. I'm just looking forward to some family time."

"Why don't I hang with you and the kids Friday night?"

"No! Don't be silly. I want you to have some fun. Take that beautiful woman out. Like I said to the caseworker yesterday, you need to have your time, too."

Anna stopped again. "To who?"

"The caseworker, Lorna, called."

"That's strange, we had a different caseworker at the house last night?"

"She said it was all routine, to just ask how people close to you felt everything was going."

"What…what did you say?" She didn't know why her heart was pounding.

"Anna, get that worry out of your voice. I told her you were doing an amazing job, she said she thought so, too."

"Oh. But why would she still be in contact if we had the new guy?"

"I don't know, maybe they like to get separate opinions. Relax, Anna."

Taking a deep breath, Anna nodded. "Yeah, you're right." When she reached the floor she wanted, she leant against the railing to wrap up the conversation. "This guy was just not as friendly. Lorna was nicer the other two times."

"Anyway, as I said, you need some fun. Not to spend even more time with your mother and niece and nephew. I'm babysitting Friday night. You don't get a choice."

A beeping made Anna look down at her pager. "Okay, *fine,* I'll take the pretty woman out to dinner. Only because you're making me."

"As if. You were taking pretty women out before I knew anything about it."

"Very funny."

"It's true. Don't think I haven't twigged about those 'sleepovers' you had when you got a bit older."

Grimacing, Anna just wanted to get off the phone. "Mum, I really gotta go."

"Yeah, nice timing. Go save lives—love you."

"I love you, too."

By the time Friday arrived, Anna was beyond excited for her date with Lane. Hanging with the kids and Lane, or Kym and Lane, or in the on-call room with Lane—these were all things she loved. But being alone with Lane again? Anna was definitely excited.

She tried not to imagine what Cathy would have to say about it.

It was so important to Anna to keep the kids feeling safe. While she had chosen to brush off what Cathy had said, it had increased those niggling concerns in the back of her mind. The ones Anna had had when she'd first heard the lawyer's words: that she wasn't cut out for this, that she was possibly the worst person to do it. Thanks to Cathy, the worries about dating Lane had intensified, too—that it was selfish to date, especially when things were so new; that the kids wouldn't cope; that they'd feel like less of a priority in her life.

So, she was taking the high road with Cathy; that didn't mean the woman hadn't gotten under her skin a little. But a pep talk from Kym and a phone conversation with her mother soon snapped her out of it. Anna was allowed a night out.

Lane was due to pick her up at six. In true form, Sandra breezed in around five, arms laden with food, and entered the kitchen with Ella in tow.

"Sweetie, hi." She dumped everything on the kitchen bench and gave Anna a tight hug, kissing her cheek.

Anna squeezed her tightly back, then turned to pull Ella in for a cuddle.

"Aunty Na, I helped cook this afternoon."

"You've definitely been busy." She eyed the bags on the bench. There definitely wasn't *just* meatloaf. "Mum, hey—how much food did you bring?"

Sandra was busy pulling dishes out and putting them in the fridge and freezer. "Oh, enough for a while, to heat up and just have on hand."

"I'm not *that* bad at cooking, Mum."

Sandra paused, arm partway in a bag, and looked sideways at Ella, who met her grandmother's eyes. Anna suddenly felt like her niece had abandoned her.

"Guys, I cook all the time now."

"I know you do, sweetie. You've gotten really good." Her mother's eyes stayed focussed on the bag she was rummaging through.

"Ella! C'mon, I can cook, can't I?"

Ella's eyes went wide. "Um—Grandma, her pancakes are really good."

A snorting noise came from the bag where Sandra's head was now buried. "You two suck. I'm going to hang out with Toby."

From the living room, she heard Ella say, "Well, they *are* good. She usually doesn't even burn them."

Ignoring the traitors in the kitchen, Anna scooped up Toby, who hummed happily at the sudden affection, and started carrying him upstairs. "You can't talk, so you can't pick on me yet. When you're older, just you remember who's changed far too many of your nappies."

Toby wrapped a chubby arm around her neck and Anna melted slightly as the fingers of his other hand grabbed at her necklace.

"Na." He murmured, smiling affectionately.

Anna cuddled him close as she walked into her room, then plopped him on her bed. His little voice was the most endearing thing and it was starting to come out more and more.

"Right, little man. Want to help me choose an outfit?"

Legs in the air, Toby fell backwards, giggling at the soft unsteadiness of the mattress.

She eyed him. "Right, you're going to be lots of help."

He blew a raspberry.

"Excellent."

Anna found an outfit and took Toby back downstairs to join the others while she had a shower. Not long before six, she emerged, walking into the dining room where her mother was feeding the kids dinner.

"Aunty Na, you look really pretty."

Anna grinned. The joy of kids was they told the truth. She had once walked out, and Ella had looked her up and down and asked, "Where did you find *that*?" There had been so much Sally in the tone it had made Anna's stomach ache. If Ella approved, she was set.

"Thanks Ella Bella. Just something I had laying around." She winked and dropped a kiss on the top of Ella's head.

"You really do, Anna." Her mother watched her, face soft.

"Thanks, Mum. And thanks again for tonight."

Sandra waved her hand. "Nonsense. We're going to have a great night."

"Grandma said we can have *two* deserts."

"*Two* deserts? Well, Grandma gets to deal with the sugar rush, so eat away."

Delighted, Ella went back to her meal with gusto, powering through as much as she could. Anna was about to tell her to slow down before she threw up when the doorbell rang.

Sandra chuckled, and Anna turned back to her. "What?"

"Your face just lit up. Go get the door."

Butterflies fluttered in her stomach as she swung the door open. Anna let her eyes drift down and her mouth dropped open at what she saw waiting in the doorway: Lane looked incredible in black slacks with heels and a white button-up shirt with a dark grey vest. She looked like a mix between office power boss and sexy secretary, and Anna thought she might need to wipe up the drool. She loved feminine Lane in dresses, but this was new.

Entwining their fingers together, Lane tugged Anna forward for a quick kiss on the lips. "Close your mouth, Anna," she said.

"You look," Anna let her eyes drop down and then back up to Lane's face, "amazing."

"Right back at you."

Doubtful. Anna had on dark skinny jeans with knee-high boots, a dark red, low-cut top and a fitted military jacket. It didn't compete, really.

"Ready to go?"

"I should really say hey to your mum and the kids."

"Oh. Yeah." The sight of Lane had made Anna's mind go blank.

Lane pushed her through the doorway. "You'll have me to yourself soon."

Anna followed happily.

"Your mum wouldn't stop grinning at me."

Wrapping an arm tighter around Lane's waist, Anna nuzzled into the back of Lane's neck as she revelled in the feel of their naked skin pressed together. Anna couldn't even care right then that it was getting late and they'd already been in bed together for hours. Bed was a haven, the only time they really got to be alone together. Especially since Lane had opened up about her ex, whenever they were in bed, they talked openly and lost hours being together, even if the consequence was exhaustion the next day.

"Lucky she doesn't know what we ran off to do upstairs the second she left. She thinks you're the best thing to happen to me. And you did take me out to an incredible meal, after all."

Shifting, Lane looked at her. "Well, I am pretty amazing. Some would say incredible."

"You, you say that."

"I like to speak the truth."

Anna smirked, kissing Lane once before pulling back. "You are pretty okay."

"It's okay to admit the truth."

Chuckling, Anna used her knee to nudge Lane. "I need to start being meaner to you. You're getting a big head."

Lane pouted. "No. No being mean."

Unable to resist, Anna leant forward and pressed another soft kiss to Lane's lips. "You pout, and it just makes your lips look even better."

"You're so easy."

"Only with you."

"Well, that's a good thing, because I can get jealous."

"Now's not a good time to tell you about my harem then?"

Lane poked her. "As long as I'm head of all those women, I'm okay."

"I'll take that as permission."

Rolling quickly so she was on top of Anna, Lane kissed her, lingering. Soft fingers traced up Anna's side and she moaned a protest when Lane turned her head away. "Damn it. It's after midnight."

Blinking blurrily, Anna, who had thought they were headed for round three, looked over at the clock with glazed eyes. "So?"

"I'm on an early shift tomorrow."

Anna wrapped a leg around Lane, heel digging into the back of her legs as she used her own thigh to mimic Lane's actions. "So?"

Lane's eyelids drifted closed as she rocked her hips. Adamantly, she pulled back as Anna tried to kiss her again. "So—I still have to get to my house, sleep enough, and go to work at stupid o'clock."

Anna grinned. "So?"

Nipping Anna's bottom lip, Lane chuckled and sat on the edge of the bed. "So…I need to sleep."

As dramatically as she could, Anna threw her arm over her eyes. "Fine. Leave me."

"I could always stay." Lane's voice was teasing. "I'd be gone by the time they woke up."

Peeking out from under her arm, Anna shook her head. "Knowing our luck, it'd be the night Toby wakes up at three a.m. and one of the times Ella climbs into bed with me."

"True. So wipe that pout off your face."

A dramatic sigh left her chest and Anna dropped her arm back down.

"You and Ella really are so alike."

A pillow hit Lane in the face. Self-satisfied, Lane threw it back and got dressed. Anna sat up and scooted to the edge of the bed, then stood and started pulling on a pair of sweats and a shirt.

Standing at the door, Lane furrowed her brow. "What are you doing?"

"Walking you out."

In a few steps, Lane was back next to Anna, wrapping her arms around her middle. "You don't have to do that. You stopped all pretence of being that romantic after the first time."

Anna chuckled, pressing her lips to Lane's neck. "True. I must be feeling more romantic tonight."

"That, and it's earlier, so you can still stand."

"Precisely."

Tugging her to the door, Lane looked over her shoulder. "Don't think you're going to bail me up at the front door for a quickie before I go."

"Damn. Onto me, huh?"

When the door was open, Lane lowered her voice to a whisper. "I'm so onto you. I have to sleep!"

Anna chuckled and followed her out.

"Stop smiling, it's not happening."

Clearing her throat softly, Anna made a serious face.

"That's better."

Barely at the stairs, they heard, "Nurse Lane?"

Freezing, Anna was still on the landing, holding hands with Lane, who stood on the first step. As one, they slowly turned to see Ella, one leg of her pyjama bottoms hiked up to her knee, her hair a cloud around her head. She stood in her doorway, squinting at them.

"Are you still here?"

Anna bit her lip and turned to look at Lane, who was gazing at Ella in such a state of shock it was almost comical.

Letting go of Lane's hand, Anna turned back to Ella. "Hey, Ella Bella, Lane was just leaving."

Ella scratched her bare knee, then tugged the leg of her pyjamas back down. "It's late."

Unable to keep the smile off her lips, Anna picked Ella up. She was getting too big for it. Big or no, Ella sleepily rested her head against Anna's shoulder as they walked over to Lane, who was still wide eyed.

"It is a bit late, which is why Lane's going home. Then I'm going to go to bed so I can get lots of sleep for the park tomorrow."

"Yeah, we're all going for a picnic with Grandma." Ella blinked sleepily at Anna, turning to Lane. "Are you coming, Nurse Lane?"

Lane finally blinked, smiling nervously at Ella. Anna tried not to laugh at her. It was her own fault, she knew—she'd made this a big deal. But Lane had frozen like a cartoon character.

"I have work in the morning, Ella, sorry."

Ella pouted, fiddling with the button on her pyjama top. "It's not until lunch time."

"If you finish up in time, you should come." Anna tried to reassure Lane with a smile.

"Okay. I could maybe finish at one-thirty. A nurse owes me a favour."

"We can go on the slide, Nurse Lane."

"That sounds like a plan, Ella."

As she put Ella down, Anna dropped a kiss on the top of her head. "Now, missy, you go to bed and I'll come up in a second and tuck you in."

"Okay, g'night." Ella took a step forward and wrapped her arms around Lane's legs.

Lane knelt down and gave her a hug. "Good night, Ella. Sweet dreams."

Once she was assured Ella had stumbled back to bed, Anna turned back to Lane.

"Your face was priceless."

"Shut up."

Giggling, Anna led the way down the stairs.

"You'll pay for that."

"Hope so."

They had just hit the bottom of the stairs, when they heard, "Nurse Lane?"

Ella stood at the top, hanging onto the banister.

"Yeah?"

"Can you read me a story before you go?"

"Of course." Immediately, Lane walked back up the stairs.

Anna followed, smiling softly.

Chapter Seventeen

"Can we have a sleepover at Grandma's again?" Ella was ignoring her food, staring at Anna with wide, begging eyes. Which weren't even necessary.

"Of course you can."

"Thanks." A smile flickered over Ella's face—which was smeared with sauce—before it faded. "I miss Grandad."

Anna's chewing slowed.

Toby, in his high chair, grabbed another meatball and put the whole thing in his mouth, cheeks bulging as he chewed. He looked like a squirrel.

They were having a night without Lane or Kym, and Anna found herself unexpectedly enjoying the time alone with the kids.

"You miss him, huh?"

Ella poked at her meatball. "Yup. He doesn't come over anymore."

Finally, Anna swallowed, wondering how to tackle this one. Honesty worked best, she was learning. "I think he's sad sometimes, Ella Bella."

"He misses Daddy?"

Stomach rolling over, Anna wondered if that would ever go away. "Yeah. He does miss your daddy."

Ella mashed the meatball with her fork, suddenly contemplative. "You miss Daddy. And Mummy."

"I do. A lot."

"And Grandma misses them."

"She really does."

"And I miss them." Ella's voice was almost a whisper. As if by saying it out loud she could never drag it back in.

Anna pushed her chair back, and that was all it took for Ella to abandon her seat and move to Anna's lap. "I know you miss them, honey." She smoothed the hair off Ella's face, holding her tightly.

Ella wasn't crying, but her face was red as she desperately tried to puzzle something out. "We all miss them, even Toby, and he's a baby."

Toby, whose cheeks still bulged and whose face was covered in more sauce than Ella's, looked up at his name. He tried to fit another meatball in, eyes twinkling.

"He does."

"So why can't Grandad miss them with us?"

Anna wanted to shake her father. He was abandoning the kids, his wife, his daughter, wallowing in his grief while they all had to hold their heads up and carry on. Another figure missing from Ella and Toby's lives.

Chin resting on top of Ella's head, Anna rocked her gently. "He doesn't know how, I don't think."

"You know how."

"Sometimes I don't. But I know I want to be with you and Toby, no matter how I feel."

Nodding, Ella picked at a loose thread on Anna's shirt. "So we can have a sleepover? Last time he sat for a little while and read a book to me. He smells nice."

Anna hugged her closer. "Of course you can. What about in two sleeps? That'll be Friday night and you can spend Saturday with Grandma and him? Maybe do some gardening?"

"Okay."

"Wanna call Grandma after dinner?"

"Yeah."

Ella was making no move to hop off just yet, and Anna was happy to let her stay as long as she wanted.

Work was a nightmare. Someone had overbooked consultations, and an emergency came in that pushed them back even later. On top of it all, Anna hadn't seen Lane in forty-eight hours, and, because of the emergency, she had missed her morning coffee with Kym and not managed any lunch. For once, she was actually grateful for her habit of eating breakfast with the kids, a meal she used to often miss.

It was after three in the afternoon when Anna emerged from the scrub room, tiredly pulling the protective cap off her head. She glanced into the second operating room as she walked past and saw that Lane was scrubbed in as float nurse. The patient was being wheeled out, the surgeons were already gone, and the nurses were doing the final count. Anna calculated she had just under ten minutes. Moving quickly, she headed for the stairs.

Just over five minutes later, she re-entered the floor with two coffees, walked to the door of the operating theatre, and snuck into the scrub room. She pushed the door open, relieved to see only Lane washing her hands.

"You had as busy a day as me?"

Lane turned, delighted, as she dried her hands. "God, what is going on today? Did the hospital gods come together to make our lives hell?"

Holding out the coffee, Anna chuckled. It really had been an insane day. Warm fingers wrapped around Anna's wrist as Lane tugged her over.

"Hey."

"Hi." Lane leant against her. "I've missed my girlfriend."

"Me, too."

"I've barely seen you since the picnic Saturday afternoon."

Arms pressed close as they drank their coffee, Anna settled next to Lane. "I know. The kids and our rosters have not allowed much time."

"Not fair. *And* I was supposed to be in emergency but got shafted up here today."

"Aren't you often in surgery?"

"More often in emergency. It's where my passion lies." Lane winked. "More hands on for me."

Mouth next to Lane's ear, Anna whispered, "What are you doing tomorrow night?"

At the insinuation, Lane's expression brightened up. "Something with you?"

"And, guess what?"

"I'm getting lucky?"

"Definitely. But also...?"

"What?"

"I'm kid-free."

A slow smile spread over Lane's lips. "All night?"

"Sleepover at Grandma's."

"Wanna sleep over at mine?"

"I really do."

"Wanna go out? Have some dinner, a date?"

Anna shook her head, smiling. "Not really."

"Wanna stay in, order Chinese, be naked in inappropriate places?"

"I love Chinese."

"Me too."

Anna wished she could wake up to Lane every morning. She'd always slept close to people when they stayed over. She liked the feel of waking up with someone's skin against hers. But she'd never woken up completely wrapped in someone before. They were on their sides, their legs entwined, Anna's face in Lane's neck, Lane's arm loosely over her waist. It was bliss.

Half-asleep, half-awake Anna just let herself enjoy the feeling of soft, warm skin. Lane was out cold, breathing deeply, and Anna brushed her lips over her skin.

They'd been up late, basking in the fact that there was no reason to be quiet, the only time they'd gotten to enjoy that since their first. And they had very much enjoyed it. There were no children waking them up, nothing to get out of bed for, no work that day. Anna didn't need to pick the kids up from her mother's until later in the afternoon.

Realising she could smell old take-out, Anna wrinkled her nose. The boxes were somewhere on the floor. They'd started eating in the living room, at least pretending they could keep their hands off each other. Instead, they'd ended up having sex on the couch, then the floor, before heading to the bed. A few hours on, Lane had sauntered out, delightfully naked, to bring the Chinese in when Anna had complained of her depleting energy reserves.

There was nowhere else Anna would rather be at that moment. No guilt was plaguing the back of her mind, no one was yelling at her to wake up, and she had spent an entire night with Lane. The guilt, the insecure feelings she had about dating so soon, had quelled for the moment.

Things could balance.

It had only been a few weeks since they had become "official," but she and Lane were solid, their connection prominent from the second they'd met. There was no insecurity from Lane. Anna had never experienced such ease before.

She felt Lane stir, arm tightening around her, and she pressed another kiss to Lane's neck, smiling as she heard Lane sigh softly.

"Wake up," she murmured against Lane's skin.

Voice low, Lane answered, "I'm enjoying waking up like this."

Anna kissed her jaw, then her lips once, before pulling back and smiling as Lane leisurely opened her eyes. A smile spread slowly across her face. Anna ran a fingertip down her cheek.

"Me too."

"Something I could get used to..."

"Me too."

Movements still sleepy, Lane kissed her. "Maybe it's something we can do more regularly?"

Running her fingers over Lane's collarbone, she stilled them there. She didn't like the hesitancy in Lane's voice, but couldn't blame her, considering how stringent Anna had been with her "rules." "Maybe we can?"

"Really?"

"Really. We could talk to Ella, explain things a little."

"Really?"

This time, the incredulity made Anna chuckle. "Yeah, really. She'll just be excited, I'm sure. It won't be something we can do all the time, at first. But we could start easing into it?"

"Really?"

Rolling them over, Anna hovered over her, weight on her elbows. "Yes! Really."

"That," Lane said, hands running up Anna's back to bury in her hair, "makes me very, very happy."

"We'll see how happy it makes you if Toby wakes up at three or when Ella comes bounding in at five asking for breakfast."

Lane's smile wavered. "Five?"

Anna's smile grew even wider. "Yup. Five."

"Like, five a.m.? Even on days we can sleep in?"

"Yup."

"You look far too chipper about that."

"Your face is just pretty funny, makes it easy to be chipper." Anna kissed her. "You do know what you're getting yourself into, right?"

"Probably not. But I know you're in it, so I'm pretty happy to find out." Lane tilted her head. "Why the concern?"

"What? No concern. Teasing."

Lane shook her head. "Don't pull that. When you asked if I knew what I was getting into, I saw it. Do you think the kids thing scares me?"

Anna bit her lip. Sometimes Lane was too perceptive for her own good. "I just…kids are a handful. And I don't mean that in a patronising way, I'm sure you know that. I love them, so much. But Toby's not always cute and delightful, and sometimes I think Ella's attitude is getting too big to fit in the door. They're still grieving, a lot; probably will be forever. They sleep like kittens on crack, they have far too much energy, and there are days I want to lock myself in my room and pretend I live alone and have nothing to do all evening but pour a glass of wine. Do you know that you can spend all day just following them around picking up their stuff? They leave a trail of destruction, and they're both still so fragile, and—"

Cutting Anna off with a kiss, Lane squeezed her shoulders. "Anna. Breathe, sweetie."

A flush swept over Anna's cheeks. "Sorry. Maybe I needed a rant?"

"You're allowed to rant. I have no idea how you do what you do."

"I love them." Anna shrugged, like it was the simplest thing in the world. Which it was. "There's so much of Jake, and Sally in them. I don't see it as a chore." She paused. "Anymore."

"I'm in, Anna. Crazy kids and your insane bed hair and all."

Anna tried to look affronted but her happiness at Lane's "I'm in" was obvious. "My bed hair is fine."

"Well, it is bed sex hair." Lane grinned. "I like it."

Needing contact, Anna kissed her, pouring everything she couldn't say into it. Anna had had such a lingering concern that Lane didn't know what she was in for, and Lane, as always, had made her feel completely reassured. She pulled back as Lane's eyes opened slowly.

"What was that for?"

"For being in."

They didn't get out of bed until after noon, finally rolling out to shower and find a late lunch somewhere. After a long, lingering kiss in Lane's doorway, Anna finally pulled herself away. Shaking her head at herself as she walked out of the building, Anna kept the memory of the morning's warmth close. Lane was going to come over for dinner that night, and they'd texted Kym to ask her to join as well. The night before, Ella had asked if they could come. Nothing, except a night like last night, beat Disney on the couch with her girls and Toby.

On the drive to her mother's, Anna couldn't stop grinning widely. Everything felt *good.* As she pulled into the driveway, she wondered if her father had managed to drag himself from his study to spend time with his grandchildren. She climbed out of the car and went to go around the front but heard Ella's giggle from the backyard, so she opened the side gate and made her way there instead.

Anna grinned when she saw Ella standing in the middle of Sandra's vegie patch, legs covered in dirt. Toby was in overalls, sitting next to Ella and grinning too, as he threw dirt at his own foot. He laughed delightedly and Anna felt warm all over at the sound. Her mother was watering the vegies and occasionally sending flicks of water towards the kids, causing Ella to squeal.

"Grandma! Don't! I can't get wet!"

Anna crossed her arms, leaning against the sidewall of the house as she watched Sandra laugh and flick more water towards Ella. Some splashed Toby, and he looked around, confused, before going back to throwing dirt.

"But you're dirty! You need a wash."

Hands on her little hips, Ella rolled her eyes. "That's what a *bathtub* is for."

Unable to resist, Anna called out, "You're not getting into the bathtub like that, Miss Ella Bella!"

Ella swung her head around and grinned. "Aunty Na! Tell Grandma to stop splashing me!"

"Na! Na!" Grinning and giggling, Toby ran at her.

Not caring he was covered in dirt, Anna scooped him up into a cuddle. "Hey, little man."

With more strength than such a small body should have, Toby wrapped himself around her. He kicked his leg out in front of him, pointing seriously to his pants. "Dirdy."

"Yup. They're definitely dirty." She looked back up at Ella. "Mum, I think you should keep squirting her, she's not getting in the car like that."

Indignantly, Ella's mouth opened to protest, but all she could do was squeal again as cold water hit her toes. "Aunty Na! You're supposed to stick up for me."

Eyes sparkling, Sandra looked at Anna. "Yeah, Anna."

"Oh good." She looked at Toby, who was gazing at her with wide blue eyes, still pointing to his pants. "I love it when they gang up on me."

Ella giggled and walked over, wrapping her arms around Anna's middle, pressing her face into Toby's stomach as she did so and blowing to attempt a raspberry. None too gently, he pushed at her head, laughing madly.

The two of them were ridiculous. Anna wrapped her spare arm around Ella's shoulders, giving her a squeeze as she said, "And now you're getting me all dirty."

The look on Ella's face was ecstatic. "Now you have to get squirted!"

Anna's eyes widened and she looked up at her mother, who was grinning almost maliciously.

"Mum, no!" She held Toby out in front of her under his armpits like a human shield, causing him to squeal happily and wave at his grandmother. "I have a baby!"

Her mother dropped the hose and walked over to turn it off. "Coward, using the baby."

Toby giggled again. "More!"

Anna hefted him up and threw him slightly in the air before putting him back down; he promptly ran back to the now muddy veggie patch and buried his hands in it. Ella squatted next to him, chattering about worms.

After walking up to Anna, Sandra kissed her cheek. "You have fun with Lane?"

"I did."

"Good. I like that one."

Anna wrapped an arm around her mother's shoulder as they stood watching the two kids. Toby poked at the dirt, Ella talking nonstop to him and drawing pictures in it with a stick.

"I do, too."

"I can tell."

She bumped her hip into her mother's. "Shh."

"I can. You're obviously smitten."

Anna couldn't really deny that. "She's easy to get smitten over."

"Obviously. Ella doesn't shut up about her and you smile any time her name is mentioned. She's a pretty welcome presence, if you ask me."

"Agreed."

"And you've clearly had sex all day."

Mouth open in shock, Anna looked quickly to the kids to make sure they hadn't overheard, then back to glare at her mother. "Mum!"

"What? You have."

Anna dropped her arm from her mother's shoulder and continued to glare at her. She was speechless. "Have not."

"Good response, Anna. Learnt that from Ella?"

Ella looked up from the dirt. "What?"

"Nothing!" They called out at once.

Face hot, Anna crossed her arms. "Anyway. How's Dad? Why isn't he here with the kids?"

"He said he had business to do." Anna saw right through the flippant way Sandra spoke. "He did watch a DVD with Ella last night, and read her a book. Then he disappeared. Toby misses him."

"Ella asks about why she rarely sees him."

Sighing, her mother shrugged. "He'll get there. He's a lot like you, like that."

"Hey, I'm here."

Her mother nodded at the kids. "Thanks to them, you are. Otherwise I think you would've disappeared, too."

Opening her mouth to object, Anna quickly closed it again when she realised her mother was right. Instead, she put her arm back around her mother's shoulder and pulled her close. They stood for a minute in a comfortable half hug, watching the kids play.

"So the sex is good, then?"

"Mum!"

Red-faced, Anna managed to bundle the kids into the car, grateful her mother still had clothes and things at the house in the kids' bedroom. It meant Anna didn't have to hunt down bags and try to con Ella into unpacking hers.

When they got home, Ella practically bounced out of the car at the news that Lane and Kym were definitely coming over for dinner. Anna got Toby out of his car seat, smiling as he fell willingly into her arms, head resting in the crook of her neck. When he yawned and rubbed his eyes, she rubbed circles on his back, pausing when she saw Ella standing on the doorstep holding a paper bag.

"What's that, Ella Bella?"

"I dunno. It was on the doormat. I think it's for me and Toby."

When Anna held her hand out, Toby craned his neck to watch what she was doing from his place on her hip. A label was on the front: "For my Grandchildren." The urge to roll her eyes overtook her—obviously Cathy had come around again unannounced. Secretly relieved they'd missed her, Anna opened the door and Ella half fell into the house.

"Your reading's getting good—it is for you."

"I got first in a writing competition at school yesterday."

"You did? Well, you can choose dinner and dessert tonight then, smarty pants."

Holding the package to Ella, Anna hid a smile as Ella bounced and took the package, already ripping into it. "Who's it from?"

"From your other grandma."

"Mummy's mum?"

"Yup."

Still tearing at the paper, Ella wrinkled her nose. "She smells funny."

Smothering a laugh, Anna coughed. "That's not very nice, Ella. What did you get?"

A book was revealed and Ella's eyes lit up. She really did love books. "It's a story. I don't have this one!"

Toby was being extra cuddly and began to climb back up Anna when she tried to put him down. Enjoying the affection, Anna humoured him.

"Well, that's awesome, a new one. Maybe we can read it with Toby tonight."

"Can Nurse Lane read it?"

Anna put her bag down on the counter. "She sure can."

"And can Kym read one, too?"

Anna eyed her playfully. "You wouldn't be trying to sneak two stories in for bed time, would you?"

Defending herself seriously, Ella said, "I don't want one of them to feel left out."

"If they want to read to you, you can have two."

Face bright, Ella put the book on the bench, already moving out of the room. "I'm going to find another story for Kym to read."

Anna looked at Toby, who was now craning his neck over her shoulder to see where his sister had gone so fast. "Your sister is like a whirlwind, Tobes."

"El done?"

His baby-speak never failed to make him sound even sweeter. "She'll be back."

After five minutes, Toby finally let Anna put him down, and she grabbed one of his cars off the bench, handing it to him.

He instantly sat down and started running the wheels over the floor, making car noises. Anna reached distractedly for the book to see what it was, smiling at the noises Toby was making. The sight of the cover made her jaw clench in anger. In her hands was a children's Bible.

It shouldn't have irritated her as much as it did. Anna had nothing personally against religion, but Sally had. They'd had long, drawn-out conversations about it, discussing Sally's oppressive childhood. Unless they chose it themselves later, Sally had been adamant that religion wouldn't be a part of her children's lives. Cathy and Sally had had a huge argument over it last year. Anna remembered Jake calling her late one evening, saying, "I need you to take the ranting for a while, it's been three hours," and suddenly Sally was on the phone, all fire and anger.

Sally had made it clear to her mother that she didn't want the kids going to Sunday School, or any of it. Yet here, from Sally's mother, was a children's Bible.

Anna sighed and looked down to Toby, chewing her lip in thought and vaguely watching him smash his car into the floor. The book could go in the bin, or to charity—but she didn't really want to do that. She'd had a children's Bible growing up, even though she wasn't brought up in a religious household. If it was her kids, she wouldn't see it as the biggest deal, she just wouldn't be emphasising it to them. But Sally had made her wishes known loud and clear. More than anything, Anna wanted to bring these kids up with every bit of Sally and Jake that she could.

She put the book on the bench and figured she'd think about it later. Cathy was not her favourite person at the moment. And Anna had a night ahead of her with Lane, her best friend, and the two cutest kids in the world.

"Alrighty, Tobes. Let's get you washed up, you're covered in garden dirt."

Face suddenly stony, he stopped his car mid-air and looked at her. "Baf?"

"Yup, bath."

He looked like he was considering chucking the car at her.

"And *then* dinner with Lane and Kym."

He perked up instantly, dropping the car and holding his arms up. "Baf!"

"Bath then Kym! Plan."

The next few hours passed quickly. Anna had the kids bathed and in their pyjamas early, and dinner—chips and pasta as requested by Ella, with some salad as negotiated by Anna—was ready.

Right on time, Kym and Lane showed up on time, Lane with a bottle of red in her hands and Kym clutching the biggest box of brownies Anna had ever seen. With much noise, Ella and Toby launched themselves at them and they all eventually settled down in the kitchen.

In between throwing sly grins at each other, Anna and Lane fluffed about serving dinner. Avoiding any chores, Kym sat at the table with Toby on her lap, the little boy completely enamoured with her, and chatted to Ella. They seemed to be debating if nuts belonged in brownies.

"Kym smiles more here than she does anywhere else." Lane spoke softly as she put chips on all their plates.

Anna looked up from where she was doling out salad and watched Kym. Whenever she came here and relaxed, the strain seemed to leave her eyes, the act of being happy actually settled into something resembling calm.

The table set, Anna was just taking Toby from Kym's arms, ready to put him in his high chair, when a knock sounded at the front door. Instead, Anna settled Toby on her hip and met the three sets of eyes owlishly blinking at her from the table with an equally confused look.

"Um—I'll just get that."

Rather than wrestle Toby into his high chair when he would only want to go with her anyway, Anna kept him on her hip as she walked through to the front door. "Who do you think it is, Tobes?"

Toby looked at her. "Pata."

"In a minute." She pulled the door open and tried to hide her surprise. "Lorna. Hi. Uh—can I help you? We just had a visit from you?"

Lorna gave a stiff smile, and it was then that Anna looked behind her to see a police officer standing calmly, hands held behind him, eyes on the ground. It seemed like he was purposefully making a point of not being intrusive. Anna moved her eyes back to Lorna, the hair on the back of her arms standing up.

"Anna, I'm really sorry."

Anna blinked at her, instinctively holding Toby closer. "What for?"

"Unfortunately, we've had some concerns raised about how you're taking care of the kids. While we investigate these, we need to take the kids into care."

"What?"

Lorna took in a deep breath. "Someone has made some fairly serious allegations, and we are obliged to investigate these, even though I've not seen *anything* to indicate the kids are being neglected."

"*Neglected?*" Anna couldn't control her tone.

Toby dug his fingers into her shirt as he held onto her, looking from Lorna to Anna and back again.

The look on Lorna's face stayed neutral. "You're aware you've had temporary custody while awaiting the papers to pass by the judge and have it all officially signed off to make you permanent guardian of the kids?"

Dumbly, Anna could only nod. "I was assured everything would be fine with that. My brother and Sally dictated in their will that they wanted me to have them."

"Well, someone has petitioned the court for guardianship over you, which they are legally allowed to do."

A humming sound rang in Anna's ears. It felt like someone had swept her feet out from under her.

"Now, normally you'd keep the kids until a guardianship hearing was held, as you're already temporary guardian, but these claims have complicated things."

"So you're taking them away from me?"

"Hopefully not permanently, Anna."

Everything was happening faster than Anna could process. "Can't they stay with my parents?"

With a shake of her head, Lorna, "Maybe, but there will be a hearing next week for temporary guardianship until the guardianship hearing. The kids will be in foster care until then."

"*Foster care?*" She didn't yell, not wanting to unsettle Toby, who had already started to cling to her. Instead she hissed, which was probably worse.

"It's a great family, and hopefully things will be sorted out next week at the hearing. We'll know the day on Monday. Call your lawyer in the morning."

Nausea swept over her, and Anna thought she was going to throw up. She held Toby harder, eyes flickering to the police officer behind Lorna. "Lawyer?"

"That's right. They can answer your questions. I'll be at the hearing, giving my input. The person who put in the allegations will be as well."

"Court?" She didn't want the kids dragged through the court system, dragged out of their *home* to be dumped in foster care. They'd just lost their parents. They didn't need this.

"It won't be like on TV. Just a judge, a table, the lawyers. And of course, the caseworkers and child protective services. We will look into these claims then, and see where that takes us."

Anna was breathing too fast. "You're going to take them into foster care? From their home? From me?"

"You know the system. The allegation was made. We have to investigate it and do what's best for the kids."

"What's best for them is being with *me*. In their home."

Hesitating, Lorna didn't say anything. Anna had to wonder if she wanted to agree.

"What were the allegations?"

Silent for a moment, Lorna finally said, "Neglect. Leaving the kids continuously. There was mention of," she hesitated, eyes going to Toby, then back to Anna, "a continuous parade of sexual partners. Among other things."

"I thought these things are investigated before something drastic is done."

Lorna hesitated again. "Some things are out of my hands."

"Aunty Na?"

Heart pounding, Anna whipped around to see Lane standing pale faced and wide eyed a few metres behind her. Ella and Kym stood in the doorway leading to the kitchen. Anna swallowed past the bile rising in her throat. "Ella Bella."

"What's going on?" Ella looked behind Anna. "Why's there a pleeseman here?"

Anna tried to look reassuring, but she didn't think it worked. She didn't know what to say.

"Hey, Ella, remember me?"

Nodding silently at Lorna, Ella stared at them as she clung to Kym's side.

"Well, we're gonna take you somewhere else to stay for a few nights."

"What? Why?"

"We have to sort some adult stuff out. So you need to sleep at a really nice older couple's house for a little while. With Toby. It'll be like a sleepover."

"No." Ella sounded incredibly confused. A panicked look was in her eye, out of place on a six-year-old. She looked up to Anna. "Don't you want us, Aunty Na?"

Anna nodded her head vehemently. "Of course I do, Ella." All she could see was the colour rising in Ella's face, the look of panic starting to take her over.

"I don't want to go anywhere. I don't know them." The hysterical edge to Ella's voice spurred Anna into finally moving.

As soon as she knelt, Ella flew into her outstretched arm; she still clutched Toby with the other. Fingers dug into Anna's back and the next five minutes passed in a blur.

Lane went upstairs and packed Ella a bag, Anna reminding her with a shaky voice to pack the panda bear. Kym did Toby's, and far too quickly, both women were at the bottom of the stairs, holding the two bags.

Ella clung to Anna the entire time; her fingers were going to leave bruises. Impressions that would haunt Anna for days. Anna tried to reassure her, but Ella wasn't listening. Her cheeks were red and her little jaw was clenched as she looked from Lorna to Anna and to the policeman in the background.

Apparently, he was there to make sure it went smoothly.

Repeatedly, Anna told Ella it would be okay, that she'd sort it out.

Choking on a silent sob, Ella didn't say a word.

Kym and Lane handed the bags over to the policeman, who took them quietly outside.

Following Lorna to a car in the driveway, Anna didn't let go of Ella's hand, Toby quiet on her hip. When Lorna opened the car door, Ella flung herself at Anna, finally breaking. Hysterical sobs heaved out of her little chest. Anna held her close and rubbed her back. She tried to hold her so tightly that Ella would know Anna didn't want to let her go.

Eventually, Lorna tugged gently on Ella, and her sobs turned into a wail. "No, no, no!"

Finally, Lorna managed to break Ella away.

Anna swallowed as she watched Ella be put in the back of the car, watched Lorna buckle her in. Ella, always well behaved, sat still in her seat even while racked with sobs. With a slam, the door shut and Ella turned, putting her hand against the glass, tear-streaked face visible even in the dark.

"Aunty Na!"

Trying to smile comfortingly, Anna raised a shaking hand to wave. When Lorna held her arms out for Toby, Anna just couldn't hand him over.

"Anna. Please."

This just made Anna hold him tighter against herself, arm across his tiny back. Anna noticed distantly that her entire body was shaking. With Lorna staring at her, with the policeman's eyes boring in to her, Anna finally stepped forward and tried to lift Toby off herself to hand him to Lorna—but Toby had realised what was happening. He started to cry. He clung on with more strength than Anna knew such a tiny human could. Lorna finally reached forward and took him, pulling him off her. His fingernails scratched her neck as he tried to hold on and he started to scream, kicking his legs and thrashing.

"Na! Na!"

Anna wanted to open her mouth, to reassure him, but it felt like all her words had vanished. Arms partially raised, she stood as if Toby were still in them, and watched Lorna expertly wrangle him into the car seat in the back. The door shut with a bang, and all Anna could hear was Toby screaming. Ella had her legs pulled up on the seat and her head pressed against her knees, hands over her ears as if she could block out the world.

Lorna stood at the driver's door; the policeman had faded into the background, gone wherever he had come from. "Call your lawyer, Anna. We'll get this sorted out."

She nodded numbly.

"They'll be well looked after."

She finally managed to ask a question. "When can I see them?"

"Call the office Monday."

Then Lorna was starting the car, and Anna could hear Toby's cries even as she reversed out of the driveway. She watched the car go down the street, saw Ella kneel up on the seat and look out the back window, hand pressed to the glass in the exact same way in which she'd wait for Anna to pick her up after work.

And then they were gone.

Chapter Eighteen

It felt a little bit like being unable to breathe. Like someone had sucked all the air out of the place, which was impossible because Anna was standing outside.

How had that just happened?

She spun slowly on her heel.

Kym stood at the bottom of the stairs that led to the house, hand raised as if to stop Lorna driving off. Lane was a step in front of Kym, one foot forward and one foot back, as if fighting with herself on whether or not to walk to Anna.

Both were pale and wide-eyed with shock; Anna imagined she didn't look any better.

She felt herself shutting down. It was like she'd just been told her brother was dead all over again. Licking her lips, she opened her mouth to say something, looking from Kym to Lane. She closed her mouth. She had no idea what to say.

"Anna." Lane's voice was hoarse. "We'll figure this out."

She'd heard those words before. She may have said them. That felt like years ago.

Lane stepped forward and Anna mirrored it with a step backwards, giving a small shake of her head, lips pursed. Lane stopped, looking unsure and helpless.

Anna realised she was picking at her nail with her thumb and dropped her hands quickly. It wasn't a good habit.

"It's a load of shit," Kym said. "There's no way this will hold up in any kind of court."

Keeping her gaze forward, Anna gave a sharp nod of agreement as she walked past a silent Lane and Kym, up the stairs, and into the house.

There was a rushing sound in Anna's ears as the hairs on her arms stood up. Walking into the kitchen, she paused in the doorway for a split second to take in the plates on the table, food probably cold by now. Toby's high chair had his little plastic Batman plate on it, his food cut into pieces the perfect size for grabbing—something Anna had only known to do because she remembered Sally doing it.

Ella's place was set with a Jasmine plate—her favourite Disney princess because she liked adventure like Ella did. There was no tomato on her plate, because Ella hated the way it felt in her mouth.

Would the foster carers know to do that? Would Ella have enough confidence to ask? Or after those hysterical sobs...would she do what she'd done the first weeks after her parents died and just retreat into herself and not talk?

Toby would be so confused, and he'd only just started to relax.

Biting her lip, Anna approached the table and started grabbing at whatever was in reach, stacking full plates on top of each other, spilling food and not caring. She took a load to the sink and dumped it in, heard a crack, then walked back to the table to grab what was left. Kym and Lane hovered in the doorway, watching her. Kym's hand was on Lane's forearm as if to stop her from moving forward. After a quick glance, Anna ignored them.

She dumped the second lot in the sink and started running water, scraping the plates into the garbage. As she turned to place some of the plates on the bench before going to grab more from the sink, she caught sight of the brightly coloured book, pushed to the side to be read later in the evening.

Suddenly, Anna could barely see through the rage that overtook her. Cheeks flushed, she turned the tap off forcefully and reached over to snatch the children's Bible. She held it in front of her, eyes darting over the cover, taking in the colourful ark on the front. Animals peeked out from all kinds of portholes, big cartoon smiles on their faces.

Anna's knuckles were white. Why was the book shaking?

She had absolutely no doubt in her mind who had done this. Those kids had been through hell. They had been through hell and had just started to come out the other side. That scene in the backyard at Sandra's, with the kids playing, relaxed, getting covered in dirt, the squeal of laughter from Ella—that had taken a long, long time to happen. Anna had worked her ass off to make sure they felt as secure and happy as they possibly could, given the circumstances. She wanted them to get through this somewhat intact; Ella, who was old enough to forever remember what she missed, and Toby, who would grow up not knowing if his memories were images he made up in his head from stories he was told, or if they were genuine wisps of the real thing.

Anna didn't know which was sadder.

No, they weren't who they had been before it had happened. But they'd made progress. Agonising but noticeable progress.

And now Sally's *fucking* mother had them torn out of their home. The only thing that had remained stable since their parents died were the beds they woke up in, the kitchen they ate in, the bath filled with their favourite water toys. And, Anna could admit now, they had her. Every morning and every evening, they had her.

The book was still shaking in her hands.

Anna put it on the bench and rested her hand on the cover for a minute, barely seeing it.

Ella had asked her if she didn't want them anymore.

She opened to a random page, the images a blur. She grabbed the page and tore it out, ripping it up, pieces falling around her. When she was left with nothing in her grasp, she did it with another handful of pages, and another. Paper confetti littered the bench around her. She didn't stop until strong hands wrapped around her biceps, firmly gripping her. Anna's flurry of movement stopped, and she realised she was breathing hard. With her fingers clenching to the edge of the bench, she felt like she was hovering on the edge of a cliff and, any moment, would fall over it. She closed her eyes for a minute, bringing herself back to the kitchen. To the pounding of her heart. To the sound of her heavy breathing. She felt Kym's eyes on her in the doorway. She felt her fingertips biting into the bench, into the curve of the edge under her palm. It was Lane's fingers that held her arms, her chest nearly pressed to Anna's back.

Anna turned slowly in her girlfriend's grip.

When Anna spun, Lane gently gripped her, Anna's hands pressed between them. The other hand stayed on the bench behind her, gripping hard on the stone. She tried to slow her breathing down as her trembling fingers tightened on Lane's shirt. Anna could feel Lane's heart racing even under the material.

"They're gone."

Lane had tears in her eyes. "I know, sweetie."

"Their parents died only months ago, and now they're *gone*."

Lane nodded. "I know."

"Sally's mother is going to try and take them."

"She won't."

"What if she does?"

"She *won't*."

Anna felt like there was no air again. "He trusted me. Jake...and Sally. They trusted their children with me and now they're in a foster home." Anna wanted to punch something. "A *foster* home, Lane."

Lane pulled Anna forward and into her arms. She wanted to resist, but, when Lane's arms wrapped around her, she felt herself melt into the embrace, hand trapped between them. Her fingers finally released the hard bench to grip Lane's back.

"I know, Anna."

She pressed her forehead against Lane's shoulder.

Lorna had said she could call the office Monday. Tomorrow was Sunday. That meant it would most likely be almost forty-eight hours until Anna would see them, or even know they were okay. That's even if they let her see them. She was being investigated. From her small knowledge on these things, she knew she might not be able to see them until the hearing later in the week.

It was a nightmare.

Anna finally stepped away from Lane, looking around at the mess in the kitchen, the ripped paper on the floor, the plates in the sink, on the bench, one of them broken from being dropped too hard. Her eyes moved to Kym, who leant against the doorframe, biting her lip.

"Sorry. About the display."

"When Simon died, I broke every plate we had chosen together." Kym gave a small smile. "Then I spent the next two days gluing them back together."

The image of Kym doing that wrenched at Anna's chest. She stepped out of Lane's arms and walked around to the table, and sat down, resting her elbows on the edge, her head falling into her hands. She heard chairs push back as Lane and Kym took seats as well.

"Right," Kym spoke first. "Well, this is bullshit and it will get fixed. We'll fix it. We'll call your lawyer in the morning, Anna. He'll know more. And he'll have access to the legal information, the complaints this bitch has put forward."

Anna nodded into her hands.

As if motivated by a plan, Lane added, "And we'll ask *him* which lawyer we need to contact."

"Yeah. I suppose the lawyer we used was more looking after Jake and Sally's will. We'll need a lawyer who actually works in this kind of family law."

Warmth spread over Anna's knee as Lane rest her hand there, squeezing comfortingly. "We'll find someone. My dad has a few lawyer friends."

"And Lane and I can testify to the fact that you in no way neglect those kids."

With a nod, Lane squeezed her knee again. "That's right. And there are so many others who will, as well. Everyone knows you do nothing but the best for them."

When she spoke, Anna's voice was hoarse. "I need to call Hayley." She didn't look up until she felt Lane's hand twitch on her knee—though to Lane's credit her expression didn't change. "It's a Sunday tomorrow, so getting a clear answer from anyone is going to be impossible. She will at least have some information, maybe make me feel better about my position in all this."

"Good idea." Lane's voice was steady.

Anna put her head back in her hands. An ache had started to pound behind her eyes.

"Toby needs a bottle of milk to settle before sleep. Do you think they'll know that?"

The silence amongst them was palpable; Lane tightened her grip on Anna's knee.

"And Ella was promised two stories tonight. She was first in a writing competition at school. She was really excited she got to choose dinner." Her voice cracked at the last word. "This isn't fair. On them."

"It's not. Or on you."

Anna loved Kym for that.

They eventually moved to the living room, putting on something to try and distract themselves. When that movie finished, they put on another, and, by about halfway through, all were asleep.

Anna woke up as the credits were rolling, looking to the right to see Kym curled in a ball in the corner of the giant couch. On her left, Lane was slouched down, chin on her chest, fast asleep.

Normally, Ella would be curled into one of them, or somehow over all three, fast asleep and probably kicking Anna in the stomach.

Easing Lane's hand off her thigh and onto the couch gently, Anna clenched her jaw and stood quietly. She made her way up the stairs and hovered outside Toby's room. The sight of the empty cot in the middle of the night had her feeling ill. She flicked the light off and walked to Ella's room, a mess from her rushing around to get ready after her shower. Anna walked in and picked up the damp towel, hanging it over the end of the bed. Two piles of books sat on Ella's bed. Undoubtedly, she had been trying to sort out the good stories from the bad to try and figure out which one to get Kym to read to her. Anna was sure all of the books there were the longest ones in her collection.

A floorboard creaked. Defensively, Anna crossed her arms over her chest and looked up.

Leaning against the doorframe, Lane stood, watching her. "How you doing?"

Anna shrugged.

Lane nodded.

Stepping into Lane's space, Anna leant her forehead against Lane's shoulder, almost sighing as Lane's arms wrapped around her. Lifting her head up slowly, she pressed her lips to Lane's, gently. Lane tilted her head to reciprocate.

Anna deepened the kiss, raising her hands up to cup Lane's face, tongue in her mouth. Responding in kind, Lane didn't question the urgency, arms tightening around Anna, pushing her backwards. Clothes off, they ended up in Anna's room, falling onto the bed, skin pressed together.

There was no way Anna would be able to sleep tonight, and she needed to not think. Because the second she did, a pit of nausea started in her stomach and *what if I don't get them back* played around her mind like a mantra.

So instead, Anna lost herself in the sound and taste and feel of Lane.

Out of habit, Anna woke up early. For a moment, when she opened her eyes, she expected to see Ella bouncing on the end of the bed and asking for breakfast.

Then the memory of last night hit her like a ton of bricks.

Waking up with Lane for the second morning in a row should have been an enjoyable bonus to a wonderful night. But she couldn't enjoy it. It wasn't happening because they'd reached that point or because they'd had a conversation with Ella about it. They hadn't gotten to talk about Lane staying, about knocking, about how the kids would always come first.

Wanting to escape this feeling, Anna sighed and pulled Lane's arm tighter around her. Had she been too selfish with her relationship? Prioritised wrong? Thought of herself when she should have been thinking of the kids more? Spent too much time with Lane?

She rolled slightly, taking in the sight of Lane behind her, face soft with sleep, hair dark against the white of her pillow. Kissing her forehead, Anna slid out of bed, grabbed some clean clothes, and headed to the shower. Not wanting to see the toys in the other bathroom, she used her brother's room. The room was chilly, and she showered and dressed quickly. A glance at her watch told her it was only six. Far too early to achieve anything productive except maybe a call to Hayley, which Anna found she didn't have the energy for just yet. She needed coffee, and she needed to know the kids were okay. How was she supposed to wait until the next day?

She padded down the stairs, a tug of guilt registering that she hadn't even set Kym up with pillows or a blanket.

As she got to the bottom of the stairs, an amazing scent hit her nostrils. She followed it to the kitchen, smiling at the sight of Kym cooking. The kitchen was clean except for the pan on the stove.

Kym immediately handed her a cup of coffee. "Sit."

A plate of eggs and bacon appeared in front of Anna the second she sat. "Eat."

Anna hesitated.

Spatula poking out ridiculously Kym narrowed her eyes. "Don't try that look on me. You didn't have dinner. Eat."

Anna picked up her fork, making exaggerated movements as she stabbed at a piece of scrambled egg and put it in her mouth, chewing dramatically.

Satisfied that Anna was eating, Kym sat down with her own plate.

On the first bite, Anna had realised she was starving, despite the nausea eating at her stomach. Kym didn't even raise an eyebrow at how quickly she inhaled her meal, making Anna love her even more.

"Did you sleep?"

Anna shrugged. "Kind of."

"Have lots of sex to try and distract yourself?"

Anna paused mid-chew.

"You are so predictable."

Sipping her coffee, Anna wrapped around the warmed china. "Kym," she stared at the mug, "I have to get those kids back."

"You will."

"This is… How did this happen?"

"People are assholes." Kym reconsidered. "*Some* people are assholes. Can you call Hayley? Not that I think you should—she's an asshole, too. But she may have some insight."

"She's not an asshole. She made a choice. One I might have made in her position." She paused. "*Probably* would have made."

"I'm your best friend. She broke up with you. I automatically get to think she's an asshole." Kym gazed at Anna over her cup. "It's how this works."

A small nod was all she could manage. "Okay. I'll call her, but it's still early." She picked up her cup but then suddenly slammed it back down. "This is so *frustrating*."

Kym blinked.

"It's fucking Sunday. Getting hold of a lawyer is going to be impossible. I can't even call the office to find out if they're okay until tomorrow. It's too early to even call Hayley. How the fuck am I supposed to fix this?"

She looked at Kym, eyes pleading.

Fingers grasped Anna's arm as Kym leant over the table. "Give it a few hours. Lane will call her father as soon as she's up, and we'll have the name of an amazing lawyer. You can call Hayley, who may also know someone and will hopefully have some reassuring information. The second you wake up tomorrow, you can start calling child protective services constantly until they answer." She squeezed Anna's arm. "I know this isn't going to help much, but they will be okay. Lorna said they were a nice older couple. The kids will be fine."

At Anna's curt nod, Kym leant back in her chair. In companionable silence, they sipped at their cooling coffee.

Anna sat up straighter when she heard Lane coming down the stairs and gave a tight smile as she walked into the room.

After receiving breakfast from Kym with a grateful nod, Lane said, "I just spoke to my father."

"It's so early."

"He's a big boy; he coped. He's going to contact his scarily large group of friends and get some names."

Gratefully, Anna touched Lane's knee under the table. "Thank you."

"Anything I can do to help."

In a slightly more polite manner than Anna had, Lane tucked in to her food. "Thanks, Kym. Starving." None of them sure what to say, so they sat silently. Distractedly, Anna picked at her fingernail, anxiety building in her stomach. As Lane finished, her phone rang, and she grabbed it out of her pocket.

"Hey, Daddy." She made eye contact with Anna before standing and wandering out of the room, listening intently.

Kym looked at Anna. "Step one. Things are happening."

Anna wrapped her hands around her coffee mug, on edge and frustrated.

A few minutes later, Lane walked back in holding her phone.

"All okay?" Anna asked.

"He gave me a name, Scott Matthews. Apparently a renowned family law attorney in Melbourne. I'll have his contact details. Dad's going to text them to me." She cleared her throat slightly. "He's also well known for working gay and lesbian cases."

Kym raised her coffee cup. "Awesome."

"Well, Dad did always like being a superhero." Lane slid her phone across to Anna, a text with a contact number for Scott Matthews on display. "He said he's contactable on Sundays from nine."

The clock showed it was only eight.

From across the table, Kym stood up. "Anna, I'm really sorry but I need to be at work in an hour."

"Stop looking guilty. We all know you take every on call you can. Go help sad people. I think I'm going to be on the phone most of the day." Horror swept through her. "God, I need to tell Mum, too. I'll have to go over there."

"Will you text me, with any news? Or if I can do anything?"

Anna nodded.

"I mean it, anything at all. Even if it's just to bring over bottles of wine tonight."

"I will. I promise."

Standing up, Kym headed for the door.

"And Kym?"

"Yeah?"

"Thank you."

She smiled at Anna. "There's no way in hell any of us are going to let them take those kids for good, Anna."

When she heard the front door close, Anna turned to Lane. "Are you okay with me calling Hayley?"

"Don't be silly. Sorry if you felt the hand twitch last night. Automatic reaction." Lane looked at her intently. "Are you okay with calling her?"

"Probably not, normally. She called ages ago, not long after we ended, to 'check-up.' I asked her to leave me alone, which she respected. But right now, she's the only one who might have some answers and I can't sit here all morning just waiting."

"I'm supposed to work this morning, too. I was thinking I'd call in sick?"

"As much as I really would like that, didn't you say there's heaps of nurses on holiday this week?"

Lane's face fell. "Oh, yeah."

"The emergency co-ordinator would skin you alive."

"He'll probably do that anyway. He's that grumpy lately."

"Probably."

Lane kissed Anna on the cheek before resting their foreheads together. She stood up.

"Don't shut down on me, Anna." The whisper against her skin was so faint she almost missed it.

"What?"

Eyes dark, intense, Lane stared at her. "I can see it. You did it last night and you've not completely come back. Which is fine, if that's what you need to do. This situation is just, painful. But I'm here, okay?"

"I know." She looked up at Lane, taking her in. "I'm sorry. It's something I do."

"I get it. Just, talk to me. Don't disappear completely."

"I won't." She raised her hand up, taking a fistful of Lane's shirt and tugging her down, kissing her softly. When she pulled back, Anna said, "Thank you. For being so amazing."

"Call me, okay? If you need anything? I'll be able to get away, if I need to."

"I will."

Obviously not wanting to go, Lane hovered, half-bent over the table where she'd leant to kiss Anna.

With a tight smile, Anna gave her a gentle push. "Go, or we'll sit here all day not wanting you to leave."

At the doorway, she paused. "Seriously—call. I'll come straight away."

"I will."

A moment later, the sound of the front door closing left Anna alone in the silent house.

She sat at the table, food sitting solidly in her stomach.

It was eight a.m. on a Sunday. Normally, they'd be planning something. Ella would be asking for things she wanted to do: the cinema, the zoo, the park, the pool. She'd be full of energy, ideas, kinetic and endearing. Toby would be clambering onto Anna's lap while she desperately tried to drink a coffee, his face covered in peanut butter. He'd press his sticky hands to her cheeks, kneeling on her legs and grinning at her.

"Na," he'd say, absolutely delighted that she was there, as she was every morning. He'd press a sloppy kiss to her cheeks, and she'd laugh, tickling him, to make his giggles come out.

Then, cartoons might be on, if Ella had managed to wear her down, or they'd put music on, classics her brother had loved that Anna, in the last few weeks, had started to pull out and play.

Anna had wanted to start telling Ella stories, soon. Not yet, but soon: stories of Jake and her when they'd been kids, brother and sister. About how Jake had hated tomato like Ella and how he could build a fort out of anything. She wanted to tell Ella how Sally had once said that Jasmine was her favourite princess too, and that she'd eat a tomato like an apple.

They'd started to move towards these things, and Anna was so angry the kids weren't there right now, chattering and loud and happily ruining what could be a peaceful Sunday morning.

The struggle to bring security to their lives had been difficult but worth it. How would they, Ella especially, feel secure again after this, even if Anna managed to get them back? With the memory that someone could turn up at night and take them away planted in her head?

Would this have happened if Cathy hadn't found out she was gay? If she wasn't in a relationship, would Cathy still have complained to child services? What complaints of neglect had she put forward, and how had it led to such a dramatic outcome?

The clock ticked loudly in the otherwise silent house. Anna needed to do something. She went upstairs and grabbed her phone, scrolling through her contacts until she found Hayley's name and hit *call*. Hearing Hayley on the voicemail after so long barely registered. At the beep, she left a message.

"Hayley, it's me, Anna. I'm sorry to call, I just need your help. Or to ask you some stuff. The kids got taken away from me last night and put into foster care. Sally's crazy mother has told protective services I'm neglecting them." Anna paused, anger making her voice shake. "I just need to know where I stand. I need them back. Can you call me, if you have a chance? Thanks."

She sat on the edge of the bed, at a complete loss.

She needed to tell her mother.

Maybe, if they wouldn't let Anna see the kids tomorrow, they might let Sandra. There was no reason they wouldn't at least let that happen. Anna, while seething with anger, knew that Lorna had to follow protocol. But she also knew that the system always tried to work in favour of the kids. People got supervised visits who maybe shouldn't even be allowed them. Surely Anna would get that, or at least her mother could. Kids needed their family, something familiar.

Nodding to herself, she took a deep breath and stood up. She'd go to her mother's.

Her phone beeped and she looked down. Lane had forwarded the lawyer's contact details, with possibly twenty *x*'s at the end. She sent an *x* back with a thank-you, walked down the stairs, grabbed her bag and keys, and got in the car.

When she pulled into her parents' driveway, she sat for a minute, hands gripping the steering wheel. Her mother was not going to take this well. Taking a deep breath, she got out of the car, opening the front door to the house without waiting for an answer to her knock, calling down the hallway, "Mum?"

"Anna? Down here!"

In the kitchen, her mother was hovering over a sink full of dishes, her back to Anna.

The sight of her mother's greying hair piled into a bun was so familiar it sent an ache through Anna's gut. Sandra glanced over her shoulder briefly.

"Hey, honey. Where're my grandkids?"

Anna opened her mouth to reply and found she couldn't.

When she didn't receive an answer, Sandra turned around, hands wet, and reached for a towel to dry them. "Honey?" She looked at Anna properly, finally, and her hands stopped, towel still clutched in them. Her face paled. "Anna. Where are the kids?"

Anna saw the panic that took over her mother's eyes and forced herself to answer. "They—they're okay. They aren't hurt."

The expression on her mother's face didn't change. "What's happened then?"

Anna ran her hand through her hair. "Cathy has told child services I was neglecting them. The kids were taken into foster care last night."

The towel dropped to the floor.

"And, on top of that, she's petitioned the court for guardianship."

Sandra's face was no longer pale—a deep red now streaked over her cheeks. "They're in *foster* care? Are they okay?" Her voice was explosive.

"I can't find out anything until tomorrow, but they're okay. I think."

"Why the *hell*," Anna had never heard her mother use that word, "would that idiotic woman tell them you were neglecting them?"

Needing to do something, Anna sat at the table.

Outraged, Sandra didn't move.

"She showed up a few weeks back, when I had to work late and they were here with you?"

"So?"

"She showed up and," Anna almost winced, "Lane had stayed over. Cathy kind of accused me of neglecting them then, implying I wasn't doing what was best for them."

"That's not grounds for any of this."

Anna shrugged. "I think she showed up Friday night, when the kids were here again. She left them a children's Bible."

Her mother's eyebrows shot up, but she stayed silent.

"No one was home that night. Who knows what she told them, Mum."

Stiffly, Sandra walked to the table and sat opposite Anna. "I still don't understand how that could mean they get taken?"

"Me too, to be honest. She's been implying I'm flaunting," Anna blushed, "sexual partners. The system works quickly, and they have to investigate anything that resembles abuse."

"That's just ridiculous. My poor kids."

Picking at her fingers, Anna shook her head. "God, Mum. They had to pull them both off of me."

Sandra blanched. "So what's going to happen?"

"Well, Lane got the name of someone who's supposed to be an amazing family lawyer. I can call him at nine."

"I can't believe that woman has petitioned to take them. And caused so much grief for them by doing this."

"I know." Anna bit her lip. "There'll be a hearing for temporary custody during the week, apparently, to look into the claims made against me and to choose where the kids go until the full custody hearing—which we need now, since she's petitioned the court."

Face flushed and eyes glittering, Sandra looked ready to explode. "That woman, is a..." she sought for the right word, "she's a bitch."

"She is."

"You look calm."

"I'm not. I just...I'm not. I tore up the book she left them."

"Good. Stupid cow."

They sat quietly for a minute.

"Mum. This is...I literally can't do anything. I want to go and get them."

"I know." Sandra looked up at the clock on the wall. "It's after nine. Call the lawyer."

Obediently, Anna grabbed her phone and rang the number.

"It's engaged."

Her mother looked ready to throw something. "For God's sake." She muttered, then stood up. "Tea?" She clearly needed to do something.

Even though Anna shook her head, Sandra went about pulling two cups out and starting the kettle.

This time, when Anna hit redial, it rang.

"Scott Matthews."

"Uh...hi. My name is Anna Foster, I—"

"Yes, Doctor Foster? I just got off the phone with Hayley Sears. She's filled me in a little on your situation."

Anna's mouth dropped open. "Um."

"We went to law school together. Now, I have most of the details, kids' names and so forth. I just need the morning to recover information. There is a branch of child services open. There's always someone in the office, these things unfortunately needing someone on them all the time. I know the guy in on Sundays personally. I'm going to get as much information about the complaints made as possible. Then I'm going to call you and have you come in this afternoon to go over what I have and what I need from you. Does this sound agreeable?"

Blinking rapidly, Anna didn't know what to say. This guy was amazing. "Yes. Yes, that sounds good."

"I know you'll have a lot of questions, but if we can save them for when you come in, we can go over everything at once."

"Uh…okay."

"Good. I'll be calling you, most likely around twelve. I have your number."

"Thanks. Wait, Mr Matthews?"

"Call me Scott."

Anna looked blindly at the mug of tea that her mother had just put down in front of her. "When you call the office, can you please try and get an update on the kids? I just want to know they're okay."

"Of course. I'll call you soon."

And he was gone.

All Anna could do was stare at her phone.

"Well!?"

Anna looked up in surprise; Sandra was looking at her expectantly. "Um. Hayley had already contacted him. They went to school together."

"You called Hayley?"

"This morning. I only left a voicemail. I wanted to ask her some questions."

"She gets stuff done."

If there was one thing Hayley was, it was efficient. "Well, he's contacting child services, some branch that's always operating that we mere mortals have no chance of contacting. He's going to get all the info he needs from them, then call me to come in this afternoon and answer my questions and get my side."

"And he'll find out about the kids?"

"Yes."

Her mother thumped her mug down in the same manner Anna had only an hour before. "This is just absurd. They're my grandkids and your niece and nephew. We should be allowed to go right now and get them." When Anna didn't answer, Sandra eyed her. "Anna. What are you thinking?"

Lost in thought, Anna kept staring at a single spot on the wall. "Nothing."

Her mother watched her, but Anna could tell she knew better than to push.

When Anna's phone rang again, she answered it as soon as she saw who was calling. "Hayley?"

"Anna. Hey. I'm sorry, the second I got your message I called my friend in Melbourne, he's a family law attorney."

"I know, he's the same guy I had recommended to me. I called him and he was already on it. Thank you for that."

"He's amazing. He's doing huge things in family law for Australia. God knows we need it. I know the issue is apparently neglect, but if I remember Sally's mother correctly, it won't be just about that."

"I think you're right."

"How are you?"

Anna swallowed, letting a breath out slowly between her lips. "I'm okay. I'm worried about the kids and what this will do to them. What if I don't get them back?"

"There are a lot of horror stories about the foster system, but I'm sure they'll be okay. Most people are doing it because they really care about the kids. As for the rest of it—you must have questions. Shoot."

Twenty minutes later, Anna put the phone down.

Her mother was back at the sink finishing the dishes. "What did she say?"

Anna took a deep breath. "Well. If things go well at the first hearing for temporary guardianship, they will probably get placed back with me in the interim until the guardianship hearing after it."

Her mother paled slightly. "Good. And if they don't?"

"They'll go to you, or to Cathy, or back into foster care. And I won't be considered at the guardianship hearing, because I will be busy being charged with neglect."

Her mother went impossibly paler. "But surely the chances are slim? You haven't neglected them!"

Anna didn't know what to say to that. She was exhausted. "Hayley said the chance of that happening is slim to none. In fact, she thinks that the judge may throw the whole thing out of court, because it seems there's been nothing that could possibly resemble neglect. She doesn't really understand how it came to them being removed."

"So Cathy is traumatising you and the kids for nothing." Her mother eyed her, and Anna shook her head vaguely; she didn't know what the woman was doing. "But we won't really know much until after this meeting with your lawyer?"

"Exactly."

"Or until the hearing?"

When Anna simply nodded, Sandra sat down heavily.

"I'll ask him about visitation, about seeing the kids hopefully tomorrow; if not me, then at least you."

Her mother stared at the table. Nausea roiled in Anna's stomach. "God, Mum. Toby will be so confused."

Eyes filling with tears, Sandra shook her head. "Anna, don't."

Anna wanted to say that Ella had looked at her and asked if she didn't want them anymore, but she didn't want to see her mother cry.

She stayed, neither of them speaking much, her father out somewhere, until Scott called and told her to come in.

Anna weaved through traffic, lost in thought.

It was incredible, really: a few months ago, she had thought she was the worst person for this, had wanted her parents to do it, anyone else, really, but her. She didn't think she was cut out for it; she was too selfish, too happy being free and childless. Anna had thought her brother and sister-in-law were crazy to leave two small children in her care.

Now? Now Anna couldn't imagine her life without those two kids. The three of them had spent months learning how to be a unit. Anna would much prefer Jake and Sally be alive, but they weren't, and this was her life, and she in no way wanted it to change. Those kids were too important to her.

When she entered the office, she was met by a polished man in a well-cut, dark-grey suit, hair stylishly groomed. He looked like he belonged in a courtroom drama, with his easy smile and charming presence. His right hand, which had been fiddling with the wedding ring on his left, reached out.

"Doctor Foster? Scott. My secretary would normally greet you, but it's Sunday, so it's just me today."

Anna shook his hand. "Please, call me Anna."

He clapped his hands together. "Great. Follow me."

The well-lit office had bookcases lining the walls and an exquisite painting of a seascape behind the desk. Anna sat in front of the dark mahogany desk opposite where Scott sat in a comfortable leather chair. The whole room smelt like a pine forest.

"Now, I won't keep you waiting on this part. I spoke to Ben in the child services office, and he had spoken with the foster family this morning, a routine follow up, considering they only got there last night."

Anna was hanging on his every word.

"I've been assured the kids are fine."

Anna slumped back into the seat slightly, relieved.

"Ella has been quiet, not talking very much. Picking at her food."

Anna nodded distractedly. "We only really just got her eating normally again after her parents' deaths."

"Another reason I am very unimpressed at this situation. Toby, he's been good. He woke up several times overnight, but is fine. Confused, of course."

"Good." Anna didn't know what to say. "I want to see them, Scott."

"I know. Call the office in the morning, speak to your caseworker. See where you go from there. Call me if you aren't happy with whatever they say."

"Okay."

Scott sat up straighter. "Now. Let's go over everything."

For an hour, Anna sat in his office. Scott got her to go over how she had gotten the kids into her care, how they had been since then, her work status, if Toby was in day care—something Scott assured her had zero weight on neglect.

"Half the families in Australia would be neglecting their kids, if that were the case." The tone of his voice showed his clear dislike of that idea.

As Scott proceeded to fill Anna in on where she stood, she learnt that Cathy had called child protection weeks ago and expressed concerns to Lorna that Anna wasn't doing right by the kids. She believed Anna was neglecting them by barely being at home with them.

That, Anna thought, explained the more frequent Lorna visits. She'd been checking in.

"I'm guessing that Cathy was unhappy with Lorna's reaction to the first complaints and went further up. There's a record of an anonymous complaint, as well."

"It would have been Cathy."

Scott raised his hands. "Probably. But they treat it as an extra one. On Friday, Cathy called again and made a serious complaint. She said no one had been home all night—"

"She watched my house?"

Grimly, Scott sat up and leant on his desk. "It would seem. She said, out of concern, she went by the hospital, where you were leaving with 'some woman' and didn't return to the house."

The hair on the back of Anna's arms stood up. "This is very creepy."

"It is, yes. She claims at least two women frequently visit your house and leave at odd hours. The complaints are numerous, but along these lines."

The more he talked, the more anger filled her.

Cathy had been watching them.

Cathy had claimed Anna worked more than she saw the children, had to work inappropriate hours—and so would "dump" the kids with their grandparents—that she'd had a parade of women over and ignored the kids. She claimed Anna was flaunting inappropriate sexual behaviours.

Scott laid it out and then had Anna give her side.

"Lane is my girlfriend—however, most of my time is spent with the kids. The only reason I was with her on Friday night was because Ella had asked to have a sleepover at her grandparents' house. Until then, Lane had only stayed over once, and it was, again, when the kids were with their grandparents."

Scott was nodding and writing in a notebook.

"Kym is a great friend, and the kids adore her. She is over often for meals and has babysat twice. She lost her husband last year and I guess we've been kind of supporting each other."

"And does she stay at the house?"

"Sometimes, yes. She sleeps on the couch. I don't think she enjoys being at home." Anna didn't want to expand too much on Kym's private issues. "The kids love her—Ella is always begging her to sleep over."

Scott's eyes scanned what he had written. "And the time Cathy showed up and the kids weren't there in the morning?"

"It was the only time my job interfered—there was an emergency, so the kids stayed with my parents. I—"

"Anna." Scott was looking at her empathetically. "That's enough of an answer. Every parent's job interferes sometimes. I'm impressed it's only been once. Look, here I am, on a Sunday." He winked at her.

Anna tried to stop the defensiveness that was overtaking her.

Scott leant back in his chair. "To me," he said, "this sounds like someone out to cause problems. It sounds like her claims are exaggerated and false, even if she believes them to be true. Nothing says neglect, and Anna, I want to reassure you that I think we'll be coming out on top with this one."

A breath Anna hadn't realised she'd been holding expelled from her chest. "Are you sure?"

"I can't give any guarantees. But it sounds like this is a woman whose religious beliefs and personal dislike for choices you are entitled to make as a guardian, such as day care, have led her to make some pretty extreme, false claims. All parents have their kids stay with grandparents at times. You've never left the kids alone, you've never beaten them, or verbally abused them. They are fed, in school, clothed—I don't think she has a leg to stand on. I'm actually quite confused as to how it's gone this far."

"The new caseworker was never friendly."

Scott's eyebrows pressed together. "That's also confusing me. It's unusual to switch caseworkers, and especially to switch them, then switch back, even if Lorna was apparently on holiday. I'm wondering if the wrong paperwork got lodged or…" he paused, "something. From what I see, things are in your favour."

Slightly reassured, Anna nodded, though the worry still ate at her.

"As for the 'sexual partners'… You are allowed to date. No one said this means you need to become a spinster. We will be needing this," his eyes dropped to his notes, "'Kym' to establish that she is in no way involved with you—in that manner, anyway."

"There will be no issue with that."

"And Lane will probably need to testify to the manner of your relationship. I'll need a list of names from you for character references. Some will be written and some I may ask to testify—people like the day care workers, your boss, your mother, teachers at Ella's school. We won't be using Lane or Kym for these, due to the allegations made against them. But anyone else is fine."

They went over names and numbers. When Anna stood to go, she looked at the photo on his desk. It showed a smiling woman with her arms wrapped around two young boys.

"Thank you, Scott. You have a beautiful family."

He smiled at the photo. "I do. I just happen to believe that everyone deserves to have what I have."

Anna nodded at him, and, as she turned to go, he called her back. "Anna! Do you mind me asking?" He grinned, and she could see the young man peek through who had probably had many a wild party with her ex in law school. "How the hell did you tie down Hayley for three years?"

Anna almost laughed. "We thought we wanted the same things."

"And now?"

"Now I just want those kids back."

He nodded. "I'll be in contact. Call me tomorrow if you have any issues with Lorna. Unfortunately, they have their own policies we lawyers don't get much say in."

Anna nodded, thanked him again, and left.

She didn't feel like she was any closer to having the kids back.

This whole thing was like a nightmare.

In her car, Anna sat for a minute, staring out the window.

It *looked* like it would be in her favour, but Scott had said there were no guarantees. And when she had asked if she *did* get them back this week, how the permanent guardianship hearing would go, he had said they'd take it one step at a time, that if she got them back temporarily, the court usually found in favour of whomever the parents had named, come the guardianship hearing. But, he'd said, their focus was the temporary guardianship hearing and disputing the neglect claims for now.

Anna couldn't help but wonder, how would the permanent guardianship hearing go with this on her record? She felt ill and like her head was spinning.

Had she, in some small way, neglected the kids for Lane? Anna hadn't thought she had. Lane had made Anna's life so much more positive during an incredibly trying time, and she didn't really understand how she was meant to have stopped it from happening. Should she have?

Her fingers gripped the steering wheel, heart pounding in her chest. In the rearview mirror, Anna caught sight of the scratches on her neck from Toby as Lorna had pulled him off her. They were tiny, thin, but long; he had not let go until forced. What if she didn't get them back, despite what Scott said? They'd been taken once. Or what if she did, and then the judge found in favour of Cathy at the other hearing? Cathy, who had a stable home life, who wasn't a lesbian in a new relationship; even scratch the lesbian part: Cathy, who was settled down, married; Cathy, who didn't work full time. It had never occurred to Anna before that being a lesbian could impact this. Even after being assured by Scott and Hayley that it couldn't, worry gnawed at her stomach.

Cathy would never use the kids having a sleepover as an excuse to stay the night at her girlfriend's.

Head hurting from beating herself up, Anna drove on autopilot. After parking in her usual spot at the hospital, she sat, staring out the window.

Jake and Sally would not want the kids in foster care, or at Cathy's. They didn't even want them with Anna's parents. And considering how her father had been since Jake had died, she was starting to understand that decision even more than she had in the beginning.

Without thinking, Anna pulled her phone out and sent a text to Kym.

Gonna need that wine tonight, please.

She climbed out of the car and took the back hallways to her office, avoiding eye contact with anyone who recognised her. Closing the door behind her, she stood in the room, looking around, bracing for something she realised she had been headed towards all day.

There was a finger painting Toby had done in day care on her wall, next to a drawing Ella had made. Toby's painting was all red, his current favourite colour. Ella had drawn a splotchy drawing of her panda teddy. The tree in the picture had pink leaves, because, "Why not, Aunty Na?"

Watching the door, Anna waited.

It didn't take long. Lane entered the office, concern on her face.

Anna straightened. She wanted to smile. Lane looked so familiar, so worried about her as she closed the door behind her. Despite wanting to meet her, Anna forced herself to take a step back. Lane paused when she saw the motion, eyebrows knitting together.

"Anna? What's happened? Did you see the lawyer?"

Anna kept her arms crossed in front of her. She cleared her throat. "I did. He's really hopeful that I'll get them back."

Lane looked relieved. "Thank God. Did you get news of them?"

"I did. They're okay, apparently. I still don't know if I'll get to see them tomorrow."

"Hopefully you can. You'll feel so much better if you can see them with your own eyes."

Anna couldn't quite make eye contact with Lane. Her stomach was churning, and Anna didn't want to do what she was about to. Her fingers clenched, nails biting into her skin.

Lane looked at her for a second. "Anna? What is it?"

Anna needed to say it, but she was having a lot of trouble doing so. She swallowed and finally looked Lane in the eye, jaw set, trying to get herself together.

Eyes darkening, Lane shook her head, her cheeks flushing. "Anna." Her voice was low. "No."

"Lane—"

"No. Don't do this."

"Lane. I'm sorry." Anna clenched her jaw. "I need to get them back."

"You will. You will!" Lane was almost wild eyed. "Anna, you said the lawyer thought it sounded good."

"He did." She licked her lips, which were suddenly dry. "But, what about later? The other hearing? I… What about if I do get them back?"

"Then that's a good thing."

"But then, the other hearing. Proving I should have them."

"What?"

There were no words to explain it. She could barely explain it to herself. "I think this was too soon, for the kids. For me, with the kids. I need to focus, on them."

Mouth open, as if she couldn't believe what she was hearing, Lane shook her head again.

"Lane…I think—"

"You can't even say it," Lane flared.

With a deep breath, Anna closed her eyes and took another. Before she wasn't able to say it, she let the words spill quickly. "I think we need to stop seeing each other."

Opening her eyes, Anna wished she hadn't. Lane's lips were pursed, tears tracked down her cheeks unchecked. "Anna…" She whispered it, her voice cracking over the word.

How had she managed to say it? "Lane…you, you are so amazing. But I just—with the kids, I'm so confused…"

Lane shook her head. "No. No. Don't do that, Anna. Don't tell me I'm amazing after ending this."

"The kids."

Lane shut her mouth.

Both were at a loss, with no idea how to fix it.

Anna's phone buzzed on the wood of her desk, and they both glanced to it. Anna picked it up. Kym.

Red or white? Hell, I'll bring both. See you at six.

Clenching her jaw, Anna looked back to Lane.

"Do you mean this, Anna?"

Anna, despite herself, said, "I do." She swallowed hard. "I have to get them back. I have to focus, on that."

Swiping angrily at her cheeks, Lane nodded. "Then you need to walk out of here, because I can't walk away from you."

The order was almost too much. Anna's urge to close the gap between them and kiss Lane waged war with her stubborn thought that this was what was best. With sheer determination, she grabbed her phone, slid it into her pocket, pulled her bag onto her shoulder and walked forward. When she was next to Lane, shoulders touching, facing opposite ways, Anna paused. Lane's scent washed over her, and her eyes closed briefly as she selfishly enjoyed it. She turned her head to look at her in profile.

"Lane." Her voice was a whisper.

Lane turned her head, and Anna almost didn't leave as she took in the utterly broken look on her face. Anna's voice cracked. "I am so, so sorry."

The tears on Lane's cheeks belied her single, perfunctory nod. Anna finally broke eye contact, finger barely stroking the back of Lane's hand before she stepped forward, pulled open the door and walked out. She let a slow breath out from between her lips as she let the door shut behind her, walking away from the sob she heard come from the other side.

Her fingers shook, and she gave up trying to do up the buttons on her jacket.

It wasn't until she reached her car that the sob in her own throat burst out. In the empty car park, hand on her door handle, she squatted slowly to her knees, forehead falling against the cool metal.

Chapter Nineteen

"Okay. So. Recap, Anna. The lawyer's went as well as it could; you still don't know for sure, but he's optimistic." At Anna's nod, Kym continued, leaning back on the couch and lifting her feet up onto the coffee table. "The kids are okay, we had that confirmed today. You will find out tomorrow if you can see them, but for now, they're okay."

Anna nodded again, staring at the empty wine bottle next to Kym's feet.

"Hayley was pleasant on the phone, but nothing happened to stress you out."

Another nod.

"And we've finished a bottle of wine, and you have just finished telling me this."

Anna nodded a third time, this time taking a sip of her wine.

"Right. So what the fuck?"

Surprised out of her stare, Anna blinked owlishly at Kym. "What?"

"Exactly—what? Things are shit, they're really, really shit, and they took the kids. I'm not disputing that at all. But why do you look ten times more messed up than this morning? Not that that's not okay, you can lose your shit. But I thought the stunt with the book last night was you doing that."

"It was."

"All right. So why? Why the red eyes when you opened the door? Why did I have to prod you to talk? Why are you clutching your wine glass like a lifeline? And why do you smell like cigarettes?" Kym sat back up. "And *where* is Lane? All she did all morning was ask me if I thought it was a good idea if she messaged you, and if I thought you were okay, and did I think she could fake the Ebola virus to get out of work? So—what happened?"

Swallowing, Anna finally said it: "I-I, uh, broke up with Lane."

Kym's mouth fell open slightly, and she stared at Anna, who simply looked back. Her mouth closed, then opened again. Finally she spoke. "You what?"

Anna didn't want to repeat it. Tears were pricking her eyes, and she really didn't want to lose it again. She looked back to the wine bottle.

"Okay." The word dragged out, as if Kym wasn't sure where to go with that information. "Okay." She approached the next question like she would approach a wild bear. "Do you mind me asking why?"

The wine glass trembled in Anna's hand and she tried to avoid Kym's wide, sympathetic eyes. She heard the rustling of Kym leaning forward, then felt a hand resting on her forearm.

"I have to get those kids back." Anna's breath came out slow and shaky, as she finally allowed her gaze to fall upon Kym again.

All Kym did was watch her.

"I do, Kym. I have to." Her voice was hoarse. "And Lane is just, *fuck.*" A tear fell down Anna's cheek, and she wiped it away with a forceful stroke of her hand. "Lane is just, amazing. She is patient and kind and loves the kids, and I think she loves me. I had to end it."

"Why? Why did you have to end it?"

"Did you not hear the explanation of why Cathy filed the charges? If I hadn't been in a relationship, if I was more focused on the kids, this may not have happened."

Letting go of Anna's arm, Kym grabbed the second bottle of wine and poured them both another glass. "Anna, you are so focused on those kids. You're allowed to date, too. All parents are allowed to date."

"I know that! It's just...It was too soon, after everything. I'm all for parents dating. I in no way believe parents' lives should end just because they have kids."

"Okay, good."

"But it was clearly too soon. Everything has still been so raw. And if, *if,* I get them back at the temporary hearing—"

"You will."

"*If* I do, what's to secure me getting them at the final hearing? Cathy has petitioned the court for custody as well. With this on my record, it may fuck it all up. If I'm having some frivolous relationship, appearing like I'm putting my own needs over the kids, why wouldn't they give them to stable, married Cathy who wants them?" Anna could feel the flush on her cheeks as she looked at Kym, begging for an answer.

"I can see where you're coming from." Kym spoke slowly. "But, it's not a frivolous relationship, is it?"

"No."

"What's wrong with two kids seeing their caregiver in a solid, meaningful relationship?"

"Kym, you're missing the point. It's too soon, it's messed the guardianship up. My brother, he wanted those kids with *me*. And now they're in foster care." She looked at Kym. "They're in *foster* care and I just, God, I miss them."

Putting her glass down, Kym pulled Anna against her, and Anna let herself be wrapped up in the comfort of her friend.

"I know you do, sweetie."

"And I miss Lane."

Kym sighed. "This is *so* fucked up."

"It really is."

"So, I kind of wish Cathy would burst through the door and see this. Then you'll really be labelled a giant ho."

This time, her laugh was genuine, the sound bubbling out of her. "She's probably parked in the bushes with a zoom lens. Come the hearing, she'll put in photos as evidence." Anna sat up, wiping her eyes and topping up her glass again, along with Kym's.

"She will. Because you know, you lesbians, you're all sleeping with everyone."

Anna managed a watery smile. "Oh, yeah. The cafeteria lady, the chick in the grocery store, everyone." Clutching her glass, Anna gave a weak wiggle of her eyebrows. "Even *you* apparently."

"Oh, you would be so lucky." She reciprocated, wriggling her brows up and down lecherously, but Anna's smile didn't last long.

"This is not fair, Kym."

Both of them looked around the living room, which was filled with Ella's DVDs, Toby's blocks, their toys scattered everywhere. A room the both of them, Lane, and the kids had all half lived in the last several weeks.

Kym sighed. "It's really not."

Waking up at eight with a sore head and a heavy heart, Anna called her boss on Monday morning to explain what had happened with the kids.

He sounded more outraged and shocked than she'd expected. McDermott told her to take the day if she needed, to let him know when the trial would be, when she'd need to see the lawyer, and he'd have her covered. He told her that he'd testify until he was blue in the face that Anna had only taken the job on the condition that she be able to be home in the evenings and on weekends when able, especially the first year, when they were all still adjusting. He said he had her work-hour statistics and that he'd compare her time spent at work to others.

Slightly impressed, she said she was calling child protective services that morning, and, if she was able to see the kids, she would take the day, but, if she couldn't, she would come in after for the distraction. She also let him know that Scott Matthews would be in touch about a character reference and that she was incredibly grateful he had her back.

The second she hung up and had nothing to occupy her thoughts, a heaviness settled over her.

She wanted to call Lane. She just wanted to talk to her.

But she couldn't talk to Lane, because she had broken up with her. The silent house was enough to remind her of why. But, God, she needed more of a reminder, because, right now, she wanted Lane. Resolved not to dwell on that feeling, Anna stood up out of bed, grabbed her phone, and pulled a hoodie on.

The house was too still, too quiet. She wanted to feel Toby's chubby little toddler arms wrap around her neck as she lifted him out of his cot. She wanted to hear Ella recount her day, sharing details that were so big and important when you were six and-a-half. Anna wanted to yell for Ella to not run down the stairs, or to have to deal with one of Toby's tantrums, or to try and pry Ella back into the world when she looked lost.

She just wanted the kids back in the house.

After wrestling so hard with the idea of having them in her life, now she was up for the biggest fight of her life to get them back. Anna needed to remind herself of that when her stomach felt hollow at the knowledge that she'd ended the relationship of her dreams.

Lane's words—*then you need to walk out of here, because I can't walk away from you*—just needed to stop playing around and around in her head.

In the kitchen, Anna started the coffee machine and quickly downed a glass of water with some aspirin. She winced at the smell of nicotine on her fingers. She was really not doing a good job of appearing like a healthy, well-put-together person who deserved to raise her brother's children. Leaning against the kitchen bench while the smell of coffee started to waft around her, Anna scrolled through her contacts until she found Lorna's office number and hit *send*.

When it rang to a voicemail service informing her that the office opened at nine, Anna slammed her phone onto the bench and glared at it. She was going to go insane without answers soon. If she could just see them, reassure Ella, cuddle Toby, she'd be calmer. She'd be able to focus on the trial.

For a moment, Anna considered calling Scott to find out if he had a date for the trial yet. Frustration bit at her when she remembered it was early and he also wouldn't be in. Plus, he'd said he'd be in contact that evening with the information. She couldn't just keep calling everyone every ten minutes.

She poured a coffee, grabbed her phone and went to sit outside on the back porch step, purposely leaving her cigarettes inside.

She felt hopeless. There was nothing she could do to speed this process up. Grabbing her phone, she dialled Lorna again, just in case she was in. It went to voicemail, and Anna left a short message to say she'd appreciate it if Lorna could get back to her as soon as possible.

The chilly morning air made her shiver as her coffee steamed on the step.

It really was too quiet.

God, what if she didn't get them back?

Her phone rang, and Anna almost dropped it in her haste to answer. "Hello?"

"Hi, sweetie."

"Oh. Mum, hey."

"Expecting Lorna?"

"I just tried calling; they don't open until nine."

"Oh." Sandra sounded as disappointed as Anna felt. "I was calling for an update. I know we only spoke yesterday evening, but, well..."

"I get it. I'll let you know as soon as I know anything."

They chatted briefly, Anna avoiding any questions about Lane, not wanting to tell her mother just yet. After hanging up, Anna took long sips of her coffee and waited. At ten to nine, she called Lorna again, left another voicemail. Anna almost hoped they'd annoy the woman. Let them question her commitment to the kids.

At six to nine, she called again and left another brief message.

At nine, she called and hung up.

At six past nine, her phone rang, and, this time, she actually did drop her coffee mug in the rush to answer it. "Hello?"

"Anna. Hi, it's Lorna."

"Hi, I've been trying to reach you."

The woman's voice was almost amused. "I know, I got your messages."

"Sorry."

"Don't be, it's fine. First things first, I spoke to the foster family with Toby and Ella on the way to work this morning, and they're doing fine."

Anna felt the breath knocked out of her. The relief she felt each time someone told her that, even if she didn't get to see them herself, was palpable. "Good." Her voice cracked. "Ella can go quiet. And not eat sometimes. And Toby, he just gets a little clingy—" She broke off.

"They're being well looked after, Anna. I am sorry about this." Lorna's voice was soft.

"Can I see them?"

There was silence for a minute and Anna's stomach dropped.

"I'm sorry, Anna. You won't be able to see them today. There's a lot of protocol in setting this up. And, uh, I may not be able to get you in to see them at all."

"What!"

"I know. I'm going to try. But if I can't get you, I will definitely be able to get your mother in. Just, unfortunately, the soonest I can get a visit would be Wednesday."

Her mouth went dry. "Lorna—they'll be so confused and unsettled. Would—can't I see them? Speak to them?"

"I'm sorry, I won't have answers for that until Wednesday."

Closing her eyes for a second to find patience, Anna counted to three and opened them again. "Can you at least pass them a message from me?"

Lorna hesitated. "All right."

"Tell…tell them I miss them, and I can't wait to see them again. Tell Ella that of course—of course I want her." She was choking up.

"I'll tell them."

"Thank you."

"We won't be doing nothing these next few days, Anna. I'll be talking to your colleagues, your family—all to testify when the date's set. Okay?"

"Yeah. Sure."

"Take care of yourself."

"I will."

Anna hung up and stared dumbly at her phone. That had not been what she wanted to hear.

To get it over with, she called her mother and filled her in, holding the phone away as Sandra protested loudly, ranting for a good ten minutes before Anna got her off the phone.

She dropped her head heavily into her hands. How was she meant to just go on about her life like normal while Ella and Toby were in foster care?

One thing was for sure: she was not going to be able to sit around all day.

After calling her boss to fill him in, Anna left for work, parking her car far from her usual place. She froze as she got out of the car. Jesus, what if she saw Lane?

It turned out that when you're trying to avoid someone and they're trying to avoid you, it's easy to not run into them. Anna threw herself into work that day.

Partway through the afternoon, she saw Lorna making her way to McDermott's office. Involuntarily, Anna's feet started walking towards her, before she forced herself to stop and walk away. No good would come from cornering the woman and losing her cool.

Later that morning, Anna's stomach clenched when she turned automatically to walk down the hallway to the day care and remembered Toby wouldn't be there, that she couldn't walk in and watch him drop whatever he was doing and run at her, delighted she had entered his little world. The last time, she'd left with paint smeared all over her scrubs, bright red, from him wrapping himself around her legs. Feeling lost, Anna turned back the way she had come and headed for the cafeteria.

In the middle of the day, Kym found her with a coffee in hand. "I saw Lane."

Anna didn't even glance up from her desk. "*Don't,* Kym. Just, not now."

Kym had a lot to say; Anna could almost feel her urge to speak as she stood near the desk. Finally, she broke. "Anna, don't you think that—"

"I've got to get to a surgery, Kym." And she slipped out of her office, leaving Kym looking torn between pity and frustration.

That afternoon, Scott called and told her the trial would be set for Friday. She told him what Lorna had said about not being able to see the kids, and he sighed, saying the system had flaws, but all their policies were there for a reason. He reminded her that by playing by the rules, they built a better case in her favour.

She told him that seemed ridiculous, that her wanting to see them should be a good thing.

"Keep phoning them for answers and check-ups on the kids, but do what they say," he told her. "Most of all, be patient."

She hung up even more frustrated.

Anna worked until past midnight that night, stealing surgeries from the on-call anaesthetist, who happily handed them over and found a room in which to sleep. Kym eventually hunted Anna down in a hallway and handed her a vending machine sandwich to share.

"You know," she said thoughtfully, "it wasn't that long ago that Lane and Tess, and then you, were following me into work and making sure I ate."

Anna swallowed an unsatisfactory mouthful of bland bread. "I'm okay, Kym. I just need the distraction."

"I know."

Anna filled Kym in on her conversations with Lorna and Scott, bitterness at the situation heavy on her tongue. Kym put her hand on Anna's shoulder; there was nothing she could say.

They finished without any more talking, Anna barely tasting her food.

As if to say something, Kym turned to her and opened her mouth, then seemed to think better of it and stopped. In the end, she just said, "Make sure you get some sleep tonight, alright?"

Anna threw her an absentminded nod.

She left the hospital around one a.m., exhausted.

Anna woke up groggily on Tuesday morning, way before her alarm—despite the late hour she'd gone to bed.

The heaviness that had been weighing on her for days was even heavier this morning.

The kids' absence was starting to take its toll.

As was Lane's.

She got to work far too early, when nurses were just starting their morning rounds. Despite the early hour, she had already left a message for Lorna requesting an update on how the kids were and to ask if there was any news on the visit.

Anna paused in her work that morning only to take Lorna's call, to hear the repetitive "the kids are okay" line. Though this time, Lorna added something else. "Ella…" she said. "Ella says she knows, because of the way your face looked when we drove away."

The sob trapped in Anna's throat almost spilled out over the phone.

Thankful that she didn't have any consultations, Anna threw herself into surgeries instead. At four o'clock, she was just collecting notes for her final operation of the day when her boss appeared before her.

"Go home, Foster."

She turned to him in surprise. "What? Why?"

The empathy on McDermott's face was worse than if he had been stern. "You were here too late last night and you came in far too early. Go. Home."

"Let me finish this one?"

"Foster—"

"I did his consult yesterday, I'm prepped. It's my signature on the anaesthetic paperwork." She paused. "Please?"

He hesitated a moment. "Last one?"

She tried not to look too triumphant. "Thank you."

But she entered the surgery with a ball of dread sitting in her stomach. She didn't want to go home, to the silence and to her thoughts.

She walked in to find the surgeons waiting in the scrub room, the nurses scrubbed in and sorting out the instruments. When she caught her anaesthetic nurse's eye, Anna tried to give her a friendly smile. She was just getting into her normal rhythm when something made her look up and she saw Lane scrubbing in, staring straight at her. Lane's eyes dropped back down to the sink. This was not the kind of work distraction Anna wanted.

The surgeons were gowned and gloved, and when Lane stepped in a second afterwards, the other nurses greeting her warmly. The surgeon, a man named Troy Fields whom Anna had never heard be overly friendly with anyone, greeted Lane like an old best friend.

"Lane! Are you my scrub nurse today?"

Lane nodded. "Yeah, I just got sent up. I heard you were one short."

Troy was already moving over to the patient. "Ah, well, always good to have you."

After the checks and safety procedures, the surgery was underway.

Lane wouldn't look at her.

Anna was spending far too much time staring. Lane was obviously incredibly respected, and she seemed to have worked often with these two particular surgeons, reading their movements and handing them instruments before they could ask. She was at home in the theatre. All Anna could think was how she just wanted Lane to look at her.

The surgery went far too slowly and far too quickly, all at once. It was painful to be so close to Lane and to feel like they were completely separated, and, before she knew it, the patient was being wheeled out and it was over.

Anna sat on her stool as the nurses cleaned up around her, torn between trying to talk to Lane and needing to be far away from her. She couldn't do this: there was no way Anna could pretend to be strong when Lane was so close that she could reach out and touch her. Pushing back suddenly, she stood and swept out of the room, washing her hands in record time before fleeing. She made it to the locker room, angry that she was being sent home and couldn't stay and distract herself from this tight feeling in her chest. Slowly dragging out the time until she would have to leave, Anna pulled on her jeans and her boots. Her hands shook slightly. She paused at the mirror, running a brush through her hair. Her eyebrows raised in slight surprise at how pale she was, at the black smudges under her eyes. She turned to leave, pausing abruptly when she saw Lane standing awkwardly in the doorway, hand on the door, as if unsure whether or not to turn and flee.

Anna gave her a small smile. "Hey."

Lane's own confused "hey" was barely audible.

Anna turned back to her locker and swung the door shut, gnawing on her bottom lip and waiting. She didn't turn around until she heard the door gently fall into place and knew Lane was gone.

She had known it would be hard to see Lane. Had known that doing what was right would be even more difficult when faced with the sight of her. In spite of herself, Anna had watched Lane more than she should have. Lane, though looking tired and a little pale, was still as stunning as always. And the look in Lane's eyes made her chest ache. Anna hadn't realised how overpowering the urge to fall against Lane would be. God, to break down and just let everything that was inside her out would be such a relief. Sighing, Anna grabbed her bag.

It seemed like the smell of Lane's perfume still lingered.

Bag on her shoulder, she turned to leave, stopping when she saw that Lane was still standing a step from the door, watching her silently. Anna took in a deep breath and started to walk forward, shoulder brushing past Lane as she walked to the door. Fingers on the handle, she paused; she could feel Lane turn around behind her. That motion was all it took.

She turned around, pressing herself against Lane, hands coming up to cup her cheeks as she kissed her. Without a second of hesitation, Lane returned the kiss, pushing back against Anna with force that felt both bruising and comforting.

Anna's thumb brushed Lane's cheek, fingers running through the softness of Lane's hair, lips hovering over Lane's before leaning forward to press one soft, final kiss on her lips.

And then she turned and opened the door, walking away before she couldn't.

"Where's Lane?"

A light flicked on in the kitchen, and Anna blinked at the brightness.

Her mother stood eying her from the kitchen doorway.

Anna tried to surreptitiously slip the packet of cigarettes into her back pocket. She pulled closed the door that led to the back porch.

"I, uh—"Anna avoided her mother's eye.

"You what, Anna Foster?"

"I broke up with her."

There was a beat of silence that actually had Anna feeling afraid.

"You what?" Sandra's voice was like ice.

Sighing, Anna looked anywhere but at her mother. "I broke up with her."

"You what!" Her voice was now more like an angry storm.

"Mum, calm down."

"I will *not* calm down! Anna Foster, you sit your ass down right now."

Anna, eyes wide, sat at the kitchen table and looked up at her mother, feeling about five years old.

"You *ended* it with Lane?"

"Yes, but—"

"The first person to make you smile after Ja… after everything?"

"Yes, but—"

"The only distraction you had from the major sacrifices you were making?"

"Yes, but—"

"The woman the kids *adore?*"

"Yes, but—"

"The woman who's been patient and who put up with all the crap that's come with dating you?"

"Crap? But—"

"You're letting that crazy old woman win!"

Anna went to open her mouth and then closed it. That hadn't occurred to her.

Her mother crossed her arms in front of herself and glared at Anna, one eyebrow raised. Anna felt like she was looking into a mirror. As she pondered those words, she practically deflated in her chair.

"I didn't do this easily, Mum." The mirthless laugh lay stuck in her throat. "Believe me, it was not easy."

Sandra kept her arms crossed, not moving.

"Mum! Stop it! I need to make sure I get those kids back, and this was one way it felt like I could help that happen."

Sandra finally spoke. "That's a load of crap."

"It's not!"

Sighing, Sandra slid into a chair opposite Anna, resting a hand on her wrist. "God, honey." Her voice was suddenly soft, understanding. "I can see why you thought this would be a solution. And I have no idea how you brought yourself to end it with Lane." She shook her head. "I really don't. But no judge is going to expect you to keep yourself single. Lane is someone any child would be lucky to have in their lives."

Dropping her head on the table, Anna sighed. "Mum, please, you are not helping."

"Good. Because you need Lane to help get you through this. And *when* you get those kids back, they're going to want Lane here, too. God, Ella doesn't shut up about her."

Sitting up, Anna clenched her jaw, frustrated. "But, the hearing, if—"

"The judge will already know you're dating someone. Whether or not you've ended it now isn't going to make a hell of a lot of difference."

"It will. It could show I'm focused on Ella and Toby."

"You *are* already focused on them, Anna." Sandra gave a sigh that made it sound like she was incredibly hard done by. "There are going to be so many people testifying to that. Don't you think it's going to look amazing to a judge that, *even though* you've started a new relationship, every single person will be testifying that you have constantly put the kids first? That you have prioritised them again and again over yourself and your relationship with Lane?"

Anna had nothing to say to that.

Sandra shook her head. "Oh, honey. You can be so useless sometimes."

"Thanks, Mum."

"Well, it's very true."

Chapter Twenty

The bathroom was the last place Anna expected Kym to corner her with a coffee, and certainly not with a look so fierce Anna was almost too scared to accept it. She slowly reached out her hand and took the cup, and they stood appraising each other for a minute.

Kym didn't even offer her a tight smile; she only spoke quickly, as if to stop Anna from interrupting. "Okay. I need to say something."

"Kym—"

"*No*. I do. Because you're being an idiot."

An indignant, "hey" was all she managed to get out before Kym raised a hand.

"You are. I get it that I don't know the legal system, but you can't end such a good thing because of this."

"I had to."

Kym's stern look remained. "Yeah, but you didn't."

"Kym, I—"

"No. Lane is too damn respectful for her own good and won't say any of this, so I will."

"Kym—"

"I said *shush*! Well, I didn't. But I meant that. You didn't need to end this. I've been good the past two days; I let it be because, well, no offense, Anna, but you looked like shit."

Anna opened her mouth, but Kym ploughed on. "I've stewed on this all night, and I need to say it." She grabbed Anna's shoulder with her free hand and stared her straight in the eye. "You are an idiot. You've got something special with Lane. Cathy is the evil one here, and no court will keep you from the kids just because you have a girlfriend! Everyone will testify that you are one hundred per cent focussed on those kids, even to the detriment of your relationship."

They stared at each other a minute as Kym's hand buried itself into her lab coat pocket.

Anna pursed her lips. "Mum pointed this out to me last night, too."

"I've always liked that woman. I'm sure she was nicer about it than I'm being."

Anna shook her head. "Actually, no, she was meaner. She may have, um, pointed out that I can be useless."

Kym shrugged. "Good. Our words getting through?"

Anna gave her back her own shrug.

"You know, Anna, if it's any help at all, everyone can see how you would call it wrong here. You were thinking of the kids."

"I *have* to think of them."

"I know."

The coffee cup shook in her hand, and she realised her fingers were trembling. "What if Lane won't forgive me?"

Kym rolled her eyes. "She will."

"She might not."

"Shut up, Anna."

They blinked at each other.

"Do we need to hug?"

Anna shook her head.

"Good."

Kym rocked on her heels for a moment, the silence suddenly almost awkward. "So. Good—I'll be off then. You, uh, you think about what I just said."

Kym exited the bathroom, leaving Anna leaning against the sink. The silence pressed in on her as her mother's and Kym's words echoed in her ears.

Everything was so very messed up, and she just wanted her biggest problem to be Lane staying overnight and how to prepare Ella, and, if Anna was being honest with herself, how to prepare Lane for what was in store with two children. She actually missed *that* hesitancy, *that* worry. She wanted to be worrying about what to cook for dinner for the kids and to be thinking about work and to miss her brother and sister-in-law. She wanted to be allowed to grieve, because it sometimes felt she'd not had the chance to.

Everything had already been a mess, and now it was just a catastrophe.

And now her mother *and* Kym were saying things that left Anna speechless. What if they were right?

Gnawing her lip, Anna checked the time. It was nine a.m., and she had to be at the lawyer's at ten; she'd cleared it with McDermott already.

She'd considered going to Ella's school, just to see if she was there and, if she was, to catch a glimpse of her heading in—to see if she looked well, if she was smiling, talking. But no, she couldn't. The lawyer had warned her not to go against child services rules, that it could—would—mess everything up.

Play by the book, and maybe, just maybe, Anna would come out of this on top.

She could call Lorna and find out if the paperwork was completed for her, or at least Sandra, to see the kids. A knot twisted in her stomach, and Anna felt nauseated. God, what if they didn't let her see them?

Walking down the final hallway towards the building's exit, she pulled her phone out, dialling Lorna's number. But the sight of Lane turning around the corner up ahead slowed her down.

Lane looked up from the chart in her hand, eyes widening when she saw Anna, and stopped dead in the middle of the hallway.

With her eyes glued on Lane's, her heart racing and the phone ringing repetitively in her ear, Anna opened her mouth to say something, anything, when Lorna finally answered on the other end.

"This is Lorna, how can I help?"

She and Lane kept staring at each other as Anna's legs continued to carry her inexorably forward.

"Hello?"

"Uh—Lorna. Hi, it's Anna Foster."

Her eyes stayed on Lane as she walked past her. She needed to get to the lawyer's office, yet, everything in her wanted to turn around and stop Lane.

"Anna, hi, I thought you'd call early."

Anna swallowed heavily. "Yeah, sorry, I just—I need to know, can I see them? Tell me I can."

Nausea played in her stomach. Anna tried to ignore it and focus on what Lorna was going to say. She breathed deeply.

There was silence on the phone.

"Lorna?"

Lorna sighed. "I am really, genuinely sorry, but I couldn't get you cleared to see the kids before the trial."

Anna refused to let it hit her, refused to stop in her tracks. Instead, she sped up, walking faster towards her car.

"There's really no way?"

"I'm sorry, no. If things don't go your way at the trial and you don't get them back into temporary custody, we'll be able to sort something out then."

Anna forced her key into the car and opened the door, climbing in and slamming it shut, leaning forward to rest her forehead on the steering wheel, eyes closed.

"That's if the reason I don't get them isn't that they find me guilty and I'm in court for neglect of my niece and nephew."

Lorna's silence answered that one.

"Can my mother see them, at least?"

"Yes. That's the silver lining, I got it cleared for her to go. She can see them this afternoon at four. I'll call her with the details."

A breath she didn't even know she'd been holding burst out. "Good. That's good."

"It is good." Lorna paused. "I really am sorry. I just want you to know that I did everything I could."

Anna's eyes welled up under her closed lids. "I really appreciate that, Lorna. I'm sorry, I've got to get to the lawyer's."

"I'll call your mother and arrange things with her. Take care of yourself, Anna. I'll see you Friday."

The steering wheel was digging into her forehead. "I'll see you then."

The thought of the trial filled her with dread, but she sat up straight, refusing to let the tears that had formed fall. So many things were whirling around her head. She started the car and pulled out of the lot, heading for Scott's office.

Her mind was a mess—the kids, the trial, not getting to see them, Cathy, her accusations. If she got them back, she'd still have the custody trial. If she didn't, she'd still have the custody trial with much more diminished chances of getting the kids permanently. Or she'd be in jail. If she didn't get them, who knew how long until the system cleared her to see them.

It had been four days, and already Anna was going out of her mind without them.

And then, of course, there was Lane. What if her mother and Kym were right? That she'd panicked and called it wrong. Thinking that was like torture. Could she really have Lane back? Could she really have Lane and maybe, come Friday, the kids?

It almost seemed too much to hope for.

That's if Lane would even take her back. Would Lane understand that it hadn't been Anna abandoning Lane, but her refusing to abandon the kids? That she hadn't wanted to do it but that she had been filled with fear and panic and done the only thing possible that had felt like action?

She pulled up to Scott's office and thought she was going to be ill with the stress sitting like a rock in her stomach. When she made it up to the reception desk, Anna realized that, for some reason, she had expected a young, sleek woman to be Scott Matthews' secretary. Instead, a woman in her late sixties who looked like she could be Anna's grandmother greeted her with a friendly smile.

"Hello, dear, can I help you?'

Anna felt like crawling onto her lap and being hugged. She blinked and tried to snap herself out of it. "Uh, yes. I'm Anna Foster. I have an appointment?"

"Yes, he's expecting you, dear. Take a seat, and Mr Matthews won't be a minute."

Anna sat down on one of the squishy chairs that made the waiting room look more like a study than an office. The receptionist peered over her desk.

"Can I get you anything, love? Some water? A nice cup of tea?"

"No, thank you anyway."

"Sing out if you change your mind. Cup of tea can do wonders." She winked.

Anna smiled, and the woman went back to her computer, typing far faster than Anna would have expected. Anna's own mother still sent her dodgy text messages that had been wrongly autocorrected and asked her regularly why her Facebook kept lighting up with red things on the top right hand corner.

Anna looked down at her phone, surprised to see she had two missed calls, one from her mother and the other from Hayley. Pressing the button for her voicemail, Anna heard her mother's voice first.

"Anna honey. I just had Lorna call me. I can't help but feel she's on our side. That Cathy woman is going down. That's what you say, isn't it? It's not that she's going off? Though she is off, off her damn rocker. Anyway, she said she's spoken to you. I'm seeing them at four."

Anna could hear the relief in her mother's voice.

"Call me to give me any messages you want for them. I-I'm so sorry that you couldn't come, sweetie. But we'll get this mess sorted on Friday. Call me back; that's an order."

It sounded like her mother was about to hang up, and Anna went to press the button for the next message when suddenly Sandra's voice came back on, much fiercer, making her jump.

"Are you back with Lane yet? You better be, young lady."

Anna gritted her teeth and pressed for the next message, her whole body tensing as Hayley's voice came over the speaker.

"Hey, it's me. Just checking in, to see if you've had any news. Hope Scott's looking after you; he really is a genius in the courtroom. Um—call me, if you need anything. I was thinking, if you needed some support, I could come down for a night or two. I know what you're like when you're stressed. Let me know, anyway…even if it's just for a night. Take care."

Anna hung up her phone and glared at it. *I know what you're like when you're stressed.* The tone of her voice hadn't left a lot to the imagination about what Hayley had been offering.

Anna leant back in her chair. Her head hurt. There was just too much going on.

She almost gave a derisive snort: Hayley had broken up with her because of the kids and, now that the kids were out of the picture for a night or two, she was offering to pop in for a quickie. The whole thing made Anna feel irrationally angry.

"Anna?"

Her head snapped up to see Scott Matthews standing there.

"Good morning. Did you want to come through?"

The meeting with Scott didn't leave Anna feeling much better. He went over the witnesses he had gathered to speak at the trial, as well as those who had given written testimonies. Speaking on the day would be Sandra, Andrew—Anna's eyebrows had risen at that; what would he have to say? He lived in his whisky bottle—McDermott, Tanya from the day care and Lane.

Anna was confused about the last one. "I thought you said Lane wouldn't be questioned, due to the allegations?"

"At first I thought that would be best, but she would most likely be called by the other side anyway, so I thought it would be a good idea."

"What about Kym?"

"She will be called as well, to testify that there is no relationship between the two of you beyond friendship." He shifted in his seat, hand rubbing at the back of his neck. "And I have to ask again, I'm sorry, there definitely isn't, is there?"

Anna gave a small laugh. "No, there's not. Kym is just a friend."

"Okay. Sorry again."

Scott let her know how the trial would run. It would be in more of an office setting, he said. The case was working as almost a "State versus Anna" situation, as it wasn't Cathy personally prosecuting her, but the state's child services following up on complaints. Nevertheless, Cathy would be there.

Anna clenched her jaw.

There would only be a judge, but no jury and no media or people able to sit in. Witnesses would sit out in the hall until called. Anna breathed easier at this. It sounded a lot less scary than the TV courtroom drama she had been imagining.

"Will Ella be called?" It was something that had been nagging at her; she didn't want Ella to go through that.

Scott shook his head. "No. We try and avoid putting kids out there like that. The school counsellor will speak, and hopefully the testimonies will be enough. Under certain circumstances, the judge will ask to have the child be called, but hopefully not in this case."

He said he'd have her in again tomorrow to go over the questions he'd ask, and then, all of a sudden, Anna was back outside, blinking in the daylight. She called her mother, keeping the conversation brief.

The most important thing she said was, "Tell them I'm doing everything I can to be with them. And I think about them all the time. And I'm—tell Ella I'm looking forward to pancakes."

Then she went back to work, to finish up her day.

Anna didn't see Lane again, and Kym was in some kind of psych emergency on the fourth floor, meaning Anna couldn't rant at her. On the plus side, it meant she couldn't give Anna the stink eye every time she walked past.

Because, damn, Kym could give a good stink eye.

Sandra called just after six with an update on Ella and Toby.

"They're…they're okay, Anna."

Anna sucked in a breath. "Why the hesitation, Mum?"

Sandra sighed. "Ella is quiet. Toby was ecstatic to see me, but then very clingy. He cried when they took him back. Ella clung to my pants leg so tight I thought they wouldn't be able to take her away."

Leaning against the wall, Anna closed her eyes and dropped her head back against it. "But they're safe? Did you meet the foster parents?"

"They're safe, and well, and they're looked after. There's some policy, I didn't meet them. Ella said they were 'okay', though. I told them what you told me to, that you're doing everything you can to have them back with you."

"Did Ella believe you?"

"Of course." Her mother's voice was high.

"Mum?"

"She believed it."

Anna balled her hand into a fist. "Mum."

Her mother sighed. "She...she asked why you didn't have your own kids before this, if you'd ever wanted them. I think she's been thinking too much."

Anna felt ill. "What did you say?!"

"I'm not new to childhood questions. I told her you didn't have kids yet because you didn't know you wanted any until you had them."

Anna let a breath out. "Did she believe that, at least? Mum—" Anna's voice cracked. "I need Ella to know how much I want them back."

"She believed that, honey."

"What else did you do?"

Toby had been incredibly attached, and even Ella had spent the entire time leaning against Sandra's side. They'd read books, and Sandra had made sure to cuddle them nonstop and to ask, without scaring Ella, as much as she could about how they were being looked after. Anna soaked in every word, closing her eyes and trying to picture the kids. When she got off the phone with her mother, she felt hollow.

At least they were okay.

As she was leaving for the day, come eight o'clock, she again went to turn down the hallway to the day care—out of habit—never mind the late hour, and never mind that the kids weren't with her.

With a heavy sigh, Anna hooked her bag back onto her shoulder and headed home, the car ride a blur as she turned up the music to try to drown out the silence. In spite of herself, her eyes kept flickering from the road to Toby's car seat in the rear-view mirror.

Anna suddenly took a U-turn, back to the hospital.

She couldn't do it. She couldn't go home and sit in an empty house, to eventually cave and have a cigarette. The rooms were suffocating as she passed the time waiting until she was tired enough to try to sleep. Coiled tension filled her body. Anna didn't know what to do about anything, and the painful truth was there wasn't anything she could do. She was completely hopeless, dependent on a system that had caused the problem in the first place.

She gritted her teeth, fingers gripping the steering wheel hard enough to turn her knuckles white.

She needed to work out what to say to Lane.

Back at the hospital, Anna walked through the entrance, itching to enter an operating room and do something constructive, to put her brain to use and to not have time to think about Ella and Toby or Lane. She was walking down towards the elevator, eyes on the ground, lost in thought. When she looked up, she saw Lane and Tess a few metres ahead, with their backs to her, about to walk into the same elevator.

Anna's stomach clenched. Tess, biting into an apple, was walking just behind Lane.

Kym suddenly stepped into Anna's field of vision, making it impossible to see Lane's face as she walked into the elevator, until Kym grabbed Tess by the back of the shirt, pulling her backwards and out of the elevator. Tess let out a muffled "Hey!" around the apple in her mouth.

With her other hand, Kym reached forward, wrapped her fingers around Anna's wrist and yanked her forward, letting go as Anna's momentum carried her towards the door. Finally, Kym gave the small of her back a shove, hissing "Fix this!" as she passed.

Anna suddenly found herself standing in the elevator, wide eyed, as Lane turned to look at her in surprise.

Glancing out the door, Anna saw Kym still gripping a pissed-off-looking Tess's uniform top as the doors started to close. With an overly cheerful wave, Kym grinned.

Terrified, Anna turned back to Lane and they stared at each other.

"Hey." Anna finally said, lamely.

"Hey."

Anna licked her lips, which were suddenly dry, opening her mouth to say something, then closing it again.

Lane gave her a small smile that did not reach her eyes. "It's okay, Anna. Kym gets excited. You don't have to say anything."

Anna took in a heavy breath and hit the emergency stop button, heart hammering in her chest. She barely knew what to say.

Confusion etched over Lane's features.

"I-I am so, sorry, Lane."

"Don't, Anna, you don't need to be. I understand."

A foot of space was all that was between them as Anna took another small step. "I am. I'm so sorry. I…" She flicked her eyes up to the ceiling before looking back to Lane. "I panicked."

Crossing her arms in front of her, Lane nodded. She took a small step backwards. "I know. I get it. I would have done the same thing."

Anna matched Lane's backward step with one going forward, trying to sort out her words. "I—"

"Actually, no." Lane's tone was still soft. "I wouldn't have. It's not what I would have done."

Dread settled over her. Lane wouldn't forgive her. Maybe she did see it as Anna abandoning her, rather than Anna desperately clutching at something that would help her keep the kids, even if it was the wrong thing.

Voice hoarse, Lane continued, "*I* wouldn't have done it. But," she sighed, "I understand why *you* did, Anna." As if trying to protect herself, Lane's arms tightened around her middle.

Anna cursed herself, and Cathy, for Lane's protective stance. What if she'd broken what they had between them permanently?

"I...I panicked. I've had it pointed out to me that I call things wrong, sometimes."

Questioning eyes met her own as Lane finally looked up from the floor.

"I...Lane..." Her voice cracked. "Can you forgive that? I was...God, I'm still so scared I'm not going to get them back."

"You...you want me to forgive that?"

Anna closed her eyes. She'd pushed Lane too far. Despite knowing it was wrong, she had really hoped Lane would understand where she was coming from enough to forgive what she'd done. Gentle hands cupped her cheeks. Anna's eyes opened, swallowing heavily when she saw Lane's face inches from her own.

"Are you asking, because you want this back? Or..." Lane bit her lip. "or because, you want forgiveness so you don't feel guilty?"

Resting her hands over Lane's, Anna shook her head. "I want this back, Lane. I can't...I can't breathe without you. Everything's been so hard."

"I thought you were just apologising."

"I was, but also...I don't want to do this without you." Anna leant forward, hesitating a second with her lips hovering over Lane's before pressing a kiss to her lips. She melted into it, relishing the feel of Lane under her after days of turmoil. Slowly, she pulled back and rested her forehead against Lane's. "I need to have them back. I can't be without them. But, God, Lane, I can't be without you, either."

"Are you saying what I think you're saying? Because if you aren't, and I'm wrong, I need to know now, because I can't take you walking away from me again."

"I am. Saying what you think I'm saying, I mean."

The smile that could always make Anna melt slowly spread over Lane's lips.

"Good," Lane murmured. "Just...don't panic again, okay?"

There was a fragility to her tone that made guilt flare up in Anna's chest. She shook her head. "I won't."

Meeting Anna halfway in a kiss this time, Lane tightened her grip. Their lips moved slowly, Anna's tense muscles relaxing slightly. Their movements were soft, gentle, not at all the frenzied kissing Anna had imagined this could lead to; it was better. When they parted, both gripped each other, fingers digging into skin.

Foreheads pressed together, Anna's voice was a whisper. "I'm so scared they're going to take them for good."

"I know. But we aren't going to let that happen."

Chapter Twenty-One

"You're thinking."

The words came out of nowhere, surprising Anna. She blinked rapidly and turned, looking over her shoulder at Lane. "How do you know that? You're being big spoon."

Warm skin enveloped Anna as she rolled over in Lane's arms, laying face to face with her on the pillow.

Lane pushed Anna's hair back behind her ears. "You're the loudest thinker I know."

"Sorry."

"You don't need to be sorry."

"Then why do you look so worried?"

Lane's brow furrowed, and she shook her head, burying her face in Anna's neck. "I don't."

This time, Anna wrapped her arms around Lane, feeling Lane's lips graze her neck.

"You do. And now you're hiding."

A sigh was Lane's answer.

"Please don't feel like you can't talk to me."

Soft, tight curls brushed Anna's chin as Lane shook her head.

Anna couldn't even really blame her. The decision she'd felt obliged to make was going to take some time to make up for. Wanting to be able to see Lane, Anna rolled over so Lane was on top of her. Black eyes met her gaze as she stared seriously at Lane, waiting for her to speak.

"It's not that I feel like I *can't*. I just..." She buried her face deeper against Anna's neck. "You disappeared. And I get why, I do. But you started to shut down in the morning, and then when you paged me, I...I honestly didn't even expect you to do it." Voice a whisper, Lane looked back at her. "It was such a shock. And now you're thinking. Loudly. And what if..."

The sentence didn't need to be finished for Anna to understand it. Kicking herself, she ran her fingers through Lane's hair, even as she felt tears on her neck. Finally, Lane drew in a quiet, shuddering breath. "And then, in the elevator, I thought you were just, I don't know, making peace. Even though part of me was kind of waiting for you. To come back. I…I kind of expected it to be when you had the kids back and things had settled."

Anna gently cupped Lane's cheeks and tilted her head up, Lane's tear-filled eyes meeting her own. "You mean more to me than that."

A tear fell down Lane's cheek.

Anna wanted to fix it all. She knew there wasn't a lot she could say, but it wasn't going to stop her from trying. "I know why you would feel like that. And I don't blame you if you don't believe everything I'm saying. But just…I just hope you know that what I did had absolutely nothing to do with you, or us, and everything to do with the kids, and my panic."

When Lane nodded, still looking uncertain, Anna was gripped with guilt. Tangling her fingers in Lane's hair, Anna kissed her, tongue running over her lip. The taste of salt mingled with her guilt, and Anna only pulled back when she couldn't taste it anymore.

Lane leant her head on her hand, elbow digging into the mattress near Anna's head. She splayed the other hand over Anna's shoulder, fingers brushing her skin, gaze intense. She was looking at her as if she was a puzzle to solve.

"It was so frustrating, because I knew why you were doing what you were doing. But I didn't know how to fight for you in those circumstances. All I could think to do was to honour what you wanted, even though not being with you felt so wrong."

The skin of Lane's hand was soft under Anna's fingertips as she stroked it. "If it helps at all…I was a mess. I just…it tore me apart. And then my mother and Kym not so kindly pointed out to me that I'm an idiot."

"So I should call your mum and say 'thanks'?"

"The last voicemail from her ended with, 'Are you back with Lane yet? You better be, young lady!'"

A chuckle from Lane made Anna smile.

"So you found me because of threats from Kym and Sandra?"

Anna could hear genuine concern behind the playful tone; she bit her lip at the insecurity Lane was feeling, especially since she knew the effect Alex had had with her lies and her distant behaviour.

With one smooth motion, Anna rolled them over, settling between Lane's legs. She looked at Lane, head cocked, expression serious. "Yes, Kym pushed me into that elevator. And yes, I needed Mum and Kym to snap me out of the haze I was in. But I said it all because I meant it. Because I was a mess without you. Because I need you with me, by my side, if I'm going to get through this. I turned around on my drive home to get you." One firm kiss, and Anna looked at Lane intently. "Okay?"

Lane gave a nod. "Okay."

Despite her words, Anna knew that it was going to be a while before Lane trusted that she wouldn't run again; Anna could wait.

Lane suddenly grinned, cheeky, relaxing slightly. "And you missed the sex, didn't you?"

"That was about eighty per cent of the reason."

Anna ran her lips slowly over Lane's collarbone, between her breasts and against her stomach, taking her time. Slowly, she worked Lane into a frenzy and showed her as best she could what she couldn't put into words.

Just having her back, Anna felt so lucky.

And she'd make sure Lane felt that, every day if she had to.

They woke up slowly. Anna had the day off to prepare for the trial and Lane called in sick despite the loud protests of her coordinator.

A small laugh escaped Lane as she hung up, and she looked up as Anna carried in two steaming mugs of coffee. The sheets were warm as she slipped back in and handed a coffee over to Lane.

"What's funny?"

"He sighed and said, 'I suppose you need tomorrow off, too?'"

Anna smirked. "What did you say?"

"I said, 'Yeah, or I could just call in sick again.' The entire hospital is behind you."

Anna sipped her coffee, looking at Lane over the rim. "Thank you."

Blowing on her cup, Lane gave her a questioning look. "What for?"

"For being here, for coming. For spending the day with me so I don't go crazy."

"Thank you for letting me."

They smiled tentatively at each other.

"McDermott made me have today off, you know."

"He did?"

Anna nodded. “I told him I’d need the afternoon to see the lawyer, and he told me to have the whole day. It’s nice and all, but at the time I was freaking out, because it meant too much time not doing anything.”

“Now?”

“Now, I have you to keep me calm.”

The kiss Lane gave her was soft, reassuring, and she settled back against the headboard with a warm glow in her chest. “So what’s your plan for today?”

Anna gave a small shrug. “Scott’s this afternoon. Maybe see my mum beforehand. Try not to think too much. And…” Anna looked up almost shyly from her coffee, “hang with you.”

“We can definitely do that.”

Anna drained the last of her mug, putting it on the bedside table and settling down on her back, head in Lane’s lap.

Silence fell over them as Lane sipped at her coffee, her fingertips running gently over Anna’s stomach and hips. Anna stared up at the ceiling, comfortable, though her thoughts were starting to wander to the trial tomorrow.

“Lane,” Anna’s voice was low. “what if I don’t get them back tomorrow?”

Soft fingers ran over Anna’s stomach as Lane kissed her cheek. “Then we fight our asses off to have them back to you at the trial.”

“It’s been so long since I’ve seen them. I just, I hadn’t even realised, in a way, just how much I need them—just how much they’re a part of my life now.”

Lane brushed Anna’s hair off her forehead, her hand soothing as it stroked along the strands. “I know.”

“I spent the first few weeks on the verge of calling Mum every night to come over so I could just run.”

Without judgment, Lane watched her.

“What if I’d caved one of those nights and done that? They could use it against me.”

“I don’t think your mum would have told them. God, my cousin did that once with her two kids. I think that’s something a lot of people have done. It’s okay that you wanted to run sometimes, you know.”

“I miss them. So much.”

Lane leant forward and kissed her forehead. “Me too.”

Their hands linked over Anna’s stomach.

“Plus side?”

“Mm?”

“You look hot as all hell lying on the bed with no shirt on like that.”

Anna even laughed.

They took their time that morning, mostly chatting idly, taking a long shower, and slowly trying to be at ease with each other again. The slight barrier between them had unsettled them both and it just made Anna even more resolved to break it down.

Lane went with Anna to her mother's. Sandra wrapped Lane in a hug but said nothing else when she answered the door to find them both standing there. Unable to stop the grin that overtook her face, she cupped Lane's cheeks a moment and then dragged them in to sit down for tea and coffee.

Anna was almost unable to hold it together when Sandra, lips pressed tight together, handed her art from Ella. There were four paintings in all, showing Anna, Ella, and Toby doing different things. Sandra was in a few of them, and so were Jake and Sally, on a cloud. Quickly, Anna handed them over to Lane. The last painting caused a lump in her throat.

As Lane looked at the picture, her own eyes glittered. Painted sitting around a very odd looking table were Ella and Toby eating dinner, with who could only be Kym, Lane, and Anna all around them.

"She wanted me to give you all of these. The teacher asked the kids in her class to paint their family." Sandra held out one more. "And this one is from Toby."

A bitter feeling of sadness rushed through her as she took the paper. It was a bright orange smear, and Anna could only imagine how much paint had ended up covering him.

"Thanks, Mum."

"They really are okay, Anna. I know how you feel, though. I wouldn't have felt better hearing you say it. It was seeing them that helped."

Anna grasped Lane's fingers where they were squeezing her knee. This ordeal had left her exhausted. Having Lane back, even though it had only been a few days that they were apart, was making a huge difference. But the only thing that was really going to quell this ache in her chest, this constant stress, was having Ella and Toby back under her roof.

Just before two, Lane and Anna went out for a late lunch before the meeting with Scott, mostly in need of a distraction. Feeling slightly bad that their reunion was tainted with all of their focus on the next day's trial, Anna pressed in close to Lane at the booth, seeking contact. They ate quietly, sharing the odd exchange of words and soft looks.

"Nervous?" Lane peered at Anna over her coffee cup.

"I don't want to be. Scott's trying to prepare me for what to expect tomorrow."

"That's what this afternoon's meeting is for?"

"Yeah."

Lane put her cup down and gently lifted Anna's chin up with her hand. Instead of resisting, Anna met her soft look.

"It's going to go fine." Anna wanted to believe her. "Anyone with a brain can see you are what is best for those kids. It *sucks* that this had to happen, but we are going to get them back to you."

Anna nodded.

With a quick kiss, Lane's fingers grazed from Anna's chin to along her cheek, which she cupped gently for a second before letting her hand drop.

"This is exactly what is wrong with you."

Anna whipped her head around at the familiar voice.

Cathy stood, eyes blazing and cheeks flushed, looking down at the two of them. Next to Anna, Lane tensed. There was a man just behind Cathy; the two of them had clearly been on their way out when Cathy had caught sight of them. He looked at them in surprise before turning his face away and hurrying out. Anna barely caught a glimpse of him—but something struck her as familiar.

"Showing *that*, in public." Cathy's voice wavered with disgust, her tone low, stony. Eyes flaming fury, she didn't even notice her friend leave. "Flaunting this, where *anyone* can see you. This is why those innocent children have been taken away from you."

Anger licked up inside Anna. She sat straighter.

"They've been taken from me because of false accusations from you, Cathy. Not for any other reason." Anna kept her voice calm.

Lane's hand squeezed her knee under the table where Cathy couldn't see it, a reminder of sorts. Scott had told Anna to steer clear of Cathy and, if she saw her, to avoid confrontation. Anything could damage their case, and Anna needed to calm down, which was incredibly difficult to do when the woman was standing over them, looking at them like *that,* when she was the cause of Ella and Toby being in foster care.

Cathy gave a snort of a laugh.

Anna could barely look at the twisted expression of hate on features that reminded her so much of her sister-in-law, who had been one of the most accepting people Anna had known, who had not wanted her mother in her own life, let alone her children's.

"They were taken because I was right. Soon they will be away from your, your," Cathy looked them up and down and Lane's hand tightened on Anna's leg, "depravity, forever."

Breath coming short and fast, Anna stood up, taking Lane's hand and pulling her up too. As calmly as she could, she walked past Cathy without looking at her.

"Really, Anna, if you love those children, *if* your kind are capable of normal, healthy love, you will let them go."

She kept her eyes forward, Lane's hand still in hers as she led them out.

Cathy, whose voice had thus far been low, called after them, "Who will you answer to, Anna, when your time comes?"

Anna called out her answer without even looking over her shoulder. "My conscience."

They exited the cafe, walking quickly, Anna's breathing no more controlled than before, their hands clasped between them. The cool air was stinging her burning cheeks.

Lane pulled them up short next to her car, and Anna leant back heavily against the door, the metal cool even through her clothing. When she finally managed to look at Lane, she saw the anger she knew was on her own face reflected back at her. They looked at each other, speechless, until Lane finally spoke, her voice terse.

"She's a crazy bitch."

Anna actually managed to crack a smile. "She really is."

"You did really well, to just leave like that."

"What gives her the *right* to feel she can judge people like that?"

"I have no idea."

"Your hand is shaking."

"I'm pretty mad. She was looking at us like we were filth. And what she said—" Lane cut herself off, too angry to continue.

Anna squeezed the hand still clasped in her own. "Thank you, for keeping your cool."

"Saying anything to that woman wouldn't have helped."

"Thank you, too, for just…"

When Anna paused, unable to put what she needed to say into words, Lane stared at her, questioning.

"I was just glad you were there."

"I'm glad you weren't doing that alone."

"I'm sorry she looked at you like that."

"Don't you dare apologise for her."

Taking a deep breath, Anna leant her head back against the car. "God, the kids just *cannot* go to her."

Lane's arms wrapped around her, comforting and warm. "There is no way in hell that's going to happen."

"Let's get to the lawyer's and get this day over with. I want it to be tomorrow already."

"Can I shoot spitballs at the back of Cathy's neck from where I'm sitting?"

Chuckling, Anna nodded. "That? That you can do."

The night air was refreshing, and the wine on her tongue even more so. The wooden step under Anna was hard, and she twirled a cigarette in her hand as she stared out into the backyard, watching a plane go over head, too far away to hear, lights flickering. Her fingers never stopped twirling the cigarette as she took another sip of wine.

Lane had gone home to get clothing for tomorrow, promising to come back as soon as she'd grabbed a shower and something court appropriate.

The meeting with Scott had gone quickly; he ran over his questions and posed the questions to her that he believed the State's attorney would ask. He reassured them, reiterated how it would be run, and answered their questions. He assured them again that being gay couldn't keep the kids from Anna. The case was based on neglect, on allegations, and also on something that their case manager had said. That was news to Anna, because Lorna had appeared to be on their side. So, how had this happened? If the caseworker was on their side, how had the kids been taken away?

Anna was wracked with nerves. No one could promise a sure thing. It could drag out for weeks if the judge wasn't satisfied that there was no neglect. Someone else could get temporary guardianship until the formal trial. They could stay in foster care or go to Cathy. Anna could go to trial for genuine neglect.

The cigarette in her hand was incredibly tempting; she kept twirling it to stop herself from lighting it.

The house was too quiet, too settled.

Before, this was where she would come to miss her brother and miss her old life. To wonder what the hell he had been thinking. To dread the sound of Toby crying or Ella waking up with sad eyes and hard questions.

Now it was where she missed them.

The plane finally disappeared, and she was left with nothing to focus on. Eyes sweeping the small backyard, she took in the dimensions. It wasn't huge, no room for a swing set or a trampoline. Jake and Sally had liked that they had a park a five-minute walk away. While the yard wasn't a huge space, a dog would be happy there. She bet the kids would love a puppy.

She sipped her wine again.

Or a kitten.

Were you supposed to start small? Maybe a hamster. Or a fish.

Anna liked the idea of a puppy or a kitten. She and Jake had never had pets. She put the wine glass down and flicked her lighter again. What if she didn't get them back?

"God damn you, Cathy," she muttered.

"I second that." Lane's voice was quiet behind her, and, though Anna hadn't heard her let herself in, she didn't startle.

"Did you find a power court outfit?"

Lane sat down next to her. "Yup, and it's awesome, if I do say so my—you smoke?"

The cigarette stilled in Anna's hand, and she looked down at it. She had meant to either smoke it before Lane got back, or play with it and then hide it.

"Uh, only rarely."

Lane raised her eyebrows.

"Like now, apparently." Anna put it down next to her and grabbed her wine glass, swiftly handing a second glass to Lane. "Don't be mad?" She tried to look charming. "I had wine ready for you."

"Hmm." After taking a sip, Lane turned back to Anna, seemingly ready to carry the cigarette conversation on.

"It's disgusting, I know." Anna bit her lip.

Soft lips brushed against her own, and Anna felt some of the tension leave her body. She pulled back slowly.

"I'm glad you didn't. You smell a lot better without the smoke."

Comfortably, they settled next to each other, Lane's arm wrapped around Anna.

"Big day tomorrow," Lane said softly.

Anna nodded.

"It's been a big week."

Anna nodded again and took in a deep breath.

"Next week will be good."

Lifting her head up, Anna looked at Lane. "Yeah?"

"Yeah."

Nothing, now, would change anything. Anna couldn't think about it anymore. Tomorrow they'd know. Her head dropped back to Lane's shoulder and another plane flew overhead. The arm around her shoulders tightened.

"Want to go upstairs?" Lane's voice was soft, gentle. "I know a stress reliever that doesn't give you cancer."

Normally she would jump at that offer. Yet, Anna burrowed in more and draped her arm over Lane's legs. Here, in the cool of evening with Lane next to her, she felt the most calm she had since Lorna knocked at the door. There was no way she wanted to move anywhere right then.

"In a minute?"

Lane turned her head, kissing the top of Anna's. "In a minute."

Chapter Twenty-Two

Anna's heart was racing, and she couldn't slow it.

"You need to breathe."

She dragged her eyes from her coffee cup and looked straight into Kym's across the table.

"I know."

"Really, you do."

"I'm okay."

"You're not. And that's okay. But seriously, breathe."

Anna sipped from her mug, both hands wrapped around it as if it could warm her completely. The more she focussed on her breathing, the harder it was to do it normally.

"Look, you have Lane back, which, I think, we can all thank me for." Kym gave her a cocky grin, and Anna even managed to roll her eyes. "And soon, you'll have those kids back. By this weekend, all going well, they'll be in this house and we'll all be planning our next movie night."

"This could go terribly."

"It could. But it won't. She doesn't have a leg to stand on. All the allegations are crap, and you deserve those kids."

It would be much easier if Anna could just believe her.

Kym watched her for a second, then sighed. "Look, worst case scenario? You never get the kids back and you act out like an idiot by breaking up with Lane again, dooming yourself to a life of loneliness. I'll buy you ten cats, you can be *that* crazy person and be alone forever, and, when you die, they can eat you from the toes up."

Horrified, Anna could only stare at her.

Kym shrugged, smirking. "Just trying to show you that things can always be worse."

When Lane walked in, fresh from her shower, Anna's shocked gaze was still locked on Kym.

"Kym! What did you do?"

Kym whipped her head around to look at Lane, feigning innocence. "What? Nothing."

"I'd just calmed her down, and I waited for you to get here to go shower so she wouldn't hype herself up again when left alone, and now, she looks absolutely terrified."

"I am terrified! And I don't need babysitting." The indignation in Anna's tone was strong and slightly embarrassing.

"I know you don't. Sorry. Just concerned." Lane pinched Anna's coffee, taking a sip. "Why do you look so terrified?"

"No reason." Anna ignored Kym's snicker. "You smell good."

With a quick kiss, Lane headed to the fridge. "Eggs? Bacon? Mushrooms? Whole lot?"

"Yes!" Kym exclaimed.

Both Anna and Lane looked at her, confused.

Kym managed to look sheepish. "I mean, whatever you want, is fine."

"You still living off vending machine food?"

Giving a shrug, Kym changed the topic. "When's your mum getting here?"

Anna let it slide as Lane went about making them breakfast, relieved that at least Kym was enthusiastic about eating.

"Any minute now." She glanced toward Lane, but a mountain of food on the counter top made her almost impossible to see her from the table. "Want a hand?"

Lane held out a packet of mushrooms. "You can chop."

Anna obligingly started to clean them. "What sucks about being me is I always get stuck with the chopping duties."

"I'd let you cook the eggs, but last time you got distracted and, rather than poached, we got rocks."

Continuing to chop, Anna poked her tongue out.

Kym smirked. "Or that morning she was going to make us pancakes and put salt in the mix instead of sugar."

"Or when she cooked us spaghetti and somehow burnt the pasta."

"Guys! I am *right* here. And it's not that bad."

Neither replied, both of them only staring at Anna.

"You guys suck."

"No, that would be your lasagne."

"Hey!"

On her way to the sink, Lane kissed the back of Anna's neck. "It's okay, you're good at other things."

Slightly placated, Anna finished up with the mushrooms. As she was washing her hands, the front door opened.

"I'm here!" Her mother's voice floated down the hall.

"In the kitchen, Mum!" Anna sat back down at the table.

"Oh my God, something smells delicious—wait, Anna, you're not c—" Sandra appeared in the kitchen doorway, a look of relief on her face as she took in the scene in front of her. "Oh, good, never mind."

"What?"

"Just—glad to see Lane in the kitchen." She turned her attention to Lane, who had looked up with a smirk. "Morning, Lane, dear."

"Morning, Sandra."

"Hello, Kym. You look lovely."

"Thanks, Sandra. You too, as always."

"Excuse me!"

They all looked at Anna.

"What is this? I am not that bad in the kitchen."

"Honey, you couldn't make cookies in your Easy Bake Oven. Admit defeat."

Anna frowned. "Where's Dad?"

Her mother avoided her eyes, bustling into the kitchen to get herself a coffee. "Oh, he's going to meet us there."

"Or he couldn't stand to be in the same room as me for five minutes." Anna was more emotional, more exhausted, and more highly strung than she had realised.

The cup in her mother's hand clattered as she half dropped it onto the bench. They eyed each other, Anna trying to ignore her guilt and her mother looking immeasurably sad.

Truth swirled around them, normally unspoken.

Then Sandra went back to making her coffee. Anna felt her cheeks flush in shame. Kym was steadfastly looking at the table, while Lane stared from Anna to her mother.

After a calming sip of her coffee, Sandra put her cup down and finally looked at Anna. "He'll meet us at the courthouse."

"Okay."

Lane cleared her throat. "Uh…breakfast is ready."

Sandra gave Anna's arm a reassuring squeeze when she sat down, stopping her from dwelling.

"Excellent. Dish it up, then, Lane. I need my energy to put this woman in the ground!" At the surrounding looks, Sandra shrugged. "What? I like a full stomach before I kick some bigoted ass."

Everyone ate in silence, Anna trying to ignore the tight feeling in her gut as she forced food into her mouth. Kym's leg bounced agitatedly under the table, and Sandra's eyes flicked over them all as she kept a strained smile on her lips.

When Lane squeezed her knee under the table, Anna felt a rush of gratitude for these people who were all about to get up and defend a situation none felt they should have to. Get it right, and Toby and Ella would be back where they belonged. Get it wrong, and who knew where they'd end up?

They took one car; Sandra drove. All Anna could do was stare out the window, her cold hand in Lane's.

Inside the frigid courthouse, Scott met them with a roguish grin. Anna was grateful for his easy charm, his comfort in a building none of them knew. Take doctors out of the hospital and they became lost and unsure.

"Ladies, you all look delightful."

All four were wearing some form of suit, Anna in a pencil skirt that made her miss her scrubs. Her mother had selected pants: *"I'm not the gay, dear. I'm not out trying to prove my femininity. On that: you shouldn't have to, either."*

Surefooted, Scott led them all through to a heavy wood door. Chairs were lined up outside, and a court bailiff stood next to the door.

"Okay, ladies, this is where Anna and I head inside. You all just need to be seated out here until you're called." Scott nodded to them. "Stay calm, big breaths. And don't talk to each other."

Sandra gave him a bewildered look. "But we could talk until now?"

"Crazy court rules." The wink Scott gave was utterly enchanting, and Anna could swear her mother swooned.

Sandra, Kym and Lane all smiled at Anna. She wanted to drag every one of them in there with her for moral support. She caught Lane's eye, and her words soothed Anna's nerves a little. "We're just on the other side of the door—okay?"

Anna nodded and tried to return their smiles.

Scott took her arm and started to lead her through the door.

"Oh, Anna!"

Anna turned her head.

Sandra was grinning. "My stomach is extra full." She winked. "It's on."

The sound that left Anna's throat was more like a strangled laugh than anything, but some of the tension in her stomach eased as she followed Scott in.

Even though Scott had told her what to expect, Anna had still pictured a huge courtroom, complete with gallery, jury section, and witness box. Instead, she walked into a room that was almost empty and lacking all the intimidating fixtures, as promised. There was a table on both the left and the right for the prosecution and defence. One long table stretched out at the front of the room, but at the same height as the two smaller tables in front of it. There was a large chair behind the table for the judge; a bailiff stood on one end and a record keeper was seated near the other. To the right, the table made a slight "L" shape where a witness could sit and give testimony.

Overall, it was a welcome anticlimax.

However, Anna was still not looking forward to this. Her sweaty hands brushed the coarse fabric of her skirt.

"I told you it was fine."

With a weak nod at Scott, she followed him up to the smaller table on the right, walking through the gate as he held it open for her.

"So Lorna will come in with the State lawyer, then the judge, and then it will start?"

"You got it." He poured her a glass of water from the jug on the table. "Here, drink this." After pouring himself one, he pulled out various papers from his briefcase and settled them down in front of her.

The door opened, and Anna turned to see Lorna walk through with a greying man in a suit and George Coleman, the caseworker who had come when Lorna had been away. Lorna smiled at her, pausing as they walked through the gate, while George walked straight past.

"Hi, Anna."

"Hi."

Her mouth opened to ask about the kids, but Anna closed it at Scott's soft touch to her arm.

Then she did it anyway. "How are they?"

Her eyes must have read as completely desperate for news, because even as the lawyer took Lorna's elbow to lead her to their table, she gave a quick answer. "Spoke to the foster family this morning; they're fine."

Anna nodded her thanks, turning back and purposefully avoiding Scott's glare. "What?" she tried to ask nonchalantly.

"Nothing."

But she could still feeling him glaring at her.

"Scott." She all but whispered it.

He looked at her sideways. "Hm?"

"We have to get them back," she said, looking him dead in the eye.

"I know."

"Good."

Suddenly, one of the bailiffs near the door straightened. "All rise for the Honourable Judge Gordon."

Fists clenched, nails biting into her palm, Anna stood.

It was finally happening.

The judge that walked in was a tall, thin man, probably in his late fifties to early sixties, with a thick head of silver hair and an air of forbearance about him.

Once he sat and nodded to the courtroom, everyone else sat down, so Anna followed suit.

The bailiff closest to the judge read out from a ledger: "Case of State versus Foster in relation to accusations of neglect against two wards in her care, pending guardianship approval, presided over by Judge Gordon."

The judge nodded, then spoke to the State's attorney, "And today, if charges are proven to be true, we are also to look at temporary guardianship of," he looked down at the papers in front of him, and Anna instantly liked him a little better for it, "Ella and Toby until the final guardianship hearing in approximately a month. Is this correct?"

"Correct, your Honour."

Shrewd eyes looked from Lorna to Anna. "Now, this isn't a trial. We don't do big opening and closing speeches. We are a family court, and we are here to do what is best for these two children, whatever that may be." He turned to the State's attorney. "Begin."

The attorney stood. "Your Honour, we are here to investigate several neglect claims that, coupled with a case manager's report expressing concern, led to the temporary removal of the children from Anna Foster's custody, and to placing the children in foster care, on a temporary basis until the custody hearing."

"And why did we need a custody hearing in the first place?"

Scott stood.

Finally realising that this wasn't a courtroom drama with gavels and yelling, Anna relaxed.

"Your Honour, originally none was needed. As you can see in the copy of the will submitted, the deceased Jake and Sally Foster named my client Anna Foster as guardian. As she accepted it, the paperwork was awaiting signing off by a judge. However, the maternal grandmother has since petitioned the court for guardianship, challenging the will, hence the need for the trial."

The judge looked back to the State's attorney. "And were the charges of neglect put forth by this woman before or after she petitioned for guardianship?"

"After."

The judge looked thoughtful, then turned his gaze back to Scott. "Did you wish to start with your character references?"

"Yes, your Honour."

Speechless, Anna watched as people were paraded in to literally sing her praises. First was Ella's school counsellor, who spoke of how Ella had, obviously, been incredibly quiet and withdrawn when she returned to school post the death of her parents. She let the court know that Anna had regularly checked in with her about Ella and asked questions about her concerns. Apparently comfortable with all eyes on her, she told the court that Ella had slowly been coming back to herself and had even started participating more with other children the last week.

"It's common for children to feel incredibly isolated from their peers in this scenario, something Ella has obviously experienced. This could be something that goes on for months or even years. Stability can help with that, as well as patience."

"And Ella seemed to be improving a little?"

"Ella's latest art work, when the teacher had them painting their families, has been showing her aunty, Doctor Foster, with Toby and Ella herself, sometimes with her parents on a cloud over her house."

"Anyone else?"

"A Nurse Lane had appeared and a Kym, who I understand are friends of Doctor Foster and have come to mean a lot to Ella."

"And do you see anything wrong with Ella forming attachments to these people?"

"No, of course not. In fact, it's incredibly positive. These are new attachments, new bonds, all showing Ella that people are still there for her, in a variety of roles, after such a profound loss. It's healthy. What is especially healthy is that Ella has more than accepted these new people in her life—she's welcomed them."

Scott leant against the desk, hands in his pockets. "Have you ever had any concerns about Ella's living arrangement since her parents' passing?"

"Never."

The State's attorney had no questions.

When Doctor McDermott, Anna's boss, appeared, Anna was grateful she'd put her foot down in the interview and been so strict with the hours she could offer.

"Her work statistics are far lower than others in the hospital; however, I hired her knowing this would happen."

"How so?"

"She walked into the interview and informed me that if she couldn't have evenings free for at least the first year, as well as weekends, she couldn't take the job."

"She sacrificed her career to be home with her brother's children?"

"Every day. Like most of the parents I employ do." He paused. "More so, actually."

When the state's attorney asked him questions, he was as blunt as Anna had expected.

"Does Doctor Foster regularly work late?"

"No."

"Not at all?"

"She has, I think, on one or two occasions. As I said already, when Doctor Foster interviewed for the position, she explained her situation with the children clearly and specified that long hours and regular late nights and weekend work would be off the table for her for quite a while."

"Only for a while though?"

"We work most parents' rosters to manage their children. It's part of the job, but Anna has been more stubborn than most in maintaining hours that let her be home with the kids, as is completely understandable in the circumstances. And I believe the one time she had to stay late, her mother took the children. Like most parents who work at the hospital, or work at all, she has a backup system."

The State's attorney didn't have any further questions.

Scott called in Tanya, and the coordinator of the day care bounced in, as peppy as ever.

"We miss Toby at the day care. He's got a little network of friends. All the kids are there full time, five to six days a week. We have them all in a routine. They get to socialise, and the biggest bonus is that the parents, or guardians," Tanya beamed at Anna, who couldn't help but smile back; the woman was like a gerbil on Ecstasy, "are right there in the building, so they can visit during the day, something a lot of parents without provided day care miss out on."

"And Doctor Foster was there regularly?"

Tanya laughed. "At first she was popping in constantly. We finally managed to reassure her that Toby was settling in fine, and she was visiting more like two or three times a day, shifts permitting."

"How did Toby react to her visits?"

"With absolute delight. He adores her."

Anna felt a tug in her chest.

"And he was adjusting fine? Considering that, before this, he had been at home with his mother?"

Tanya nodded. "Oh, he took some adjusting, though I think a lot of that wasn't just because he wasn't at home, but because of his loss. He was quite clingy with Doctor Foster at first, but this was slowly settling." She paused for a second, then quickly added, "Lots of these kids come into day care, after being at home with their parents for up to two years. Parents coming back from maternity leave and so forth. They all settle in, make friends, and get to see their parents. Day care isn't a negative experience."

Scott thanked her, and the State's attorney, again, had no questions.

The bailiff called Kym, and Anna's stomach flipped. The clack of heels on the wood floor sounded out, and then Kym was seated. Scott, obviously deciding to beat the State's attorney to it, asked about the nature of their relationship.

Without batting an eye, Kym threw her answer back at him. "She's my best friend."

Anna smiled when Kym caught her eye.

"Can you elaborate?"

"Anna and I met at work and bonded over mutual loss. I lost my husband about nine months ago now, and she had just lost her brother and sister-in-law, plus was going through massive life changes with taking on the kids. We supported each other."

"How regularly were you and Doctor Foster seeing each other, outside of work?"

"Two or three times a week."

"And you'd go out?"

Kym shook her head. "No. Mostly, we would be at Anna's house, with the kids."

"So Doctor Foster wasn't floating off to have a social life to the detriment of the kids?"

"God, no. It's getting her to take a break that's the problem."

Anna resisted the urge to roll her eyes.

"Do you get along with Ella and Toby?"

"A lot. I really miss them, actually."

"And I'm sorry. I just have to ask blatantly, to save the State's attorney the question. Have you ever been romantically involved with Doctor Foster?"

If the situation wasn't so serious Anna was sure Kym would have laughed. "No, I've not."

"Nothing further. Thank you, Doctor Drew."

The State's attorney stood. "I have on record that you've been seen leaving the property in the early hours of the morning. Has there really never been any romantic link? I'm sorry, Doctor Drew, but this is part of the complaints and we need to ask. Uh…again."

Kym looked pissed. "Who's spying on the house at six a.m.? That's creepy."

The judge cleared his throat and looked at her.

Kym quickly went back to the question. "No, there has never been anything more than friendship between Doctor Foster and me. Sometimes I stay the night on the couch, either because it's one of the rare times I've babysat or because I don't like to be in my dead husband's home. Anna is nice enough to let me do that."

Obviously not wanting to go down the deceased husband route, the attorney pried further elsewhere. "So you babysit as well? Does Doctor Foster regularly leave the children in your care?"

"Why? Do you believe that someone with a double medical degree majoring in psychiatry isn't someone a responsible adult would leave two children with for a few hours?"

The judge actually smothered a laugh with a fake cough. "Just answer the question, please, Doctor."

"Twice I have babysat the kids, for about four or five hours each time. Anna always has Toby settled and in bed, and I hang out with Ella, who is six. Between us, we manage not to get into a lot of trouble besides eating too much ice cream."

Love for Kym filled Anna's chest, and she was fairly certain Judge Gordon was covering a smirk again.

"Only twice?"

"Only twice, in the last couple of months."

"For work?"

Kym sighed. "No, Anna went on two dates."

"With Lane Bishop?"

"Yes."

"What is the nature of this relationship?"

Scott stood up. "Your Honour, that's not for this woman to proclaim. Miss Bishop is next to be called, and Doctor Drew is here as a character reference only and to clear up her own links to Doctor Foster."

Standing straighter, the State's attorney interrupted, "Your Honour, Doctor Foster's 'sexual promiscuity' has been raised in the complaints put forth to child protective services. If we can clear some of the questions up now, I figure why not?"

Despite herself, Anna couldn't shake the vibe that the guy was actually on her side. She glanced at the table and saw Lorna nodding, but George scowling.

Kym looked from one lawyer to another, then to the judge.

The judge spoke to the State's attorney. "Continue."

Smothering a sigh, Scott sat back down.

"Right. Again, what is the nature of their relationship?"

"As far as I am aware, they're dating."

"How long has that been going on?"

Scott stood up again. "These are still questions for Miss Bishop and Doctor Foster."

"Stick to questions from an outsider view, please."

The attorney took it in his stride. "Have you seen Doctor Foster dating various people?"

Kym shook her head. "No, just Lane." She paused. "Um, *Miss* Bishop."

"And does she regularly see her…that you are aware?"

"They see each other when they can, but Anna has always, to Lane, to me, and to work, made it very clear that the kids come first."

"Can you give me an example of this?"

"I had to talk her into it being okay to date Lane at all. I had to talk her into letting me babysit for them so she could have a break and go out with Lane. I had to remind her that she is still allowed a life, to date, even if she has kids under her care."

"She was reluctant?"

"Very. She didn't ever want the kids to question their place in her life. And that's a direct quote, by the way. When the kids got taken…" Kym hesitated and looked at Anna, who nodded. "When the kids got taken, Anna broke it off with Lane because she thought it might help. Considering the allegations, I think she thought her relationship was playing a role in having the kids removed."

"But they're together again?"

Kym grinned. "I talked sense into her."

"Thank you."

Dismissed, Kym stood up. Anna caught her eye as she walked out and Kym shot her a thumbs up.

And then Lane walked in, looking more anxious than Kym had. She took the oath, then looked at Anna. They shared a nervous look, though Anna tried to look encouraging.

Scott started the questions after the initial introduction and run down. "Can you tell us, in your own words, the nature of your relationship with Doctor Foster?"

"We're together. We're dating. Uh...we're girlfriends."

Sympathy flared in Anna. Lane looked extremely nervous and fidgety.

Scott smiled at Lane. "How long have you been dating?"

"We've been seeing each other about two months. It's been, uh, very slow."

"Why's that?"

"When we met, Anna had only just taken on the kids. She didn't want to rush into anything; the kids were her priority."

"How exactly did she put it?"

A genuine smile played at Lane's lips. "'The kids are my priority.'"

"And you were okay with this?"

Lane nodded. "There was no reason to rush it, and I could understand where she was coming from. I slowly met the kids and then would have dinner sometimes, hang out with them."

"You get along with them?"

"Ella and I got along instantly. Toby, though, he warmed up a bit slower. He likes to get a grip on people. Now he's on me like a rash."

"Do they know the nature of your relationship?"

"Um...we hadn't gotten to talking to them about it. That was actually what we had just talked about doing right before this. I never stayed over, because we didn't want to confuse Ella. And Anna repeatedly said she didn't want the kids to think they weren't her number one priority."

"Does she prioritise the kids over your relationship?"

Anna flinched.

Without hesitating, Lane stated, "Of course she did. She still does. She prioritises the kids over anything. Anna has always thought of the kids first in everything she does."

"And you support that?"

"I don't think I could feel the way I do about her if she didn't. It's amazing, the bond the three of them have."

"Thank you, Miss Bishop, that will be all."

The State's attorney stood up. "How often were you seeing Doctor Foster?"

"Almost every day. We work together."

"Outside of work?"

"It would depend on my hours, or hers, but anything from twice to four times a week. She liked to spend one-on-one time with the kids."

"And you hadn't spoken about the nature of your relationship with the kids?"

"No. We were talking about doing that, but hadn't gotten there yet."

"And Ella never guessed? You weren't overtly affectionate in front of her?"

"Not overtly, no. From what I know, though, Ella's parents had explained that Anna dates women to her already, as Anna had a long-term partner the kids had met before. I think Ella's at an age where she doesn't think in terms of things like that, she just likes to hang out and watch movies and play games with us all."

"Thank you."

Shakily, Lane stood and caught Anna's eye, mouthing something she couldn't get. Anna looked at her, confused, but Lane was being ushered out.

The questions with Anna's mother passed in a blur, and she raved for so long about how good Anna was with the kids that Scott had to interrupt her.

Her mother would always fight for her.

And then, her father was called up.

A nervous pull in her stomach distracted her from wondering what Lane had tried to mime to her.

"How much do you see Anna and the kids?"

Andrew looked down before answering. "Not very often. The kids have the odd sleepover with us. It's something they've always done, since Ella was a baby, and I see them then."

"Were you surprised when Doctor Foster got guardianship?"

"My son had spoken to us about it previously."

"Do you think she's suited to it?"

Her father hesitated. "I didn't."

Anna looked up sharply.

He was still looking down towards the ground.

The judge had his eyes on him. Anna reminded herself to breathe.

Andrew cleared his throat. "This may sound like a strange statement, but I didn't think I'd raise a lesbian daughter. Yet I did." He gave a self-conscious shrug. "But I learnt quickly that who she was dating had nothing to do with anything. Both my children were good people." He paused, and Anna just wished he'd look at her. "Being the girl she is, she was career driven, brilliant at her job. She and her brother were fiercely close and incredibly loyal to each other. Jake was the family man, and Anna was ambitious. She adores her job." He paused, clearing his throat. "Then Jake...and Sally...Well, I dropped off the face of the earth. Anna, she looks so much like him. And Toby, he does, too." Voice cracking, her father cleared his throat. "Losing a child so young, it takes a part of a man away. Everything that reminds you of him just hurts. I, uh, I disappeared on my family." He looked up, and, for the first time since Jake died, looked Anna in the eye.

They held each other's gaze, and she felt her heart break for the grief she saw in his eyes.

"I disappeared." He pressed his lips together. "But she didn't." He turned and spoke to the judge directly. "Anna stepped up. I don't think she planned on having kids, but my son, her brother, asked it of her, and here she is, fighting tooth and nail for them. Losing their parents could have destroyed those two kids. I'm sure it's altered them, of course. But destroyed? Anna's held them together. She's held my wife together when I all but left her to her grief. And through it all, she's held herself together for those two kids. She's the best thing to happen not only to my grandchildren but to this entire family."

Silence rang around the courtroom until finally Scott broke it.

"Uh—thank you, Mr Foster. That will be all."

The State's attorney shook his head when the judge looked at him.

There was a lump in Anna's throat she could barely swallow past, and she watched helplessly as her father started to walk awkwardly out of the room. As he walked past her, Anna couldn't help herself. She stood up and walked towards him, wrapping her arms around him and burying her face in his chest. Only for a moment, he hesitated. Anna was fairly certain the last time he had hugged her had been when she was small, but she didn't care. His arms wrapped around her, tight over her shoulder blades.

Anna pulled back and stared into eyes the same shade her brother's had been. Her father's hands rested on her shoulders for a moment. With an uncertain look, he nodded to her. Anna quickly slipped back to her seat.

The glare Scott gave her didn't have much effect behind it.

Looking down at his papers, the judge acted like he hadn't noticed someone standing up in the middle of court proceedings. "Right. I think we'll take a ten-minute recess before resuming."

They stood as he walked out, and Anna turned to Scott. "How are we going?"

"Good. We just have to see what Cathy and the caseworkers have to say."

"George is speaking? He was only there once."

Scott frowned. "I know. We'll see."

"This judge? Is he a good one?"

"He's a religious man, but he has a lot of respect for the law. We could have done a lot worse."

Religion made her nervous. "Can I talk to the others?"

"They've all been called, so yes. Just be back here in five minutes. We won't be calling you unless the judge has specific questions for you."

Mind already out the door, Anna nodded. She walked out and was quickly hit with the rocket that was her mother, whose arms wrapped tight around her. "Did I do okay? Oh, I was so nervous, I don't even remember it now; it's a blur."

Anna pressed her face into her mother's neck. "You did great, Mum, thank you." She looked around. "Where's Dad?"

"He left for home, said he had business."

Of course he did.

Anna nodded, resigned. "Kym?"

"She said she mentioned it the other night, that she had to get in to work when she was finished testifying. She said you have to message her as soon as you know."

Lane stood behind Sandra, fidgeting with her bag, appearing even more anxious than she had in the courtroom. Untangling herself from her mother, Anna gave Lane a searching look. "Are you okay?"

"Anna, that man in there, at the table with your caseworker."

"George Coleman?"

"He was at the café with Cathy yesterday."

Freezing, Anna stared at her. The memory of the scene in the café, the man who had seemed vaguely familiar, washed over her. "Oh, my God. You're right."

"Do you think—"

"Who's George?" Sandra cut in, but they ignored her.

"Everyone has been saying this reaction was extreme. Lorna wouldn't speak more about it." Thoughts whirring, Anna didn't take her eyes off Lane's.

Lane nodded vigorously. "Do you think he was the one that pushed for this?"

"They said there was an issue from someone at the office. I never really thought it could be George. Why would he be talking to Cathy?"

"Anna, you have to tell Scott."

"I'll go now."

Shrilly, Sandra cut in again. "What? Who's George? What is going on?"

Anna whipped her head around. "Lane will explain, I have to run, Mum." Heart pounding, she turned on her heel and rushed back in. Everything began making more sense. She sat down next to Scott and grabbed his arm, turning him towards her.

His eyes widened when he saw the look on her face. "What?"

"Scott," she said, trying to keep her voice to a whisper, "George was at a café with Cathy yesterday. We saw him there. Lane just recognized him. He only came to my house once, and Lorna did *not* express any concerns about the kids. He appeared *after* Cathy first came over and got scary."

Processing this information, Scott stared at her for a second. Excitement gleamed in his eyes. "Got it."

"This is good, yes?"

"That is all far too much of a coincidence."

When the bailiff stood straight and said his piece, Anna didn't even hear what was said. There was a ringing in her ears. Everybody stood up again.

Scott winked at her. "Leave this to me."

"Okay." Her mouth was dry. Half-elated and half-nauseous, Anna felt helpless, but finally one step closer to getting the kids back.

Lorna was called to the stand first.

The State's attorney rose and started questioning. "Lorna, you've worked for the department of child services for how long?"

"Eight years."

"And you've been on the Foster case from the start?"

"Yes."

"Have you yourself had any concerns in this matter?"

"No. None."

"So why are we here today?"

"An order came from above me, and I had to follow the protocol."

"And you saw nothing that had you concerned all that time?"

"No."

The lawyer nodded. "That will be all."

Anna glanced at George, who was trying to hide his glare at Lorna.

Scott rose. "So you had no concerns, Lorna?"

"Not really, no. It was very straightforward. A guardian had been allocated. Doctor Foster accepted taking in the kids. It was mostly paperwork and routine follow-up visits. I went on two and a colleague on another."

"A different colleague—isn't that unusual?"

"It is a little unusual, but not unheard of. The senior caseworker in my office, George Coleman, had the initial neglect complaint cross his desk. He took over from there."

"Ah, I see. So he did the third visit, the visit post the first neglect complaint you received from the maternal grandmother?"

"Yes. I wanted to do it, but he insisted a higher-up wanted a second pair of eyes on it. It's not completely unheard of."

"Okay, let's go back to the beginning. Did you have any concerns raised at any of your visits?"

"No. I was there twice in that short time, and the kids were adjusting as well as could be expected. Doctor Foster seemed to be juggling them and work. After moving states and starting a new job, she seemed fairly settled. I spoke to the school counsellor about Ella, and no red flags were raised."

"Ella broke her arm, yes?"

"Yes, early on, at the park. There were witnesses; there were no concerns about this."

"So when the complaint was officially lodged, it had nothing to do with the broken arm?"

"No. That wasn't even mentioned; in fact, I'm not even sure if the grandmother had been aware of it."

"So what were the concerns put forth?"

"Neglect. She said that the kids were being 'dumped' with many different people. She went so far as to hint that the children had been left at home alone. The second complaint, an anonymous one, claimed that many different women were in and out of the house at all times and that the children were being left alone, or in other places, as Anna was frequently at home without them."

"And this triggered the unscheduled home visit and checks on the school and day care?"

"Yes."

"And you still weren't concerned?"

"I wasn't at all. The kids appeared on the way to healing, as well as they could be expected to be, and, again, I saw no red flags when I made the visits and calls to the school and family members."

"So what led to the kids being removed from the home?"

"My colleague raised red flags after his home visit. The complaint crossed his desk after my second visit. That was when he decided to go. He raised concerns, and that, coupled with a new complaint from the maternal grandmother, led to it going over my head and the kids being removed."

"I see. One last question, Lorna. What would your recommendation to the court be?"

"I believe these kids need to be back in their home, in a stable environment. I think Doctor Foster is the best person to be providing that."

"Thank you."

Lorna went back to her seat.

The State's attorney called Cathy, and Anna felt every hair on her arms stand up.

Accompanied by a bailiff, Cathy walked down the aisle. Anna gripped her knee tightly. Cathy was dressed like a president's wife, wearing a day suit with pearls at her throat that had a silver cross hanging from the centre.

As soon as she was sworn in, the State's attorney started. "Mrs Larsen, you've petitioned the court for guardianship, is this correct?"

"Yes."

"Was this before or after you lodged your concerns with the department?"

"Before."

"What drove you to lodge for guardianship, considering the parents' wishes had been for guardianship to go to Doctor Foster?"

"My concerns were always present." Cathy glared at Anna. "She has no children of her own, she can't know anything about raising two young children. She has always appeared focused on her career and relationships, never on having a family. I visited one day, and was appalled to find out Toby was in day care during the week when he should be home, and she was working full time."

"Understood. And you were concerned enough to lodge a complaint?"

Cathy shifted uncomfortably in her chair. "I was concerned she was not doing well by the children, and then, not only this, but Toby was with his other grandmother that day, a Friday, while Anna had clearly slept late and was entertaining her—" she clearly struggled with the word, "*girlfriend* in the house."

"Is this when you lodged the complaint?"

"Yes, and started the process of petitioning to challenge the will. I could see the children were not getting the attention they deserved, and Anna was clearly still focused on her career and conquests, rather than the kids. It's obvious I can provide a much healthier atmosphere."

Anna stiffened at the harsh words. Scott whispered out the side of his mouth, "Breathe."

She tried.

"So what led to you to lodge the second neglect complaint?"

Blinking rapidly, Anna turned to Scott in confusion, but he simply watched what unfolded with a smile playing at his lips. The second complaint had been anonymous. Surely the State lawyer wasn't actually trying to trip Cathy up?

Eyes back on the pair, Anna actually felt hopeful.

Cathy pursed her lips. "I kept an eye on them, after that."

It was as if Cathy had forgotten it had been anonymous. She didn't even deny it.

"There were *two* separate women I saw coming out of the house at various times of the evening and early hours of the morning, which is no way to influence a child. Not only this, but Anna was working full time, when Sally had been home with the kids previously. Some nights, Anna got home later than others. I went by one evening to drop off a present for the kids and no one answered the door. I was concerned. Where would someone with a toddler and a six-year-old be at eight in the evening? Giving her the benefit of the doubt, I stayed to see if they would get in so I could give them the present. I gave up after midnight. It was then that I realised I needed to get these children out of this destructive environment and with my husband and myself, to somewhere more stable."

"Okay. Thank you." The State's attorney sat down, an odd look on his face.

Scott stood up, and Anna sat up straighter. There was no way to know how this was going to play out—what would Scott do with the information she had given him?

"Mrs Larsen." He smiled at her, and she frowned at him. "Were you ever concerned Ella or Toby were not being fed? Clothed? Housed? Sent to school?"

Cathy's lips pressed together in a tight, white line, and it surprised Anna how she could go from looking like Sally to looking like a completely different person. "No. But—"

"Did you ever think they were being starved? Abused?"

"They are being abused! That woman lives in sin, and she is perpetrating to *my* grandchildren that it is okay and *normal* to live that lifestyle."

"It's not illegal to be gay in Australia, Mrs Larsen. Nor does it mean you can't parent. I'll ask in a different manner. Did you ever think they were being hit? Yelled at? Blackmailed?"

Nostrils flaring, she glared at him. "No."

"Yet you deemed it fit to make three complaints, one 'anonymously' to make it seem as if others had concerns."

"I never said I made the anonymous complaint."

Spreading his arms wide, Scott smiled. "You all but admitted it to the other counsellor."

The flush that spread over Cathy's cheeks gave Anna a warm feeling in her chest.

The judge was watching Cathy with a dark expression on his face. He cleared his throat. "One moment, Counsellor." And then he was looking at Anna.

"Doctor Foster, if you don't mind me asking: this evening Mrs Larsen was at the house and neither you nor the kids were home, where were the children?"

"Uh..." Anna was taken off guard. "Having a sleepover with my mother. Ella had specifically asked if they could. It was something they used to do regularly when my brother was alive."

"And the other day she came over, when Toby was at his grandmother's?"

"That was the one night I'd had to work late, until three a.m. My mother took the kids."

"And in two entire months, it was the only time you agreed to work late?"

"Yes. A truck had hit a school bus and, being a senior on staff, I felt obligated to stay. Half the staff on shift that afternoon stayed late."

"I saw that on the news, a tragedy. Though I also heard your hospital didn't lose a single patient."

"They're all doing well."

The judge eyed her for a second, then said, "Thank you for answering."

Cathy piped up. "And where were you, afterwards? Using the advantage to instantly be with a woman? And the other night you were out, was it even one of the two you're already stringing along, then?"

The vehemence in Cathy's voice made Anna's eyes widen and her stomach roll over. Never in her life had someone looked at her like Cathy was looking at her now.

Everyone looked to the judge as he cleared his throat. "You will stick to answering questions, thank you. If the children were safe and looked after that evening, I have no concerns about what Doctor Foster was doing with her free time."

A lemon could never be as bitter as Cathy looked in that moment. "Those children deserve to be raised by God-fearing, Christian parents. My daughter had already gone so wrong, and now here we are, an opportunity to raise them as they should be, not in sin, but—"

"Please stick to the questions, Mrs Larsen."

Anna had a slight, awkward crush on the judge.

With a benign expression, Scott said, "No further questions."

He sat back down.

Staring at the judge, Cathy was apparently unable to contain herself. "You are a Christian man, I can tell," she said. "How can you want to put these children back into her care? The law needs—"

"The law is as I see fit in my courtroom, Mrs Larsen." The judge had clearly had enough. "Please step down and refrain from speaking to me about

Christianity. I would like you to remain in the courtroom for the rest of the hearing, since it is mainly on the basis of your complaints we are here today. Take a seat."

The anger radiating off Cathy as she took a seat behind the lawyers' tables was palpable.

The judge looked back at the lawyers. "Continue, please."

The second case manager was called. Refusing to look anywhere near Anna, George Coleman took the witness seat.

The State's lawyer stood, cleared his throat and said, "Please let us know when you first became aware of the Foster children."

"I first became aware when the first neglect complaint was lodged. I'm the senior caseworker in my department, and these things usually come across my desk. Sometimes they are handed straight off to the caseworker in charge of the case and others I take a personal interest in."

"And you took an interest in this one?"

"It was a known case. The car accident was on the news, the kids were spoken about in office meetings. The call of neglect in these circumstances concerned me."

"And when you went to the home visit, what caused you to lodge a complaint?"

"The form I lodged was not a complaint, nor an official statement of neglect. It's like a 'red flag' warning, a form we fill out to let people know the caseworker had some concerns."

Rising from his chair, Scott interrupted. "May I ask a question?"

Momentarily taken aback, the State's attorney gave a nod and sat down.

As if asking about the weather, Scott continued, "But what were your concerns?"

Barely noticeably, George shifted in his seat. "The children were strangely quiet. They appeared withdrawn. Miss Fost—"

"Doctor Foster, actually."

George grimaced. "Yes, ah, Doctor Foster did not seem very interested in the kids or talking to me. I had a feeling with this, so I simply put the paperwork in that there were some concerns; that was all."

Completely relaxed, Scott nodded. "Okay. And how long have you known Cathy Larsen?"

George tried to hide the fact that his mouth had dropped open in surprise. "What makes you think I know Mrs Larsen?"

Scott smiled easily.

Anna pursed her lips and tried to quell her rising excitement.

"Please just answer the question, sir."

"I, ah, don't know her well."

"The question was how long have you known her."

"We go to the same church. I suppose I've known her six or so years, but not well."

"Well enough to have coffee yesterday?"

George's face paled, and his eyes finally flitted to Anna, who looked back at him, expression stony. He obviously thought he had gotten away without being spotted. "I did have coffee with her, yes."

"Was this the first time the two of you have had a meeting?"

George was silent.

"Answer the question, Mr Coleman." Anna had thought that Kym gave a good stink eye, but that was before she met this judge.

"I have met with her several times over the last four weeks."

"And were you, by any chance, advising her on how she could work the system to ensure the children could be removed and assuring her you could lodge certain paperwork and give the right nudges to ensure that would happen?" Scott asked.

The silence was thick. "Answer the question, please," Judge Gordon said "You are under oath."

"I gave her advice, yes. She had many, legitimate concerns about her grandchildren."

"And you helped her manipulate the system to lead to their removal from the custody of Anna Foster and, you hoped, to lead to the placement of them in the care of Cathy Larsen and her husband?"

"I never lied."

"Do you really think it was surprising that the children were reserved around you, a stranger? Especially considering the death of their parents only two months previously?"

Visibly sweating, George seemed to realise he would have to answer. "No."

The glimmer of hope that Lane had ignited in the hallway flickered brighter in Anna's chest.

"During your investigation, did you see any sign that the children were being neglected or abused in any way?"

"...No."

Anna couldn't tear her eyes away from the scene unfolding between the now profusely sweating man in the chair and the calm, collected lawyer.

"And where do you think these children will be better off?"

"Cathy Larsen."

Anna was sure that Scott almost rolled his eyes. "Why?"

"Because I spend my entire job fighting against a system that doesn't always do what it should do. Because I return children to homes they should never be returned to and take children from homes they should stay in. And here, well, here is the easy option of putting children in a God-fearing, stable environment and thereby removing them from an unstable environment with no religion and, it appears, no morals. The choice is logical!" George Coleman was red in the face, straightening as if his beliefs gave him strength.

Scott let a meaningful beat of silence fall around them before saying coldly, "No other questions." He sat down.

The judge turned to George. "Please take your seat, Mr Coleman."

Breathing heavily, the man walked over and sat next to Lorna, who was staring steadfastly ahead with a very red face.

The judge looked down at the papers in front of him for a minute. Anna stared at him, waiting for him to speak.

After what felt like an eternity, he looked around the room and opened his mouth.

"Mr Coleman speaks only the truth." The indignant voice of Cathy Larsen rang out, cutting off whatever the judge had been about to say. "If you have any belief in God at all, you'll put those children in a home that will teach them true family values."

Glaring, the judge spoke in a level tone. "Sit down, or you will be removed from this room."

Anna didn't even turn around to watch as she heard Cathy slowly take her seat.

"And I'll have you not lecture me on Christianity, either," Judge Gordon said. "The question in this court today is of the allegations of neglect directed at Doctor Foster in regards to Ella and Toby Foster. From the evidence put forth today, I see absolutely no sign of neglect or abuse. In fact, the only thing I can think of as harming them is removing them from what was obviously a stable and loving environment to be placed in foster care to investigate what are obviously nuisance claims put forward by a woman with her own vendetta—a case which should never have even ended up in my courtroom. The only reason it did is because a government employee has manipulated a system put in place to protect children to cater to his own religious beliefs."

He looked directly at George Coleman. "You knew that your notice of concern, coupled with exaggerated and blatantly false accusations and your power in the department would lead to this knee-jerk reaction; and I'm guessing you pulled some strings. I will see that this is investigated and your actions prosecuted."

He paused, sitting up straighter. "Sexual orientation plays no role in someone being legally fit to raise children in Australia, and it's plain that this is what the allegation is. If I see you in my court again, Mrs Larsen, without genuine proof of abuse or neglect, I'll have you arrested for false allegations and for purely wasting my time. I hereby put forward that Doctor Anna Foster will have temporary custody of both Ella and Toby Foster until the permanent guardianship hearing in one month's time. However, these court proceedings will be going on record, and I wish anyone luck contesting the wish of the biological parents and of this court."

The judge stood, looking across the room to Anna. "Good luck, Doctor Foster. You're going to have your hands full with two young children and a full-time job. It's refreshing to see someone with such an excellent support network, all of whom are so committed to doing what is best for the children in your care." And with that, he swept off and left the room. Anna was left staring at his empty chair.

Scott, having stood up the second the judge did, looked down to Anna, beaming. "We won."

Breathing hard, heart fluttering in her chest, Anna looked up at him. "We did?"

"We won!"

Unable to stop herself, Anna launched from her chair and hugged him. "Thank you! Really, really, thank you." Then she was turning and walking down the aisle as fast as she could, pulling the door open, joy flooding her chest.

Her mother stood outside, watching the door as if willing it to burst open with news. She blinked, and a grin grew over her face as Anna powered towards her.

"We won?"

Nodding even as she pulled her mother into a hug, Anna felt torn between laughing and sobbing. "We won, Mum." And she felt it then, a sob, escaping her chest, sheer relief finally making her crack. She pulled back, and her mother beamed at her. Over Sandra's shoulder, Anna saw Lane walking towards them, three coffees in a carrier tray in hand and a hesitant smile on her face as she took in the sight in the hallway.

Without knowing how it happened, Anna was in Lane's arms, grinning wide enough to burst, even as tears streaked her cheeks. She felt ridiculous, but it was as if all the tense, terrified emotion of the last six days had finally been allowed to break.

As Sandra rescued the coffee, Lane's lips pressed against her ear. "You get them back?"

Anna nodded, unable to speak, and Lane picked her up, swinging her around. Both of them were laughing, even as Anna let out another half sob. Back on her feet, Anna squeezed Lane tighter.

Anna choked out words, needing to hear them again. "They're coming back."

"They are!"

Even while returning the kiss Lane gave her, an ecstatic laugh escaped Anna's lips. "I love you."

Lane's grip slackened in surprise, then tightened around her, breath hot against Anna's neck as Lane buried her face against it. "Good, because I'm pretty in love with you, too."

Anna grinned against the soft curve where Lane's neck met her shoulder. It was probably the most absurd place to say it, in a courthouse with her mother a few metres away. But the high Anna was on dominated any such thoughts.

"Anna?"

Remembering where they were, Anna pulled away, hand still clinging to Lane's. "Lorna." She swiped a hand over her cheeks, not used to tears in public. "Hi. Thank you."

Lorna shook her head. "No, don't be silly. Everything I said was true. Just...I can pick them up and get them to you anytime."

"Now?"

Lorna laughed. "Now is good. Are you headed home? I'll drop them there."

"We'll go home now."

"I'll meet you there." She turned to go, and Anna turned back to Lane and her mother. "Oh, and Anna?"

Anna turned. "Yeah?"

"I am so sorry this happened to you."

In spite of the serious moment, Anna couldn't stop beaming. "Thank you."

"Want to know a secret?"

"Always."

"He's needed to go for a long, long time. The good thing coming out of this is he finally will."

Cathy walked out of the courtroom past Lorna, her eyes straight ahead, handbag clasped to her side as she marched down the corridor and left the building.

Lorna winked at Anna, pulling her keys out of her pocket as she walked away. "I'll see you soon."

Lane and Anna, hands still clasped, were joined by Sandra as they started walking out of the building.

"What about the other hearing?" Concern was clear in Sandra's tone, but Anna just gave a slight shrug. "It's in a month. But, uh, it sounds like the chances are good I'll be keeping them." She took a deep breath. "I just want to enjoy the fact that I'm about to see them again."

Lane squeezed her hand.

"Did I see coffee, Mum?" Anna asked.

"Uh..."

Lane turned to look at Sandra as they were walking. "Oh, yeah, you took them. Can I have one?"

"Um."

"Mum?"

"Well, I was excited, and you two were having a moment."

"You drank them?"

"I drank one of them and dropped the others in the bin because I was so nervous. I had to do something; the excitement was overwhelming!"

Anna shook her head, climbing into the passenger seat of the car as Lane took the back.

"Anna."

Anna turned to look at her mother. "Yeah?"

"So what the hell happened in there?"

Anna filled them in on the proceedings as they drove home.

Sandra shook her head. "But those people are supposed to be preventing these things from happening."

They pulled up to the house. "I think most of them are there for that," Anna said "From the sounds of it, this guy isn't going to be there much longer."

"Good!" Sandra was bouncing from foot to foot on the walkway and looking uncomfortable. "Oh, good God, I have to pee."

With a grin, Lane watched her go. "Serves her right for throwing away our coffees."

Anna looked at Lane as they took a seat on the front step. "They're coming back," she said again, still not quite able to believe it.

"On their way now, in fact."

Anna turned back to the road, finger picking at her thumbnail.

Lane put her hand over Anna's, stilling the nervous habit.

"Are you okay?"

Anna shrugged. "I am."

"Really?"

"I'm…I'm so excited to see them. Just…are they going to be okay?"

Lane pulled her hand onto her lap. "They won't be, completely. But they'll be back with you, and they'll slowly be okay again. They weren't okay when you came here, but you helped them, then. Like you will this time round."

Anna let out a slow breath.

A car turned onto the street, silver and new. Tyres crunched on the road, and Anna's heart sped up.

The grip she had on Lane's hand was probably too tight. "Lane."

Unable to tear her eyes off the car, Anna felt Lane push her up so she was standing.

Ella turned her head in the back seat just then, eyes wide and her hand pressed to the glass. Before Anna knew what had happened, the door pushed open and Ella was flying over the grass in an orange Conversed blur.

Anna squatted down, and Ella hit her at full force, arms and legs wrapping around her so tightly that Anna fell backwards, sprawled on the grass and not caring that the damp ground was soaking through her skirt. Ella's fingers dug into her back and it didn't matter one bit; all Anna could do was hold her.

There was a hiccup in her ear, then a sob, and she held Ella tighter, auburn hair pressed into her face as Anna gripped the little girl with everything possible. Somehow, through Ella's sobbing, she heard a sound that made her split into a huge grin even as it brought forth another sob. She looked up from Ella's neck.

"Na!" Somehow smaller and yet bigger than she remembered, Toby was fighting to get out of Lorna's arms.

He slid to the ground, grinning so hard his dimples showed; he was clearly delighted to see her. Like every time he got too excited and ran, he tripped and fell, then pulled himself back up, still smiling. The next moment he was in her arms as well, half climbing her and Ella to be closer.

And Ella finally pulled back, hands grasping Anna's cheeks as she stared at her, almost nose to nose. Toby was buried in her neck and Ella's green eyes were bright as she stared at Anna.

"Hey, Ella Bella."

"Aunty Na." Lips trembling, Ella finally gave her a slight smile. "Can we have pancakes for dinner?"

Anna couldn't help but laugh.

Chapter Twenty-Three

Feet up on the coffee table, back against the couch, Anna let herself truly relax for the first time in a week. Her hand rubbed slow circles on Toby's back; he was fast asleep on his stomach, face against her collarbone and legs to either side of her waist. She should have taken him up to his bed, but he had been incredibly clingy since getting back, and, if she was honest, she felt pretty clingy herself. He smelt of baby shampoo and was warm against her chest, his breathing deep and even.

Ella was pressed tight into Anna's side, wrapped in her other arm. They had *Aladdin* turned down low, Ella only half watching as her hand clung to Anna's.

Anna's mother had left after half an hour, hugging the kids and telling Anna that she had spent that Wednesday with them and Anna needed to get them settled. Lane had gone home even sooner. She'd whispered in Anna's ear that they'd talk later.

Ella was mostly quiet.

And that was okay.

Quiet was something Anna got, especially with her niece. Unfortunately, everyone was right in saying they were similar. She'd seen it the weeks after her brother passed away. And she'd been concerned, but had let it play out, understanding more than anyone what Ella was doing. The counsellor at school hadn't been too concerned, so Anna had left it. And slowly, ever so slowly, Ella had reacted and lashed out and responded and had started, Anna hoped, to heal.

Anger bubbled up again inside her, and Anna had to swallow it back down. Whatever Cathy and George's motivations, it had been damaging, to all of them, but Anna worried especially for Ella, who had been eating dinner when someone had turned up and all but ripped her from her house.

So Ella was quiet.

And Anna was letting her be, tonight.

But Anna also wanted Ella to talk to her, so she could reassure her. The look on Ella's face when she had asked, "Don't you want us?" still haunted her. Because, God, this little girl was going to have abandonment issues if she didn't realise that of course Anna wanted her—she wanted the two of them more than she had ever even realised.

But tonight wasn't the night for that. Anna was just soaking up the joy that she had them back, that the kids were delighted to be back.

Stilling her movements, Anna cupped the back of Toby's head, the silky soft strands of his brown hair in her hands. Just as Jake's hair had in his baby photos, Toby's was starting to curl at the ends. She tugged her arm tighter, hugging Ella against her, and she heard a small giggle.

"Why you laughing, Ella Bella?" She spoke softly, mindful of Toby.

A shrug shifted Anna's arm slightly. "You were squeezing me."

"Because I don't want to let you go, that's why."

Ella was quiet.

Anna didn't push it, then. But she would need to soon. Wriggling her fingers, Anna tickled Ella again, smiling softly at the little giggle it caused. Ella settled back into Anna, and Anna rested her cheek against her head, dropping a kiss on top of it first.

There was nowhere else she would rather be.

A small foot had dug into Anna's back, and a hand was flung over her face when she woke up. Opening her eyes, she relaxed as she saw Ella sprawled on her back, arms and legs thrown out, her auburn hair a cloud around her head. She looked so young when she slept.

While Anna had put Toby into his cot, Ella had done the fastest job of brushing her teeth ever. Anna had walked into her room and found Ella curled up in her bed. Not saying anything, Anna had crawled in beside her and wrapped her arms around her, pulling the little girl into her. She hadn't fallen asleep until she'd heard Ella's breathing even out.

At one a.m., Toby had woken up almost hysterical. His cries had scared Anna awake, and she'd run into his room in a panicked state. He had settled when she pulled him to her arms and soothed him, but his hiccups had taken too long to slow, and she'd finally brought him into bed with her and Ella. He fell asleep in her arms as she sat up against the headboard, looking down at him.

Ella blinked sleepily at her. "He did that every night we were gone. But he didn't stop this quickly then."

Anna swallowed the lump in her throat and brushed her hand through Ella's hair as she drifted off again.

Now, she had two tiny bodies half crushing her. Rolling over, desperately trying not to wake the kids, Anna reached for her phone.

Lane.

> *First night back with them...you must be ecstatic. Still want to hang out today? It's okay if you want one-on-one time with them. x PS Even though it's totally okay, I missed you last night. :)*

Anna smiled and wrote a quick reply, adding a photo of Ella and Toby sprawled out over her and the bed.

> *So happy to have them back. Park this afternoon? I'll ask Kym and Mum. You finish at three this afternoon? Say four? And I missed you, too.*

She opened a text from Kym.

> *When can I see them? When can I see them? When can I see them? When can I see them?*

There was a second one from her, too.

> *Seriously, when can I see them?*

Anna laughed quietly and wrote back.

> *Park at four? Meet here and we'll all head over?*

The reply was almost instant.

> *Yay!*

A message came through from Lane straight after that.

That sounds like the best of plans. Can't wait to see you and the kids again. :)

Warm fuzzy feelings had taken over Anna's chest. She put her phone back down after texting her mother about the park and rolled over to see Ella watching her with sleepy eyes.

"Heya, Ella Bella."

Ella blinked at her. "Hi."

She snuggled into Anna's chest, and Anna wrapped her up in her arms. Soft clouds of hair tickled Anna's neck, and she gave her a kiss. "I missed you."

Ella only shook her head slightly against Anna's neck, silence her response.

"I *did,* Ella Bella."

While Anna wanted to let Ella process on her own, she wasn't going to leave her stewing on whatever was going on in her head that whole time. She at least needed to ensure Ella understood that what had happened had been out of Anna's hands.

Before Anna could say anything else, Ella spoke in a whisper: "Why didn't you come find us then?"

A lump filled Anna's throat instantly. She closed her eyes and took a deep breath, then wrapped her arms tighter around Ella. "Honey, I wanted to."

Another head shake.

"I did." Anna didn't know how to explain this to a six-year-old. "Ella? You know when you get in trouble at school?"

"I don't get into trouble."

In any other moment, Anna would have chuckled. "Okay, you know when other kids get into trouble? And there is all this stuff the teachers have to do? Like tell their big boss, the principal? And then the teachers send the kid there? And then the principal has to tell the kid's parents? And they have to wait for the parents to come in so they can all talk, and the kid has to wait in the hallway?"

This was making no sense, but Ella nodded.

"Well, you got taken by people who had to make sure I was looking after you properly. And to get you back, I had to wait for those people to talk to their boss—he was called a judge, though, not a principal. And I had to sit outside until I could find out what they said." She sighed, hand on the back of Ella's head. "Does that make sense?"

Ella half shrugged in her arms. Pulling back, Anna saw that Ella's face was pinched together as she tried not to cry, her cheeks a blotchy red. Anna welled up herself, swallowing past the lump in her throat.

"If it were up to me, I would have pulled you out of the car when Lorna came that night. All I was doing while you were gone was fighting alongside all the people trying to get you back. I love you, Ella Bella. You and Toby and me all belong together." She stared intently at Ella, who had finally given a hiccup and started to cry, staring into Anna's eyes.

"Oh, honey." Anna wrapped her back up and pulled her right into her, tears on her own cheeks as Ella came undone in her arms. The little girl sobbed, and Anna had no more words to give her. Instead, she rubbed her back and smoothed her hair and held her as tightly as she could.

They lay for a while, Ella's hiccups slowly fading, her breathing evening out. The fingers that were clenched in Anna's tank top eventually relaxed. Ella sniffled, rubbing her nose against the material of Anna's shirt and making it wetter.

"You okay?"

Ella nodded, still pressed against Anna. This time, she pulled back on her own. Watery eyes searched Anna's face. "You cried, too?"

"Yup."

Delicate eyebrows scrunched together. "I don't like that you cried."

Anna gave a low chuckle. "I don't like you crying, either, because I don't like you being sad; but some of it's happy tears, Ella. I got you and Toby back."

"But you smile when you're happy."

"Sometimes your body gets confused. I'm smiling now, though." Slowly, Ella smiled too, and when her green eyes lit up, she looked so much like Sally that Anna's chest ached. "And now you are."

Quickly, Anna blew a raspberry against Ella's neck; she giggled and tried to squirm away as Anna did it again and again.

"Aunty Na! Stop it!"

"Nope!"

"Please!"

"Never!"

"Aunty Na!"

"Fine."

Ella flopped back dramatically on the bed, breathless and grinning.

"Can we have pancakes now? We didn't last night."

Anna smiled through the aching in her chest. "Sure."

They both turned their heads as they heard Toby make grumpy, baby-waking-up noises.

Ella looked at Anna. "Toby's up."

"Okay. Plan of attack. We get Toby up, eat pancakes, go do some grocery shopping, go to the library and get you some new books. Then we'll come home for Toby to nap and for us to read the books. Then," she paused for emphasis, "Kym, Lane and Grandma are coming over and we are going to go to the park."

Ella's eyes lit up, and she sat up on the bed. "Really?"

"Really." Anna sat up too, pulling the still-half-asleep Toby into her and rubbing his back gently. "So, you take Toby and make pancakes, and I'll wait here for breakfast in bed."

The way Ella rolled her eyes made her look sixteen, not six. "I can't do *either* of those things."

Anna made sure to sigh as dramatically as she could. "Okay. Fine. You go get the things out of the cupboard we need and *I'll* deal with Toby nappies."

Ella slid off the bed and raced out the door. "Okay!" Her voice called out loudly, even from the hallway.

Looking down, the sight of Toby blinking up at her, grinning around the pacifier she'd used in a desperate attempt last night, confronted Anna. Sleepily, he pushed up and snuggled into her neck, his fingers playing with the material of her shirt. With her eyes closed, Anna leant back against the headboard. She'd missed morning cuddles with Toby. He held his ratty blue blanket close between their bodies while his other hand continued to grip her shirt. "Shall we get you ready and go get some pancakes, Tobes?"

He sat up, eyes wide. "Cakes?"

"You bet."

He wriggled excitedly in her arms.

As she changed his nappy, she made a secret oath she doubted would last very long to never complain about doing this task if it meant she had the kids with her. Then she got him dressed in denim overalls and a striped green shirt underneath, pulling his shoes on while he kicked his legs cheekily. She poked his tummy and pulled him back into her arms, where he settled back in, blue blanket grasped firmly under his arm.

The blanket. Anna tried to not make a big deal of it. When Sally and Jake had first passed away, the blanket had gone everywhere with him, as it had most times since he was a baby. As time had passed and, Anna supposed, he got a little older, the blanket had started to be left behind, increasingly only used for sleep. Leading up to the trial, he'd been using it and his pacifier a lot less. Mostly at night it would make an appearance, but for the last month, that had been it.

And now it was back, Toby clutching it firmly.

Anna plodded down the stairs, chatting to Toby until the scene in the kitchen brought her to a stop.

At the bench, Ella stood on her footstool, eggs, flour, and milk in front of her with the mixing utensils fanned out. A measuring cup was buried in a jar of flour. She looked up. "One of these cups?"

Anna nodded, walking over with Toby and plopping him down on the floor. Immediately, he started to try climb up her legs, making whiny noises.

She looked down. "Wanna stay down there with some books, Tobes? We'll get your trains?"

Fingers clasped her pyjama pants as Toby tried to scale her leg. "Na."

Indulging him for now, Anna bent down and picked him back up. She had no idea what was normal for this situation and felt at a loss all over again. But there was no way she could say no at the moment.

Content back on her hip, Toby peered over to watch Ella.

Anna watched her, too, smiling when puffs of flour billowed up in the air. "That's it, Ella. I'll help with the milk."

They made pancakes, passing the morning by eating far too many of them. They all hung out in the living room, playing with Toby's trains while Ella studiously coloured in. Relieved it was Saturday and she didn't have to keep Ella out of school for this bonding time, Anna took the kids in the late morning to the grocery store, then the library. It didn't take long for her to start to hate the fact that it was Saturday, though: two hours later they returned home, Anna frazzled by the amount of people at the stores and the library. That experience was not one she would be repeating with two children any time soon.

Toby, full from the lunch they'd had while out, fell asleep on the drive home. Anna settled him in his bed, rubbing circles on his back until he was deeply asleep.

By the time it was four o'clock, Toby was awake again. He and Ella sat on the floor next to the table in the kitchen, playing with his cars and trains as Anna drank a coffee. It wasn't long before Toby was back on her lap, train in hand.

There was a knock at the door and Anna looked up sharply as she heard a small crash.

Ella sat there frozen, eyes wide, peering towards the hallway, the train she had been holding now upside down on the floor next to her crossed legs.

"Ella?"

She didn't look at Anna. Her cheeks were pale, chest rising and falling rapidly.

"Ella Bella?"

Ella blinked and looked at her. "Who's here?"

The panicked look in Ella's eye made Anna react instinctively. She held out her hand, and Ella hesitated only a second before standing up and leaning into Anna in a rush, half sitting on her lap.

"It'll be Lane or Kym or Grandma." Anna smiled reassuringly. "Let's go see, hey?"

Ella nodded, still wide eyed, and took her hand. Anna led her to the front door, Toby on her hip.

"Who is it?" Ella called after Anna poked her.

"Someone bearing treats!"

Anna grinned, looking down at Ella. "Who did that sound like?"

"Kym!" Already kneeling to wrap Ella in her arms, Kym hugged her tightly the moment the door opened. "Ella! I missed you!" As she hugged Ella, she looked over her shoulder to Anna and the baby. "Toby!"

With an excited shout Toby lunged himself forward until Anna put him down. He ran at Kym, leaving Anna without a child on or directly next to her for the first time all day.

"Did you bring treats?" Ella looked at Kym with all the love and adoration of a six-year-old promised chocolate.

Kym laughed loudly. "I did! They're for a picnic at the park though. Know anyone who would be interested in coming to the park with me?"

"Me!"

"Oh! You want to come? I thought you hated parks. Especially ones with a picnic."

"No. I love parks! Who told you that?" She turned and glared at Anna. "Did you tell Kym that?"

Hands held up, Anna shook her head. "Nope. Not me."

As Kym stood, Toby looked at her like she was the second coming.

Still looking worried, Ella looked back to Kym. "Well, I love parks."

"Then you can definitely come."

Before they could move inside, Lane pulled up, waving through the window.

"Nurse Lane!" When Ella bolted for Lane, Anna felt some of the lingering tension in her chest relax as she watched them greet each other.

Kym looked to Anna, rubbing her nose on Toby's cheek to make him giggle.

"Hey," Anna said.

"Hey." Leaving Lane chattering with Ella next to her car, they walked inside. "You know, Ella just adores her."

Anna looked over her shoulder to Kym. "I know."

"Good. So, all is right with the world?"

While Anna put the kettle on, Kym settled at the table, bag dumped on the floor and a clinging Toby on her lap.

"All is very right."

Kym "oohed" at Toby, who had pulled one of his books off the table and was pointing at a random page to show her. "I was so relieved for you guys. Not that it should have gone any other way."

Completely comfortable, Toby leant back against Kym, and Anna nodded as she watched them together. "I was relieved, too."

Kym looked up at her over Toby's head, turning pages for him, her face concerned. "How are they?"

Anna shrugged and checked that Toby was absorbed in his book. "Blanket's going everywhere." An indication with her chin showed what she meant. "And I can't put him down. And E...well, she's unsettled. Quiet. We had a chat, which will hopefully help. The knock at the door made her panic."

With a sad nod, Kym said, "That will calm down. She'll realise she's safe eventually."

Anna gnawed her bottom lip, wanting to believe her.

"No *way*!" Ella's voice cut through the silence.

"Yes way!"

"I don't believe you!"

"Ella, who's the nurse here?"

"You."

"Exactly."

They entered the kitchen, and Lane looked up from Ella. "Hello, ladies."

Kym waved at her and went back to Toby.

"What were you two talking about?" Anna asked.

Lane walked over to Toby and kissed his neck in a quick flurry of kisses, making him giggle. In moments, Lane was in the kitchen next to Anna, and soft fingers trailed down her back. "Ella doesn't believe me that there's a *Finding Nemo 2* coming out."

"What does being a nurse have to do with that?"

Lane shrugged, smirking. "I use what I have."

Anna chuckled.

Ella's voice interrupted them.

"You two really like each other."

They both looked to Ella, who was staring at them blatantly.

Amused, Kym glanced up. Flicking her eyes from Kym's smirk to Ella's honest face, Anna had no idea where that had come from.

"What, Ella?"

"You two. You really like each other. You're always staring and smiling with gross looks on your faces. Kind of like how Aladdin looks at Jasmin."

Not even attempting to cover the sound, Kym cracked up. Anna resisted the urge to throw something at her. Needing help, Anna turned to Lane, who had nothing to offer with a blank look. With no one else to go to for help, Anna gave her attention back to Ella.

"Uh…yeah, we do really like each other."

"*So* obvious."

"Right, Ella? They're *so* obvious."

Anna was sure Lane was also staring at Ella with her mouth wide open.

"What?" Ella asked, looking from one to the other.

Finally closing her mouth, Anna shook her head. "Nothing."

Kym snorted again, and Ella looked at her. "What?"

"Nothing."

Mouth still slightly agape, Lane still stared at Ella.

"*What?*"

Lane shook her head. "Nothing, Ella."

"You guys are weird."

The lights were off, and they were all washed in the flickering blue glow of *Finding Nemo*, because they apparently needed to "be on top of it all" for the sequel in a year.

The afternoon in the park had been relaxing, and Sandra had looked so happy Anna thought she might cry. Through use of expert puppy dog eyes, Ella had convinced Lane and Kym to stay for DVD night, since it was Saturday and it was tradition.

Now, with Toby in bed, all four of them were struggling to stay awake on the couch. Ella was half-asleep with her head on Anna's lap, legs stretched out over both Lane and Kym. Kym kept drifting off and snapping her head up, while Anna and Lane blinked heavily. As she looked at them all, Anna couldn't help but think about the toll the last few days had taken on all of them.

Kym jolted herself awake again.

With a smirk, Anna poked her. "You sleeping here tonight, Kym?"

"That okay if I crash on your lovely couch?"

"Definitely. We can all have breakfast in the morning."

Through her yawn, Ella asked, "Pancakes again? Lane, you're staying, too? You make the best pancakes."

Slightly panicked, Lane looked to Anna.

"We're kind of running out of beds, Ella."

"She can sleep in *your* bed. You like each other and stuff. Hayley and you used to sleep in the same bed here." Her eyes were back on the screen, problem solved in her mind.

With a look at Lane, who was trying not to look too hopeful, Anna turned back to Ella. "Would that be okay with you?"

"I get pancakes."

"Okay then." She looked to Lane. "Wanna have a sleepover?"

"Yes, please."

"Ugh."

With a roll of her eyes, Ella looked up at Kym. "I know, right?"

Kym grinned.

Ella fell asleep sprawled over them all on the couch, delighted to know she'd be waking up in the morning with her three favourite people. A glance to the right showed Anna that Kym had also drifted off.

"You take the big one and I'll take the small one?"

Lane chuckled. "Deal."

Lane found a blanket while Anna woke Ella and guided her, half-asleep, to the toilet and then to bed. As she tucked Ella in, she gave her a hug, and, when Anna pulled away, Ella clung to her shirt. Not having the heart to leave, Anna sat stroking her hair until Ella fell back to sleep, her hand falling away on its own as she drifted off.

Anna sat for a minute longer, hand stilled on the sleeping Ella's forehead, and watched her.

The relief that Ella was back and in her bed, that Anna could touch her, was almost overpowering. Ella was like a doll when she slept, an adorable mix of Sally and Jake—gangly limbs, the soft curve of her nose, and the smattering of freckles that covered it.

The sick sense that she'd failed her brother and Sally had started to disappear now that the kids were back under the same roof as her. Anna still ached to have Jake there, to ask him how she was doing, if everything was how he would want it. And then the sick feeling would wash over her again, because what Jake would want would be to be alive with Sally and his kids.

As she watched Ella sleep, she thought about how she had Jake's slow smile, his inherent curiosity about everything, and a serious, introspective side. This was balanced by the sheer energy she'd taken from Sally, along with the way Sally would look at someone and sometimes know exactly what they were thinking.

What would fade without their influence? What would stay?

Anna kissed Ella's cheek and pulled the blanket up. The light that washed over the bed dimmed as Anna pulled the door over. She listened in at Toby's door and heard soft sleeping sounds.

Finally exhausted, Anna fell in to bed next to Lane, sighing contentedly as warmth enveloped her.

"Ella and Kym are going to be ganging up on us from now on."

Anna attempted a laugh at her comment, but choked on emotion.

"Hey," Lane whispered. "What's up?"

Burying her face in Lane's neck, Anna kissed the skin there, then kissed her lips with more fervour than she'd realised she had building.

An hour later, they fell asleep, wrapped in each other. Anna had to poke Lane awake enough to pull clothes on, reminding her that Ella sometimes liked to crawl into her bed.

It was a habit she'd have to get Ella out of, or she'd at least have to teach her to knock first and wait. However, with the fragile state she was in, Anna wasn't going to give Ella any hint that she couldn't come to her whenever she wanted.

If Anna had anything to do with it, Ella would never feel like that.

Chapter Twenty-Four

Crying rang out and Anna's eyes snapped open.

The loud groan that came from behind her made Anna chuckle.

"What is that?" Lane's voice was choked with sleep.

Anna pulled Lane's arm tighter around her middle as Lane curled more snugly against her back. "That, was Toby."

"Na!"

Lane groaned again, and the arm slid away as Lane rolled onto her back.

The sheets rustled, and Lane pulled a pillow over her face. Her muffled voice floated out. "Why is it Toby?"

"Cause he's a baby?"

"He's almost two!"

"He's eighteen months."

Lane made a grumbling noise, then pulled the pillow up and looked at Anna. "What time is it?"

Anna grimaced. "Five." Any earlier and she might have had hope of getting him back to sleep for another hour or so, but this late, he could be up for good.

"Ugh." Lane pulled the pillow back over her face.

"Welcome to your first sleepover when the kids are here." Anna sat up, resting her hand on Lane's stomach. "I'll be right back."

Lane just grunted from under the pillow.

Amused, Anna padded down the hallway to get Toby before he woke up Ella. Often, he'd sleep much later than this. On the odd occasion, however, he woke up bright and early, ready to go. And while Anna didn't hate mornings as much as Lane clearly did, she found it was always easier to cope with one cuddly toddler rather than a cuddly toddler and his six-year-old sister. It *was* five a.m., after all.

Stifling a yawn—she'd only gotten four hours sleep—she pushed Toby's door open to find him sitting up, looking even sleepier than she felt. The grin he aimed up at her melted her. Maybe he would go back to sleep.

He pushed himself up to stand, unsteady on the softness of the mattress, and she scooped him up before he could fall over.

"Na," he said happily.

She pulled him against her, his little legs wrapping around her and his head resting heavily on her chest.

"Morning, little man."

Chubby fingers grasped her shirt, as they always did, and he yawned against her neck.

"It's very early, you know."

He burrowed into her.

Anna turned to carry him through to her room when he sat up straight in her arms, hair sticking out every which way. "Blank!"

"Of course." Anna turned back to his cot. "Can't forget your blanket." The second she held it out to him, Toby grabbed it and settled against her, clutching it to his chest. His head thunked back down against her chest and he cuddled in.

Another yawn and Anna could practically feel him falling back to sleep in her arms. She carried him through to the bedroom, rubbing his back. A lump was all that Anna could see of Lane in the bed. The pillow was still over her head.

Whispering in Toby's ear, Anna pointed, "Who's that?"

Curiosity coloured Toby's features as he sat up straighter in Anna's arms. He looked at the lump, then back to Anna, then back to the lump. Toby pointed at it, then looked to Anna to make sure she'd seen it.

"I know! Who is it?"

When he craned forward, she stepped towards the bed to plop him down. Blanket in hand, he crawled across the mattress and sat down heavily, then smacked his hand down on the pillow. Nothing happened, and he looked at Anna, concerned.

"Try again, Tobes."

So he did. And he jumped when the pillow moved, then looked delighted as Lane emerged from under it, hair a cloud around her head.

Lane, even half-asleep and hating everything at five a.m., smiled at the delighted toddler. "Hey, Tobes."

As Toby fell down in a full body cuddle, Lane manoeuvred him under the covers with her.

Comfortable, Toby snuggled in, then suddenly sat up, grabbed his blanket and lay back down, cuddled right into Lane's chest. Toby turned his little head to look at Anna, who was trying not to explode with the cuteness of the scene.

"Na."

She took the hint and slipped back under the covers. Anna threw one arm over Toby, resting her hand on Lane's hip, effectively encasing Toby in a sandwich. He burrowed in and yawned.

Lane caught Anna's eye over the top of his head. "Is he always this cute in the morning?"

"About nine times out of ten. Every now and again, he's a nightmare."

"Never! Look at him!"

Right then, cuddled between the two of them, he looked like an angel.

Anna pressed her face into the back of Toby's head, breathing in his baby smell. "Mm. He's good at looking innocent. You slept through the one a.m. thing this morning." She caught sight of Lane's guilty look. "Or you pretended to sleep?"

Lane had the decency to look sheepish.

Unable to feign being indignant, Anna yawned, and Lane caught it, yawning too. Toby joined in, and Lane chuckled, slipping her arm over him so her hand mirrored Anna's, fingers stroking the skin at Anna's hip.

They all drifted back to sleep.

"Wake up!"

The bed lurched and Anna opened one blurry eye. Lane groaned and rolled onto her back, pulling the pillow over her head, while Toby sat up, clapping at the sight in front of him.

Ella stood on the end of the bed, with Kym kneeling next to her. Their hair was wild around their heads, and both looked ecstatic.

Kym was the one chanting: "Wake up, guys!"

"Hi, Aunty Na! Kym told me to yell and wake you up, but I said I wasn't meant to, so she said she'd do it."

"Way to drop me in it."

Sensing an opportunity as Kym mock-glared Ella, Anna sat up, grabbed a pillow, and threw it, hitting her right in the face.

The glare Kym had been directing at Ella turned onto Anna. "Well, that was just rude."

With a loud, "Morning!" Ella half sprawled in Anna's lap. Anna smoothed her crazy bed-head off her forehead. "Morning, Ella Bella."

"El! Lan!"

"Morning, Toby."

Desperate to share his news with his sister, Toby smacked his hand down on the pillow over Lane's head. "Lan!"

"Hi, Nurse Lane."

Finally emerging from her hiding spot, Lane gave a wiggle of her fingers. "Morning, Ella."

"I slept in!"

Anna looked at the clock. "It's barely after seven, Ella."

"That's totally a sleep-in."

"Well, I appreciate you waking Kym up first."

Kym, who had flopped down on her back at the end of the bed, turned her head. "Happy to be of assistance. Why's the tot in your bed?"

Toby was crawling his way over to Kym. Soft hands patted her stomach, and then he lay his head on it, fat fingers gripping her shirt.

"He woke up early."

Unable to hold back a smirk, Kym looked at Lane. "How early?"

Lane answered through gritted teeth. "Five."

"Nice work, Tobes."

Toby giggled.

The week passed and became the next week too quickly for Anna to keep up. In some ways, it was like their routine was never broken. In the mornings, Anna dropped Ella at her mother's and Toby to day care. After work, she picked Ella up and they had dinner. During the day, she visited Toby in day care, had coffee with Kym, and paged Lane to her office at inappropriate times.

However, some things made it glaringly obvious that they'd had six days of hell—and other things were subtle, barely noticeable unless you knew to look for them.

At night, Toby's cries when he woke were the hysterical ones of the first few days. By the end of the first week, it turned to just a desperate cry of Anna's name and tears, but was a long way from the twice-a-week, half-asleep cry of before. The blanket still went everywhere, and he clung more than ever when she dropped him off at day care. He spoke a little less, words he'd picked up no longer yelled out in delight.

The real mystery was Ella. At times, she was the Ella that had started to re-emerge right before she'd been taken into foster care. Other times, she was quiet, contemplative. She clung for longer when Anna tucked her in at night. When

Ella heard tyres over the gravel in the driveway, her whole body tensed and she stared at the door as if she expected to be dragged through it.

Four times in ten days, Anna had gotten up to comfort her after a nightmare, and, in the end, had taken Ella to her bed. One night, Ella had been almost inconsolable. Her choked cry of "I want Mummy" had made Anna's chest ache and her own tears fall. She had rubbed Ella's back, wanting to give her whatever would comfort her, and unable to give the only thing that would truly make everything okay.

Lane was a ray of sunshine for all of them. She had stayed over twice more, and she and Kym had joined them for dinner even more times than they stayed. The kids loved waking up to Lane in the house, and, thus far, Anna and Lane had remembered to put clothes on before falling asleep each time.

There were days Anna felt like she was exactly where she wanted to be, Lane moving around the kitchen and Ella telling them about the baby bird they'd saved at recess. Toby would sit on Anna's lap, leaning into her and sucking at a sippy cup they were trialling.

And then there were days Anna felt like pulling her hair out and screaming.

Ella would be sullen and refuse to pick up her toys. Toby would be clingy and whiny, hanging off Anna until she couldn't remember what it felt like to be alone for more than thirty seconds. Work would get hectic, and she'd be running around, trying to finish in time to get Toby from day care and stop by the grocery store and get Ella from her mother's and, God, what was she going to do for dinner tonight and there were six loads of laundry she had to get done and, if Ella whined she wanted another bowl of ice cream one more time, Anna was going to lose it.

Moments would rear up out of the blue so solid and painful in which Anna wanted to talk to her brother, to ask Sally questions, to giggle with her over wine, to punch Jake in the arm when he said something annoying—to have her brother, her best friend.

But without everything that had happened, Anna wouldn't have the life she had now. And that would mean no Toby and Ella. And no Lane.

Toby would look at her sometimes, head cocked and forehead all scrunched up, and she would swear Jake was looking at her with his "you're insane, little sister" look, and it made her chest ache until she couldn't breathe. Giggling, Ella would tell her a story from school like a conspirator, leaning forward so her hair fell around her face, and she was the mirror image of Sally doing the same.

Without the distraction of the trial, missing her brother and Sally seemed to drop on Anna like a tonne of bricks; she couldn't explain why.

One day, hands clasped around a coffee, Kym looked at her from across the cafeteria table, eyes intent. She leant across the cool metal tabletop and rested a hand on Anna's forearm.

"Don't beat yourself up."

"What?" Anna was genuinely puzzled.

"You miss them. And you're allowed to—grief is funny like that. It's more like a wave than something you, I don't know, progress through in steps. It recedes, then hits you again, sometimes weaker and sometimes stronger."

Nodding slowly, Anna gave an awkward shrug. "I thought it was getting better."

The smile Kym offered was soft and deep with understanding. "It was. And it will again. It takes a long time."

"What do you do when it's like this?"

Kym sat back in her chair and grinned. "Either sob in the shower or come hang out with you guys."

After having a psychiatrist tell her it was normal, Anna felt marginally better, though she still missed them constantly.

She knew Lane had noticed, but found herself waving the concern away and saying she was fine. The third time she did it, Lane looked at her and said, "No you're not. No running."

Staring at her, Anna finally gave in and shook her head. "I'm not. But I'm not ready to talk about it."

Lane pulled her into a hug. "And that's fine. Just no disappearing."

Surrounded by the softness of Lane, Anna buried her face in her neck. "I'm not going anywhere."

There were the days she'd stand in the kitchen, when Toby would be pulling on her leg and Ella would be calling something out from the living room, when she wouldn't have gotten to have more than five minutes with Lane in days, and Anna would close her eyes and take a deep breath and count backwards from ten.

But these days, when it felt like she didn't know what she was doing, she genuinely didn't question *why* she was doing it or if she *wanted* to be doing it. Not anymore. Anger at her brother for putting her in this position didn't bubble up, and Anna didn't wish him back purely so she could scream at him. But now that the anger was gone, she was left aching with the sadness that Jake wasn't there.

When she finished counting back from ten, she would open her eyes and lean down to pick Toby up. He would pat her face with his open palm and say, "Na," with layers of affection in his voice.

Ella would wander through from the living room and say, "I just wanted to tell you that the teacher asked who we wanted to talk to every day, and everyone said a friend from school, but I said Mummy and Daddy, because I remembered you told me it was okay to talk about them."

And Anna would be able to keep doing it; because those two kids made all the rest completely worth it.

On the bad days, a glance at her phone would show a text from Lane that would make her smile. Then she'd order pizza and they'd pull out a blanket and have a picnic on the kitchen floor, the kids chewing messily and getting pizza all over their colouring-in things.

Anna would leave the laundry to the next day.

And that was okay.

"Ella asked me at dinner if you're my girlfriend."

Disengaging her lips from Lane's neck, Anna looked up. "When?"

She was sprawled over Lane, trying to find the energy to get up and get clothing on before the aforementioned Ella could burst through the door.

One arm under her head and the other tracing lazy patterns over Anna's back, Lane shrugged. "When you were doing the dishes."

"What did you say?"

"Um…I didn't want to lie. But I didn't know if it was my place to say anything. I don't know how much detail you wanted to go into, or how much detail Ja… I didn't know."

Anna smiled softly. "You can say his name, Lane."

Hand gliding up Anna's back and over her shoulder to push the hair behind her ears, Lane took her time to answer. "I didn't want to upset you. You've seemed extra…sad about it this last week or so. Which is totally fine. I just didn't want to make you talk about it."

Normally, Anna would change the subject and not talk about it—and that's exactly what she wanted to do again. But Lane was looking at her with utter concern, and she was wrapped in warm skin, lying between Lane's legs, and Anna didn't want Lane to think she couldn't bring up this topic.

At times, it seemed Lane was still walking on eggshells since they had gotten back together. It had only been a few days, but it had impacted them. Anna didn't want Lane to have to be careful.

"I have been."

Lane looked at her, waiting for her to go on.

"I...I'm not angry anymore."

Brow furrowed, Lane looked at her.

Leaning her cheek in her hand, Anna moved so she could still look at Lane, whose hand was softly stroking the skin between her shoulder blades. "I was so angry, at Jake for putting me in this position. God, even for...for dying; I just wanted to yell at him." Anna didn't know if it made much sense, but she kept talking. "And now, it's kind of hard to explain. I'm not angry at him anymore. I wouldn't want the kids to be with anyone else and I have you and I actually *really* like my life. And then I feel guilty, because I like my life and it's a life where my brother and Sally are dead, and that is *not* okay." It came out in a rush, some of it things Anna hadn't even really realised she had been thinking.

Dark eyes soft, Lane just watched her, expression empathetic.

Eyes burning, Anna looked Lane in the eye, feeling tortured. "Those kids don't have their parents and I don't have my brother or my best friend and we are all starting to move on, and that's not *fair*, Lane." Her voice broke over the words. "It's not fair."

A sob escaped her, and Lane pulled her up and into her arms. Anna buried her face in Lane's neck, and her fingers dug into her back as she clung on. She had no idea why she was feeling like this, why now.

But she missed her brother.

Lane's hand ran down her hair and over her back as she threw her leg over Anna's hip, pulling closer.

Another sob heaved out of her chest, and Anna's eyes stung with salt. "And Lane, God, I love you." Her hand gripped the back of Lane's neck. "Do you have any idea just how much better you make everything else?"

With a shake of her head Lane pulled Anna up, kissing her, cheeks wet. Fingers wrapped in Anna's hair, Lane drew her closer for another kiss.

When they finally parted, Anna gripped her arm. "I know I don't always talk. It's okay to push me, sometimes."

Avoiding her eyes, Lane nodded slowly. "I just, didn't want to push you away."

Foreheads together, their breath mingled between them. "You couldn't do that."

Lane took in a deep breath; Anna did the same, hers shuddering slightly.

"I just miss them."

Making soothing sounds, Lane wrapped her back in her arms. "I know you do."

They lay quietly for a minute before Anna kissed the skin under Lane's lips. "And you can tell Ella we're girlfriends. You're a part of the kids' lives, too. I trust you to tell her whatever you want."

Touch soft, Lane tilted Anna's face up and kissed her.

Chapter Twenty-Five

"Why don't you sleep in the big room?"

Anna looked up at Ella as she tried to sneak the last few bites of Toby's meal into his mouth. Every time she thought she was about to succeed, he clamped his lips shut and turned his head away, then laughed almost maniacally.

"Uh…in your mommy and daddy's room?"

Ella took a big sip of juice. "Yeah. The room you're in is for when people have sleepovers. But you're not a guest. You live here."

Anna managed to get a mouthful of food into Toby, which he promptly spat back out. The glare she attempted was ruined by the charming grin he gave her as half-chewed peas stuck to his chin. Anna started wiping him up. Sometimes it was easier to just give up.

"Would it be weird for you, Ella Bella, if I slept in that room?"

Ella just shrugged and went back to her fish.

Later that night, when Toby was fast asleep and Ella had weaselled three stories out of Anna, Ella grabbed her hand as she stood to go. That wasn't unusual these days, but her words left Anna speechless.

"Mummy always liked people being comfy when they stayed over." Her big green eyes looked up at Anna sincerely. "And I think you'd be more comfy in their room. And then Kym can be comfy in your bed when she stays."

Anna crawled onto the bed next to Ella and pulled her into a cuddle. Quiet and contemplative, Ella played with the pendant around Anna's neck.

For a moment, Anna considered where she wanted to take this conversation. "How about I move some things from there tomorrow? And then you can pick things that you want to keep safe, of Mummy's and Daddy's. And then we'll find a special place for you to keep them?"

"Can I tell you a secret?"

"Always."

With a sniffle, Ella pulled away then, and leant over her bed, pulling out Jake's hoodie, the one Sally had kept under her pillow for when he was away. Guiltily, she held it out. "I took this after that time me and Toby threw up everywhere. Sometimes I wear it when I can't fall asleep."

Brushing the hair off Ella's face, Anna let her fingers trace her soft cheeks. "Ella Bella, why do you look worried?"

Eyes on her lap, Ella picked at the hem of her jumper. "'Cause I took it and it's not mine."

Gently, Anna took the hoodie, pulling it over Ella's head swiftly as she slipped her skinny arms through the sleeves; it was miles too big for her.

"It can be yours if you want it to be."

With the hood over her head, Ella lay back down, tugging at Anna's hand so she'd lay with her. Anna tried not to think about how it still smelt a little like her brother.

"Can I keep Mummy's teddy from when she was a kid?"

Pulling Ella in tighter, Anna nodded against the soft material of her brother's once-prized jumper. "You can keep whatever you want."

"What about Toby?"

"We'll choose some things for him, too."

Taking a deep breath, Anna pushed open her brother's bedroom door.

The room was clean, now. No slight layer of dust. Even though she didn't like stepping into this room, Anna included it when she ran the vacuum over the rest of the house. Since the night with Ella and Toby when they'd been sick and miserable, the room wasn't always shut off. Anna used the bathroom sometimes; she left the door open. But no one regularly went in there.

Lane was at work and Anna had a day off in the middle of the week; Ella was at school and Toby was asleep. So now, Anna stared into the room and prepared herself to start to pack it up.

When he woke, she'd bring him in to "help," thinking if anything grabbed his attention, she'd keep it aside for him. Boxes sat in the hall, gathered from a grocery store that morning.

All she had to do was step in and start.

She jumped when the doorbell rang.

Relief spread through her. She walked down the stairs, pulling open the door to find a red-eyed Kym. Her hair was in sloppy braids, and she was wearing sweats. She didn't look like she'd slept. "Kym—what—are you okay?"

Kym folded her arms across her chest. "Uh. I am. I'm okay."

Anna watched her, hand still on the door.

Kym made no move to step in. "I called in sick to work today."

"You sleep last night?"

Kym shook her head. "Kind of. I packed it up. Everything. Yesterday afternoon and all night, I packed it up. And then I put in a rental application online at one a.m. And then I drank two bottles of wine. And I slept in our bed for an hour and woke up, and he wasn't there."

Anna let go of the door, stepped forward, and wrapped her arms around Kym, gripping the thin woman to her.

For just for a second, Kym's fingers dug into her back before she pushed Anna away and nodded once. "So, I'm moving."

Anna's fingers curled around Kym's forearms. "Yeah. You're moving."

"What are you up to?"

Anna shrugged. "Trying to be as strong as you and pack up Jake and Sally's things from their room."

"Seriously? Like, right now?"

"Yup. You rang the bell and gave me the perfect excuse to stop standing in the doorway, staring into their room and achieving nothing."

"Want a hand?"

"Don't be silly—you look exhausted."

"Anna—let me help."

The look Kym gave her was almost pleading and, not for the first time, Anna wondered how she was still standing. "Okay."

Anna stepped back, and Kym walked in and followed her up the stairs. They both paused in the doorway, Anna looking into the room apprehensively. Kym turned and looked at her profile, then did what Anna couldn't: she grabbed a box and stepped in, turning to look at Anna.

Grabbing a box herself, Anna followed. She looked around at Sally and Jake's things spread out, the touches of objects that made up their room—photos, ornaments from travels, the bottle of sand Jake had sent Sally from Iraq, Sally's collection of first-edition novels passed down from her grandmother. All of it just *stuff* really, just things. But all of it was a collection of them, mapping out the moments of their meeting, falling pregnant, getting married, starting a family.

This room was *them*, in a lot of ways. It was their space.

Kym tilted her head as Anna watched her look around. "Let's start with the socks. Can't get sentimental about socks."

With a shaky laugh, Anna nodded. "Socks it is."

"Hello?"

The sound floated up the stairway, and Anna felt relieved. Lane was here.

"Upstairs!" Anna tried to call out quietly.

She heard Lane's footsteps on the stairs and looked up from where she sat cross-legged on the floor in the middle of Jake and Sally's room.

Lane paused in the doorway and took in the scene in front of her.

The room was filled with boxes, drawers opened and empty, the wardrobe door open, and nothing but dust inside. There were boxes in two separate piles, one along a wall, and the other near the bed. The dresser was barren and most of the boxes were taped up.

A concerned smile hovered on Lane's face. "How you doing?"

Finger to her lips, Anna indicated the bed. Passed out over the covers lay Toby and Kym.

"That is possibly the cutest thing I've ever seen."

"Kym didn't get much sleep last night. She lasted four hours before falling asleep."

"Toby's sleeping late?"

Anna gave a slight shrug. "He woke up far too early from his nap from the noise and then passed out again. He'll be fine."

Leaning her shoulder against the doorframe, Lane watched Anna. Lost, Anna looked around the bedroom.

"You going to move in here?"

Anna sighed, leaning back on her hands. "I suppose." She looked up at Lane. "I mean, that's what makes sense. It just feels...weird, like I'm trying to replace them."

"I don't think it's like that at all. It makes sense for you to be in here. It's your house now, Anna. They left it for you, because if this happened, they wanted you to feel like it was yours."

Anna nodded, staring at a box.

With a sigh, Lane walked forward, sitting cross-legged in front of her and resting her hands on Anna's knees. "It sucks." Anna looked up at her sharply. Lane continued. "It sucks, to put it all in boxes."

"It does."

"I'm glad Kym was here."

"I don't think I would have started without her. You would have gotten here tonight to find me surrounded by empty boxes." Anna looked down at her watch. "Actually, on that...it's only four?" A smile spread over her face. "You're early."

"I escaped."

"Are you playing hooky?"

Coyly, Lane grinned. "I may have found out I'm stuck on a random night shift tomorrow and so *may* have taken the liberty of claiming extensive hours to the coordinator, who panicked when he looked at my roster and sent me home, scared I'd call the union."

Chuckling, Anna wrapped her arms around Lane's neck. "Sneaky."

With a soft kiss, Lane closed the distance, arms tightening around each other.

Lips trailing down Lane's neck, Anna grimaced when Lane said, "Haven't got to do that in a few days."

"I know. Life has a habit of getting in the way."

Lane's hands came up to lift Anna's head. "Just makes it more worth it when I see you."

"Okay, seriously, you two are repulsive."

They both turned to see Kym sitting up on her elbow, rubbing her eyes and making a face.

A smirk played on Anna's lips, and she reached for the box she had next to her, pondering the inside of it. Her expression turned uncertain.

Kym sat up on the bed, crossing her legs. "Stop. It's fine."

All Anna could do was shrug. She cast a worried look at Toby, still fast asleep, then back to the box.

Lane looked at Toby, too. "Thinking of putting him in there?"

"Funny. It's a box of things to keep for him, of both their stuff."

"How do you choose something like that?"

"Exactly. What if I keep the wrong things?"

Moving to the edge of the bed, Kym spoke up. "Anna, nothing you keep for him will be wrong. You kept the things he kept grabbing at in here and added the things you thought he'd like."

Anna chewed her lip and passed the box over to Lane, who peered inside. "You're giving him the sand in the glass?"

"Yeah."

Lane had a look through, noting the dark black jacket Anna had kept of Jake's that might one day fit Toby, the odd ornament, the photos, the shaving kit, and the bottle of aftershave. "This is perfect, Anna."

Still worried, Anna gnawed her lip.

With a squeeze of Anna's knee, Lane smiled. "It's a big responsibility, choosing this stuff. You've done well."

Anna sighed and looked up to the bed where Toby was sleeping soundly. "He's just so little."

Kym turned her head and looked at Toby, curled up next to her leg. She ran her hand through his curls. "He is." She looked up at Anna. "But he'll be okay. The sand is a great idea, and so is the jacket."

Toby stirred then and sat up, hair tousled. He rubbed his eyes and looked around, face splitting into a sleepy grin as he took them all in. Finally, he zeroed in on Anna, grabbed his blanket, and half crawled to the edge of the bed, turning onto his stomach to slide off. Toddling over, he fell into her lap, wrapping his arms around her and burying his face into her neck as he yawned widely, not quite awake.

Anna brushed the hair off his forehead.

When she looked up, both Lane and Kym were gazing at Toby with smitten looks on their faces. "You two are ridiculous."

They both looked up at once, surprised. "What?"

"You're both only here to use me for the cute toddler. Admit it."

They looked at each other and shrugged. "We were hoping you'd take longer to clue in," Kym said.

Poking her tongue out, Anna tugged Toby closer; he quickly became indignant and squirmed to be put down. When Anna set him on the ground, he stood for a minute, blinking and looking around, before sitting soundly back in Anna's lap.

Lane rolled her eyes. "He adores you."

"Jealous?"

About to reply, Lane was cut off as they heard the door open downstairs.

"I saw Nurse Lane's car! And Kym's!" Ella's voice came yelling up at them.

"Ella! You don't have to scream it out." Sandra's voice reached them, and Toby stood up, looking delighted at the sound and bolting for the door.

"Well, where are they?"

All three stood up and followed Toby out into the hall, where the toddler was about to launch himself down the stairs.

Anna raced forward. "Toby! Wait for us or take the rail!"

Blanket clutched in both hands, he didn't even look at her as he started to climb down. Quickly, Anna reached forward and grasped the back of his shirt. "Toby!"

He looked up and tried to keep walking forward, Anna holding tight to his shirt so his little legs kicked at air. "Toby Andrew Foster!" She tugged him up, and he squirmed in her arms. "You know you need to hold the rail or wait for me."

He squirmed more and made a whiny noise as Anna gripped him.

"I do it!"

Secretly delighted he'd just thrown out a sentence, Anna held onto him and started walking down. She could practically *feel* the amusement coming off Kym and Lane behind her. Her mother looked up at them, Ella bouncing from foot to foot next to her in her school uniform.

Anna looked at Toby, who had half twisted around trying to get down. "Nope. Now you get carried because you didn't listen."

She blew a raspberry on his neck, making him half giggle and half whine before she set him on the ground at the bottom.

Instantly, Toby ran to Sandra, his goal since he'd heard her voice. Anna's mother bent down and picked him up. "Toby! Are you being naughty?"

"Nan!" He looked absolutely delighted with himself, his little chest puffed out.

Unable to be grumpy at him, Sandra chuckled and kissed his cheek, looking up at Anna. "Hello, and hello to you two," she greeted Lane and Kym.

Bouncing forward, Ella attached herself to Anna's legs. "Hi!"

Anna chuckled and ran her hand over Ella's braided hair. "Hey Ella Bella. How was school?"

"Boring." She looked around Anna's legs to Kym and Lane. "Are you guys staying for dinner?"

Plopping down on the stairs, Kym reached forward to pull Ella between her legs, wrapping her arms around the girl. "Sure are."

Whispering in Kym's ear in a voice that everyone could hear, Ella said, "Is Nurse Lane cooking? 'Cause Aunty Na cooked last night, and it was covered in black bits."

As soon as everyone sniggered, Anna threw her hands up in disgust and walked down the hallway to the kitchen, calling after Ella, "I was going to offer you an after school snack, Ella, but I might burn the banana."

Her niece's confused voice floated down the hallway, "How can you burn a banana?"

The group appeared in the kitchen doorway.

Lane looked down at Ella. "Your aunty was being silly."

"Oh."

"And yeah, I was going to cook. What did you want?"

Anna chose to ignore them all and start cutting fruit.

"Pancakes."

Scooping Ella up and tickling her, Lane said, "You're going to turn into a pancake soon!"

"Am not!"

When Kym sat down next to Sandra, Toby instantly squirmed from her lap and made a beeline for the basket in the corner filled with trains and cars. Content, he ran one over the floor, making crashing noises.

"Are too! We can't have pancakes. There has to be at least three different food groups."

Back still pulled into Lane, where she half hung with Lane's arms around her waist, Ella pouted. "Um—sgetti!"

"Spaghetti? Okay. Deal."

"Yay!"

Lane looked up. "You staying, Sandra?"

"Twist my arm."

As Anna dropped banana into two plastic bowls, she eyed her mother. "Twist your arm to not have to cook for once?"

"Have to pretend to not jump at a free meal, dear. Don't want to look cheap."

A squeal of protest from Toby had Anna looking up sharply, eyeing her niece, who was holding a train. "Ella, did you just grab the train out of his hands?"

As quick as she could, Ella dropped the train back into Toby's lap; the little boy clutched it to his chest, looking at his sister like she'd utterly betrayed him.

"I wanted to show him something cool!"

"So don't snatch it from him. You know that."

Ella reached forward and grabbed a different train out, grumbling, "Fine. Sorry, Toby."

With a smile, Toby held the train out to Ella.

Happy the kids weren't about to kill each other, Anna went back to the fruit, smiling as Lane kissed the back of her neck on her way to fill up the kettle.

Sandra turned to Kym, resting a hand on hers. "You look tired, Kym."

She said it with a mother's concern, and Kym gave a weak grin. "I had a long night."

Patting Kym's hand, Sandra murmured something that caused her to nod. Anna didn't quite catch what it was as she dropped some apple into the bowls and walked around the bench, holding them out to the kids, who both grabbed at their fruit instantly.

"Ahem?"

"Thank you!" Ella's voice had turned singsong as she bit into a piece of apple.

"Tobes? Ta?"

Bulging cheeks impeded his "Ta."

"You're welcome."

Taking a seat, Anna thanked Lane as she put a mug down in front of her. Kym was looking a little better, and Anna sipped her hot drink, wondering how Sandra could murmur words of comfort so easily. After so many months supporting her mother as she fell apart, Anna liked to see that she could still get it together to comfort Kym.

The afternoon passed easily, and Lane started to prepare dinner, Sandra joining her in chopping vegetables, while Kym read stories to an enthralled Toby.

Anna slid behind Lane and murmured something in her ear, loud enough for Sandra to hear. They both nodded as Anna slipped over to the table where Ella was colouring in. "Ella Bella? Is that a unicorn?"

"Yup. She's even going to have wings."

"Wow. That's way too cool. Kind of like *My Little Ponies*?"

Ella looked at her blankly. "What?"

God, Anna was old. She heard both Sandra and Lane chuckle behind her. "Nothing. Wanna come upstairs with me for a bit? I wanted to talk to you more about what we talked about last night?"

Instantly, Ella's demeanour changed. She kept her eyes glued to her picture for a second. Anna didn't push it, waiting for her to make the first move.

Finally Ella put her pencil down and pushed her chair back, standing up. She was eye to eye with Anna, who leant forward, kissing Ella's cheek and smiling at her reassuringly.

When she stood, Anna patiently waited for Ella, who stood staring into the kitchen where Lane and Sandra were busy pretending nothing important was happening. Eventually, she held her hand up for Anna to take. Wide green eyes stared up at Anna, and Ella suddenly looked a lot older than her six years.

"Did you pack their stuff?"

"Yeah. I've started to. But I wanted to make sure you got all the things you wanted. Did you want to go look now?"

"Yes, please."

"Okay. Let's go, honey." They started walking to the hall and up the stairs. "Toby chose some things, you know."

Halfway up, Ella paused. "Did he?"

Wanting to be eye to eye, Anna sat down on the step. "Yeah."

Fingers fiddling with the zip on her jacket, Ella looked up the stairs almost nervously. "Good. 'Cause he's just a baby and he needs stuff to remember them."

Watching such a young child be so contemplative was humbling. "Aunty Na, do you remember things from when you were a baby?"

Anna shook her head slowly. "No, I don't."

"I don't really, either." Ella was gnawing her lip, and Anna sat still, letting her work out where her thoughts were going. "Toby's really little."

"He is, yeah." Some hair had fallen loose from Ella's braids and Anna tucked it behind her ear gently.

Ella's eyes searched Anna's face, and her voice came out a whisper. "He's not going to remember Mummy and Daddy, is he?"

"No, not really, Ella Bella."

Ella's forehead furrowed and her eyes shined. "But I remember them."

"Yeah, you do."

"And you do. And Grandma."

"Yeah."

"But Toby won't?"

Anna shook her head. "He'll have a feeling about them, though."

"A feeling?"

"Yeah. A feeling of them. Of how much they loved you and him."

Ella nodded absently. "And we'll help him remember. I'll help him. I'm his big sister, I can help him remember all about them."

Pulling Ella between her legs, Anna wrapped her arms around her tiny frame. With a sigh, Ella leant into her.

"You can definitely do that."

They sat for a minute, Ella playing with the pendant around Anna's neck. Anna kissed the top of her head and waited.

Ella finally took a deep breath. "Can we go up now?"

"Yeah, we can. There are lots of boxes, and a lot is packed up, but if you think of anything I haven't kept out, you ask and we'll dig it out, okay?"

Hand in hand, they walked up the stairs, pausing in the doorway. Ella's eyes flicked from the bed to the boxes, taking in her parents' things packed away. Without looking at Anna, she whispered, "How does it all fit in boxes? They're so *big*."

Not sure what she meant, Anna looked around at the medium-sized boxes. With a stab in her gut, it occurred to her: Ella meant her parents, the memory of them, was so big. To Ella, nothing that huge could fit in a box.

"I don't know Ella. I wonder the same thing."

"Are we gonna throw it all away?"

Anna shook her head adamantly. "No. I was going to put a lot of it away, for now. But I thought—you know how at Christmas we collect things to put in boxes and give to people who can't afford stuff?"

"To the poor people?"

"Yeah."

Ella looked back into the room. "Yeah, Mummy always gave lots of stuff. We'd go to the stores and pick out toys I thought other kids would like and we'd wrap them, and they'd get given to kids who couldn't 'ford presents."

The story tugged at Anna's heart. Sally had been such an exceptional person. "Well, I was thinking, their clothes? Maybe we could give most of them to a charity? So people who can't afford clothes can have some."

Ella was quiet again before she finally nodded. "Yeah. Mummy would like that."

"I thought so, too."

And finally, they stepped into the room together, Ella's hand tight in her own.

Anna felt like she could conquer a mountain. She felt like she could climb freaking *Everest.* She felt like, finally, everything was settling. The ball that had been sitting heavily in her gut had completely dissolved, and she was left feeling jubilant.

Two weeks on from clearing out her brother's room, Anna marched through the hospital on a mission. At the elevator, she hit the *up* button, tapping her toes impatiently. She adjusted her blazer and tugged at her shirt, making sure her outfit was straight. Lane had insisted on the black pants with the white stripes down the side, and Anna had to admit that she did feel like she was dressed in a power outfit, which had been the point. The elevator finally opened, and she made her way to her office, opening the door to see Lane standing inside, leaning against her desk and waiting for her.

Lane's eyes raked down her body and back up again. "Hey. Nice outfit."

As Anna pressed Lane back into the desk, her hands cupped Lane's cheeks and her lips pushed against hers. Lane swiftly buried her hands in Anna's hair.

With kiss-bruised lips, Lane finally pulled back, grinning. "It went well then?"

Anna, ecstatic, grasped Lane's forearms purely for the need to hold her closer. "The judge didn't even deliberate. That's it—it's done. I have permanent guardianship!"

A laugh bubbled out of Anna's chest as Lane wrapped her arms around her.

Not caring that they looked ridiculous, huge smiles plastered on their face, Anna pressed their foreheads together. "Lane! They can't take them now."

"I know. That's it, it's done."

"I love you." She kissed Lane. "God, I love you. Thank you."

"Why are you saying thank you?"

"Because I'm allowed to."

"I love you, too."

There was a knock at the door, and it swung open behind them.

"Oh, for God's sake. Am I stuck forever looking at the two of you?" Anna turned around at the voice, letting go of Lane and launching herself at Kym, tackling her in a hug. Kym wrapped her arms around her and looked over her shoulder at Lane. "I take it the final guardianship hearing went well?"

Dusk was settling in when Anna picked up Ella from her parents'. Her mother was already aware of the outcome; Anna had called her as she left the courthouse. Anna had asked her not to tell Ella.

While Ella gathered her things, Sandra turned her attention to Anna, who stood in the doorway. "Did you see Cathy?"

Anna snorted. "She ignored me."

"Well, I suppose that's better than reciting Bible verses at you."

A chuckle forced itself out of Anna's chest as she made her way to the car with the kids. It was easier to see the funny side now it was over.

They drove home, Ella talking about her day at school and Anna nodding, asking the right questions. When they pulled up to the house, Anna pulled Toby out of his car seat and put him on the ground so he could run over the grass to the front door.

School bag in hand, Ella was already waiting when Anna reached the door and let them through, Ella and Toby half tripping over each other to get inside. Toby went for his blocks in the living room, and Ella dumped her bag at the stairs and moved for the kitchen.

"Ella!"

She stopped and turned, walking back. "All right, I'll put my bag in my room."

With a chuckle, Anna sat on the step and pulled Ella to her. "That too. But I have something to tell you." Settling against Anna, Ella furrowed her brow, uncertain. "Okay, sweetie. Remember how, for a little while, you got taken to another house?"

Ella nodded.

"Remember how I told you I had to wait for the judge to make some decisions, and that's why it took days for me to finally get you back?"

The panic that rose in Ella's voice made Anna squeeze her tighter. "Is that why you're dressed all fancy? Is he going to take us again?"

"No, sweetie. No." She brushed the hair off Ella's face. "Today I saw the judge again. But it was a good thing. Today he signed a special piece of paper that means no one can ever take you again." She put her hands on Ella's cheeks, looking at her with utter sincerity. While the kids had been slowly settling the last month, she hadn't made clear-cut promises to Ella, just in case. But now, she wanted her to have some security, and Anna could finally offer it. "Hear that, Ella Bella? All the police and all the judges have a piece of paper that says you stay here, with me."

"So…they can't come and put us in a car again?"

"No."

"And—and we stay with you, all the time? For good?"

"All the time, sweetie."

The way Ella hugged her took Anna's breath away.

Chapter Twenty-Six

Warm lips were running up Anna's spine. Naked thighs straddled her legs. Anna burrowed her face into the pillow and yawned, relishing waking up in such a manner. The lips reached the back of her neck, and warm breath washed over her skin, making her shiver.

"Morning." Lane's voice husked out next to her ear.

"Morning." Anna rolled onto her back, and Lane straddled her hips, hands pressing either side of Anna's head so they lay flush against each other. Anna gently tucked a tendril of hair behind Lane's ear.

"You were sleeping late."

When Anna glanced at the clock and saw it was after ten, her eyes widened slightly, and she looked back at Lane, voice low with sleep. "I really was."

"I thought I'd wake you up."

Anna wrapped her hands in Lane's hair and pulled her down, kissing her. The appreciative hum Lane gave made Anna smile.

"I never sleep later than you."

"Yeah, well, you had a rough week."

"Yeah. It was long."

Lane rubbed her nose against Anna's neck and kissed behind her ear before pulling back again. "Long, and with no time for us."

"I'm sorry."

"No, don't be. It wasn't your fault."

"You got stuck with the girlfriend with a crazy life."

Lane kissed her once. "I like my girlfriend and her crazy life."

"Even the crazy kids?"

"I love the crazy kids."

"Even though Toby threw up on you?"

Lane made a face. "That was not my favourite Toby moment, I won't lie."

With a chuckle, Anna tugged so she was laying on her side, half-sprawled over Anna, head resting in her hand to look down at her. "They were so sick." Anna wrinkled her nose. "It was so gross."

As Lane finally flopped her head down on the pillow, Anna rolled onto her side, hooking a leg over Lane's hip as she snuggled in, face pressed into her neck. The stroking of Lane's hand in her hair relaxed her, and she was able to close her eyes.

"It was really gross. Days and days of stomach flu and crazy hours were a fair excuse to not have much time for us," Lane said.

A lazy grin made it's way onto Anna's lips. "We made up for it last night."

"So maybe it wasn't just your crazy week that made you sleep late."

"We *did* only fall asleep after four."

"Yeah we did. The joy of the kids requesting a sleepover at your mum's."

Opening her eyes, Anna settled back so she could look at Lane. "They do love a sleepover at Grandma's."

Lane pushed Anna's hair back, hand resting gently against her neck. "I have missed you this week."

"Me too. I liked going out to dinner last night. We actually got to have a conversation."

They lay for a few minutes, enjoying the silent house and time just for them, naked and warm in the morning. Anna loved the kids, but not being jumped on at six a.m. was feeling especially nice. Two months on from the trial, Ella was sleeping better than she had been, while Toby was mostly back to his old self. Anna brushed her lips to Lane's chest, sighing contentedly. While it was great the kids were returning to normal, even slowly, it meant lots of energy and early wake-ups.

The silence was broken when Lane said softly, "I wish I didn't work at one."

"Yeah, me too. I have to get the kids in about an hour anyway. Mum has an appointment."

Lane's fingers trailed up and down her sides, fingers tracing ribs. "What are you going to do with your afternoon?"

"Meet Kym and take them to the zoo."

Lane's eyes lit up. "I love the zoo!'

"You are such a kid sometimes."

Shrugging, Lane didn't even look embarrassed. "It's why Ella and Tobes love me."

"True."

A more serious look replaced the playfulness on Lane's face. "And it's twelve months today?"

"Twelve months since Simon died. I'm, uh, going with her, before the zoo, to the cemetery. I was going to take the kids to see Jake and Sally."

"That's a good idea. I wish I could come."

"You'll be there next week when we go with Mum."

"You want me there?"

Lane smiled as Anna leant forward and kissed her again. "Of course."

The touch of Lane's fingers along her hip made Anna fall back against the pillow. "If we start we won't stop." Her murmurs of protest didn't hold much conviction as Lane's lips started to trail against her jaw and her neck.

"I see nothing wrong with that."

"Work and, uh—" She moaned softly as Lane sucked on her pulse point. "I have to get the kids."

The kissing paused. "Shower?"

"Shower. We'll be saving time."

"Yeah, let's look at it like that."

Without warning, Anna rolled away, Lane half falling into the warm spot she left behind. The bewildered look on Lane's face made Anna smirk. She swung her legs over the edge of the bed and stood up, Lane's surprised face switching to a grin as she stared at her.

Anna winked and started walking towards the bathroom. "Join me in five?"

"Twist my arm."

Anna threw a smile over her shoulder and shut the door.

In the shower, hot water came quickly just as Anna heard Lane call out, "Your cell phone's ringing!"

Not caring, Anna stepped into the hot water, sighing at the sensation against her skin. "Can you see who it is, in case it's Mum?"

There was silence, and then the sound of the door opening. Lane entered with a strange look on her face.

Anna pushed the shower door open completely to look at her. "Who was it?"

Lane didn't step into the shower, instead leaning stark naked against the wall and looking at Anna with an odd expression on her face. "How often does your ex call?"

If Lane was trying to sound relaxed and neutral, she was failing. Anna looked at her quizzically from the shower, rubbing shampoo into her hair. "What?"

"I'm just, you know, wondering, for future reference. Does Hayley call a lot, or..." Lane was trying to appear calm, but Anna could see the mental freak-out occurring underneath.

"That was Hayley?"

"Mhm."

"Did you answer?"

"Of course not." Brown eyes avoided hers even while Lane smiled. "Though it did occur to me to answer with, 'Sorry, Anna can't talk right now, I'm about to take her against the shower wall after hours of sex last night.'"

With a chuckle, Anna asked, "Can you come in here so we can at least have this naked conversation next to each other?"

Lane shook her head. "Not yet."

Anna gauged her. She definitely wasn't mad. "Wait...Lane, are you jealous?"

Lane gave a shrug. "No, I just, you know, want to know if you guys chat all the time. Catch up."

The clear-cut jealousy all over Lane was almost funny. "I haven't spoken to her in months."

"Really?"

"Really."

Lane took a step forward. "So I shouldn't worry about her trying to get you back?"

It occurred to Anna, finally, that the messy ending Lane had had with Alex could be contributing to this reaction. Anna tried to control the look that flashed over her face, but, apparently, she was too late.

"What was that?"

Anna widened her eyes. "What?"

"That look?"

Anna sighed. "She's not trying to get me back. She's being an idiot. A well-meaning one, I think. But still being an idiot." She dipped her head under the spray and rinsed the shampoo out.

When she re-emerged, Lane was basically twitching. "Has she tried?"

Anna held her hand out. "Would you come here so I can calm your inner panic?"

Thankfully, Lane reached a hand out and stepped forward. The second that Lane was in the shower, Anna wrapped her arms around her. She kissed Lane's neck once.

"Are you breathing?"

"Yes. Just...she tried?"

Wet hair flew as Anna adamantly shook her head. "No, not to get me back. Though she did call me and leave a voicemail before the trial, when you and I were broken up."

"Okay! That was like three months ago! And you never told me?"

Reminding herself that this was more about Lane's stuff than about Hayley, Anna tried to quell the defensiveness that rose up. "I completely forgot. She basically offered me sex as a distraction."

Lane's mouth dropped open. "She called *you*, my girlfriend, and offered sex, and you never told me?"

Squeezing Lane tight, Anna looked straight at her. "Lane, I never replied. I ignored her and completely forgot about it. There were bigger things going on, and I forgot." She brought her hands up and cupped Lane's cheeks. "I'm sorry."

"I'm not…I'm not mad at *you*." She paused as if trying to figure out what she *was* feeling. "Just…she propositioned you!"

"To be fair—I don't know if she knew I was seeing someone; because I *haven't talked to her*."

The pout on Lane's face made Anna purse her lips together to stop herself from smiling. "So why is she calling you?"

"I don't know. She texted me last night—"

As Lane's eyebrows shot up, Anna rushed to finish. "And I got it as I was dropping the kids off at Mum's and then clear forgot about it because I was in a rush to get home and be with you for the first time since Toby threw up on your lap."

Clearly trying to relax, Lane pursed her lips. "So what did she want?"

Anna grabbed some body wash and poured it on a loofah, running it over Lane's chest and back. "She texted me to say she was sorry for the message during the trial. Since she hadn't heard back from me, she figured she had made me angry. She said she wasn't trying to offend me. She just felt like she had dropped me in all this when we broke up and she wanted to support me."

"With sex?"

Anna shrugged. "I don't know. Apparently."

Realisation dawned on Lane's face. "Because she knows how you deal with emotions with sex. Because she was with you for three years and knows that."

"She doesn't know me. Not anymore, not really. In fact, I wonder if we ever knew each other. We were so focussed on our careers." Anna dropped the loofah to the floor and pulled Lane in. "You know me. You know me, not her. And when she left me a voicemail the first time giving such a bad offer, all I was thinking about was how I wanted Ella and Toby back and how much I missed *you.* I didn't even entertain the idea."

Running wet hands over Lane's side and over her shoulders to bury in her hair, Anna slipped her tongue into her mouth and felt Lane moan, then return the kiss with as much force.

Eyes sparkling, Anna pulled back. "Lane, do you have a jealous side?"

"I…no."

"Sure."

Lane's hands dropped to Anna's hips, pushing her back against the wall, pressing herself flush against her. Pulling her in tighter, Anna wrapped her arms around her waist. Wet thighs pressed together as the water streamed onto Lane's back. Jealousy apparently made Lane want to make a point, and Anna was very okay with that, more than okay. She took hold of Lane's hand and ran it down her stomach, looking at her with darkened eyes. "Only you see me naked now."

Anna closed her eyes and leant her head back against the shower wall, Lane's lips on her neck.

"Good." Lane dragged her teeth against Anna's skin, and Anna let out a low moan as Lane's fingers ran between her legs.

They emerged from the shower thirty minutes later, Anna slightly wobbly as they dressed quickly and Anna grabbed her phone, looking down at the missed call. She started tapping at the touch screen.

Lane threw her a quizzical look as she towel-dried her hair, wearing just her underwear. "You look very serious."

One finger held up in the air told Lane not to interrupt, and she closed her mouth. Anna typed furiously at her phone, then finally scrolled back up to the top of the message.

Anna read from the text: "Okay. 'Sorry I missed your call, Hayley. I wasn't mad, just very caught up in the trial. I understand you were trying to help, but propositions from my ex weren't really very helpful in that situation. Also, I'm seeing someone and have been for the last few months, so, between the kids and her, I'm kept happily busy. I hope all's well with you, take care.'"

She looked up to Lane and her thumb moved. "Sent."

A slow smile spread over Lane's lips, and she sauntered forward, pulling Anna into her arms. "Happily busy, huh?"

A grin playing over her lips, Anna nodded emphatically. "Very."

Lane kissed her then, hands curling into Anna's hair. She rested her forehead on Anna's. "Sorry about the minor freak-out."

"You can be crazy sometimes."

With a light tap on Anna's ass, Lane stepped away, slightly flushed.

They finished getting dressed and parted ways in the driveway with a quick kiss, Lane headed for the hospital and Anna for her mother's to get Toby and Ella. Anna drove with the radio off, enjoying her last few minutes of silence for the day.

Her ex was not a bad person at all. But it did kind of make Anna amused to see Lane get jealous, if only because it was incredibly hot and gave her a warm feeling in her chest that Lane cared so much.

Anna pulled up and got out of the car, smiling when she saw Ella pressed up against the window in the living room, hands to the glass. Toby, so much smaller, was kneeling next to her. They both waved. Toby got a tad too excited and smacked his open hand against the glass, his head turning as, Anna assumed, he was told off by his grandmother.

When the door opened, Sandra warned her, "Brace yourself."

Even as she frowned, Ella tore around the corner, Toby hot on her heels, and they both collided with her knees. The force of the two children almost knocked her backwards. "Hey, guys! Miss me?"

Ella shook her head. "Not till just now, then I remembered I do!"

"Well, good, 'cause that means you had fun with Grandma."

Tiny fingers were gripping the material of her pants and tugging as Toby tried to scale her leg. "Cake, Na! Gama cake."

Anna acquiesced to the unsubtle request Toby was making and picked him up. "You made cake with Grandma?!"

"Cake." His little face looked troubled and he held his foot out. "Owie foot."

"What happened?"

All he did was point at it. "Owie."

"He had his first stubbed toe," Sandra informed her.

Anna grimaced and cupped his foot gently, giving it a soft squeeze. "Poor Toby. Did you get a Band-Aid?"

"He did." Gripping Anna's hand, Ella puffed her chest out. "I put a Dora the Explorer one on his toe for him."

"*You* put it on! Ella, soon you can go to the hospital and work instead of me."

"No, don't be silly, I have to go to school."

"Hm. True." Anna slid Toby down to the floor. "Okay, you two go get your things. Ella, you help Toby, and we'll go meet Kym."

"Zoo!"

Ella ran off and Toby followed her. Ella, obviously remembering what had been asked of her, stopped and held her hand out for Toby to take; the two headed up the stairs. Toby held the rail with one hand and Ella's hand with the other, taking the steps one at a time, while Anna and Sandra watched them go.

Toby's blanket was down to bedtime again now, not being dragged everywhere unless he was having a tantrum day. And the most uplifting thing was, he no longer panicked if Anna was a few metres away from him.

Ella was bouncing in her excitement. "We're going to the zoo, Tobes. What sound does a lion make?"

"Rar!"

Anna chortled and turned back to Sandra. "You guys had fun then?"

Her mother nodded and started walking into the kitchen. Anna followed after closing the front door behind her.

"We did. Ella ate more cake batter than went into it, and Toby smeared it on the bench, but we managed to make something out of it. You want some?"

Anna shook her head. "No, thanks. We're meeting Kym, and I need to stop by the shops first."

"Today the day?"

"Yeah. One year since Simon died. I was going to get her a flower to give from us? Do you think that's a good idea?"

"It's a really good idea."

"I was going to go with her, with the kids. I thought we could all put a flower down for Jake and Sally."

The glass her mother held out to Anna trembled slightly. "That's a beautiful idea. I took Ella last month after school."

"It's good for them, right?"

"It is."

"Did you want to come?"

"No, thank you. This is more for Kym. I was going to go next week, at the six-month date for Jake and Sally."

Lips pale, Sandra gave a nod and tried to smile.

Anna put her glass down, pulling her mother into a hug. She ran her hands up and down her back, but Sandra pulled away fairly quickly and swiped at her cheeks. As the kids came back in, Anna squeezed her arm and let her hand fall.

"Ready!"

Distracting the kids while her mother took a moment, Anna said, "Great job, guys."

Just as she was about to tell them to cuddle Grandma and say *goodbye* and *thank you*, her father walked around the corner and into the kitchen.

He stood awkwardly, looking at them all.

Since the trial, after all he had said, he had been trying. He had come to the odd dinner with Sandra, and, when Anna picked up Ella after school, she'd often find them reading the paper together or in the garden. Occasionally, he picked up Toby, and he spoke to Anna now—basic conversations and pleasantries.

Anna wasn't sure whether to hope for more from him or not.

He had finally met Lane at dinner the other night and had put his hand on Anna's shoulder as he left, with just the words, "She seems nice."

Now, he smiled tightly at his grandchildren and looked to Anna. "Can I speak with you?"

Anna hadn't been alone with him since before Jake's death.

She looked to Ella and Toby. "You two smother Grandma in as many hugs and kisses as you can, and then we'll go when I'm back, okay?"

Ella moved quickly to Sandra, who had squatted down with her arms open; Toby barrelled in after his sister.

Anna followed her father down the hallway, hating that feeling nervous with him was a habit stemming from long before Jake died.

In his office, Andrew stopped beside his giant desk, standing straight with his arms by his sides. He looked at her for a minute, his head tilted slightly to the side, and, in the gesture, Anna saw how Jake would look at her when trying to make a point—how Ella and even Toby looked at people sometimes.

A gesture she herself did.

Anna met his eye and waited.

He cleared his throat. "The kids are doing well."

"Yes—Toby is hitting a delightful point of tantrums."

Andrew managed a small smile. "He's what, twenty months?"

"Twenty-one now."

"Same age that you and Jake became nightmares."

Anna laughed. "That's what Mum said."

"Especially Jake. He threw a good one."

"That's where Toby got it from, then."

Her father looked sad, his expression softening; it was strange to see on him. He was so good at schooling himself into a hard outer coating that Anna sometimes forgot that, buried underneath, he must have feelings.

Her mother was right; they were so very alike.

Jake had gotten their mother's softer side. He had been a bit more sensitive, open to emotions; he had always been a touch more like their mother, while Anna had taken after their father and his tendency to bury anything unpleasant.

Lately, though, Anna had started to realise she had a lot more of both of them than she had originally thought.

"He's got a lot of Jake in him." His voice didn't waver, not once.

Anna nodded. She wasn't sure why she was in here.

Her father opened a drawer on his desk and pulled something out, holding it in his fist. Walking around the desk, he stood in front of her, and, Anna noticed, *he* was nervous being near her. She knew she reminded him so much of Jake.

He held his hand out, and she held her palm under his fist; it didn't open. Instead, he cleared his throat again. "I…I wanted you, to have this. Jake and you, you were close; I know that." He looked her in the eye. "I know you lost him, too. And I know I've been absent. But I wanted you to have this."

When he finally opened his fist, Anna felt something warm hit her hand, and she looked down as he dropped his hand back to his side. Sitting in her open palm, the metal warm from his skin, were Jake's dog tags.

Anna's fingers curled around them.

Jake might have stepped down to an administrative role because of his worry about leaving the kids and his wife. But the Air Force had still been his life. His friends, his sense of duty—those dog tags symbolised what made her brother *her brother* as much as those two kids in the kitchen did.

The lump in her throat made it difficult to swallow. Anna looked up.

Her father's blue eyes were unchanged. He gave her a nod and she returned it.

"Are you sure?"

"You need something of his."

Smiling softly, Anna said, "I have Toby and Ella."

"You need something for you, too."

Anna managed to swallow, and Andrew gave another nod, walking around his desk and sitting down, opening up his laptop.

She watched him for a minute, lifting the chain up to slip around her neck, the tags tinkling together as they fell to sit under her shirt, settling over her sternum.

He was focussed on what was in front of him.

"Bye, Dad."

He looked up. "Bye."

Anna went to walk out.

"Oh, Anna?"

She turned, hand on the door handle. "Yeah?"

He kept his eyes on his laptop screen. "That woman's a keeper."

Shaking her head in disbelief, Anna left. Her hand rested over her shirt, where she could feel the outline of the tags sitting. She hadn't been expecting that.

She found her mother sitting on the floor, leaning against the cupboard doors with Toby on her lap and Ella seated next to her. All three had giant pieces of cake in their hands. They all stopped mid bite and looked at her.

Anna narrowed her eyes.

Her mother leant over and whispered loudly in Ella's ear, "We obviously didn't eat fast enough. We were caught out."

Ella looked panicked. "Quick! Scoff!"

They downed the last of their cake.

Anna put her hands on her hips, looking at her mother, who looked back at her innocently as she licked frosting off her thumb. "So I get the sugar rush?"

Sandra winked. "Exactly."

They got the already hyper kids into the car, and Anna hovered at the driver's door, giving her mother an extra hug. "So, next week? We all go on Saturday?"

"I'll come by your place, and we'll go with the kids?"

"That sounds like a plan. Ella wants to take a painting to leave."

"They would love that."

"Would you mind if—"

"If Lane didn't come, I'd be horrified."

"Really?"

"Really."

"She offered, and I hadn't realised I wanted her to until then."

Her mother squeezed her arm. "Sometimes it takes someone giving you a nudge to realise what you want."

Anna heard the door downstairs open and close and felt her pulse speed up, knowing Lane had just let herself in with the spare key she kept in a fake rock.

A glance at the clock told her it was eleven at night.

The afternoon had been draining, though not in the way it would have been months ago. Anna, Ella and Toby had sat between the two headstones. Ella, who had been before, liked to talk to them. The first time she had gone, Ella had been nervous and jittery. Now, she settled in, comfortable in a place where she felt closer to her parents.

Anna had sat with her chin resting on Toby's head, listening to Ella tell her mother and father about school.

Kym stayed at Simon's grave on the other side of the cemetery. She wanted to go alone, and she wore a red top, which she'd smilingly said always made Simon forget whatever he'd been thinking.

Anna's hands left Ella's hair to rest between her small shoulder blades as she talked. Softly, she kissed Toby's head as he chewed on a muesli bar before resting her chin back against his soft hair.

More than anything, she wished those two children didn't know what death was. Not like this. She wished it wasn't a part of their lives, that Ella didn't have this understanding about cemeteries, that she didn't have the knowledge that came with it. When Ella found out Kym's husband had passed away, she had hugged Kym and then said, "I think my daddy and your Simon will be friends in heaven."

It had been almost peaceful at the cemetery. The grass was kept green, it was filled with trees, and a soft breeze always seemed to be blowing. The dog tags had made a soft sound when she moved, and Anna wished she could ask her brother if he found it weird that she was wearing them.

Toby suddenly pushed up from Anna's lap, and she watched him, steadier now on his little twenty-one-month-old legs, run up to Kym as she approached. She scooped him up and sat right next to Anna, her cheeks dry and her eyes clear.

Relaxed, Ella stopped talking and leant back into Anna. "Do you think they hear?"

Anna wrapped her arms around her. "I think they do. Do you?"

"Mummy always listened before, so why would she stop?"

The words that fell from Ella's mouth sometimes blew her away. Anna kissed the top of her head and rested a hand over Kym's.

"Exactly."

The bedroom door opening brought Anna back to the present, and she heard clothes dropping to the ground. She lay still as Lane brushed her teeth in the bathroom. Cool air brushed her skin as the covers lifted, and Lane settled on her side, flush against Anna. Her fingers ran gently through Anna's hair, then came to rest splayed over Anna's lower back. Lane's touch was always soft.

"Hey."

"Hey. You're awake."

Rolling over, Anna nodded. "I was waiting for you."

"Bold move with hospital hours."

Through a yawn, Anna said, "Very."

"How was today?"

"It was okay. Ella likes going to see them, I think. Toby doesn't get it."

"How was Kym?"

Anna kissed Lane's jaw before pulling back and answering, "Honestly? She was okay."

"Yeah?"

"Yeah. You could tell it was hard, but...she's okay."

"Good."

When Anna leant over and kissed her again, the dog tags made a slight noise as they fell between them.

Lane's fingers ran along the chain around Anna's neck. "Is this—?"

"Jake's dog tags. Uh...Dad gave them to me."

Lane ran the chain through her fingers before taking the tags and moving them back and forth, unable to read them in the light. "That's nice."

"It was, actually."

The chain fell back between them, and Lane shifted so she could wrap her legs around Anna. "Did you still want me to come next week?"

"Definitely."

Kissing Lane, Anna ran her nails lightly up her side, rocking her hips and swallowing Lane's soft gasp. As Lane's hand buried in Anna's hair, Anna rocked her hips again, slowly.

A knock sounded at the door.

They stopped, foreheads resting against each other.

"Was that—?"

Lane nodded.

"Thank God we finally taught her knocking."

Anna smirked, stood up, and grabbed Lane's shirt, throwing it to her. "One second, Ella," she called softly.

Quick as she could, Anna opened a drawer and pulled out two pairs of shorts, one she threw at Lane and one she pulled on herself. When she opened the door, Ella stood there, blinking at them blurrily. Anna squatted down and opened her arms, and Ella stumbled into them. Tousled hair fell over Ella's cheeks, and Anna smoothed it off her face. "What's up, Ella Bella?"

Ella shrugged. "I can't sleep."

Anna wrapped her up tighter. "Well, that's no good. Want me to come read you a story?"

At first Ella nodded, then shook her head.

"No?"

"Can Lane read me one?"

Anna smiled. "Let's ask Lane."

They both turned to the bed, but Lane was already standing up and walking over to them, holding her hand out. "Come on, Miss Ella, I think we're up to chapter six in *Matilda.*"

Sleepily, Ella took her hand.

Lane looked back to wink at Anna, who mouthed, *thank you.*

She stood and watched them walk down the hallway, then checked on Toby, who was sprawled out in his cot, sleeping soundly. Soon, she would probably have to get him a big bed.

The idea of that made her a little sad and also slightly horrified about how on earth she was going to keep him in it at bedtime.

As gently as she could, Anna pulled his blanket up over him, fingers trailing softly over his hair, and went back to bed. Wrapped in her blanket, she listened to Lane's soft voice come from down the hallway. Despite how sleepy Ella was, Anna heard her giggle softly.

The chain lay warm against her skin.

About G Benson

Benson spent her childhood wrapped up in any book she could get her hands on and—as her mother likes to tell people at parties—even found a way to read in the shower. Moving on from writing bad poetry (thankfully) she started to write stories. About anything and everything. Tearing her from her laptop is a fairly difficult feat, though if you come bearing coffee you have a good chance.

When not writing or reading, she's got her butt firmly on a train or plane to see the big wide world. Originally from Australia, she currently lives in Spain, speaking terrible Spanish and going on as many trips to new places as she can, budget permitting. This means she mostly walks around the city she lives in.

Connect with G Benson

E-mail: gbensonauthor@gmail.com

Tumblr: http://gbensonauthor.tumblr.com/

Other Books from Ylva Publishing

www.ylva-publishing.com

A Story of Now

Emily O'Beirne

ISBN: 978-3-95533-345-4
Length: 367 pages (128,000 words)

Nineteen-year-old Claire knows she needs a life. And new friends.

Too sassy for her own good, she doesn't make friends easily anymore. And she has no clue where to start on the whole life front. At first, Robbie and Mia seem the least likely people to help her find it. But in a turbulent time, Claire finds new friends, a new self, and, with the warm, brilliant Mia, a whole new set of feelings.

Once

(revised edition)

L.T. Smith

ISBN: 978-3-95533-399-7
Length: 295 pages (77,000 words)

Beth Chambers' life is no fairytale. After four years in a destructive relationship, Beth decides enough is enough and leaves her girlfriend, taking Dudley, her dog, with her. At her lowest point, she meets Amy Fletcher, a woman who appears to have it all–and whom she believes would never want more than friendship. Beth needs to believe in magic once more for her dreams to come true. But can she?

Barring Complications

Blythe Rippon

ISBN: 978-3-95533-191-7
Length: 374 pages (77,000 words)

When a gay marriage case arrives at the US Supreme Court, two women find themselves at the center of the fight for marriage equality. Closeted Justice Victoria Willoughby must sway a conservative colleague and attorney Genevieve Fornier must craft compelling arguments to win five votes. Complicating matters, despite their shared history, the law forbids the two from talking to each other.

Coming Home

(3rd revised edition)

Lois Cloarec Hart

ISBN: 978-3-95533-064-4
Length: 371 pages (104,000 words)

Rob, a charismatic ex-fighter pilot severely disabled with MS, has been steadfastly cared for by his wife, Jan, for many years. Quite by accident one day, Terry, a young writer/postal carrier, enters their lives and turns it upside down.

Coming from Ylva Publishing

The Red Files

Lee Winter

Ambitious journalist Lauren King is stuck reporting on the vapid LA social scene's gala events while sparring with her rival—icy ex-Washington correspondent Catherine Ayers. Then a curious story unfolds before their eyes, involving a business launch, thirty-four prostitutes, and a pallet of missing pink champagne. Can the warring pair join together to unravel an incredible story?

Popcorn Love

KL Hughes

Her love-life lacking, wealthy fashion exec Elena Vega agrees to a string of blind dates set up by her best friend Vivian in exchange for Vivian finding a suitable babysitter for her son, Lucas.

Free-spirited college student Allison Sawyer fits the bill perfectly.

Elena and Allison bond over tales of Elena's disastrous dates, and Elena begins to realize that perhaps she should have been dating the babysitter all along.

All the Little Moments

ISBN: 978-3-95533-341-6

Also available as e-book.

Published by Ylva Publishing, legal entity of Ylva Verlag, e.Kfr.

Ylva Verlag, e.Kfr.
Owner: Astrid Ohletz
Am Kirschgarten 2
65830 Kriftel
Germany

www.ylva-publishing.com

First Edition: July 2015

Credits:
Edited by Michelle Aguilar and Alissa McGowan
Proofread by Melissa Tapper
Cover Design by Streetlight Graphics

This book is a work of fiction. Names, characters, events, and locations are fictitious or are used fictitiously. Any resemblance to actual persons or events, living or dead, is entirely coincidental.